Advance  **W9-CAI-557**

RUMORS

✻

"From the Depression, through World War II, into the bitter era of McCarthyism and beyond, *Rumors* tells the tale of a woman who survives scandal and heartache. Ms. Fitzgerald's heroine loses one love, one life, only to find and to forge another."

—Nora Roberts, author of the *New York Times* bestseller, *Carnal Innocence*

✻

"Sara Fitzgerald has written a wonderful book. It's filled with intriguing characters that you'll love and despise and a plot that keeps you turning the pages eagerly. I literally couldn't put it down."

—Haynes Johnson, *Washington Post* columnist, author of *Sleepwalking Through History*

✻

"A sensitive and satisfying portrait of a proud, tough, and loving woman. Sara Fitzgerald's writing is as intelligent as it is entertaining."

—Diane Chamberlain, author of *Secret Lives*

✻

RUMORS

SARA FITZGERALD

WARNER BOOKS

A Time Warner Company

WARNER BOOKS EDITION

Copyright © 1992 by Sara Fitzgerald
All rights reserved.

Photograph by Nancy Palubniak
Cover design by Diane Luger

Warner Books, Inc.
1271 Avenue of the Americas
New York, N.Y. 10020

W A Time Warner Company

Printed in the United States of America

First Printing: September, 1992

10 9 8 7 6 5 4 3 2 1

To my parents

An author who writes a book in her spare time over the course of several years has many people to whom she is indebted when the work is done.

First, thanks to my aunt, Annie Laurie Ellis Horsfall, whose memoir, "With Love, Lollie" inspired me to start my book where she spent her early years, in rural Mississippi.

Thanks, also, to my friends and colleagues Jean Parvin Bordewich, Judy Mann, Karen Coe, Belle Elving, Jamie Baylis, Diane Chamberlain, Meryl Gordon, Haynes Johnson, George Mair, Dennis McAuliffe, Marylou Tousignant, Ken Greenberger, Jean-Yves Heyer, Ken Bredemeier, and Don Phillips for their encouragement, for answering my questions or both. A special thanks to Howie Kurtz for sharing his insights about investigative reporting.

Special appreciation must be reserved for my critique group, Judy Yoder, Tommye Morton, Mary Blayney, and Pat McLaughlin, who provided not only encouragement for a flagging spirit, but useful advice as readers, authors and editors. Thanks to all the members of Washington Romance Writers for their friendship and support.

My appreciation also goes to Marcia Rowen, Chong LaRocque and Susan Cavanaugh, whose friendship and help over the years has enabled me to juggle the many things that I do.

To my agent, Denise Marcil, my thanks for keeping

me on the right track and sharing her excellent editorial instincts. Thanks, too, to my editor, Jeanne Tiedge, for useful suggestions at every stage of my writing career.

And finally, thanks to my family; to my parents for nurturing the writer in their midst, and especially to Walt and Steve, for their patience and advice and for tolerating the grinding of a computer printer in the early hours of the morning.

"Good name in man and woman, dear my lord,
Is the immediate jewel of their souls;
Who steals my purse steals trash;
    'tis something, nothing;
'Twas mine, 'tis his, and has been slave to
    thousands;
But he that filches from me my good name
Robs me of that which not enriches him,
And makes me poor indeed."

                    —William Shakespeare

Prologue

There were, by Aurore Callahan's count, just a few decisive moments in a woman's life.

You chose a school and a lover, a husband and a career, and, in the end, whether to be faithful to him—and to yourself.

And even though tonight had been billed as a "dinner with friends," she knew that it was one of those moments.

She reached across the cluttered vanity table for the palette of eye shadow that matched the taffeta cocktail dress and the steel green of her eyes. At forty-nine, she was not the kind of woman who wasted hours in front of a mirror or weeks at a spa. But she was a realist, and long ago she had accepted the fact that when a man met a woman for the first time, he was more likely to be seduced by her eyes than by her IQ.

She thought back to that afternoon, when Andrew had joined her in front of the fireplace that made her office the best place in their law firm for a heart-to-heart talk.

They pulled up matching wing chairs, covered in chintz—a touch of feminine whimsy in their otherwise buttoned-down world. Then, because the day was cool and drizzly and there were no more clients to see, she opened her liquor cabinet and offered him a glass of sherry.

They talked for more than an hour, like the best friends they had become after working together for nearly twenty years. And there, within the womb that was her office, they dissected her scheme one last time.

Andrew played the prosecutor, peering at her over the wire-rimmed reading glasses he'd been forced to accept as he approached fifty. He poked at the weaknesses of her plan, pointing out where events could take a different turn—and the possible consequences if they did.

Aurore, in turn, played the defendant, providing, in practiced words, the answers to all of his questions.

All of them but one.

"What will he do if he finds out you're the one who's really behind all this?"

She stared into the fire. "I'm not sure."

"Don't go through with it then."

Andrew's words echoed as she rode home, oblivious to the cabbie's battle with the dense traffic of K Street. She thought of them again as she slipped into the bathtub that Inez had filled with warm, violet-scented bubbles. She heard them then one last time as she pulled the place cards out of her desk drawer. Then, her mind made up, she put the one that read "Thomas Feigan" at the place setting next to hers.

All these years she had waited, hoping someday to strike back at those who had tried to ruin her: the man who had crafted the lie and the man who had printed it.

She had almost given up that hope that she would find out who was responsible. But now she knew—and she was determined to pay him back.

The reporter had long since retired, and that was a pity. But his son was trying to follow in his footsteps. And she was determined to teach him the lesson his father had never learned.

Andrew was right—her plan was far from perfect. But that didn't matter anymore. It was time now to even the score.

For Robert and the life they might have had together. For the child she had never really known. But most of all for the guileless young woman who had disappeared in a sea of scandal in what seemed like a lifetime ago.

She checked her reflection in the mirror, then the thin gold band on her wrist. The time had come. She lifted her chin and headed for the stairs. Her pawn was about to arrive.

PART ONE

Mississippi, 1925

One

She remembered the red-gold hair, gathered up in haphazard loops, an antidote to the hot, muggy summer.

She remembered her mother's hands, white, silky, and cool. Hands that never seemed to tire of fussing with her daughter's cinnamon-colored curls. Hands that didn't belong on a poor dirt farmer's spread.

Most of all she remembered a hot, muggy day when she was five, and the town of Homer celebrated its centennial. There was a parade and a picnic, but all the red, white, and blue faded now. Instead she remembered it as the day when her life changed forever.

"Katharine Aurore Callahan, if you won't be still, I'll never get this bow tied." Her mother fiddled with her new gingham pinafore. "There," she said, giving her daughter a twirl. "You look very pretty today. Don't you think so, Emory?"

He stood silently in the bedroom doorway, wearing only his singlet and trousers. Kate twirled a few more times for her father's benefit.

"Yes," he said, ruffling his hand through her hair. "I think my little Katie looks mighty pretty."

"I pressed your uniform this morning, dear." Charlotte's eyes brightened. "It's hanging in the bathroom."

He scowled beneath his dark mustache. "I don't want to wear it."

"But, Emory," she pleaded, "all the men will be dressed for the parade. Why can't you get in the spirit of things?"

"Because I don't want to," he bellowed. Kate jumped back, bumping into the hard ball where her mother's lap used to be.

Her father stepped closer, his coal-black eyes narrowing. "What's wrong, Miss New Orleans fancy lady? Do you miss the gallant fighting lad you married?"

Charlotte wrapped her arms around her daughter. "No, Emory." Her voice was soft, but controlled. "You know that's not true. I only thought you'd enjoy marching with the other men. I thought it would give your spirits a lift."

"Well, think again," he said, slamming the bedroom door.

Charlotte knelt quickly and held her daughter's face. "Daddy has a lot on his mind these days, Katie. You know, the new baby coming and all. He didn't really mean to be so angry."

Kate wanted to believe her. But her father seemed to be angry all the time now. Her mother said it was just that he was working too hard. But it had been months since he had led her around the yard on the back of Bessie, their horse. Or told her a story about her grandfather and the war. Or even remembered to bring her a piece of candy when he came back from town.

But he'd promised he'd buy her some today. He was even going to let her stop by Doc Marston's store to pick it out.

What's wrong? Do you miss the gallant fighting lad you married? The words had stung Charlotte with the force of truth. Now, as she sat beside her sullen husband on the ride into town, she wondered how things had managed to go so wrong.

Eight years before, Emory Callahan had swooped into New Orleans a few weeks before he would be sent to the muddy fields of Belgium. He was tall and lean, all spit and polish, with shiny black hair that was darker than his boots.

She was Edmund Dellaplaine's younger daughter, a girl

who had acquired the manners of a convent education but none of the guilt over her romantic longings.

All the best young men in New Orleans knew the red-haired beauty with a laugh as light as a song. And they all knew better than to pursue her too single-mindedly under her father's stern eyes.

But Emory didn't know that. He was just off the train from boot camp, fresh from his father's farm. New Orleans stretched before him—a final fling before he headed for the western front. He found a party and he found a girl, a strawberries-and-cream girl who was prettier than any woman he had ever met.

He asked her to dance. She accepted.

He was nothing like the tongue-tied young men her mother ushered into their parlor. His black eyes danced with a passion for life that she found tempting. And when he took her hand to lead her onto the dance floor, she felt a jolt, a sensation unlike anything she had ever experienced before. She knew Emory Callahan was not going to abide by her parents' rules.

"What makes your hair such a beautiful color?" he asked.

She struggled to breathe. "I don't know."

"I know," he said, pulling her close. "It must be the fire burning in your heart."

He acted as if there were no tomorrow, as if the world existed for the two of them alone. And by the time they had danced the last dance of the evening, she was crazily in love.

"Where can we go?" he asked.

"I know a place."

He was not a wealthy banker nor a smooth-tongued lawyer. He was not even a Catholic. He was, in short, everything that her parents would oppose in a man—which made him even more perfect in Charlotte's eyes.

She sneaked out of the house to see him when he returned the next two weekends. They held hands and went for long walks and kissed in the moonlight. And when, on the eve of his departure, he asked her to marry him, she didn't hesitate for a moment before saying yes.

They went out into the country to find a judge who wasn't

a friend of her father's. Then they spent their last afternoon
together in a tawdry hotel down by the river, far from anyone
who might know Charlotte. They made love, over and over
and over again, till she thought the rusty springs in the old
bed would break.

He unleashed something in her, a wild woman who was
ready to try whatever he wanted to teach her. And each time
he took her to the brink of ecstasy, she laughed out loud,
thinking of the twitching faces of the nuns at school and
imagining how shocked they would be.

And when the afternoon shadows grew long, and she had
to button her new husband back into his uniform, Charlotte
wondered how she'd ever learn to survive back in her parents'
prison.

But survive she did.

She didn't tell her family she had married. Instead she
feigned polite interest in the men who came around to their
house, making sure that none of them grew too attached to
her. And all the while she hid Emory's locket in her dresser,
between the folds of her silk underwear.

Each night she prayed for Emory's safe return, that the
two of them would be together again. And in the end, her
prayers were answered. In the early months of 1919, he rode
the train back into town for her.

But he was different now. She couldn't define it at first.
She was simply too happy to see him, to find out that he was
still in one piece. Whatever it was that was bothering him,
she was certain it wouldn't matter as soon as they were in
their own home together.

Naturally, her parents were horrified to discover that she
was already married, and to a Mississippi farmer they'd never
laid eyes on before. They screamed at her, threatened to
disown her, and finally, in desperation, prepared to go to the
Church to get the marriage annulled.

But after all the cruel words were spoken, Charlotte rode
out of town without looking back. She sat beside her husband
in their rented wagon, wearing her favorite Parisian bonnet
with her head held high. She had chosen Emory Callahan's
life. Now she would have to live it.

* * *

When the last unit in the parade had passed, they headed to the Baptist church, out on the edge of town. The families had gathered in clusters across the wide green lawn of the white clapboard building. Charlotte picked out a sycamore tree, set down her basket, then pulled out the red-checked tablecloth and snapped it to attention.

"How about a piece of fried chicken, Emory?"

"I'm not hungry," he muttered.

"But Matty fixed it just the way you like."

"I said I'm not hungry." He stalked off to join the men.

Kate perked up. "I'll have a piece, Mama."

Her mother smiled weakly, then piled up her plate with chicken and pickles and a fat slice of bread.

They ate silently as the midday sun burned down. Charlotte leaned back against the tree, trying in vain to create a breeze with a tiny parchment fan. As she closed her eyes, she felt the baby stir. *If it's a boy, it will all be better. We'll all be happy then.*

Something moved beneath Kate's head. She blinked open her eyes, then focused on her mother's face. But Charlotte no longer wore the serene mask she'd donned that morning. Her face was pale, and her lips were white where she had bitten them.

"Mama!"

"It's all right, Katie." Charlotte's words came in a rush. She took a gulp of air. "Now listen carefully. Go find your daddy. He's probably over with the men watching the ball game. Tell him my time has come."

Kate was too stunned to move.

"Hurry, dear!" Charlotte's eyes squeezed shut.

Kate dashed toward the noisy crowd gathered around the makeshift diamond. She wove her way through the clusters of people, searching in vain for a mustached man in a brown suit.

"Hey, what are you up to, Katie Callahan?" Horace Malone grabbed her by the elbow.

"My father," she panted, "have you seen him?"

"Emory?" The minister rubbed his chin. "No, I don't believe I have."

"Try down by the creek," another man suggested. "I saw him going that way."

She sped off without another word, heading for the steep bank that marked the rear boundary of the church.

"Daddy!" she shrieked as she reached the soft muddy creekbed. She listened, but all she heard was the trippling of the water over the ford the boys had built. "Daddy!"

She listened again. This time she heard a different sound. It was a kind of groan, sort of half animal, half human. It frightened her, but she picked up the hem of her skirt and tiptoed carefully through the grasses at the water's edge.

Then she saw him, sprawled out on his back, his eyes closed and his collar unbuttoned. She ran to his side and gave his arm a shake. "Daddy, wake up. Mama needs you."

She saw the bottle then, lying empty by his side. She had seen them before—they always made her mother angry.

Now she stared down at her father's lifeless form. Was Mama dying? Was Daddy already dead?

She closed her eyes, opened her mouth, and screamed louder than she ever had in her life.

Two

The soft black hands tucked the starched sheet up around Kate's neck.

"Is she going to be all right, Matty?"

"Of course she is, chile." Matty smiled tenderly at the little girl. "Having a baby is hard work, dat's all."

Kate looked up into the big woman's chocolate-brown eyes, not ready to believe her. For months, her mother had spent almost every afternoon in bed, leaving Kate with no one to talk to but their plump cook. Sometimes Matty brought her daughter, Lucy, along to play, but if the little girls squealed too loudly, Matty would rush out to shush them.

Now she thought of those afternoons as her mother's painful cries echoed in her ears.

"Remember, sugar. I've known your mama since she was a girl. She'll be awlright. But you know what your mama would want if she could tuck you in herself? She'd want you to close your eyes and go to sleep."

"Yes, Matty."

"Good night then, sugar." She stroked Kate's cheek with a callused hand, then bustled out the door.

Kate stretched out beneath the stiff sheet. She closed her eyes, and yet she couldn't dispel the memory of that afternoon.

At the sound of her screams, the men had come running to the creek. When they saw Emory, some of them laughed. "It's my mama," Kate said quickly. "She needs help."

"Where is she?" Rev. Malone asked.

Kate glanced back at her father, wondering if she should leave him.

"Don't mind your daddy," she heard a voice say. "He'll be all right—after he sleeps it off." Another round of laughter stung her ears.

"Remember," her mother had told her more times than she could count on her little fingers, "you are a Dellaplaine, too. And no matter what happens, Dellaplaines hold their heads up high."

"Come," Kate said, resolving in a moment which parent needed her most. "I'll show you where she is."

Now she could hear her mother groaning again from her room down the hallway. It had started to rain, and the air crackled with the tension of lightning. Kate buried her head under her big feather pillow. "Please, God," she prayed, "let it all be over soon."

The room was gray when she awoke. Her dress was hung on the peg across the room. Her rag doll still sat in the rocking chair. The white cotton curtains dangled limply at the window.

It seemed the same—and yet it wasn't. Now it was too quiet.

She swung her legs to the floor and crossed the rug to her door. She opened it a crack and looked out.

At the end of the hall, Matty was slumped in a chair, her face masked by a corner of twisted white apron.

"Matty," Kate whispered as she slipped down the darkened hall, trying not to wake her mother. "What is it?"

Matty looked up, her face awash in tears. She pulled Kate close to her skirts. "Oh, Lawd, what's gwine to happen to us?"

The door to Charlotte's bedroom squeaked open, and Kate looked up eagerly. But it was Dr. Howard, who'd come the night before.

"Matty," he said, his voice grizzled with fatigue, "did you. . . ?"

The black woman shook her head, then let go of Kate.

"I'm sorry, Kate." The doctor knelt beside her. "But your mother had a very difficult time of it. We did all that we could. But she died early this morning."

Died? Her mother? Bobby Revell had a dog that died. Chickens died when you chopped off their heads, and bugs died when you swatted them. But her mother? Who would kill her mother?

Maybe if I tiptoe back to my bed very quietly, I'll wake up and find that this is just a bad dream. Maybe if I say nothing, Mama will come into my room in the morning. She'll pull back the curtains, laugh and say, "Wake up, my little sleepyhead."

But Dr. Howard opened the bedroom door, just long enough for her to see the horrible scene inside. There was her father, sprawled over her mother, sobbing and pawing like a crazed hound dog. And there was her mother, eyes closed, a sheet pulled up to her neck, and her skin, the color of cold cinders.

The house filled up with people, people who came bearing sympathy along with early summer squash and sweet potato pies. They passed through the Callahan parlor to view Charlotte and her dark-haired infant son, dressed in a lacy christening gown and nestled in the crook of her lifeless arm.

Someone asked what the child had been named, but there was no answer. It was up to his father to name him, but it was obvious that Emory couldn't make a decision like that. Hour after hour he sat, staring at the red-haired woman in the simple pine coffin, oblivious to the neighbors who filed in behind him.

But Kate would not look into the long wooden box. The woman lying there bore no resemblance to her mother. She had the same red hair, but she had no smiles, no words of comfort, no lilting laughter. This was another woman. A woman whose silence frightened her. A woman she couldn't bear to see.

Matty explained that once they took her mother to the church, she wouldn't come home again. But what did that mean? Who would feed her dinner, and brush her hair, and make her dresses? Would Matty become her mother now? Or would her father take care of her?

On the third day, they buried Charlotte and her son in the cemetery behind the Baptist church. As Matty's brother and his friends filled in the hole and shaped the mound with the backs of their shovels, Kate looked across the yard to the spot where her mother had fed her chicken and lemonade, only days before.

She took hold of her father's hand and rubbed it against her cheek. She looked up, hoping he would notice her. His jaw twitched, but that was all.

Their friends came forward to cover the mound with flowers, and Matty took her hand. It was time to go home now. Kate turned back for one last look at the pile of red-brown earth. And for a moment she wished that she could trade places with her nameless brother and be the one to sleep with her mother forever.

Three

"Eat your cereal, Kate."

The little girl stared at the bowl of cold oatmeal. "I'm not hungry, Daddy."

Emory sighed as the familiar pain began to climb up the back of his neck. It had been eight months since Charlotte had died and still Kate wouldn't mind him. "I don't care if you're not hungry, Katie, you must eat your cereal!"

"Really, Daddy, I'm not hungry."

He grabbed her by the scruff of the neck and pushed her nose into the bowl. "You eat it all up, you hear?"

He stormed out onto the back porch, slamming the door so he wouldn't hear his daughter whimper. He reached in his pocket for a cigarette, then shakily lit a match.

It was just his nerves, he reminded himself. That damn war had shot them to hell. Now the angry words seemed to spill out before he could stop them. Hurting Charlotte, hurting Katie.

It was just that it was all so overwhelming. He didn't know how to raise a five-year-old girl, not properly at least. Just as he didn't know how to raise cotton.

The farm. The memory of it had kept him from losing all hope in those dark days in France. Amid the mud and the stench and the death all around him, it reminded him of what he was fighting for. And Charlotte, too, of course. But the farther he traveled from her perfume, the more he knew that when he returned, she would realize the mistake she had made.

There was none of that in her letters—they were full of love and passion and plans for the future. But still he worried. In all his life, he had never expected to meet a woman like

Charlotte Dellaplaine—much less discover that she wanted to marry him.

How would he keep her happy? His only hope was that he could take his father's land and turn it into one of the best spreads in western Mississippi. Then he'd be able to give his laughing redhead all the things she'd have to give up when she left New Orleans.

But it was all a farce, every last bit of it. The western front had none of the glory that the army recruiters traded on. You'd gain a few yards of burnt-out countryside and lose your best buddies. There was no triumph, only death and despair.

But Emory had survived and he had come home, home to a wonderful woman who still professed to love him.

He tried to escape the awful memories in farm work, getting up early and working long after the sun went down. But after the first two years, he learned the secret his father had taken to his grave—their beautiful Mississippi land was dying.

Emory tried different crops, but it didn't seem to matter. Each year's production was lower than the year before, each year there was less money to bring home to Charlotte.

But she never complained. She always insisted that next year would be better, that their fortunes had to change. Somehow her relentless optimism only seemed to make it worse. It would have been easier if she had nagged him, told him to find another job. But she didn't. And it only made him feel guilty, guilty that he could never give her the things she had dreamed of, guilty that she had traded in the comforts of her youth for this.

It was last March when he'd discovered Charlotte's secret: that her mother was sending her a check every month. Charlotte insisted that she only used the money to buy special things for Kate. But it made no difference to Emory. In his eyes, he might as well have been a kept man.

But now all their arguments seemed silly. He had sent word to her people when she died, but they didn't come to the funeral. And after a few weeks, the checks stopped coming, too.

Emory didn't care at first; he'd never counted on Mrs.

Dellaplaine's money. But long days in the field and late nights huddled over the farm's ledger books had changed his mind.

He needed the money now.

More than that, though, he needed Charlotte.

The shock of her death had turned into a dulling pain that never seemed to dissipate. When he came in from the fields, he still expected to see her there, tidying up the house or learning a new recipe from Matty. And when he looked at Kate, all he saw was Charlotte's proud chin and her haunting deep green eyes.

Nighttime was the hardest part of the day, when their big bed seemed so empty, when his dreams taunted him with visions of Charlotte, her creamy skin, her laughter, and her love. And now that the harvest was over, there was less work to fill his days. So he turned, more and more, to the cure that he had found was better than sleep.

He pulled out his father's pocket watch. Johnny Revell had said he was going to make some more mash whiskey last night. If he rode over there now, he could probably still get some.

He pulled on the coat he kept in the barn and saddled up Bessie.

"Daddy," a voice called from the kitchen. But it was lost in the clatter of hooves on the road into town.

The little girl came out on the porch. "I finished all my cereal!" Too late, Kate saw the figure disappearing into a cloud of red dust.

She was all alone now, deserted. Eight months ago, she would have been terrified. But her father's departure meant nothing to her now. It had happened too many times before.

Matty Brown had been surprised when "Mistuh Emory" had let her go. She knew he would have trouble making ends meet, but she reckoned that somehow he would find a way to keep her on.

But three weeks after Charlotte died, he told her to leave. "What about Katie?" she'd wanted to ask. But instead she held her tongue. The Mansons had told her there would always be a job with them—just on the strength of her dewberry pies. Within hours she had gathered up her things and left the Callahans for good.

She hadn't been back since, though a day didn't go by without her thinking about Miss Charlotte and her daughter. She didn't like the things she was hearing around town. About Mistuh Emory not paying his field hands on time. About how Mistuh Emory didn't show up for church anymore. About how Katie Callahan hadn't started school that fall.

So at last, Matty decided to see for herself. It was a cold day, even for February, and the horses' leather reins sliced across her worn hands like knives. The wind whistled across the fields, and as she rounded the bend, the house came into view.

From a distance, it looked no different from before, its white shingles fading into the gray sky. The red fields lay fallow around it; in town they were saying "Mistuh Callahan's crops gone bad this year."

She rapped briskly on the door in back, then again, a little harder. At last, she heard a little voice from the other side.

"Who is it?"

She smiled with relief. "Miss Kate, it's me. Matty."

The door swung open, and the little girl threw her arms around Matty's ample waist. "Oh, Matty, I've missed you so."

"I've missed you, too, sugar. Here, let me come into the kitchen and get warm."

As she stepped inside her former realm, a fetid odor assaulted her. At first, she thought it was the contrast between the closed-up house and the cold fresh air. But it was worse than that. The sink was stacked with dirty dishes, and in the pantry, she knew food must be rotting.

"Where's your daddy?" Matty asked stonily.

"I don't know," Kate said, tugging at her hands behind her back. "He never tells me where he's going."

"Is he gone a lot?"

Kate hesitated, then nodded.

Matty sighed as she looked around her. It was worse than she had imagined—the dust, the cobwebs, the garbage piled up as if it were prepared for a reunion of rats.

And the little girl. Matty reached down to brush Kate's matted hair from her cheek. What would Charlotte say if she could see her child, left alone like this?

"What's wrong, Matty?"

"Nothing, chile." She knew her first job was to comfort Kate. She needed love, and someone to pay attention for a change. "Why don't we go up to your room and I'll tell you a story, the way we used to."

"I'd like that!"

The two of them passed several happy hours, talking and singing and laughing. Matty knew she could keep Kate happy for now. But what about tonight—and tomorrow?

It was late now. She had to leave.

"Will you come back and see me again, Matty? Can you bring Lucy next time?"

Matty bent to kiss her. "I'll try, sugar. I'll try."

She embraced Kate one last time, then freed herself from the little girl's grasp and ran for the wagon. It was growing darker now. She didn't know when Mistuh Emory would be home, and she didn't want to meet him.

The day had haunted her, sickened her. Didn't anyone care about the child? But what could she do? She was just a poor colored cook, who couldn't read or write. What business did she have messin' with a white man's life?

But then she thought of Charlotte. Sweet, beautiful Charlotte. Matty had loved her like a sister. And, she thought, Charlotte had loved her about as much as a white woman could.

Charlotte had trusted her so much that when she decided she had to tell someone she had gotten married, Matty was the person she'd told. "His name is Emory," she said breathlessly, pulling out a locket from her drawer. "Emory Callahan."

Matty smiled at the memory. Charlotte had counted on her then. And as sure as she was of the Lord Jesus, she knew Charlotte was counting on her now.

Four

Amanda Dellaplaine McNeil pulled the velvet wrapper close to her pale skin as she sat down at her desk in the morning room. Overnight the temperature had dipped into the teens, and though Washington liked to pretend it was a southern city, it was a chilly reminder of how far from home she really was.

By the capital's standards her face was pleasant enough, long and thin, with piercing blue eyes. But the golden tresses of her youth were turning brown now, rather like first-of-the-autumn leaves. To a stranger, she had the air of a rose that had been left standing too long in a vase of water that no one had bothered to change.

She took a sip of tea and savored the warmth it sent to her fingertips and toes. Then she set the cup down and pulled out the curious letter one more time.

She pondered for a moment what stationery would be proper for the reply. It depended, she decided, on what that reply would be.

"Dear Mrs. McNeil," the letter began in a precise script.

> *I am the pastor of the Baptist church in Homer, Miss., and am writing at the request of Matty Brown, who served as housekeeper to your late sister.*
>
> *Mrs. Brown asked me to write you because of her concern for the welfare of your niece, Katharine Callahan. Since your sister's death, it has become clear to many of us that Emory Callahan is unable to care for his daughter as a proper father should. Mrs. Brown is hoping that you might be able to intervene. . . .*

Amanda put the letter down. What kind of a man was
Emory Callahan? No one in her family knew for sure. Charlotte had given her only glimpses in the letters they had
exchanged. But Amanda had always sensed that she was
holding something back.

She had only a vague memory of Matty. All of her parents'
servants tended to blend together in her mind. All of them
had liked Charlotte better anyway.

"You're thinking about your niece again." Stephen
McNeil kissed his wife lightly behind the ear.

She folded up the letter quickly. "Are you off to court?"

"Yes"—his eyes twinkled—"and you're trying to change
the subject." He smiled. He was too smart for her. But then,
that was one of the things that had attracted her in the first
place. He was twenty years older, a widower whose hairline
was now receding in inverse relationship to his waistline. But
he was kind and comfortably wealthy—and tolerant of her
idiosyncrasies.

"What do you think I should do?"

He bent down and took her hands in his. "I think you
should do whatever you want. We have room for your niece.
And Margaret might enjoy having a cousin to play with. But
if you don't want to make that kind of commitment, you don't
have to. Ultimately her father must bear the responsibility."

"How would we arrange it?"

"We could hire a lawyer. Ask the minister to approach
Emory. If he agrees, we should get him to sign a document.
To protect ourselves, of course."

"Do you think he'd agree?"

He nodded toward the letter. "Reverend Malone seems to
think so."

She rose and attempted to straighten his tie. "I'll think
about it. In the meantime, you'd better hurry. We wouldn't
want the Honorable Stephen J. McNeil holding up court over
a silly domestic matter, now would we?"

He kissed her quickly on the forehead. "We can talk about
it more tonight."

She watched him leave, then returned to the pile of cor-
respondence that awaited her. A wedding invitation that had

to be acknowledged. A thank-you note to a congressman's wife for her dinner party. A letter from her mother.

She had never forgiven her parents for abandoning Charlotte, even as she had understood why. There was nothing more basic to the Dellaplaines than family and reputation—and Charlotte had scorned them both. Still, Amanda thought, her parents should have gone to Charlotte's funeral. She would have—if anyone had bothered to tell her in time.

She remembered when she and Charlotte had learned they were both pregnant. "Maybe someday our children will get to be friends," her sister had written. Amanda had wondered about that. Their lives were so different, as were the men they had married.

But when you stripped all of that away, Amanda knew, Katharine Callahan was still a Dellaplaine.

Amanda reached into the drawer and pulled out two sheets of crisp ivory paper, a bottle of India ink, and the fountain pen with the new nib.

"Dear Rev. Malone," she wrote. "Thank you for your kind letter. I have thought about the matter for several days now, and I have decided I would like to help my niece. . . ."

Emory watched as the two men pulled out of his driveway. He went to the pantry to pour himself one last drink, then turned off the lights and climbed the stairs to his bedroom.

But he didn't stop there. Instead he went on down the hall and quietly opened Kate's door.

A ribbon of moonlight brushed her forehead and the sight of her moved him so much that he could not bear to leave. He picked up the doll in the rocking chair, then sat down, being careful not to creak the floorboards.

With her hand curled on her pillow in peaceful innocence, Kate had never looked more like Charlotte. He remembered the nights he had lain awake, calculating the farm's accounts over and over in his head. Then he'd look across the bed and see Charlotte, pale brown feather lashes closed and a red curl grazing her cheek.

A sob welled up in his chest. In the morning, they would come to take Kate away. Deliver her to the Dellaplaines.

Take her away from him. He buried his head in his hands. *Oh, Charlotte, have I done the right thing?*

"I know it has been difficult," he remembered the minister saying. "Carrying on without Charlotte, trying to raise the little girl the best you can. But tell me this, Emory: Does Kate go to school? Is there someone watching her when you have to go into town? Do you get home each night to fix her dinner?"

The questions had pummeled his heart like stones.

"Your sister-in-law wants to take Kate," the minister had continued. "She can provide her with a good education, a home that's safe and secure."

A home with money, Emory had thought.

But in the end, he had gone along with them. It would be better for Kate. He'd be able to devote all his energies to the farm then. And someday, when it was making money again, he would bring her home. Those papers they'd had him sign didn't mean anything. She was still his flesh and blood.

She was still his only tie to Charlotte.

He sat and rocked on into the night. And for the first time in a long time, he didn't finish his drink.

Kate rolled over sleepily and propped open an eye. Across the room, she saw her father, swaying slowly in her rocking chair, cradling her doll as if it were his child.

"Daddy?"

"Good morning, Katie. Did I frighten you?"

"No," she lied, shaking her head.

"I came in to kiss you good night, and the next thing I knew I fell asleep in your rocker."

He seemed different this morning. Kinder. Quieter. But why?

"What are you going to do today, Daddy?"

He clasped his hands in front of him and stared at the floor. "I'm going to work in the barn, sweetie."

"Can I help you?" she ventured shyly.

"I don't think so, Katie." He forced a smile onto his face. "You're going to start off on a long trip today."

"Me?" He nodded. "Where are we going?"

Emory swallowed hard and stroked his hand along his grizzled jaw. "I'm staying here, Katie. . . . You see, I haven't been a very good father to you since your mama died. Your Aunt Amanda, Mama's sister, wants you to come live with her. In Washington. Where President Coolidge lives. It won't be forever, sweetie. Just long enough for Daddy to get the farm going again."

Kate said nothing for a moment. Leave her father? Leave Homer and everything she knew? Who was this Aunt Amanda anyway?

But then another voice took over. *Maybe she knows how to cook like Mama did. Maybe she'll play with me and tell me stories. Maybe she'll sing me Mama's songs.*

"Will you miss me, Daddy?"

"You know I will, sweetie." He rose from his chair and came over to hug her tightly. "Always remember that no matter what happens, you will always be my little girl."

Then why, she wondered, *does he want to get rid of me?*

They were waiting for her at the station, Matty and Lucy, Rev. Malone and two strange men, one white, one black.

"This is Mistuh Cowpet," Matty whispered. "He's a lawyah. And this is Ezra." She nodded to the tall black man who stood proudly at her side. "He's come to take you to your aunt's."

"You're not coming with me?" Kate asked. Suddenly she was confused. *What have I done wrong? Why are they sending me away?*

Matty's voice was quiet. "Lucy and I have to stay here."

The train came around the curve up ahead, steam billowing from its engine.

"But I don't want to leave you!" Kate wailed, her eyes filling with tears.

The train screeched as it pulled into the station, drowning out her words.

The men looked on helplessly. Finally, the white lawyer growled at Matty: "Can't you do something?"

She knelt down and took hold of Kate's shoulders. "Listen, Katie. What would your mama think if she could see you carrying on so? You're going off to see your aunt Amanda. She's a nice lady who lives in a big house in a big city. And you can always come back and visit ol' Matty whenever you want.''

She hesitated, then said solemnly: "Remember what your mama used to say. Hold your head up. You *are* a Della-plaine.''

Kate sniffed loudly, then straightened her back. At the far end of the station, the train blew its whistle.

"You'd better get going," Mr. Cowpet said.

"Good-bye, Katie.'' Her father hugged her tightly, his cheek wet against hers. "You be a good girl, you understand?''

She nodded.

"Good-bye, sugar,'' Matty said, wrapping her arms around her and squeezing hard. Kate hugged Lucy quickly, then someone took hold of her arms and pulled her on board the train.

It pulled out of Homer, away from everything in the world she had known: her father, her mother, Matty, and her friends. A sultry world that seemed to change as slowly as the cotton blanketing its fields.

Kate looked back as that world disappeared into a haze of confusion and tears. Then the train rounded a curve and steamed off to a faraway city and an aunt she knew only by name.

Five

Overnight, Amanda's calm confidence had disappeared. What if Katharine were ill? What if she got homesick? Or worse, what if she turned out to be a little hooligan?

Perhaps they should have all gone to meet the train. No,

it was easier here, in the quiet of her home. Besides, you never knew who you might run into at Union Station.

"Mother!" Margaret's shriek pierced the silence. "They're here!"

The front door swung open and Ezra led a young girl in. She came forward slowly, clinging tightly to his hand. So small, Amanda thought, and yet struggling so hard not to be afraid.

"Hello, Katharine." Amanda knelt down to her niece's height. "Welcome to Washington."

"Hello," she replied shyly.

"Here," Amanda said, pulling Margaret to her side. "This is your cousin, Margaret."

Margaret stuck out a pudgy hand. "I'm glad you're here."

"Thank you," Kate said.

For a moment Amanda couldn't speak. There was no doubt this was Charlotte's daughter. It wasn't obvious at first glance, because Kate's brown hair was so much quieter than the vibrant red of Charlotte's. But there was something about Katharine's eyes and face, the stubborn pride of her uplifted chin and straight shoulders that belonged to her mother. And forced Amanda to remember just how jealous she had always been of her.

Then she noticed her niece's loganberry coat. It was a size too small, and in need of mending under the arm.

I ran away from you, Charlotte. I could never compete with you in New Orleans. But I did all right for myself. I married a judge who bought me a beautiful home and gave me a lovely child. What did your husband ever do for you?

She turned to Ezra. "Please collect Katharine's bags and take them to her room."

"No problem, ma'am," he replied. "She only brought one."

Kate's room was straight out of a young girl's fantasies. She had a canopy bed, covered with ruffles of white dotted swiss. Across the room were two tall windows that looked out on the tops of newly budding trees and beyond them, Dupont Circle. A window seat had been built between them

and covered with a soft cushion. On a rainy afternoon, it was
the perfect place to leaf through a book.

And, oh, did Margaret have books! There were fairy tales,
and Aesop's Fables and Robin Hood and Ali Baba and the
Forty Thieves. Kate couldn't read them, but she loved looking
at the pictures—colors so rich that a little girl could get lost
in them.

Margaret had dolls, too. Rows and rows of china-faced
things, dressed in fine silk and velvet. Aunt Amanda had
given her one, too, but Kate didn't like it much. It was a doll
to look at, not one to dress and feed and hug and take to bed
with you at night. Not a good rag doll like Jenny.

Most of her old clothes had disappeared, replaced by fine
embroidered dresses and fancy party clothes. Her brand-
new red leather oxfords had shiny buckles on the straps, and
they made a wonderful noise when she tapped her way down
the curving staircase. Just the same, she wished she still
had a pair of overalls to wear, the kind that were fun to get
dirty.

She had never really worried about coming home dirty
before, but now she did. She was always careful to say
"please" and "thank you," "yes, ma'am," and "no, sir."
If she made her aunt and uncle cross, they might decide to
send her away, just like her father had. But here at least, she
never went hungry. And she was never left alone.

Sometimes, though, she wondered when she would go back
to Homer. If she could only figure out what she'd done to
make her father so angry. Maybe then he would come back
to get her.

She still missed Matty and Lucy and riding bareback
and playing Red Rover with the kids down the road. And
she missed her mother and her father and the days when they
had all been together. The times when they had all been
happy.

And sometimes late at night, when she burrowed underneath the covers so the McNeils wouldn't hear her cry, she
wished that she could rub a magic lamp like the one in Margaret's storybook, and make her world go back to the way
it used be.

* * *

Margaret was already enrolled at St. Peter's, the school, Amanda had determined, to which most of Washington's "better" families sent their daughters. But to Kate, it looked like a prison, a dank stone building that squatted behind the church that gave it its name. Slivers of sunlight managed to sneak through the thick windowpanes, but they only high-lighted the dust motes, rising up to the ceiling, trying to escape.

The uniforms seemed to match the building: heavy jumpers of gray serge that hung shapelessly over scratchy blue cotton blouses and were much too hot for the warmest days of fall.

But it was the other girls who made St. Peter's truly un-bearable for Kate. They mimicked her accent and called her names. And they all seemed so much smarter than she was. Why, some were already reading—and doing sums.

There seemed to be no way to escape the fortress. Not until the afternoon when Kate's teacher excused her to go to the bathroom in the middle of her grammar lesson.

As she hurried into the lavatory, two older girls looked up from the pictures they were drawing on the wall. The pictures were not very good, but one drawing was unmistakable. It was a cartoon of Miss DeVore, the school's aging headmis-tress.

The girls dropped their chalk and ran out the door. Kate went into the stall and locked the door. When she came out, a teacher was blocking her exit.

She had tiny eyes and a tight, mean mouth. "Come with me," she said.

She ushered Kate down the hall and into the main office. "Wait here," she ordered. She disappeared, then reappeared a few moments later. "Miss DeVore wants to see you."

The older woman sat straight in her chair, her hands folded primly on top of her desk. Her face was framed by the frill of white lace at her neck and marcelled curls that punctuated her chalky cheeks.

"Sit down," she commanded.

Kate did as she was told.

"Did you see who was drawing the pictures?"

Kate nodded.

"Then I know you'll tell me who they were."

Kate remembered when Bobby Revell tattled on his older brother—and the shiner he'd gotten in return. "No, ma'am, I can't."

Miss DeVore glared at her. "You know, young lady, that St. Peter's Academy has an honor code and that all offenses must be reported to me. If you don't, you will be expelled."

You will be expelled. The words were the key to her prison. This time her voice was stubborn. "I don't know, ma'am."

Miss DeVore's eyes narrowed. "I'm sure you will know by Monday, Katharine. You are dismissed."

That night, after supper, Kate was summoned to her uncle's study. It was his private sanctuary, a room the girls were not allowed to play in. He was seated on the leather couch beside the fireplace, her aunt on the tufted chair to one side.

"Miss DeVore called me today." Amanda's voice was stern. "I told her you probably didn't understand what would happen if you refused to tell her the girls' names. Do you?"

"I won't be able to go to St. Peter's anymore."

Amanda's lips formed a chilly smile. "Then why won't you tell her, dear?"

"Because I don't want to!" Kate sputtered.

"Now listen." Amanda rose, shaking a finger in Kate's face. "I am not going to put up with this behavior any longer." She grabbed Kate by the wrist and spanked her toward the door. "You go to your room and you stay there until you're ready to tell us those names!"

As she climbed the stairs, Kate worried: Was her aunt angry enough to send her away? No, she hadn't threatened to do that. No matter how long she had to wait, Kate was not going to tell the names. She could outlast her aunt. If she could survive all those months with her father, she could survive this. She was not going back to St. Peter's.

The next morning Tillie, the maid, delivered her breakfast on a tray. As Kate munched on the dry toast, she heard the front door close. Now she remembered. It was Saturday, the day her aunt had promised to take her and Margaret to the National Museum.

There was a knock at the door. "It's Uncle Stephen, Kate. May I come in?"

"Yes, sir."

He opened the door and crossed the room to sit on the edge of her bed. He was older than her father, and certainly not as handsome. But even now, she wasn't afraid of him.

"I've been thinking about you and your school since last night, Kate." It was his solemn voice, the one she'd heard when Aunt Amanda had taken the girls to visit his courtroom. "And I've been wondering why a good little girl like you would be so stubborn about something as important as this."

She didn't speak.

"I can only think of two reasons," he continued. "Either you're afraid of those older girls or you don't want to go to school." Then he looked straight at her. "Am I right?"

"I don't want to go back," she blurted out.

"Why not?" His voice was gentle.

The tears began stinging her eyes as she spoke. "Because the girls make fun of me. They make fun of the way I talk and they laugh and they call me names."

He handed her a linen handkerchief. "Like what?"

She sniffed. "They call me 'po' white trash.' And they call me an orphan. I'm not an orphan, Uncle Stephen!"

"I know you're not, Kate." He thought for a moment. "I'll have to talk to Aunt Amanda first. But if you're so miserable at St. Peter's that you would try to get yourself expelled, well, I think we'd better see about moving you somewhere else."

Her heart leapt.

"But I'll tell you something important, Kate." He stood up beside her bed. "You know how you have one good red velvet dress and you try very hard not to get it dirty?"

She nodded.

"Well, just like your dress, 'Katharine Callahan' is a very nice name and it's the only name you'll ever have. So you have to be very careful not to do anything that will make people think Katharine Callahan is a bad girl, because we both know she isn't. Do you understand?"

"Yes, sir."

"So if you leave St. Peter's, we don't want it to be because you were bad, do we?"

"No," she said, but she wasn't convinced.

"Then if I promise to work on finding you a new school, will you promise to tell Miss DeVore the names of the girls?"

She hesitated. "I promise."

She kept her word and her uncle kept his. They transferred her to the public school that was an easy walk away. It seemed like heaven compared with the tyranny and teasing of St. Peter's, and she quickly made several friends. Not the children of the city's finest, Amanda was quick to note, but still children of good, middle-class parents.

A few years later even Margaret joined her. Her aunt and uncle wouldn't say why, but Kate decided it probably had something to do with the "Crash" everyone was talking about.

The McNeils let some of their servants go. Aunt Amanda finally learned how to drive. And her aunt didn't talk as much anymore about her family back in New Orleans, and the money her daddy had promised would all be hers on the day he died.

Six

It was as hot as the inside of a teakettle the summer of 1932. Or at least it seemed that way when you were twelve and had to pass the steamiest months of the year cooped up in town.

It wasn't that they couldn't afford to rent a summer cottage, Stephen had assured the girls. And he certainly wasn't in any danger of losing *his* job. It was just that Amanda felt safer if they stayed in town and saved up the money.

It seemed to Kate that her aunt was never sure what she

should worry about these days—and so she worried about everything. How were they going to keep the maid on? Where was Mabel Baylor's brother going to find a job? Would her stocks ever be worth anything again?

"And now," she said in a pique over dinner, "what are we supposed to do with all those hooligans who've arrived in town?"

Stephen took a slice of cold beef. "Are your referring to the Bonus Army, dear?"

"Bonus, my foot," she replied. "If they were a real army, they'd be home watching out for their womenfolk."

"I think Hoover should at least talk to them," Kate piped up. "After all, they traveled all this way to see him."

Stephen's eyes lit up. "You've been reading the papers, haven't you, Kate?"

She nodded.

"Well, I happen to agree with you. All the men want is for someone to listen to them. But they're not going to sit still all summer." He tugged at his well-starched collar. "Not in this heat at least."

Darkness fell very slowly, like a worker staggering home from the office. Across the street from the McNeils', a stranger paused underneath the streetlight and pulled a crumpled paper from his shirt pocket. He smiled. This was the place. It had been easy to find, once his buddy helped him figure out the pattern of Washington's streets.

He leaned back against the lamppost and pulled out a cigarette. Had he always planned to come here when he set out for Washington? He wasn't sure. But somewhere in those long, restless nights on the mud flats by the Potomac, the idea had come to him. He knew he had to find her.

He retreated into the shadows where no one could see him. He was prepared to wait—a long time if he had to. But she had to come out eventually. And if his luck stayed with him, she would be alone.

Stephen looked up from the morning paper and smiled. Across from him Kate was engrossed in a newspaper story, oblivious to her breakfast, her spoon suspended in midair.

He'd given up pushing Amanda to have another child. But if he couldn't have a son, Kate was the next best thing.

His gaze turned to his blond-haired daughter, concentrating on painting her short fingernails. He loved Margaret, of course, but as she grew older, she seemed to have adopted all the traits of her mother that he found most annoying. When she wasn't trying to figure out how to catch the eye of that Brown boy down the street, she was papering her room with more photos of Valentino. And he'd been dead for years!

Kate, on the other hand, couldn't get enough of school. Often when he came home, she would be waiting in ambush with a fusillade of questions. "What caused the stock market to crash?" "Why did they approve Prohibition?" "How does an airplane fly?" Sometimes after a long day in court the questions exhausted him. But more often than not he felt a ridiculous kind of pleasure watching her young mind at work.

"What are you up to today, Kate?"

She marked her place with a finger. "Well, I have my tennis lesson this morning. After that, I'm not sure. . . . I may stop over at Ruth's."

"There's a case coming up in my courtroom next week that I think you'd be interested in. Maybe we can talk your aunt into letting you sit in on it."

"I'd like that, Uncle Stephen."

"Margaret, would you. . . ?"

"Thanks, Dad, but I think I'll pass."

Kate glanced over at his watch. "Oh, gosh, look at the time." She gulped down the rest of her orange juice. "Gotta run or I'll be late." She planted a kiss on Stephen's forehead. "Bye, Margaret."

"See you tonight," Stephen called as she grabbed her racket and dashed for the door. "And serve well!"

It was nearly a mile's walk to the courts, but Kate didn't mind. She liked the freedom of being out on her own, of strolling down the tree-lined streets like a queen surveying her kingdom.

In her new white tennis dress she felt pleased with herself, and as she walked she swung her racket through the air, trying out her forehand, her backhand, and then, just for fun, a smash.

As she waited to cross Connecticut Avenue, she looked back and saw a man approaching, about half a block behind. He was dressed strangely, she thought, in baggy, khaki-colored pants and a shirt without sleeves. Maybe he was some sort of workman. Or maybe he was out of work.

The light took an eternity to change. She headed across the street. She tried to walk more quickly, but whenever she turned to look, the man had managed to narrow the distance between them. He was following her, she was sure of it.

She decided to stay on Connecticut Avenue—there were more cars and people there—but she didn't look back anymore. She kept her head down and picked up her pace. There were only a few blocks left.

She could hear his footsteps now, drawing closer. What could he possibly want? Her legs were getting heavy, she was nearly out of breath. And then he grabbed her arm.

"Hey, slow down, Katie."

How did he know her name? She spun around, trembling, and looked the dark-haired stranger in the eye.

"Don't you know who I am?"

And then it hit her. Like a blow to her head—and her heart. She was six again, and this man was all she had left in the world.

"Daddy?" she said in a shocked half whisper.

"That's right, honey." He swept her into his arms. "Oh, Katie, it's been too long . . . much, much too long."

Her tall, thin body remained rigid within his embrace. She felt confused, confused and embarrassed that he would grab her like this on a busy street.

It was a long moment before she could speak. "What are you doing here?"

"I joined up with the Bonus March," he said, lifting his chin. "I figured my country owed me something more after all I've gone through. And once I got this far, I said to myself, 'I want to see my little Katie' " He held her at arm's length. "How you've grown! You're turning into quite a young lady."

"You never wrote me, Daddy." She felt the anger welling up in her. "All those years and you never even once wrote me!"

"I know, honey, and I'm sorry . . . but I've changed. I really have."

She tried to pull away. "I have to go, Daddy." She spoke slowly, as if she were talking to a crazy person. "I'm going to miss my tennis lesson."

"All right," he said, letting go of her arm. "We'll talk more later on. But I've done a lot of thinking, Katie." He paused, looking at her intently. "I want you to come home with me. It's time you came back to Homer where you belong."

A chill ran through her body. She stared at her father, searching his wild dark eyes, studying the face that seemed to belong to a stranger.

"I've given up drinking," he said quietly. "I had to sell off the farm, but I still have our house. I rent it now. I work for Doc Marston, doing odd jobs, that sort of thing. Do you remember his store? That's where I used to buy you candy."

Cinnamon sticks and gumdrops. "I'll bring you a piece of candy when I come home, Katie." Her stomach churned with a desperate sort of emotion. "Daddy, I'm late. I have to go."

"All right, Katie. We'll talk more later on."

What did he mean, "later on"? When? Where? What was there to talk about anyway? "Good-bye," she said with finality, then turned and ran pell-mell toward the park.

But she never made it to the tennis courts. Her head felt light and her legs trembled. She wouldn't be able to hit a tennis ball if she tried. She stopped under a maple tree to catch her breath. She had to have a chance to think.

Her life, as she thought of it now, began the day she came to Washington. Homer was but a distant memory, a sort of fog in which she could still see the faces of her parents and Matty and Lucy, but only dimly. Aunt Amanda had some photos of her mother, of course. But they were from an earlier time, of a sister who was still more a girl than a woman. When Kate left that wintry morning six years ago, she didn't think to ask for any pictures. She never expected to be gone this long.

There was little that was happy to remember from back home. There were only scenes of her mother dying, and of her lonely father forgetting that she was still alive.

The McNeils, on the other hand, had been good to her. She loved Uncle Stephen—and looked up to him. Aunt Amanda probably would never treat her like a real daughter, but by now she could accept that.

But Emory Callahan was still her father. And she was puzzled now by the haunting feeling inside her that made it impossible to move.

He had never visited in all these years, never even written. And yet suddenly, she was filled with a profound curiosity over what he was really like—and what part of him was in her.

She left the cool shade of the tree and began walking, out to Rock Creek Park and along the paths that twined alongside the dwindling stream there. She walked for hours, for miles, trying to organize her feelings into one coherent whole that would tell her what she should do and what she should say when she saw him again. As long as she kept walking, she knew he wouldn't be able to find her. And as long as she kept walking, her aunt and uncle wouldn't be able to send her away.

But at the end of the day, she had to go home. It was late, and the McNeils had already sat down to dinner.

"Where have you been?" her aunt asked as Kate shuffled into her seat. "I've been frantic, calling around, trying to find you."

"I've been walking," Kate replied. She picked up her fork and poked at her salad.

"Walking! What kind of an answer is that?"

Kate chewed her lip, then said, "My father followed me to my tennis lesson."

"Your father!" This time Amanda and Stephen spoke together.

She nodded. "He's in town with all those veterans. He says he wants me to come back home with him."

"What did you tell him?" Stephen asked.

"Nothing, really. I said I had to get to my lesson and he said we'd talk later and then I left."

"Did he say when he would come?"

Kate shook her head. "He just said 'later.' "

No one spoke for a moment. A fly circled the strawberry shortcake on the sideboard, its buzz crescendoing, daring someone, anyone, to swat it. But nobody lifted a hand.

"Well," Stephen said at last, "there's nothing we can do about it now. I suggest we all eat dinner."

They ate in silence, a hurried sort of meal that everyone seemed to want to finish. Kate yearned to talk to someone, to Margaret, to Uncle Stephen, even Amanda. She wanted to explain how she felt, see if it made any sense. But she was not about to put her emotions on the table like a vase of flowers for all of them to sniff and pluck and rearrange. Now, more than ever before, she felt she didn't belong. And for all she knew, they just might decide that she *ought* to go back to Mississippi.

The front-door buzzer sounded. Again they said nothing, waiting for Tillie to answer it. Amanda's fingers fluttered up to pat the back of her hair; Stephen stared at his half-shorn corn cob. They didn't know anyone who would show up uninvited at this hour—and so they all knew exactly who it was.

"It's a Mr. Callahan, ma'am," the maid dutifully reported.

"Stephen?" Amanda's raised eyebrows begged him to take charge.

"Show him into the library, Tillie. Mrs. McNeil and I will have coffee in there." He turned to Kate. "Would you like us to talk to him first? Find out exactly what he is proposing?"

"Oh, would you, Uncle Stephen?"

"Certainly." He reached over and patted her hand. Then he pushed back his chair. "Come, Amanda. Let's see what the man really wants."

They filed down the hall and disappeared into the study.

"I caught sight of him," Margaret said, craning her neck for another view. "He's good-looking, your father is."

Kate nodded dumbly. She went to the sideboard and cut a piece of shortcake, then drowned it in thick fresh cream. Her aunt would scold her if she could see her now. But then it might be years before she'd see another shortcake like this one.

"Do you remember your father very well, Kate?"

She looked at her cousin, surprised. It was a subject Margaret had never broached in the six years they'd been together. Parents dying and parents leaving and parents who failed to keep you fed—it was an image that was much too frightening when you were six or seven.

But now a future was beckoning, a future in which a girl could begin to imagine leaving her parents and marrying, or, perhaps, forging out on her own. And all that really mattered then was who you were deep inside.

Who was Katharine Callahan? she wondered.

"Do you remember him?" Margaret persisted.

Kate shook her head. "Not very well. I almost didn't recognize him. I guess I don't remember very much about my parents. I don't remember very much about Homer."

Margaret said nothing. Kate listened for a moment, hoping to hear something—shouting perhaps?—from behind the closed study door. Then she pushed away her bowl. "I don't feel very good," she said. "I'm going to my room."

She darted up the stairs, afraid that that would be the exact moment the adults would choose to open the door. But their conversation went on, interminably it seemed. She peeked down the stairs occasionally, catching sight at one point of Tillie carrying in the shortcake. But the door remained closed. What *were* they talking about?

She tried to read, but her mind wouldn't take in the words. So she sat on her velvet window seat and watched the lights of Dupont Circle come up as the day faded into night. And she thought about how different her life would have been if her mother had never died.

At last she heard a murmur of voices downstairs, and then the front door closed. She watched her father disappear down the street. He was wearing a jacket now. At least he seemed to be trying.

There was a knock at her door.

"Come in."

It was Uncle Stephen, followed by her aunt.

"We've spoken to your father."

Kate nodded.

Stephen sat down on the edge of her bed, Amanda remained standing.

"It was as you said. He feels that he can take care of you now, that he's turned over a new leaf. But we said we had to talk it over with you first."

He waited, but she said nothing.

"Your aunt and I, we want to do what's best for you. We love you and hope you know you'll always have a home with us. But if you decide you want to be with your father, we'll understand that, too."

"Does he have any right to claim me?"

"No," her uncle replied. "When you came to live with us, your father signed papers that declared we were your guardians. We reminded him of that tonight, and he acknowledged that. But he said he thought that you were old enough now that you should be able to decide for yourself." Stephen pulled out his handkerchief to mop his forehead. "I think we should make some inquiries if you decide you want to join him. Make sure his story holds up. But he sounds as if he's prepared to accept your decision."

Kate's eyes widened as the words registered. It was up to her? They were going to make her decide?

"He wanted to talk with you tonight, but we suggested he come back tomorrow. So it comes down to this, Kate: What do you want?"

She stared at her hands, clasped tightly on her lap in front of her. How could she choose? Her father, her flesh and blood. Yet he represented an unknown future and the pain of the past. Who could say it would be any different now?

Then there was this life, the life she knew. It wasn't perfect either, yet she could trust it, she could count on it. Her uncle and aunt would always be there, with a nice house and plenty to eat. And, what was more important, love. Even now, when they could have sent her away, they weren't trying to.

She thought about the choices, like she had all day in the park, but the answer still came out the same. "I want to stay," she said at last.

Stephen let out his breath in a soft whistle. "I'm glad."

He stood up. "But I think you ought to be the one to tell your father. I don't think he'll accept it otherwise."

"But I don't know how to tell him."

He winked at her. "Don't worry, we'll find a way."

Amanda reached down to brush the hair from Kate's forehead. "It's late, Kate. You ought to be getting to bed."

She turned and headed for the door, but Stephen hesitated. Then he bent down and hugged Kate, and planted kisses on both cheeks. They were wet and sloppy—and yet they were wonderful. When her uncle kissed her, Kate knew that he meant it.

Her father came back the next evening. Once again they met him in Stephen's study, this time with Kate.

All day long she had sat in her window seat, telling herself she was doing the right thing. But it wasn't fair. Why did she have to decide? None of her friends had ever faced a choice like this. Why was she always different?

But when she saw him again, she knew she had made the right decision. It was his eyes that convinced her. She didn't doubt he had changed. But his eyes had seen too much—and she had seen too much in them. The crazy widower. The surly drunk. Her mother had loved something in this man, but now she wasn't sure what. When Kate saw him, she felt anger and—what was worse—pity.

"Have you thought about what I said, Katie?"

She nodded.

"And?"

"I want to stay here, Daddy."

He swallowed hard, his Adam's apple bobbing out from the sinews of his throat. He looked at his hands, then asked, "Will you tell me why?"

She had hoped he wouldn't ask, the answer was so difficult. She spoke carefully, painfully. "This is my home, Daddy. I know it, and I know it will always be here. I can't depend on your home . . . and I can't depend on you."

Emory crunched up the cap he held in his hands. "No, I reckon you can't." He stared at the floor. "Maybe you could come down sometime, just for a visit."

Stephen rose to his feet. "I'm sure we can work something

out," he said quickly. "But I think now, Mr. Callahan, the time has come for you to leave."

Emory did not object. He stood up, then extended his hand. "Good-bye, Kate."

She reached for it, then he pulled her into his arms and hugged her tightly. She felt the tears well up in her eyes, but struggled not to show them. "Good-bye, Daddy."

He turned and walked out of her life without saying another word. And she wondered how long his eyes would haunt her dreams this time.

While her family slept, Amanda paced, the gnawing pain eating away at her heart.

Stephen had never asked her.

It was her niece, her decision—and yet he had never asked her if she wanted Kate to stay.

If he had, she probably would have gone along with him. But he hadn't—and she knew why.

He loved Kate too much. Perhaps it was simply the love of a man for a daughter, but if so, it didn't matter. It was clear he loved Kate more than Margaret. It was possible he loved Kate more than he loved her.

Charlotte had won again.

Perhaps she should feel smug. Eye to eye, it was clear that Emory Callahan wasn't half the man that Stephen McNeil was. She had beaten her sister at her own game.

But now she saw it was only a skirmish. The reinforcements had been sent in, and Margaret was no match for Kate. Kate was smarter and, in her own way, prettier. She was shyer, but when she discovered the boys, she would have her pick.

And until then, Kate had her adoring uncle, and Stephen had Kate.

Why didn't you let him take her, Stephen?

The city was still reeling from the heat, so they had no trouble claiming one of the courts by the Washington Monument.

"Ladies first," Stephen said, tapping the balls over the net.

Kate took her place on the baseline, then smiled, remembering what her instructor had said the day before: "You don't have a lot of power, Kate, but you've got two things that are more important. You know how to concentrate. And, down deep, you really want to win."

She tossed the ball, then whacked it, catching the corner of the forecourt, beyond the reach of her uncle's backhand.

"Hey," he said with a laugh. "Remember this is an aging man you're playing!"

"Sorry," she said gleefully. She moved to the left and hit her next serve, but this time he was ready for it. They settled in, Stephen trying to make up in power what he lacked in Kate's placement. At last he beat out a 6-4 set, but only after three games had gone to deuce.

They paused by the fence for a sip of ice water.

As they rested, they heard a commotion across the Ellipse. A small army seemed to have appeared out of nowhere. Row after row of soldiers, guns held high and bayonets at the ready. Six tanks, testing their engines. And up front, a tall, proud man, riding a beautiful horse.

"My god," Stephen said with disbelief. "They're going after the Bonus Army."

Without a word, they swept up their gear and moved in for a better view. The soldiers started marching, down Pennsylvania Avenue toward blocks where tired-looking men crouched at curbside. An order was sounded, and then the soldiers began lobbing canisters into the crowd.

"Tear gas," Stephen muttered. "Hoover's gone absolutely mad." He took her by the elbow. "Come on, let's go home."

"But what's going to happen?"

"I don't know," he said sternly, "but it's not going to be pretty."

It was after midnight when Stephen finally got home. He had dropped Kate off, ordered Amanda to keep her inside, then disappeared.

Kate tiptoed down the stairs in her thin cotton nightgown. She found him in the kitchen, pouring a glass of milk.

"What happened, Uncle Stephen?"

He took a sip. "It seems the government decided today was the day it had to force the Bonus Marchers out of its buildings. They cleared out some over by the Capitol, but then some of the men decided to try to get back in. When the police came back, they started throwing bricks. The police fought back." He took another sip. "One of the marchers was killed."

She gasped.

"It was a man from Chicago," he said quickly. "Hoover ordered up MacArthur and the troops from Fort Myer. It was as if they decided to fight the war all over again. After they swept down Pennsylvania Avenue, they headed over to the marchers' camp across the river."

"And then?" she prodded, sensing he was holding something back.

He hesitated. "They ordered everyone out," he said, "and then they began burning the place down."

"My father. . . ."

"He probably left town already, Kate. A lot of them have."

"Yes," she said dumbly. Why did she care anyway? She had sent him away. She hadn't heard from him in six years. Why did it matter now?

But it did matter. He was real to her.

"I'd like to find out for sure," she said. "Do you think we can?"

Stephen downed the rest of his milk. "I'll see what I can do."

It took two days and a phone call to Cowpet, the lawyer down in Jackson, before Stephen got his answer. When the government had offered the marchers a free ticket home the week before, Emory decided to take it. He was back in Homer, working in the drugstore.

Stephen called Kate into his study to make his report. When he had finished, she burst into tears.

"What is it, honey?"

"I don't know," she said, sniffing loudly. "One minute I don't want to see him again, then the next I'm terrified that he'll turn out to be dead. And now . . . now I just don't know what I think."

"If you're having second thoughts. . . ."

"No," she insisted. "I just . . . I just wanted him to be all right."

He put an arm around her. "I understand."

Summer dragged on. Kate wondered when she'd hear from her father. If he'd write and ask her to come visit next year, like he said he would.

But the weeks and months went by. Fall came, and with it the start of school. But the letter never did.

So she knew her father hadn't changed after all. She couldn't depend on him, she never could.

She knew then that she had made the right decision.

PART TWO

Washington, 1938

Seven

Franklin D. Roosevelt swept into town the spring of 1933 with a can-do crew and a smile that lit up the country. Within weeks, it seemed, Washington swelled with eager young job-seekers. And over the next few years, agencies sprouted like weeds in the cracks of the concrete of Pennsylvania Avenue, their names a mishmash of capital letters.

All of it served to energize Kate. It made her want to see the world, right the wrongs, make a difference. Just like the president's wife.

Amanda and Margaret told her she was being silly. Now-adays, nothing got Amanda on her high horse more than Eleanor Roosevelt. And with a glass of brandy or two, she could launch into a mocking imitation of the First Lady's nasal voice. The only thing that quieted her was Stephen's gentle reminder that if he was ever going to get a seat on the U.S. Court of Appeals, Roosevelt would be the one to appoint him.

Kate knew she and her cousin had drifted apart over the past few years, and that made her sad. Yet they had so little in common these days. Sometimes it seemed as if Margaret cared only for boys, clothes, and herself—not always in that order. She was going to go to Sweet Briar next year, but not with any hope of getting a degree. Stephen had been reluctant to place the phone calls that got her in, but Amanda had been insistent. She wanted her daughter to find a suitable husband, U-Va stock or a frat man from Hampden-Sydney. A husband not unlike her own.

Kate, on the other hand, viewed her world as a limitless mystery, where everything was a possibility. As for young men, they were merely the standard by which she measured herself—in school or on the tennis court. No matter where she met one, she loved trying to beat him. And that, she knew, horrified her aunt as much as it amused her uncle.

She had developed a passion for languages—first French and now German—as well as European history and politics. As she entered her senior year of high school, Stephen had pushed her to apply to Radcliffe or Smith. But she had decided to attend George Washington instead.

She told her aunt and uncle that she didn't want them to spend the extra money for her to go away—they'd already given her so much. But she also realized that she didn't want to leave Washington; that no ivy-choked campus could provide her with the kind of real-world excitement she found right at home.

But there were some things that she would have been happy to leave behind. Like the ridiculous notion of her aunt's that she and Margaret would make their debuts during the Christmas season of 1938.

"Do I really have to go through with it, Uncle Stephen?" Kate had cornered her uncle in his study and waited so his after-dinner brandy could have a mellowing effect. "I mean, Margaret will love it, but you'll just be wasting your money on me."

Her uncle laughed heartily. "I'm sorry, my dear, but when I pick a battle with your aunt, I do it carefully. And this is one issue on which she is not about to be moved.

"But cheer up," he went on. "It's not the end of the world. Besides, I tend to agree with Amanda that it's about time you started meeting some more young men. Not only are you a very intelligent young woman, you are also very pretty."

"Oh, Uncle Stephen. . . ."

"I'm serious. And if no one else has told you that yet, it's about time they did."

"What would you know about it anyway?"

He chuckled softly. "Kate, you may think I'm an old coot, but I can still remember the first time I fell in love. There is nothing in the world quite so wonderful—or so painful."

She smiled. "Tell me about it then."

He hesitated. Not a day went by that he didn't think of Cecily, and how different his life would have been if she had lived. But he had always tried hard to be loyal to Amanda. "Not now," he said. "Perhaps another time."

So in the end, Kate gave in. And as she stood in the receiving line at the Sulgrave Club on a frosty December evening, she tried to make herself believe that aching feet were a small price to pay for all the things the McNeils had given her.

Her aunt, she knew, had spared no expense. The six-course dinner for fifty guests at their home had been catered. The club, already decked out for the holidays, was not judged to be ready until Amanda had ordered up more poinsettias, pine garlands, and red candles. And now upstairs in the mirror-lined ballroom, Sidney's Orchestra, one of the capital's best, was beginning to warm up.

She and Amanda had finally compromised on a relatively simple dress off the rack at Garfinckel's. It was ivory-colored satin, with a fitted bodice, full sleeves, and a square neck. Stephen had provided the final touch: a bouquet of red roses.

Now, as she stood by her aunt and uncle and extended a gloved hand to each guest, she felt as if she were playing "dress up" again with Margaret.

The band swung into "Paper Moon" as what seemed like the six hundredth guest passed by. "I think that's just about everyone," Amanda said. "You girls ought to get upstairs for the dancing."

Kate turned to her cousin. "You go ahead. I want to stop in the powder room."

"Oh, Kate," her aunt sighed. "Must you? Right now?"

"I'll only be a minute."

The room was a lavender-scented haven, and despite its

feminine fussiness, Kate wished she could stay there all night. She dallied as long as she dared, straightening her dress, powdering her nose, reapplying her lipstick, patting her page boy into place.

At last she left, but she paused at the foot of the staircase. Upstairs the band was playing a fox-trot. Slow-slow-quick-quick-slow. The pattern came back to her like a multiplication table, remembered from the ballroom dancing classes Amanda had forced her to take. How many dances would she have to endure before the evening was over?

"Excuse me. . . ."

She turned and saw a young man, dressed in black tie, with a fine white silk scarf tossed around his neck.

He flashed a broad smile. "Could you please tell me where the party is?"

His face was a study in black and white. Jet-black hair and dark eyes, contrasted against pale skin. A face sculpted of cool, fine marble, with a well-chiseled nose and a chin held at a deliberate angle. Yet his skin was soft, pampered-looking.

"What party are you looking for?"

He reached into his jacket and pulled out the engraved invitation with a flourish. "The ball," he read, "for Miss Margaret Dellaplaine McNeil and Miss Katharine Aurore Callahan."

"Let's see"—she began counting off on gloved fingers— "last night was Patricia Halloran's dinner. Tomorrow is Mildred Byers's tea. This is Saturday night, so it must be . . ."

"You've made your point."

"You'll find the dancing upstairs." She turned to leave.

He reached out and caught her by the wrist. "Don't go away."

The move took her by surprise, made her catch her breath. For some reason, she did as she was told.

The stranger deposited his topcoat in the checkroom and returned to the foot of the stairs. She had climbed up several steps so for a moment she towered over him. He tilted back his head, regarding her with eyes that were a smoldering gray.

"And who do I have the pleasure of meeting?"

She bowed deeply, in an exaggerated curtsy. "Why, Miss Callahan herself."

"Indeed," he said. "Then I am honored."

"And who, may I ask, are you?"

"Jason Rush," he replied, bowing at the waist. "At your service."

She leaned forward, feeling drawn into the game. "So tell me. How did *you* rate an invitation?"

"My father went to law school with Stephen McNeil. What's your connection?"

"Stephen McNeil is my uncle and guardian."

"Ah," he said, nodding.

"Well, Mr. Rush, as much as I'd like to stay and chat. . . ."

"You've got a party upstairs."

She nodded.

"Well, then allow me to escort you. . . . That is, if you'll stop calling me 'Mr. Rush.' "

He offered his arm. Kate hesitated, knowing that they were about to step over the line between friendly banter and something else, something new and uncomfortable. But there was no time to agonize. She looped her arm through his, and let him lead her up the stairs.

But at the entrance to the ballroom, she nearly stumbled. No one had started dancing—they were all waiting for her.

"Where have you been?" Amanda hissed into her ear.

"Is this your aunt?" Jason stepped forward. "It's a pleasure to meet you, Mrs. McNeil. I'm Jason Rush."

Amanda looked at Kate, then back at the young man. "Well, Jason"—her voice turned buttery—"it's very nice to meet you. We've known your father, of course, for years."

"My parents were very sorry they couldn't be here tonight. But, say, if your lovely niece would permit me, I'd like to have the first dance with her—that is, if she hasn't already promised it to someone else. . . ."

Kate felt all eyes on her. "Why yes," she said. "I mean, no, I don't have a partner."

"Then that settles that." Without asking, Jason took her

bouquet and handed it to her aunt. Then he took Kate's hand and led her onto the floor. The band struck up "Embraceable You" and he put his arm around her waist.

"You seem to be an old pro at these things," she said.

"I've attended a few in my time."

"I appreciate the way you saved me from my aunt."

His lips turned up in a wicked sort of smile. "Older women are my specialty."

He pulled her close, her chin nearly resting on his shoulder. Kate felt a little dizzy, twirling in his arms, feeling her own heartbeat and sensing his, as new couples crowded onto the dance floor. This was new, this feeling. It was strange and disorienting, but not unpleasant. Who was this Jason Rush anyway?

"Mind if I cut in?" Her uncle broke the spell.

Jason winked at her. "Of course I mind, Judge McNeil." He let go of Kate's waist and gave her hand to her uncle. Then his dark eyes caught hers. "I'll see you later, Katharine."

Kate watched him disappear into the crowd, then turned to catch her uncle smiling. "What's so funny?" she demanded.

"Nothing," he replied. "Except I think young Rush rather intrigues you."

She tried not to smile as they began to fox-trot. "What do you know about him?"

"Well, I've known his father for nearly forty years. Good solid family. From Boston originally. If I'm not mistaken, Jason is finishing up his senior year at Harvard. And beyond that"—he smiled slyly—"you're on your own."

They danced until the song ended, then he led her off the floor. "Still sorry we forced you into this?"

She hesitated, then shook her head. "No, Uncle Stephen. It's really very lovely." She planted a kiss on his cheek. "Thank you for everything."

He smiled. "It's been my pleasure, dear."

She danced one number with Richard Smart and another with Alec Hayes, both old friends of her cousin's. And she tried not to wonder where Jason was and who he was talking to.

Then, as suddenly as the first time, he reappeared by her side, a glass of cranberry punch in each hand.

"I thought you might be getting thirsty." He gave her a cup, then took hold of her elbow. "Let's see if we can find someplace to talk."

He led her out to a red couch at the far end of the hallway. She sat down at one end and arranged her skirt around her.

"I hope you don't mind if I tried to improve the recipe." He opened up his jacket, revealing a silver flask.

"I guess Prohibition is over." She tried to sound sophisticated, but doubted that she had succeeded.

"What did your uncle tell you about me?"

"What makes you think I asked?"

He smiled. It was a velvet smile, a smile that conjured up everything that she imagined Boston and Harvard to be. "Experience," he replied.

She ignored the implication of his remark. "He told me about his friendship with your father. And he said he thought you were finishing up your senior year at Harvard."

"Right on that score."

"What are you going to do when you graduate?"

"I plan to go on to law school. Hopefully Harvard."

"That's nice," she said politely.

"How about you? You strike me as"—he paused, as if he was riffling through a catalog of his previous flirtations—"a Mount Holyoke girl."

"Actually, I go to George Washington."

"That's rather déclassé, isn't it?"

She bristled. "As a matter of fact, that's where I wanted to go. I love this city and wanted to stay here. Besides, I felt my aunt and uncle had already spent too much money on me."

"Like this party, for instance?"

"Believe me," she sighed, "it wasn't my idea. It seems absurd to waste money like this, particularly when people all over the country are still struggling."

"Don't you think the upper classes need to maintain the illusion that all's right with the world? You know, give the downtrodden something to aspire to?"

"Is that what they're teaching at Harvard?"

"No," he said, smiling. "Just asking . . . for the sake of debate."

She sipped her drink. "It's not just the appearances. I would have rather spent the money on something else. Like, say, a trip to Europe next summer."

"It's not exactly a great time for a young woman to be sauntering off to Europe."

"Now you sound just like my aunt."

As she took another sip of the punch, Jason studied Katharine Callahan. Her protests on behalf of the poor amused him. And yet in his many years of attending debutante balls he had never met a woman who held the same low opinion of the affairs that he did. He sensed, too, that that was only the first difference he would discover between her and all the others.

She seemed totally unaware of how beautiful she was. Her skin was creamy white, with a flush to her cheeks that he knew had not come out of a jar. She wore her hair like all the girls did, just a fluff of curls around her neck. And yet her hair had a golden sheen that transformed "brown" into "special."

She argued like a prizefighter, except she led with her chin instead of her left. It gave her stubbornness an endearing quality. He could only imagine her legs under the folds of that maddening dress, but her arms had the lean, hard muscles of an athlete—an attribute he did not find at all unattractive. As for her breasts, they were just the way he liked them, not too small, yet not Rubenesque either. Suddenly he was desperate to press them up against his chest again.

Kate stared at her empty glass and wondered just how much liquor Jason had added to her drink. She had never been intimidated by a young man before, and she was determined not to let Jason Rush become the first.

She set down her glass. "Thank you. I think that was just what I needed."

"Me, too." He finished his drink. "Would you like to dance again? That is, if your social conscience will permit you."

"I think it'll suffer through somehow." She presented her

hand to him, the way she imagined Margaret would. He led her back to the ballroom, where the band had just begun playing "You Go to My Head."

He took her in his arms and pulled her close, whispering the words of the song in her ear. Champagne and wine, mint juleps and romance.

The crowded room seemed to sway as one mass of humanity. It made her want to cling to Jason more tightly, as if he were the only steadying thing in the place.

She felt the smooth wool of his tuxedo caress her cheek and the warm touch of his hand against her neck. And despite the dozens of couples, old and young, who had crowded onto the ballroom floor, it seemed now as if she and Jason were the only people there.

Was this how it feels? she wondered. Was this how it was supposed to feel when a man takes you in his arms? Or was this how it feels when he's slipped you too much gin or rum or whiskey or whatever Jason had in that flask?

He gave her a final twirl as the band ended with a flourish of trumpets and woodwinds. Then he leaned back and studied her face intently.

"That was nice," she said, feeling breathless.

"I thought so, too."

There were other dances, fast and slow, as the evening spun on. If any other young man thought that his invitation required him to dance at least once with Katharine Callahan, the possessiveness in Jason Rush's eyes seemed to deter all but her oldest, most avuncular friends. But she didn't mind; in fact, she reveled in Jason's attentions. And when the band started playing "Good Night, Sweetheart," it seemed much too soon.

As they rejoined Stephen and Amanda, Jason spoke up, "If it's all right with you, Judge McNeil, I'd like to see your niece home."

Stephen looked to his wife, but Amanda said nothing. "That's fine, Jason. But don't dally. And be careful. The roads are getting slick."

"Yes, sir."

Amanda watched Jason offer Kate his arm, and her heart

lurched with a memory. It was the memory of another girl and another ball, in the Christmas season of 1913. It was to be her special night, her night in the spotlight, as her parents presented her to the cream of New Orleans society.

Of course, Charlotte was there. She could hardly exclude her younger sister. But that was precisely the problem. While the young men dutifully wrote their names on Amanda's dance card, it was Charlotte they had really come to dance with. Amanda might have been the one with the big bouquet of lilies, but Charlotte was the flower of the affair.

Margaret's high-pitched giggle carried over the babble of the crowd. Amanda sighed. When would her daughter stop wasting her time on boys like Alec Hayes and Jack Swayze? They could set Margaret's head aspin with their fast talk and fast cars. But they had about as much substance as the exhaust in a tailpipe.

If only Margaret had met Jason first . . . she thought. Amanda had included him with that thought in mind. And she had it all worked out: how she'd introduce Margaret and Jason, and get them dancing, and then invite him back for coffee.

And then practically before she could say "good evening," it was Kate who was in his arms.

It's not fair, Charlotte. It's just not fair.

Kate waited until she was bundled up inside of Jason's sports car. "You might have asked me first."

He didn't turn the key. "Would you rather ride home with them?"

She hesitated, then shook her head.

He started up the car. "I didn't think so."

She wondered if he would take her straight home, or drive somewhere and talk. The annoying thing was, she wasn't sure which she wanted more.

But he made good on his promise to her uncle. He asked her for directions, then navigated the short distance to her home.

On the steps, she stopped and turned to him. It was hard to see his face—it was lost in the shadows of the streetlight and the fog of their breaths in the chilly night air.

"Thank you, Jason. I had a wonderful time tonight."

He took her hand and cupped it between both of his gloves as if to warm it. Then he lifted it to his lips and brushed the bare skin of her wrist where her long glove was unbuttoned.

The gesture was over in a second, and yet it spiraled a tingling message up her arm to her brain.

"I've been to dozens of parties like this before," he whispered, "but this one was different. It was better than all the rest—and that was because of you."

He stepped back down a step.

"Will I see you again?" she asked.

"Of course," he replied. "Now, go inside, Katharine Callahan, before you catch a death of a cold!"

"Good night," she said, then disappeared inside.

Jason retreated to his car, but let the engine idle while he rubbed his cold hands together.

He was a man who knew what he wanted—and was used to getting it. He knew what he usually wanted in a woman, and more times than not he could find it after sharing a flask of bourbon in the backseat of his car.

But tonight that hadn't interested him. He had wanted Kate, but he had wanted all of her, body—and soul.

He knew the time had come for him to find himself a wife. Up to now, he had never met a woman he considered good enough, a woman who he'd want to be the mother of his children, a woman who was perfect enough to please his mother.

But Kate just might be that woman. She was beautiful—and she was smart, a combination he rarely found in the women he dated. She was naive, of course, but this time he found that refreshing. The raw material was there, that was the important thing. He could take care of the rest.

But how and when? He would have to return to school after the holidays. And yet, as he thought about it, he didn't worry that he would "lose" Kate. She would wait. Not for him necessarily. He could sense she wasn't ready for that kind of commitment. In the few hours he had known her, he had seen how serious she was, about herself and about life. She was clearly not a girl who was going to rush into marriage.

But, Jason thought with a smile, between a quick peck and a proposal stretched a long list of possibilities. And when Kate was ready to get married, he was going to make damn sure that he was the man who would be there.

Eight

Jason set his coffee cup on the corner of his mother's bed tray. Saturday morning had been his time with her ever since he was old enough to climb out of his bed and into his parents'. It was his hour alone with his mother, his chance to tell her all about his world. And for Audrey, it was her time to bestow her only child with the precious gift of her approval.

As Jason had gotten older, even after he had been away at school, their Saturday morning ritual had become more important, not less. It was an unspoken thing between them, a kind of mating dance between would-be lovers. Audrey always arose early to apply her makeup; Jason always knew to knock precisely at nine. And the maid always knew that on Saturday mornings she was supposed to place a second cup on Mrs. Rush's tray.

He'd always thought of his mother as a queen, arrayed as she was now in a silk robe against a backdrop of pale pink pillows. At fifty-five, she looked ten years younger, the result of a careful regimen of tennis and massage. Every movement she made was chosen with care: the way she picked up her teacup so as not to ruin a manicure, the controlled way in which she smiled so as not to crack her skin.

Sometimes he wondered if his restless flitting from girl to girl, from deb to coed, was simply a quixotic search to find a young woman who could replace her in his heart.

"Would you mind if I invited someone down to the Cape

this summer?'' he asked. He had already led his mother on a verbal waltz through the parties of the holiday social season. All of them, that is, but one.

"Who? One of your law school friends?''

"No,'' he replied, his mouth turning up into a smile. "A girl.''

"Jason,'' she said, wagging a finger at him, "you've been hiding something from me.''

He pushed aside the morning papers to stretch out on the bed. "She's Stephen McNeil's niece.''

"Do you know anything about her parents?''

He shook his head. "Apparently Judge McNeil is her guardian.''

Audrey studied her son as she sipped her coffee. "You know what I'm driving at, Jason. Is she good enough for you?''

He snorted. "Would anyone be?''

"What do you mean?''

"Nothing, except that I rather think any potential daughter-in-law of yours, Mother, is going to have a hard time living up to your standards.''

"I just want the best for you, Jason.''

"Trust me. I've found it. And I mean to have her.''

"Do you now?'' Audrey put down her cup and swung her feet out of the bed and into a pair of maribou-feathered pumps. Then she reached out and took his chin in her hand. "You know, Jason, you could be very happy in life except for one thing. . . .''

"What's that?''

"You never get enough.''

Then she flashed a smile, the smile that in his eyes would make her youthful forever.

"And in that,'' she added, "you're too much like me.''

He had never been much of a letter writer, but this time Jason intended to keep his promise to write. He sent Kate a letter once a week, conducting a careful campaign to woo her with words because he couldn't court her face-to-face. He was determined to keep himself foremost in her mind. So far—if he could trust her replies—the strategy seemed to be working.

Kate looked forward to Jason's letters, anticipated them, really. When one arrived, she would retreat to the window seat in her room, then study it carefully before composing her answer. She wanted to be honest about her feelings.

For she didn't know what to make of Jason Rush. Up to now, she had thought boys were a waste of time, a diversion from studies and work, the serious business of life.

But after all, she seemed to intimidate most of them. Not Jason. His aggressiveness and his quick wit served up a challenge to her. And as always, she relished that.

But there was something else, something new and disturbing. It was the way her heart had raced when he had kissed her good night, or the excitement she had felt when a letter arrived.

Yet, Kate felt as if Jason had chosen her. And if she were choosing a man, she was not sure she would have chosen Jason.

In April, his mother wrote Amanda: "We would be so happy if Katharine would join us at our cottage at the Cape for a few weeks this summer."

"What do you think?" her aunt asked.

"I guess I'd like to go," Kate replied.

"No one's asked me," Stephen said, "but I think it's a great idea."

Amanda smiled. "I think it's a marvelous idea."

And so she had gone—with her family's blessings as well as their cheers from the sidelines. It was time, Amanda told her pointedly, for her to be finding herself a husband.

She had known Jason was wealthy, but his "cottage" by the sea confirmed it. It was a large clapboard structure, weathered to a powdery shade of gray, which had sprouted extra bedrooms and porches over the years it had been in his family. A broad lawn swept down to the sand dunes, wide enough to hold a tennis court.

His parents welcomed Kate warmly, but most of the time they left the two of them alone. The whole family seemed to relate to each other with a polite, yet chilly formality.

Jason's father returned to the city each Monday to go to work, while every morning his mother would disappear through the tall grasses to the beach. Yet even from afar, Kate couldn't shake the feeling that Audrey was watching her very closely.

On the third day, Jason suggested they play tennis. Kate was curious to see what kind of game he played and it didn't take long to find out.

He was all power, no finesse. He served the ball hard, but a third of the time he served it long or wide. When he tried to put her away with a shot down the line, he usually ended up putting his ball into the net.

She focused on playing the game her way: consistency, patience, concentration. And the strategy worked. By the time it dawned on Jason that he might actually lose, it was too late for him to salvage the set.

"Good game," he said as they met at the net.

"Thanks."

"You know," he said, "I've never been beaten by a girl before." He hesitated, just long enough for her to wonder whether she should have let him win. But then he looped his towel around her neck and pulled her close. "Still, I liked it."

He kissed her then, a light, playful kiss. He did not, however, ask her to play tennis again.

Still, she enjoyed herself that summer. The lazy days were filled with swimming and lying in the sun, easy conversation and laughter. They'd walk hand in hand along the beach as the foamy waves nipped their ankles. And they'd kiss late at night when the summer sky was a shower of stars.

And oh, could Jason Rush kiss! Unlike the other boys' mouths, which always seemed to grab her lips like some sort of mechanic's vise, Jason's lips were gentle, soft, and supple. He nibbled at the edges of her mouth, then followed with his tongue, teasing and tempting, then tasting inside. She surprised herself as her tongue followed suit, knowing, without ever asking, what it was supposed to do. And just as she was feeling breathless and ever so vulnerable, he'd give her a quick hug or a kiss—and leave her wondering what the next step would be.

The last night of her stay, they went with his parents to a dance at the Yacht Club. Kate had saved a dress for a night like this, a pale green moiré that was cut low across her shoulders and brought out the color of her eyes.

They lasted through the cocktail hour, the seafood buffet, and a couple of dances. Then Jason made their excuses and got the keys to his father's car.

They drove out to the north end of the Cape, where the sea and the landscape grew wilder. Then Jason pulled the car over to the shoulder and turned off the engine.

They said nothing for a moment. She felt the salty breeze against her face and listened to the rhythmic roar of the surf, a counterpoint to her heartbeat. Was it trying to tell her some secret message?

"I hope you realize," he said at last, "how much you've come to mean to me."

His inky eyes stared out at the water; his jaw, the cords of his neck, were stretched tightly, as if he were struggling for control.

"Yes," she said softly.

"I'd like to think we had some sort of commitment," he went on. "It would make it easier for me."

She hesitated. She liked Jason, she liked him a lot. But when she asked herself if she loved him, the answer always came back no. Was it him? Was there something about him that made her get close, but not too close?

Or maybe it was her. Maybe she just needed more time. She'd known him for what?—seven months?—and had hardly seen him for most of that time. Whenever she had tried to imagine being married to Jason, or even coming to the Cape every summer, she simply couldn't.

But what if there was more to it than that? What if she was incapable of falling in love? What if she was the kind of woman who could never get close to a man?

But she couldn't sort out all of that now, not on a moonlit night on an isolated beach with a man whose hand was gently stroking her bare shoulder. Nor could she pretend to feel something she didn't. It was one thing to play the role of the blushing debutante for an evening, quite another to lead on a man like Jason.

And so she waited for a moment. And when she spoke, she tried hard to pick the right words.

"I'm touched, Jason. Really I am. But I'm not ready for that sort of thing. I want to finish school. I want to go to Europe. I want to know something of life."

"But I won't stop you!"

"I know you wouldn't try. But it would. . . . I can't explain it. I just know me. I know I would feel tied down."

He shifted in his seat. "Is there someone else?"

"No, there's no one. Just you, Jason. And you are very important to me. I care about you. . . ." She took a deep breath. "But I'm just not ready to say I love you."

"You'll never go to Europe," he sputtered. "Not anytime soon at least. A war's going to break out any day now, despite what all those fools at the club were trying to convince themselves tonight."

"You may be right. But I just can't let go of my dreams."

He said nothing then. His hand jerked down to the ignition, then the car hacked back to life. He shifted clumsily, making it lurch into reverse. Then they careened back down the road toward home, the engine's roar blessedly saving them from talk.

When they arrived home, he helped her out of the car, but said not a word. Nor did he make any attempt to kiss her good night.

That night Kate lay awake, tossed by waves of doubt and dreading. Had she played it all wrong? Had she ruined what they had? And what would she do if she lost him?

In the morning he drove her, stone-faced, to the train station. She tried to make innocuous small talk, but he only mumbled in reply.

Finally they arrived at the station, and shortly after came the announcement of her train. "It's been a wonderful summer, Jason," she said, turning toward him. "Thank you . . . for everything." She hesitated, then added, "I'll write you as soon as I get home."

She waited, wondering if he'd kiss her one more time. When he didn't, she asked: "Will you write me?"

"Sure. Now you'd better get on board."

Two weeks passed and a letter finally did arrive. It was

the Jason of old: warm, witty, affectionate. But not pushing her anymore. And, she had to admit, she was relieved to hear from him. But most of all, she liked knowing he was there.

Nine

Jason had been right about one thing: It would be a while before she would get to Europe. The invasion of Poland that September was followed in short order by the invasion of Norway and Denmark, then the Netherlands and Belgium. The next summer, she cried when she watched the newsreel films of German tanks rolling down the Champs-Élysées. How many times had she imagined herself, pausing at a sidewalk café and telling a waiter, "*Une pêche Melba, s'il vous plaît*"?

Each day's unbelievable headlines were followed by another set. At night, she and Stephen would retreat to his study and pore over his maps of Europe to chart the paths of the armies. Then they would tune in the radio and listen in silent horror as Edward R. Murrow described the bombs raining down all over London.

In Boston, Jason studied the news reports with a different kind of horror. His parents' friends could talk all they wanted to about staying out of Europe's wars, but he knew that his friends would end up fighting them. The only question now was when—and how was he going to avoid it.

Before the draft lottery was held in the fall of 1940, he prayed—for the first time in years. His prayers were answered, in a fashion, when his number was not among the first to be picked. He had won a reprieve, but he knew it couldn't last forever. He had both of his arms and both of his eyes and, unless his dithering grandmother was doing the talking, perfect hearing. He was not about to pretend to be crazy, and he knew he had no conscience with which to pretend to be an objector.

He told none of this to Kate, of course. In his letters, he spoke of "preparing myself mentally to fight when my time comes." Ever the optimist, she always told him she was sure he wouldn't be called up.

Jason, however, was not about to relax. Finally, when he had exhausted all his other options, he turned to his father for help. Jonathan Rush called his friends (except, on his son's orders, Stephen McNeil) to see what they could do for him. In the fall of 1941, four months after Jason finished law school, salvation came in the form of a job in Washington.

The job had less to do with the law than with strategic imports and exports and the Lend-Lease program. But Jason had taken some economics courses and he was prepared to learn fast. At last he would be close to Kate. And he probably would be eligible for the one thing that, for now at least, he coveted even more than her: a deferment for a civilian job that was essential to the war effort.

The forecast for that Sunday was for a warm, windy day. For that, Kate was grateful. She was not much of a football fan, but if she had to spend three hours in Griffith Stadium on a December afternoon, she would rather it be warm than snowing.

"Are you annoyed," Stephen asked, "that I invited Jason's father down for the game?"

"No. Why?"

"I was afraid you would think I was pushing you."

"Are you?"

He smiled. "Well, maybe. Just a little bit."

Perhaps someone should be pushing her, she thought. After all, it had been three years since she and Jason had met. She had other male friends at school, but none of them meant to her what Jason did. Still, she felt she would know when she was ready, when the time was just "right." And she knew that, for whatever reasons, it wasn't yet.

The stadium was half full when they arrived. The crowd

was expected to be smaller today because the Redskins had lost four straight.

"There's Jonathan," Stephen said as he spied his friend.

"I'm sorry Jason's not here," he said as they joined him. "He's been working so hard lately. But he should be along soon."

Kate smiled at the older man. "I'm sure he will, Mr. Rush."

As it turned out, Jason slid in beside her just as the national anthem came to a close. He gave Kate's arm an affectionate squeeze, then turned to watch the opening kickoff.

Kate held up her thermos. "Want a cup of coffee?"

"No thanks," Jason said, stifling a yawn.

"You have been working too hard!"

"Maybe just a little." He put his arm around her shoulders and settled in to watch the game.

"First and ten for Philadelphia on the Redskins' forty-one-yard line," boomed the announcer over the stadium's public address system. "Admiral W. H. P. Bland is asked to report to his office at once."

Philadelphia edged its way toward the Redskins' goal line.

"The Resident Commissioner of the Philippines, Mr. Joaquim Eilzalde, is urged to report to his office, immediately!"

"Something has happened," Jason said quietly.

"Bob Hutchinson and Stuart Lytle, please call your offices," the big horns blared high above the field.

"What could it be?" Kate asked.

The crowd booed. Philadelphia had scored a touchdown.

"Perhaps Japan has finally declared war," Stephen said solemnly.

"Surely," Kate said, "they would announce that!"

The Redskins began to march down the field toward them, Sammy Baugh leading the way. But the four of them sat silently, lost in their thoughts. The announcer called off more names, more admirals, more generals, more police officials. And around them the crowd buzzed with rumors . . . "the Philippines . . . bombed at dawn . . . Hawaii . . . talking to Hull."

At halftime, Jason stood up. "I'm going to find out what's going on."

"I'm going with you," Kate declared.

"No, stay here," he said. "I'm going to try to sneak into the press box."

This time, she obeyed him. She sat down next to her uncle and tried to pay attention to the band strutting through its halftime routine. She poured herself a cup of coffee, but then hardly touched it, letting it grow cold like the fear in her heart.

Jason was gone so long that Kate began to wonder if he was ever coming back. But just as the teams were taking the field again, he returned, with a face so gray she knew the news could not be good.

"What is it, son?" his father asked.

Jason sat down and stared out at the field. "The Japanese bombed Pearl Harbor this morning."

"Hawaii?" Stephen asked, incredulous.

Jason nodded.

"How . . . how many were hurt?" Kate whispered.

Jason shook his head. "They don't know yet," he said. "But most of the fleet was in port."

The scene froze in her brain. A stadium awash in burgundy and gold. Like blood, she thought, and the flares of bombs, filling up an ocean half a world away.

The crowd roared; Baugh had passed for another touchdown. *How can they cheer?* she wondered. *How can they pretend not to feel it?*

The sun dipped behind a cloud, sending a chill through her bones.

"Let's go home," Stephen said at last. And this time, no one objected.

As night fell, they all gathered in Stephen's study for brandy and coffee. John Carson, a friend of Stephen's from down the street, came by with his wife. Kate had spent many a night arguing with Stephen and John over Roosevelt's strategy in Europe. But there was no debate tonight. The men huddled quietly in a corner, while Amanda and Karen Carson dabbed at their eyes.

How strange, Kate thought as she sipped her drink. *In the space of an afternoon, or an hour at dawn in Hawaii, the*

*fate of the world changes. And my life probably has changed,
too, in ways I don't yet recognize.*

She thought of the men who had died that morning—still
nameless, faceless boys—and wondered how many more
would die before it was all over. Then she looked at the men
in their little cluster, and felt a profound frustration that as a
woman she could do so little to help.

"Why don't we listen to the news?" she piped up.

She turned on her uncle's radio and caught the tail end of
a report. Casualties were in the thousands already. Tomorrow
the president would go before Congress to seek a declaration
of war.

She twirled the dial and caught the unmistakable timbre of
the First Lady's voice.

". . . To the young people of the nation I must speak
tonight." Kate looked up, her eyes glistening. "You are
going to have a great opportunity—there will be high moments in which your strength and your ability will be tested.
I have faith in you! Just as though I were standing upon a
rock, and that rock is my faith in my fellow citizens. . . ."

When Mrs. Roosevelt finished, Jason flicked off the radio.
"Come on," he said to Kate. "Let's go for a walk."

The night was eerily quiet, except for the wail of an occasional siren. Neighbors had closed their curtains and it
seemed like the streetlights glowed more dimly now. Jason
took her hand and tucked it into his pocket to warm it.

"Do you suppose they're serving tea at the Japanese embassy?" he cracked.

She said nothing.

"What's bothering you?" he demanded.

"What's bothering me?" she lashed back. "Our whole
world is going up in smoke and you're asking what's bothering me?"

"I didn't mean it that way. . . ."

"I'm frustrated, Jason. I want to do something and I
can't. I feel like going to the nearest recruiting office and
enlisting."

He snorted. "Well, that's about the last thing in the world
I want to do."

Even in the faint streetlight, he could tell she was looking at him strangely. Stupidly, he had let down his guard.

"You don't want me to go get killed, do you, Kate?"

"Of course not, Jason. . . . But . . . but don't you think we have a responsibility to defend our country? To protect all those rights we've taken for granted all our lives?"

"Of course, I do," he said, trying to reassure her. He put his arm around her shoulder, then pulled her close. "Give me a kiss, Kate." For a moment he wondered whether she would, but at last she complied, her moist, soft lips meeting his. And as he tasted them, it occurred to him that the war might actually turn out to be useful to him.

"Kiss me again, darling," he whispered in her ear. "Who knows how many nights we'll have left together?"

On New Year's Eve Stephen and Amanda went to a dinner party at the Carsons'. Margaret went to New York to say good-bye to Jack Swayze, who'd decided over Christmas to enlist. Kate and Jason were invited to a party, but Kate didn't feel in the mood. Instead, she suggested that he come by late in the evening to share a quiet drink together.

She wore a white angora sweater, and despite the tension of the past few weeks, Jason thought she had never looked lovelier. She had pulled back her hair on one side with a silver barrette; it caught the twinkling lights of the Christmas tree, beckoning above her ear like a star.

It was time to make his move. He could tell she was getting restless, the way she had talked that night after Pearl Harbor, her lack of interest in every date he had suggested since. But then, as luck would have it, the answer had come to him.

"I've been thinking about what you said the other night and I've got an idea," he said. "They're reorganizing our agency—they've already changed the name. And today my boss came and said they're going to give me a new job. . . ."

"What?"

"It's a little complicated, but, say for instance, they're going to send bombers over Germany. They want to try to figure out where they should drop the bombs, how to destroy the supply lines, the factories, that sort of thing. Anyway, my boss told me to keep an eye out for anyone who might be useful. Naturally I thought of you.''

"Me? But I don't know anything about bombing."

"That's not the point," he said. "You speak French and German. The job involves talking to people who've been there. Businessmen, recent émigrés, that sort of thing."

Her face lit up as she began to think out loud. "They announced the other day that they're going to expand the night school at GW to help more boys finish up early. I could work for you during the day and go to school at night."

"Sounds perfect."

She hesitated. Perhaps it would be awkward, working for Jason. She had felt differently about him the past few weeks. Maybe she was being unfair, but she had been profoundly disappointed in the way he had reacted to the war.

Still, she couldn't bear the thought of going back to school next week, with nothing more to her life than four increasingly irrelevant classes. At least this way, she'd be doing *something*.

"When can I start?"

Jason swept her into his arms. "Whenever you're ready."

He kissed her full on the mouth. The radio announcer proclaimed, "Happy New Year!" and then came "Auld Lang Syne." He kissed her again, this time more sweetly, like the old times.

Kate handed Jason a bottle of champagne, then held out two glasses. He popped the cork cleanly, then filled them.

"Happy New Year, Jason," she offered in a toast. "May 1942 be all you want it to be."

"Happy New Year to you, Kate."

Their glasses met, and then their eyes. And as he sipped his drink, and the bubbles stung his throat, Jason made a promise to himself. This, at last, was going be their year.

Ten

And so Katharine Callahan went to war.

Her battleground was a cramped room deep inside the Commerce Department—an office, Jason liked to say, with all the charm of a janitor's closet. But until the new "tempos" opened up across Constitution Avenue, they would just have to make do.

If she couldn't be close to the front lines, Kate decided her job with the Board of Economic Warfare was the next best thing. She had a security clearance, and her task, like most of the division, was to study Germany, to identify the most important rail lines, the biggest steel mills, the places where Hitler was building the most destructive weapons.

By April, there were four of them. Delilah Alberts had arrived in town the month before on a train from St. Louis. Her brother was somewhere in the Pacific and she was determined to help him. Jason had asked for a secretary; the government responded with an eager young girl who could hunt and peck.

And there was Elliot Ingraham, a shy man in his midtwenties, who was always careful to say that he really *had* tried to enlist after Pearl Harbor, but the army had said he was too short. With his blond hair and freckles, he looked like somebody's kid brother.

It should have made for a collegial atmosphere: four people in tight quarters, working on a common goal. Except for one factor.

"Ruhr, Delilah," Jason bellowed as he threw the report down on the terrorized secretary's desk. "How many times do I have to tell you? R-U-H-R."

If the seeds of Kate's doubt had been sown the night of

73

Pearl Harbor, a few weeks of working with Jason had brought them to full flower. When he wasn't harassing Delilah, he bullied Elliot with taunts. But with Kate, he was polite, obsequious really, and attentive to the point of fawning. And nothing could have made her more uncomfortable.

One day over lunch she decided it was time to bring it up. "You know," she said, "you really ought to be nicer to Delilah."

"Why?"

"Because she tries so hard, Jason. And every time you yell at her, she only makes more mistakes."

"That girl thinks that just because there's a war on, I can tolerate sloppy work. What if everyone was like that?"

"Well, you can't say that about Elliot. He does excellent work—and you know it."

"There's something about that guy I don't like. . . . I wish I could get him transferred." He took a bite of his sandwich, then studied her face. He did it all the time now—as if he were searching for some emotion that she knew he was not going to find.

He put down the sandwich. "Why have you suddenly become the mother hen of the office?"

"Because I like them. And I don't think you're being fair."

"Talk about being fair, what about you? You haven't been out with me in a week."

"I'm so tired, Jason."

"That's what you said last Friday."

"Well, it was true then and it's true now."

"But I'm working longer days than you are."

"But you're not going to school, too. You forget that when I go home, I still have books to read and papers to write and exams to study for."

He stirred his coffee, his face set in a frown.

"Look," she said at last, "if it will make you any happier, I'll go out with you Saturday night."

"You promise?"

She nodded wearily.

He took her to the Blue Room of the Shoreham Hotel for dinner and dancing. He tipped the maître d' for a table near the band, then made a point of ordering filet mignon for two and a bottle of wine.

They had been here once before, shortly after they'd met. That evening had seemed so special, but the mood was different now. The little tables were crowded with soldiers and sailors, men in navy and green and brown, and women with a desperate sort of gaiety. The familiar uneasiness began to well up in Kate and she knew she couldn't ignore it for very long.

Jason leaned across the tiny table. "You look lovely tonight." His voice, as ever, was whiskey-smooth.

"Thank you."

He studied his plate for a moment, then reached out and took her hand. "I've been worried, darling. Over the past few weeks, I've felt as if you've been growing apart from me." He paused. "You must know how much I love you, Kate."

Her hand felt like a cold rock in his. There might have been a time when she would have told him she loved him, too. But no more. His warm words brought forth no response from her heart—other than a growing feeling of dread.

Had she led him on? She hadn't meant to. But she had never been able to find the right time or right words to tell him how she felt. That there were too many sides of him she didn't like. That she could no longer look up to him, the way she had that night when they'd danced across the ballroom of the Sulgrave Club.

She had always assumed that no matter what happened they would remain friends. But now she wasn't sure. Amid the din of the room and the effects of the wine, she tried to form the words to explain herself. But even now, like a coward, she avoided the real issue.

"Jason, I care for you," she said softly. "But I find it hard to work for you during the day and be something else at night."

She hesitated, then pressed on. "I think that as long as you're my boss, we'd both be better off not seeing each other like this."

She withdrew her hand and looked up at him. His face

was rigid, betraying no emotion. He reached for his wineglass—very deliberately—and took a long sip. Then his lips turned up in a tight smile. "Would you care to dance?"

She nodded, wondering whether he'd heard a word she'd said.

He pulled her close, splaying her soft breasts against the hard muscles of his chest, forcing her to gasp once for breath. His fingers crept up her neck, tangling her hair, and his thighs seemed glued to hers—if she moved, he moved, if she didn't, he didn't. Beneath his suit coat, she could feel his heart beating wildly and his breath growing ragged. And lower down, he was growing hard.

She had never seen him like this before, like some sort of wild animal, pawing her in public. Her aunt had warned her once, "Men are like that." But Kate hadn't believed her. Other men perhaps, but not Jason. Not Jason Rush.

The smell of her Arpege filled his senses again. *She's confused*, he thought. *This damn war's made her all confused. . . . "We'd both be better off"—hah! What horseshit! This little girl needs to get laid—that'll solve her problem.*

He smiled into her soft brown hair. He had been a patient man, after all. He had waited—what was it?—more than three years already. But now he could tell. Kate Callahan was ready for him. Oh, sure, she came up with excuses, but all the girls did that. It was their way of pretending that they didn't really want it. They did want it, they just didn't know it.

Jason twirled her in his arms. It was time now. Katharine Callahan *would* be his. All he had to do was push the right buttons. And he was confident that he would be able to find them.

Eleven

When Monday came, Kate wasn't ready to face Jason again. Fortunately, though, she didn't have to. She was scheduled to go to New York to interview Walter Bernstein, a German industrialist and a Jew, who had managed to escape across the border to Switzerland.

She cooled her heels for three days, waiting for the OSS to finish grilling the elderly man, and by the time her turn came, he was obviously exhausted. But she prodded him gently and in the end he knelt down by the maps she had spread out on the floor and carefully located factories for her.

She arrived back at work early the next morning, eager to get started on her report. Delilah was already at her desk, painting her nails a bright shade of crimson.

"We've got somebody new," she announced.

"Really? Who?"

Delilah lowered her voice to a whisper. "His name is Robert Kaufmann. He just got back from Europe."

Kate glanced around the room. "Where are we putting him?"

"He used your desk while you were gone. Jason said we'd all just have to share. Everyone, of course, but Jason."

"Big of him, don't you think?"

The secretary giggled. "Anyway, I wanted to warn you. This guy is gorgeous."

"Gorgeous" was not the word Kate would have chosen to describe Robert Kaufmann. Distinctive perhaps. Or striking.

She was bent over her typewriter when she became aware of someone standing beside her. She looked up, knowing it would be him.

He was very tall, very angular. He had dark brown hair,

a shade longer than was fashionable in Washington. He had a sharp jaw and a nose that some might think was too long. But Kate decided it suited him. It directed her gaze up to his eyes, the most haunting set of dark brown eyes that she had ever seen. They invited you in, and yet they seemed to guard many secrets.

"You must be Robert. I'm Kate Callahan."

"I know." He smiled. "I kept your seat warm all week."

She felt his fingers take her hand, fingers so long that she was sure they could stretch out and time her racing pulse.

She cleared her throat. "Delilah tells me you've just returned from Europe."

"Yes."

"Were you traveling there?"

"No."

"Were you working for the government?"

"If you don't mind, I'd rather not talk about it."

Awkwardly, she turned back to her typing. "Suit yourself."

Delilah found a spare desk in another office that they squeezed in on the far side of the room. But despite that separation, Kate found it harder to concentrate when Robert was around. She was self-conscious when she spoke, worried that for some unknown reason he disapproved of her. The last time she had felt this uncomfortable was the first time Jason asked her to dance.

As the weeks went by, Kate picked up more fragments of Robert's story. His family was from New York City. He had graduated from Columbia eight years before. He had recently recovered from pneumonia—a fact that seemed to have something to do with his abrupt return from Europe.

But the rest remained a mystery. He was unfailingly polite, and occasionally very funny. But he didn't talk very much, especially about himself. And especially not to her.

Kate wasn't aware of it at first, but as the months went by, it was clear a subtle change had occurred in the office.

Perhaps it was because Robert was older than Jason, and clearly knew more about Europe. Perhaps it was because of his quiet confidence. In any case, Delilah and Elliot were treating Robert like he was the boss now. It was as if he had become their protector, and as long as he was there, Jason wouldn't bother them.

Robert's protective circle, though, did not include Kate, a fact of office life that puzzled—and disappointed—her. She figured someone must have told Robert she was Jason's girl, and he had decided to keep his distance. Then again, perhaps Robert simply didn't like her.

She had stopped going out with Jason months before, but that didn't stop him from asking. She wondered when he would learn, then she wondered whether he was capable of learning.

One cold night near the end of February, she stayed late to try to finish a project. The others had left hours before, but Jason was still at work in his office.

She buttoned up her coat and tied her scarf tightly around her neck. Then as she reached up to put on her hat, a pair of arms slithered around her waist. "C'mon, Kate," Jason whispered thickly in her ear, "give me a kiss."

She tried to laugh him off. "Don't be silly, Jason."

His lips worked their way under the hair on her neck as his hands groped upward toward her breasts. "C'mon, Kate. We both know you want me."

Her knees felt weak with terror, yet she couldn't scream. "I mean it, Jason, that's enough. Let me go."

He grabbed a breast greedily. "No, it's my turn to say that's enough." He began unbuttoning her coat. "I'm fed up with your playing hard to get. Now we're going to play the game my way."

"Stop it, Jason!" She tried to struggle free. "Stop it right now or I'll scream!"

"Hold it right there, Jason."

Jason swiveled around. Robert stood in the doorway, glaring at them icily.

Jason relaxed his grip. "Why don't you stay out of this, Kaufmann?"

"I will," he replied, "if the lady tells me to."

Jason let go.

"Thank you," she whispered to Robert, trying to regain

her composure. She rebuttoned her coat nervously. "I think I'll be going home now."

She didn't look at Jason.

"I'll walk you out," Robert said.

"No, really, it's not necessary."

She tried to brush past him, but he stepped in front of her. "Please," he said softly. "I want to."

She looked up into his eyes and knew in an instant that she could trust him. "Thank you," she whispered. She grabbed her purse, then left the office, with Robert close behind.

They went out into the frosty evening and stopped underneath a streetlight. By now, her fear had been replaced by a sense of shame and a rage that flooded through her body. What had gotten into Jason? How could he treat her like that?

Robert studied her closely. "Would you like me to take you home?"

"I'll be all right." It was all she could think to say. She reached up to straighten her hat. "I'm just sorry you had to be dragged into the middle of that."

He smiled. "I'd say you were pretty lucky I was."

She looked up at him. "I guess you're right."

"Take my advice and stay away from him."

"It's over," she said. "It has been for a long time. He just won't accept it."

"I see." There was an awkward silence. She wanted to explain everything to Robert. To tell him she wasn't really like that, that Jason wasn't really her kind of man. But she didn't know where to begin.

At last he spoke. "Shall I try to get you a cab?"

"That would be nice."

She could have stood there forever, feeling safe in his presence. And normally she might have. Taxis, at least empty ones, were hard to find in Washington these days. But at that very moment, one came rolling by.

Robert flagged it down, then opened the door. But she hesitated, not wanting to say good-bye yet.

"Will you go home now?" she asked.

"Eventually. But I usually like to take a long walk before I go to bed. I find I do my best thinking then."

Kate smiled, imagining him. "Then be sure to keep warm." She climbed inside. "Thank you again, Robert . . . for everything."

The taxi pulled away into the inky night.

Three floors up, Jason watched until the cab disappeared around the corner. Then he went to his desk and took out a glass and a flask of whiskey. He filled the glass, quaffed it down, then filled it again.

He despised her.

He had waited years for her. He had been prepared to give her everything, his name, his wealth, his child, his life. And she had thrown it all back in his face.

He took a sip of the drink. He wasn't dumb. He had seen how her cheeks had flushed when she looked at Robert. He had watched them huddle closely on the sidewalk below. *She probably loves him. She probably thinks he's her knight in shining armor. Well, go to him, Kate. See if you like how HE touches you!*

He downed the rest of the glass, then coughed as the heat of the liquor—and his anger—constricted his throat. Then he threw back his head and straightened his shoulders. She was just a girl after all. Another tight-assed girl. There were thousands of 'em in this city, lovely and lonely. Far from home. Far from the men they loved. Far from any man their age.

Who needed Kate Callahan anyway?

Still, the whiskey burned the pit of his stomach, like bile eating away the lining. But he didn't stop to analyze it. The night was still young, after all. He checked the knot of his tie, then smoothed down his hair with the heel of his hand. Then he went out into the black of evening, knowing already where he could find the next one.

Twelve

This, Elliot concluded, was no way to win a war.

The bureaucrats were squabbling over the mission of their agency. Was it supposed to get hold of rubber and tin and cinchona for quinine any way it could, or was it supposed to make sure that the workers of South America weren't exploited in the process? The bickering made the headlines every day—and Elliot bet FDR wasn't going to put up with it much longer.

But their own office was even worse. It wasn't that people were fighting—they weren't even talking anymore.

Something had happened, but no one would tell him what. Jason and Robert had never gotten along, but what was Kate's problem now? Each day she came in and did her work carefully and efficiently. But she never joked or laughed anymore—and at night, more times than not, she was the first to leave.

More than anyone, Elliot wasn't about to start poking around in other people's business. It was safer to keep his mouth shut and his nose clean.

Yet he couldn't help feeling that they were all under siege. Like Corregidor or Leningrad, their little outpost was doomed. But as Elliot dreaded the day when all the polite walls they had built up would finally crack, he also yearned for it. At least then this awful war of no words would end.

Kate also longed for something to happen, she just wasn't sure what.

Jason had apologized and seemed to stay out of her way. Still, he made her nervous, and she was careful not to be left alone with him again.

But Jason no longer was her main concern—Robert was. When he had escorted her out on that starry evening and paused to say good night, she had felt the flickering of an unnamed something between them. Perhaps it was the way he had smiled, his dark eyes gazing down with a mixture of concern and amusement. Or that instant when his hand had brushed hers as they both reached for the door of the cab. Or perhaps it was the way he had stepped in to stop Jason. Would any man have done that? Would Robert have done it for any woman?

Whatever it was, she had, for the first time, allowed herself to hope that she meant something to him.

Yet everything she had experienced that evening had dissipated by the next day. Robert was polite, but still distant. Never once did he suggest they have lunch together. Never once did he offer to see her home.

The five of them were tackling a new and difficult subject: the German oil supply, particularly the refineries in Rumania. This time their old sources weren't much help.

"A proposition," Jason declared one afternoon, appearing in the doorway of his office.

Kate looked up from her typewriter.

"I can understand why we're fighting Japan," he said. "They did bomb Hawaii, after all. But what about Germany? Until we went after them, what did they ever do to us?"

No one said anything. Kate felt ill, and wondered if Jason had been drinking.

Finally, Elliot said softly, "Jason, you can't be serious."

"Oh, just for debate. Isn't the monotony of the war starting to drive you crazy?"

Again, there was no response.

"Well, what do you say, Elliot?"

The short man sighed. "As a matter of historical fact, Jason, Germany declared war on us."

"Oh, details, details." Jason laughed with a wave of his hand. "Look, this is my point. This war is over the stinking Jews. If it weren't for all the damn Jews Hitler thinks we're hiding, he would have left us alone."

Kate gasped. Then, out of the corner of her eye, she could

see Robert, his fists clenching and arms tensing. Suddenly he sprang forward like a tiger, grabbing Jason by the shoulders and slamming him into a filing cabinet.

"Robert!" she screamed.

He smashed Jason's back against the metal. "Don't you ever"—he jerked him again—"spout horseshit"—the sound echoed—"like that again."

"Stop it, Robert!" Kate said as she and Elliot tried to separate the men. She was mad enough to slug Jason herself, but she was more worried about Robert. She could see the fury in his eyes, hatred that was wild enough to kill someone.

He shoved Jason to the floor and stormed out of the office.

"Did you see that?" Jason looked up, rubbing his jaw. "I may have to file charges."

"You just try it," Kate said.

She ran out into the hall. There was no sign of Robert. She went down the stairs to the lobby, then outside onto the street. Then she spotted him, about a half block away.

"Robert, wait!"

If he heard her, he ignored her. But she wasn't about to give up. She trotted to try to catch up with him, doing the best she could in her high-heeled pumps and long straight skirt.

"Robert. Please!"

He slowed his pace then. A block later she drew even.

She reached out for his arm. "Stop for a minute." She took a deep breath. "Please."

This time Robert obeyed. But he said nothing. He only stared off into the distance, his arms folded defiantly across his chest as if he were braced for another blow.

"What Jason said was unforgivable."

Robert didn't move.

"It won't happen again."

He kicked a stone fiercely. "I feel like a prisoner here."

"I know what you mean. . . ."

"I'm not talking about the office," he said, turning away from her. "I mean all of it—Washington, America." He looked back at her. "But you wouldn't understand, would you?"

His eyes flashed like warning lights, telling her to stay away. But she pressed on, speaking softly. "I want to understand. Please tell me."

He studied her face, and was stunned to see her green eyes starting to fill with tears. He turned away. "Let's walk."

He knew he had turned off his emotions in the past few years—Europe had done that to him. It was easier not to feel, because when he did, all he felt was anger. Rage at the enemies he could name and those he could not. Pain at the remembrance of those who were gone.

So he had retreated, like a snail in a shell, away from the laughter and joy of other people. Away from women like Kate.

He knew she threatened his self-imposed exile. She could hurt him, even if she didn't mean to. And yet he couldn't bring himself to say "leave me alone."

They headed south, past the pencil-thin monument, starkly white against the clear spring sky. The daffodils had bloomed. And around the Tidal Basin, the fragile pink buds of the cherry trees, an ironic gift from Japan when it was still a friend, were about to burst open.

"So try me," she dared. "See if I really can't understand."

Could she? In this world, there were people who were Jews and people who weren't. He had never expected to be attracted to a woman who wasn't like him. But that was before Kate.

"It's a long story. . . ."

"So let Jason wait."

He smiled at that, liking the rebel in her.

She raised an eyebrow. "What's stopping you?"

He hesitated for a moment, and then began, gazing at his feet or the cherry trees in the distance. Anything but her disturbingly green eyes.

"The summer I graduated from Columbia—it was 1934 —I went to Europe, to visit my relatives in Germany. We . . . have a lot of them there—my mother's parents and an aunt and uncle on both of my parents' sides. Lots of cousins.

"I had planned to stay only for the summer. But I had been feeling at loose ends and I liked them all so much, I decided to stay longer. My uncle put me to work in his import business, and with my passable German I managed to do all right.

"But that didn't last long. One thing after another happened—the new laws and the yellow stars and Kristallnacht. Hitler made it pretty clear he didn't want any Jews in his country. So I told my relatives to come home with me."

He paused. "And did they?" she asked.

Robert shook his head. "My parents offered to pay their way, to give them a home and help them find jobs. But they wouldn't budge. They insisted they were Germans first, not Jews. And it wouldn't be long before the German people would rise up against Hitler."

They reached the Tidal Basin, and found a vacant bench.

"What did you do then?"

"I was torn," he admitted. "My parents ordered me to come home. But I wanted to stay and help my relatives. So I compromised. I went to Switzerland and talked my way into a job with the American embassy. I started doing intelligence work in France and Germany. Nothing flashy, mind you, but at least I felt I was doing something."

His brown eyes, she noticed, grew darker, angrier. He seemed to lose himself in his memories, and she wondered whether she had any right to disturb them.

A question formed on her lips, but she was almost afraid to ask it. Then she looked at him and knew that she had to ask it, even if she already knew the answer. If she didn't, if she let him hide the rest away, she would never really know him.

"What happened to your relatives?"

He stared at his hands, the anger in his eyes giving way to helplessness. "I don't know," he said at last. "They've disappeared. As best I can tell from their old neighbors, the Nazis packed them off to camps in the East. . . . I'm sure I'll never see them again."

She tried to say, "Of course you will," but the words died in her throat. Instead, she remembered the day she watched the soldiers go after the Bonus Marchers, and imagined how she would have felt if they had taken her family away. She closed her eyes, then murmured, "I'm sorry."

He reached down and picked up a twig, then snapped it and threw the pieces away. "I managed to come down with pneumonia then. I was in a sanitarium in Geneva for a while. After several months, I felt better, but they said it could come back anytime if I wasn't careful. And so they sent me home.

"I argued, I pleaded with them, but they said they had to go by the rules. I was supposed to get transferred to the OSS here, but when my papers finally came through, I found myself in your office, checking maps and writing reports and working for a jackass named Jason Rush."

Kate said nothing for a moment. There was no way she could make it up to him, no way she could apologize for a world that had a Hitler, an office that had a Jason. But if he only understood that he wasn't alone in all this. That other people cared, just as much as he did.

She rose from the bench and walked over beside the water. "You know," she said softly, "we're not all that different."

He snorted. "Come on!"

"No, I mean it." She whirled around to face him. "You feel like no one has seen the things you've seen, that no one can understand the way you feel. You're plunked down in the middle of an office, thousands of miles from where you want to be, surrounded by people who are so pleased to be making their own little contribution to the war when the last thing you want to be doing is pushing papers. . . ."

For a moment he was silent. "Go on."

She hesitated. "For as long as I can remember, I've felt like I was alone, that no one could understand how I thought or why I did the things I did."

"I always thought you were a rather conventional person."

"I am in some ways," she said.

She turned back toward the water. She had always avoided talking about her childhood, but suddenly, with Robert, it was what she wanted to do.

"It feels like I've been on my own ever since I was a young child. My mother died, and then my father sent me off to live with my aunt and uncle. Don't get me wrong.

They've been very good to me. But I've tended to keep to myself. I guess it's sort of a form of self-defense.''

"How did you get to know Jason?" There was an edge to his voice.

Kate sighed. "His father went to college with my uncle. My aunt and uncle invited him to my . . . a party for me."

He looked at her strangely.

"He didn't used to be like this," she added quickly. "Back then he seemed witty and charming and polite. But after the war started, things were different." Her voice trailed off. "I guess you could say that about a lot of things now."

"Yes, you could." He paused. "Has there been anyone else?"

The question startled her. "You mean other men?"

He nodded.

"No."

"Why was that?"

She hesitated. "I'm not sure. . . . I always seemed to have other things I wanted to do. . . . Maybe I was just trying to protect myself . . . from getting hurt." She looked up at him then. "What about you? Have you ever been in love?"

"There was a girl in Germany, a friend of my cousin's. But even now I'm not sure whether I was really in love with her or whether I was in love with a time and a place and she was just part of all that."

He looked out across the water, and Kate knew that the girl had disappeared, too.

"Would you rather be over there now?" she asked at last.

"Yes," he said. "I don't feel a great urge to go off into combat and try to kill some poor sucker before he kills me. But I want to do something to end all of this. I want to make a difference."

She looked up. "I'm always wondering how much longer the war will drag on, and how many more people will be killed before it's all over."

"And all you and I do," he said, "is sit around all day, writing reports for generals who will never have time to read them. . . .''

He stood up then. "But just in case someone is reading them . . . I guess we ought to be heading back now."

"I guess so."

She hated to leave. She hated to have to stop just when he was beginning to open up.

But it would take time, she reminded herself. Just like the war. One battle at a time. The victories counted in hills, not cities or countries. Hoping all the while that the casualties didn't climb.

They walked back to the office, but hesitated before going in. He reached out and brushed back a lock of hair that had blown across her cheek. "You know, you really are a stubborn woman."

She looked into his eyes, eyes that no longer were as mysterious as they had been that morning.

Then he added, "But I'm glad you came to find me."

And she knew that when he said it, he meant it.

Thirteen

Jason offered an apology; silently Robert accepted it.

Kate thought that was the end of it. But it also was the end of whatever had happened between her and Robert that afternoon by the Tidal Basin.

If she suggested that he join her for lunch, he always had too much work. When she told him she liked his new suit, he smiled, murmured "thanks," then went back to plotting bombing runs. If he had a life outside of the office, he never spoke of it. And so each day Kate tried to persuade her head—and her heart—that the most they could ever be was friends.

She made a point of meeting her uncle for lunch. She pushed herself to go shopping after work. She tried to track down old friends to play tennis. But after the diversions were over, the emptiness remained.

It bothered her, this purposelessness. She had always

known where she was going, she had always set out after her dreams. But now she seemed stuck, stuck in an office and stuck in a crowded town that was ruled by the rhythms of war. Stuck with two men, one who had wanted too much of her and one who had wanted too little. Both of whom, in his own way, had disappointed her terribly.

Some days she yearned for a place of her own. Sometimes she thought she ought to join the WACS. Those women in their smart uniforms certainly looked like *they* knew what they were doing. But she could never bring herself to sign up. Someday, she told herself, the war had to end. That was when she'd go abroad or go back to school. That was when she'd get on with her life.

But first they had to win the war. So for now, Kate poured herself into her work. They all knew they were working on the invasion of Europe, even though no one had told them so. Her job was to piece together scraps of information from the Resistance into a report on food supplies in France.

It was hard work, so hard, in fact, that for the first time in a long time she decided to stay late. Robert stayed late, too, reading the papers, so she didn't worry about Jason. And as engrossed as she was in her work, she almost forgot Robert was there.

She kept at it for more than two hours, but the codes and chopped-off sentences began to spin before her eyes. Her head ached, her shoulders sagged. Her stomach was beginning to rebel.

She looked up and was startled to see Robert, stone-faced, staring out through the venetian blinds. He turned to her and said, "I can't believe it."

"What?"

He began pacing the room. "You know that meeting that's going on in Bermuda, where the Allies are trying to figure out what to do with the Jewish refugees?"

She nodded.

"They did their damnedest to keep the press out, but *The Times* did a story. And it says they're going to do nothing."

"Are you sure?" She came over to look for herself.

"Oh, they say they're going to establish a camp in Africa for five thousand refugees. Five thousand, Kate! Hitler probably killed that many Jews yesterday."

He wadded up the page of newsprint, then hurled it across the room. Then he turned to her, his eyes aflame with the anger that she knew was in his heart. "You could put ten thousand Jews in Washington tomorrow and no one would ever know the difference."

Then he cocked his head and looked at her strangely. "But maybe you would."

She shook her head, speechless.

He grabbed hold of her shoulders. "What is it about us, Kate? Is it our strange last names or our kinky hair or our crooked noses? Or maybe it's just the way we smell. . . ."

His fingers dug into her arms, but his words stung even deeper. "Stop it, Robert." She started to cry. "Stop it. You're not being fair."

His body froze, his hands released their grip. Pain transformed the hard edges of his face. "I'm sorry." His voice cracked as he folded her into his arms, burying his cheek into her hair. "I didn't mean you, Kate. God knows I didn't mean you."

She pressed her cheek into his chest, struggling to stop her tears. She gasped for the breath his anger had pummeled out of her. She was afraid to venture out of the cave of his embrace.

But then she realized, she was in Robert's arms. The pain became joy, the tears melted into rejoicing. And yet she wondered, how long could it last this time?

He raised his head and gazed into her eyes, searching them in a way he had never allowed himself to before. He lifted his hand to her face, and with the side of his thumb traced along her cheekbones and down the side of her face. "How could I be so stupid?" he whispered. "How could I hurt you so?"

His finger reached her lips. He bent his head to meet her upturned mouth and brushed her lips gently, once, then again and again. *Such sweetness,* he thought. *Like a treat—sugar*

*or butter—that's been rationed: the taste of it after such a
long time only makes you yearn for it more.*

He reached down and turned off the gooseneck lamp on
his desk. The moon shone through the venetian blinds, painting their faces in stripes of white and black. He hesitated,
then placed his palms lightly on her breasts and bent to kiss
the valley in between. Then he pulled her close again, holding
her tightly to remind himself that she was not about to disappear. Not like the others had.

Then he remembered that other night, the awful night when
he had found her here with Jason. He kissed her quickly on
the forehead. "C'mon," he whispered. "Let's get out of
here."

They raced down the stairs. Then came the dilemma.

"Where shall we go? Your place?"

She hesitated. "My aunt and uncle will be there."

He laughed. "And all of my roommates are home, too."
He thought for a moment. "I've got an idea."

He tried to hail a cab, and finally one came to their rescue.
He opened the back door, then crawled in beside her. Then
he took her face between his hands and kissed her, very
tenderly.

But it had been so long, and she had wanted him so, she
pressed herself into his strength. It could have been a dream,
and yet she knew it wasn't. This was him. This was Robert.
How many times had she imagined the feel of him? And yet
the real thing was so much better.

"Hey, kids," the cabbie growled, "are we gonna smooch
all night or are ya gonna tell me where ya wanna go?"

Robert smiled down at her with longing. Then he looked
up and said, "To Paradise, please. And take all the time you
want."

Mays come and go, but in Kate's memory there had never
been one like the May of 1943. The azaleas burst forth with
a siren of color, pinks and whites and purples, as if they were
heralding her happiness. And the last warm days before the
steamy summer months seemed to stretch on without a
thought to the calendar.

It was hard at first, trying to find a way to be alone together. At work, they wanted to be discreet. Robert's place was a madhouse, with roommates coming and going at all hours of the day. And Kate still wasn't ready to subject him to a cup of tea in Amanda's straitlaced parlor.

So they caught their moments when they could. But it still gave Kate pleasure to look up from her work and see Robert sitting nearby. This giddiness, this desire to be with him every moment of the day, this was what she had never felt all those years of going out with Jason. This, she knew now, was what people called love.

Their nights and weekends were filled with discovering the other sides of each other. It was impossible to get gasoline that summer, so they took long bike rides along the C&O Canal instead. She taught him to play tennis, but never tried to humiliate him on the court. They held hands in the dark to watch *Casablanca* and argued for hours afterward over whether Rick should have let Ilsa go.

"But they were meant to be together," Kate protested.

"Ah, but Rick knew her too well," he retorted. "He knew she would always feel guilty about leaving Victor. And if he couldn't re-create what they had had in Paris, he didn't want to try."

She smiled. "I wonder if he'll still feel that way tomorrow."

They had been together a month, Kate realized, when she bothered to stop and count the days. It was hard to remember when Robert hadn't been a part of her life.

"I've come to a profound conclusion about love," she declared one afternoon as they lay on a blanket near Hains Point. "The only people who keep track of the days or months or years that they've been with someone are the ones who are really worried that it's not going to last. It's as if they can't believe they've lasted that long already."

"Either that or they're celebrating," he said. "Remind me not to remember our tenth anniversary."

She liked the sound of that. "That's not what I mean." She reached over and touched his lips. "It's like . . . it's like every day's the first day . . . and yet every day gets better."

He kissed her fingertips. "I know what you mean." He leaned up on one elbow. "When did you first know?"

"Would you laugh if I said from the day I met you?"

He gave her hand a squeeze. "No, I'd say it only proves that you're smarter than I am."

She bent her arm up to shield her eyes from the sun. "It's hard to believe on a day like today that there's anything wrong with the world." She curled up close to him. "I'm so happy right now I almost feel guilty."

He reached out and stroked the curve of her hip. "Now that'll never do." He leaned over and kissed her. "You're sounding too much like I used to."

That night he took her to the Library of Congress to hear a string quartet play. She watched, fascinated, as he closed his eyes and drummed his fingers, reading the music in his head.

Afterward, they walked out into a star-filled evening.

"I'm glad," he said, "that someone in America is still playing Beethoven."

"How do you know that music?"

"I studied violin for ten years."

"You did?" There were so many things to learn about him. "Will you play for me sometime?"

"Maybe." He hesitated, then said, "The truth is I used to play all the time with my cousins. But I haven't played a note since I left Germany."

Would the ghosts always be there? she wondered. Lurking in the most unsuspecting places? Waiting to devour all that they shared?

Or could love defeat them? Could it light the dark recesses of his heart and warm the chilling memories?

The stars didn't answer. And she was careful not to ask him again.

Fourteen

Margaret was getting married. She and Jack Swayze had decided they would do it the next time he made it home on leave. She had a dress, a minister, and an anxious mother standing by. All she needed now was the groom.

Kate, however, had a young man in town. And one morning over breakfast Amanda said, "I think it's about time we found out more about him."

"His name," Kate said slowly, "is Robert Kaufmann. He's an economist who works with me."

Margaret looked up from the new issue of *Bride*. "Is he good-looking?"

Kate laughed. "Well, I think so."

Stephen winked at his niece. "Maybe instead of interrogating Kate, we ought to invite Robert to dinner."

"All right then," Amanda said. "How about Friday night?"

Kate hesitated. Robert was her treasure, a sort of secret that she didn't want to share with just anyone. But this was her family after all. What was she afraid of anyway?

"I think Friday will be fine, Aunt Amanda."

"Now tell me again what his name is."

"Robert. Robert Kaufmann."

"It sounds Jewish," Amanda observed.

"It not only sounds Jewish," Kate whispered, trying not to smile, "it is."

Friday was hot and sultry and by the time Kate and Robert had made it home on the crowded streetcar, Kate's reserve of optimism was nearly depleted.

"You're not mad at me, are you?" she asked as they slogged up her front steps.

"No. Should I be?"

"I'll ask you again when dinner's over."

Stephen and Margaret greeted Robert warmly, Amanda offered her hand and a well-practiced smile. After a round of cold drinks in the study, her aunt led them to the dining room, where the huge table was set with her finest linens, china, and flowers.

They made small talk for a while, and then Amanda turned to the topic of the evening. "Katharine's told us you're from New York originally, Robert. How did you end up in Washington?"

"It's a long story, but I was working for the government overseas when I became ill. After I recovered I was assigned back here."

"You're lucky not to be off fighting like Margaret's fiancé."

He winced. "Actually, I find civilian life to be quite frustrating. I often wish I was closer to the action."

"I know how you feel," Stephen spoke up. "Sometimes it seems like I'm the only man in Washington who's not in uniform."

"Oh, but, dear," Amanda said, "you're much too old to be going off to war."

Margaret giggled, Stephen coughed. "Yes," he said, "and getting older by the minute, I'm afraid."

Tillie brought in a serving platter. Pork chops and asparagus. Kate shifted in her chair. Either Amanda didn't know any better or she was deliberately trying to offend Robert. With her aunt, Kate wasn't sure which.

The maid offered the platter to Robert; he took a small piece of the meat and thanked her.

"Tell us about your family," Amanda prodded.

Robert put down his fork. "My father is a lawyer, my mother is an organizer for the garment workers' union."

"Does your father have a specialty?" Stephen asked.

"Yes, sir. Labor law. He represents several large unions."

"I see," Amanda pronounced. "Union activists."

"You might say so," Robert said with a hint of a smile.

"Where are your people from originally?" Amanda asked.

"Depends what you mean by originally," he said, pausing to take a sip of water. "My parents emigrated from Germany when they were in their early twenties. 'My people,' as you put it, are thought to have originated in a place they call Palestine."

For a moment no one said anything, the silence underscoring the curtness of Robert's reply. Kate tried to think of something to say, something clever or light to pierce the tension. But finally Amanda herself stepped in.

"That's very interesting," she said, dabbing at her mouth with her napkin. "Margaret, would you please pass the pork chops."

Afterward, Kate asked if they could be excused. It was still light out so they strolled up Connecticut Avenue, their arms wrapped around each other's waists. They stopped at a sidewalk café for another round of coffee.

"Your aunt doesn't like me," Robert said.

Kate sighed. "My aunt is my aunt. What can I say?"

He laughed. "At one point I considered leaning over and saying, 'But you know, there haven't been any known cases of syphilis in my family.' "

She laughed. "You're terrible! . . . But so is she."

"I liked your uncle, though. He seems like a regular sort of guy."

"Yes, he is."

The waiter brought their drinks.

"So when am I going to meet your parents?" she asked.

He circled a spoon around his cup, saying nothing.

"I'm serious, Robert. We could make a trip to New York some weekend. Don't you think it would be fun?"

"No, I don't."

She put down her cup. "Why not?"

"My parents are old and set in their ways. They'd never understand."

"Understand what?"

He sighed. "You forget, Kate, that it works both ways. . . . It would kill them to know I had fallen in love with someone who wasn't Jewish."

The words hit her like a mortar, hard and unexpected. She

had known it wouldn't be easy. She had known the two of them would have problems. But it had never occurred to her that she would be one of them.

"But surely, Robert, in this day and age. . . ."

"In this day and age, Kate?" His face turned grim. "My parents have watched a madman destroy their family. My brother and I are all they have left, their only link to the future. We're the only ones who can keep their family alive."

He hesitated, then added, "The way my mother talks it's like she thinks anyone who marries outside the faith is in cahoots with Hitler."

A chill raced through her heart. Did people really think that way? "I guess I'm kind of naive," she said very softly. "I guess that's what I thought we were fighting this war over. That people would learn to understand one another."

"My mother would understand you fine," he said. "Just as long as you didn't marry me."

Just as long as you didn't marry me. Where did that leave the two of them? Where did this lead if not to marriage?

But she couldn't push him, not yet, at least. She was only just beginning to enjoy it, to revel in this feeling of love. It was too precious to challenge, too fragile to shake.

And so she said nothing for now. But as she sipped her coffee, a thought singed the edges of her heart: *You can talk all you want about mothers and fathers and Hitler, Robert. But what about you and me?*

It was late when he finally walked her home, and paused on the front porch to kiss her good night. He held her close, stroking her hair. She clung to him tightly, afraid for the first time that in the end she would lose him to forces she could not understand. Emotions that were as strong as love, beliefs that were as old as time.

"I love you, Kate."

"And I love you, Robert."

The others had already gone to bed when she climbed the stairs to her room. Now, even though she had outgrown its frilly white fussiness, it was still her haven from the storms around her.

She changed into her nightgown and climbed into bed. Then there was a knock at the door.

"Katharine." It was her aunt. "May I come in?"

Amanda was wearing her blue silk robe, with her hair brushed out loosely around her shoulders. When she wore it that way, it reminded Kate of her mother.

"Thank you for the dinner."

"You're welcome, dear. Robert seems . . . like a very nice young man."

"But you're not exactly thrilled about him, are you?"

Amanda sat down at the foot of her bed. "It has nothing to do with Robert personally. It's just that he's not our type."

"Oh, gawd." His side, now her side. It was too much for one night.

"These things are important," her aunt persisted.

"You should talk," Kate parried. "You left the Catholic Church when you married Uncle Stephen."

The line of attack stunned her aunt momentarily. "Yes, but he didn't care one way or the other. It just seemed to make more sense for me to become an Episcopalian."

"More socially acceptable you mean."

"Now hear me out." Amanda's voice rose. "I know what I'm talking about. You can't ignore such differences in up-bringing. Take your mother. She was beautiful, intelligent, talented—just like you are. She could have had any young man she wanted in New Orleans. But that wasn't enough for her. Oh, no, she had to have adventure. She had to have some . . . some . . . sort of grand passion in her life. So she married someone who was different. And he took her to a hellhole of a farm that killed her."

"Amanda, that's unfair."

"Is it?" her aunt replied. "Ask yourself this: Why Robert? Why is it that of all the young men you've known, he's the one you've fallen for now. How many years did you date Jason Rush? A young man from a good, respected family? And then suddenly it's all thrown away on this Robert Kaufmann." She paused, then added softly, "I just don't want you to make the same mistake your mother did."

"Don't worry," Kate said firmly. "I won't."

"I'll say good night then."

"Good night."

Kate flipped off the light by her bed. It was silly, she told herself. Robert was no more like her father than he was like Jason. Her parents' differences were differences of class, not religion.

And yet Amanda's words echoed again and again. Her mother remained in her memory as an angel, a mythical princess; her father, a weak-willed cad. She could not begin to understand why Charlotte Dellaplaine had ever married Emory Callahan.

Was she rebelling against something? Was it some sort of grand passion, like Amanda said? She would never know for sure. For Charlotte hadn't lived long enough to provide her with the answer. Nor long enough to reassure her: "Don't worry, you're not like me."

There was no more talk about trips to New York or visits to Robert's parents. The subject was dropped, but Kate knew that it hadn't gone away. It hovered beneath the surface of everything they did or said. It clouded all the fantasies she had of the life they'd have together.

It didn't matter now, but someday she knew it would. He would have to make a choice: his parents or her. And as much as she wanted to hope, as much as she wanted to believe in love, she couldn't be sure that in the battle for the heart of Robert Kaufmann, she would come out the winner.

Fifteen

Time felt suspended as 1943 drew to a close. People spoke about today and yesterday and "when the war is over." But no one could say when that would be.

It seemed dishonorable to talk about marriage and houses and children and such, when all around Kate young women were losing young men and young men were losing their lives.

Yet it nagged at her. How long would she and Robert go on like this, stuck in a sort of no-man's-land between love and marriage? Was it the uncertainties of the war? Was it the differences they kept trying to ignore? Or was it something else—battles still to be fought, deaths to be avenged—that kept Robert from making that final commitment to her?

She knew he still wanted to go back to Europe. Each month he slipped out of the office during lunchtime to take the army physical. He never told her where he was going, but she could tell by his sullen expression when he returned that he had failed it again. But how long could she count on that happening?

Someday, she kept telling herself, the war *had* to end.

"Where are we going tonight?" She liked to let Robert surprise her.

"I've decided," he replied, "that there are some major gaps in your education."

"Like what?"

"Have you ever heard Norman Thomas speak?"

"The socialist? No, actually."

"Then I think it's about time you did."

The hall was hot and crowded when they arrived. The days when Thomas could be a factor in a presidential race were long gone, but he could still weave a spell around his audience.

Why was it, he asked the crowd, that the army was allowed to segregate its soldiers? Why was it, he shouted, that Americans who just happened to be Japanese had been sent away to internment camps? He built to a crescendo at the end. "Maybe our battle for freedom and justice ought to begin at home!"

"What did you think?" Robert asked as they left.

"I can see why he has a following."

He took her arm to lead her through the throng. "My

parents used to take my brother and me to listen to him when
we were growing up. I liked it because it meant we got to
stay up late."

But that night was just the beginning. He took her to union
meetings where it seemed that half the people in the place
recognized "Jake Kaufmann's little boy." He took her to a
picnic where men and women reminisced about the days when
they'd fought side by side with the Loyalists in Spain.

He took her to another meeting, located in an abandoned
warehouse in a run-down part of town. As the agenda un-
folded, she listened with a growing sense of shock. "Robert," she whispered, "they're Communists!"

He smiled. "I know."

Afterward she asked, "You're not a member of the party,
are you?"

"Don't worry. I just find some of their ideas interesting."

So they went back occasionally, and talked with the people
they met. Kate thought some of them were impossibly stri-
dent, but others she genuinely liked.

They were always circulating petitions, petitions against
this atrocity and petitions for that cause. Robert almost always
signed them; Kate did, too, if they didn't seem too radical.

One night a voice called out from the center of the crowd:
"Robert! Robert Kaufman!" A bear of a man with a dusty
blond crew cut lumbered across the room toward them, his
florid face growing redder with the exertion.

Robert seemed to tense. "Hello, Karl," he said when the
man joined them. They shook hands, then Robert turned to
introduce her. "Katharine Callahan, Karl Wagner."

"Quite a comer you're bringing 'round here," Karl said
with a broad wink.

"Nice to meet you," Kate replied, withdrawing her hand.

The man's muddy blue eyes darted back to Robert. "How
many years has it been, Robert? Fifteen? Twenty? Why, I
remember how your dad used to bring you over to our
house. . . ."

"Yes, I remember, too, Karl. How's your mother doing?"

"Fine. Still living in the Bronx."

"That's nice. Say, I'd like to stay and talk but Kate and
I were just on our way out the door. . . ."

"Why don't we all go out and get a couple of beers together? Talk about old times?"

"That sounds great but . . ."

"I know this place downtown that's got cheap food and a great band. We could just . . ."

"I'd like to, Karl, but I'm afraid we've already made some plans."

Karl's smile faded into a sneer. "Well, sorry, Mr. Bigshot. I guess ever since your family went uptown, you've got no time for your old friends."

"You know that's not true, Karl. Look, I'd like to get together. But let's do it another time, okay?"

"Forget it," the big man said with a wave of his hand. "Just take your fancy girlfriend and get out of here."

"Karl, wait . . ." Robert said, but the man had already stormed off, knocking down a few chairs in his path.

Robert sighed and shook his head.

"What was that all about?" Kate whispered.

He frowned as he led her outside. "Our families used to be close friends. We lived in the same neighborhood. Dad and Werner, Karl's father, were both working for the same union.

"The company they were dealing with was really anti-union. Negotiations were getting tense, and a strike vote had been taken. And Dad discovered that Werner was spying for management. He caught him red-handed with the payoff."

Robert pulled his coat a little tighter. "That was the end of our dealings with the Wagners. I suppose it's not fair to Karl, but I've never really trusted him ever since. I just can't help remembering how it hurt my father."

Suddenly it struck her how different his world was: Everything was black and white. Our side and their side. Labor and management. Liberals and conservatives. Jews and Germans.

Jews and Christians.

"So," he said, stopping under a stoplight to look at her, "other than tales from my childhood, have you learned anything from all these meetings I've been dragging you to?"

"It's funny," she said, taking his arm. "I used to always think that Stephen was such a great liberal. But he was never involved with any of this. I guess I always thought that as a judge he had to stay above the fray. But I'm not sure he ever really had to take a difficult stand."

"So what do you believe in, Kate?"

She stopped and thought for a moment, about what she'd been raised to think, and what she had been taught in college, and what she had learned since then. Then she knew the answer.

"I believe that someday the world will stop fighting. I believe that someday people will have to learn to live together." She paused and then added, "And I believe in you, Robert."

The words were a little corny and she was afraid he would think they were the first thing that popped into her head. But as she looked up at his face, haloed by a street lamp, she knew that she meant them with all her heart.

On a Monday morning in early March, Jason summoned Robert into his office and asked him to close the door.

"I have something you might be interested in. You know about that War Refugee Board FDR just approved?"

Robert nodded.

"I have a friend at the Treasury Department who's trying to find some people for it. He's looking for men who know their way around Europe, fellows who can land there and get moving fast. Naturally, I thought of you."

"I'm flattered," Robert replied icily.

"Well, are you interested?"

"What's in it for you?"

Jason shrugged. "I help a buddy, that's all. I figured you'd jump at the chance, the way you've been wanting to get back over there."

Wasn't it strange, Robert thought. A year ago, he would have given anything to be free of this place. But that was before Kate.

"I don't know," he said.

"Hell, I thought this would be right up your alley," Jason

said. "Going over there, rescuing Jews. . . . But I guess I read you all wrong. You're not the crusader I thought you were."

His aunts, his uncles, his cousins, his people.

"I guess I'll just tell my friend that you weren't . . ."

"No, wait." Robert hesitated. "Tell him I'm interested."

"Are you sure?"

"Yes."

"Great!" Jason reached for the phone. "I'll call him right now."

Robert stood up. "There may be a problem. I still can't pass the army physical."

Jason shrugged. "They're bureaucrats, not soldiers. They won't give a shit."

As Robert returned to his desk, Kate looked up, curious. "It's nothing," he mouthed.

He sat down and tried to resume his work. How would he tell her? He didn't know, but there was no point worrying about it now. Hell, the job probably didn't even exist. Probably just another trick of Jason's to torture him.

Robert shared a townhouse on Capitol Hill with six other men, but there were always more passing through. Space and—more important—privacy were as rare as the tin and rubber their agency worked to procure.

But tonight—Kate's twenty-fourth birthday—it was different.

"Where is everyone?" she asked.

He smiled. "I bribed them all to get out of here. For one night of this war, I wanted to bring you home to my place. Alone."

"And just what did you have in mind?" she teased.

"Sit there," he said, indicating a squat velveteen armchair that was coming apart at the seams. He got out two glasses and filled them with scotch. Then he crossed the room and opened the front closet. "I have a present for you."

"The pearls were more than enough." Kate reached up to savor the necklace's perfect smoothness.

"Shh," he said.

He pulled out a leather violin case and opened it. He was going to play!

He smiled as he tucked the instrument up underneath his chin. "Didn't anyone ever teach you not to talk when the orchestra was about to start?"

He pulled his bow across the strings, launching into a song she'd never heard before. His touch was feather-light, sending forth a stream of precise, even tones. The back-and-forth strokes of his bowing arm mesmerized her, casting a hypnotic spell.

The long fingers of his left hand darted up and down the strings, while his right hand held the bow tenderly, as if coaxing it to take over and play by itself. He seemed to be communicating with the instrument, caressing it almost, like he had rediscovered a long-lost love.

The violin's burnished wood began to dance with the lights of the room around them. And as the phrases tumbled out, he transported her to a new world, a world of sensitive, beautiful things. A world that was at peace.

She heard in the music a theme that returned, over and over in different forms. It was sweet, incomparably sweet at times, and yet it was tinged with sadness. The sadness that hung over Robert's world, the sadness that clouded his heart.

She had never seen him like this, so lost in his music. This was not Robert the office leader nor Robert the rabble-rouser. This was Robert the artist. This was a gentler man.

He moved on to a second section. It was angrier, and the tones and rhythms more discordant. It reminded her of the way he had been when she first met him. The man who had locked up all his anger inside of him.

And yet this Robert had started playing his violin again. Her heart swelled with love—and just a touch of pride.

He paused briefly, then plunged into a new section. It was happier, almost soaring. It made her think of the past few months, the happiest months in her life really. For the first time, she had learned to put aside all of her defenses. She had learned to open herself to the possibility of love.

And Robert? She gazed then at the man she loved. He

moved his bow in a frantic final cadenza, and then with a flourish he stopped.

Kate was transfixed.

"Well, what do you think?" he asked.

"Robert, that was beautiful."

He stood before her, shyly clutching his instrument. "Did you really think so?"

She nodded. "I'm so glad you started playing again. I wanted to hear you so much. And that music—it was wonderful. Who was the composer?"

He put the violin back in the case, then refastened the latches. "Me," he said quietly.

"You?"

He turned and pulled her into his arms. "I wrote it for you, Kate."

For her? He had written all this music for her? She never would have guessed he was blessed with such talent. And where had he found the time?

"Robert, what can I say? . . ."

"Say you've had a very happy birthday."

"It's been a wonderful birthday. An indescribable birthday."

He laughed and kissed her on the forehead. But then the laughing stopped.

The room seemed to whirl around her. Her heart was still dancing to his song. His eyes burned bright with yearning, then posed the question. She nodded, silently.

He took her hand and led her up the stairs to his room. She had been there before, but it was different now. The house was so quiet. Waiting. Watching. There were no radios blaring the latest news from the front. No boisterous male voices, enjoying their last hours together. Just the two of them, the racing of their hearts, and the imprint of his music on her soul.

He doused the light overhead and then, to her surprise, lit a candle by his bed. It filled the room with a dim warm light, and cast large shadows of the two of them on the far wall. In the world of his room, they were the only thing that mattered.

He smiled, then began to unbutton her blouse. So many furtive moments, she thought. Kisses in the backseat of cabs, embraces in the stairwell at work. Never enough time to be together. Never enough time to be alone.

He undid her bra, and stroked her breasts, teasing her nipples into expectant points. She noticed the difference in his hands now, the callused fingertips of his left hand built up by hours of practicing. It reminded her of his gift of love, and made her want him even more.

He lowered her to his bed, then stripped off his shirt and joined her. He took a nipple in his mouth and sucked it hard, then covered her breasts with kisses. Then he reached up under her skirt to tease the edge of her panties.

She was hot with the need of him, every part of her wanting to feel him, every part of her wanting to be touched. Nice girls didn't, they always said. But this was different. This was Robert. And wherever he wanted to lead her, she would follow.

But he didn't push her any further. He didn't strip off her clothes. He kissed her breasts and their legs intertwined and he rubbed the hard knot on his leg as his breath blew hot in her ear. Then he came to a shuddering stop. And she came to a shuddering realization.

He's never going to marry me.

Oh, yes, he loved her. He loved her enough to be kind and gentle. And he loved her enough to worry about her reputation. But if she came to him as a virgin, what difference did it make if she remained one?

Unless he knew there would be someone after him.

He reached down to stroke her again, but she shook her head. "It's not going to work for me."

"Are you sure?"

She closed her eyes tightly and nodded. "I'm sure."

He kissed her tenderly, then got up to go to the bathroom. She waited for him, wishing she could ask, wishing that her fears would go away. But she couldn't push it. Nice girls don't.

He came back then and sat down beside her. He studied her face quizzically. "Are you all right?"

She nodded, but said nothing, afraid she might burst into tears.

He leaned down to kiss her and it was almost more than she could bear. The softness of his lips, the hardness of his chest, those deep chocolate-brown eyes.

"It's almost midnight," she whispered. "I think I'd better be getting home."

"If you say so." His voice was sad.

Later, as he took her in his arms on her doorstep, she tried to put her doubts away.

"It was a wonderful evening, Robert. I'll always treasure your music."

He smiled. "Happy birthday, darling." He kissed her one last time.

Happy birthday, she thought ruefully as she closed the door. She was twenty-four now. Next year she'd be twenty-five. It was time, as Amanda was forever telling her, for a girl to be thinking about marriage.

Sixteen

Jack Swayze finally made it home to marry Margaret in the spring of 1944. They had a small wedding in the McNeils' parlor, with the reception in the backyard.

Afterward, Margaret climbed the staircase to throw her bouquet into the swarm of single women down below. She took a careful aim, then flung her white orchids straight at her cousin. And as much as Kate wanted to, she couldn't avoid catching them.

"Congratulations," Robert said as she rejoined him.

"Just lucky," she said, feeling a twinge.

As Margaret and Jack dashed out of the house under a pelter of rice, Kate made up her mind. It was time to confront

Robert. She couldn't go on like this forever. She had to know where she stood.

They wandered out to the backyard, where the caterers were clearing off the tables. She brushed off a spot on the back steps and sat down. "What did you think of the wedding?"

He sat down beside her. "It was . . . interesting."

"Is this the first time you've been to a Christian wedding?" He nodded.

"How are they different?"

"Well, most of the Jewish ceremony is in Hebrew, and the bride and groom stand under a canopy. But the wedding also has religious significance. When two Jews marry, they reaffirm the covenant God made with the Jewish people at Mt. Sinai."

When two Jews marry. The words seared her heart.

He looked out across the yard. "I'm going home next week for Passover."

"Why don't you take me with you?" She said the words without thinking. "Why don't you try to teach me what it's all about?"

He shook his head. "It wouldn't work."

"Why not?" Now she was beginning to get angry. "If I'm willing to bend a little, why can't you?"

"Because it's different for us. It's not just a matter of 'bending a little.' " He hesitated, then plunged on. "If we got married, would you be willing to convert?"

If we got married. Maybe it wasn't hopeless. "I don't know," she said. "It's a hard decision."

She *had* thought about it. She wasn't much of a churchgoer, but all her life she'd been taught to believe in Jesus, and Easter and all the rest. She wasn't sure she could disavow it, overnight.

"You see," he explained, "according to Jewish law, a person is a Jew if his mother is Jewish. If we were to marry, my children wouldn't be considered Jewish."

"And that's all that matters, isn't it?" she said quietly. "Not me or you or the love we share. Just parents and traditions and laws handed down by bearded men with sandals."

"Kate, don't. . . ."

"Why don't we just face up to it, Robert. You can't accept me the way I am. You never had any intention of marrying me and you never will."

"That's not true. . . ."

But she didn't hear him. She was crying now, and she couldn't stop. She brushed past the last of the wedding guests and ran upstairs to her room. She threw herself down on her bed and muffled her tears with her pillow.

Was she being unfair? Had she exploded too fast? No, it was the same old thing. He expected her to make all the changes. But that wasn't right, and she wouldn't do it.

But how was she ever going to live without him?

The rumbles from northern France answered the rumbles of her heart. After months and months of waiting, the Allied invasion had begun. All around Kate, people listened for the latest news from Normandy and talked about when the war would end. But there was no room for hope in Kate's heart.

It was so painful now to work with Robert and remember how things had been. They moved around each other like machines, barely talking, never touching. Trying to forget.

Each day she considered telling him that she was wrong, that she hadn't meant all the terrible things she had said, that she wanted to give it another try.

But no, that was just postponing the inevitable. It was his turn now. And if he changed his mind, he would know where to find her.

Jason smiled as he studied both sides of the government form, savoring every word of the fine print. Everything was in order. Just a shame it had taken so long. But no matter. All that was left now was to break the news to Robert—and to Kate. And he knew just how he wanted to do that.

Did they really think he didn't know about them? Did they really think that they could hide? No, he had seen it all. The secret smiles. The coy glances. The furtive touching as they passed in the office. Now and then he had even followed them—at a distance of course—just to know where they were going. It was masochistic, but he couldn't stop himself.

At 8:05 on the dot, Kate breezed in.

He rose from his desk and walked out beside hers. "I've got some news," he said with nonchalance.

"Oh?"

"Robert's going to be leaving us."

She looked up at him, her face frozen. "What do you mean?"

"He requested a transfer to the War Refugee Board. It just came through. He's been assigned to Switzerland."

"I see," she said woodenly. She turned back to her typewriter and fumbled to remove the cover. She stuffed a piece of paper behind the roller. "That's ve-very nice for Robert." Then she looked up at Jason. "Does he know yet?"

"No, the papers just came in."

Kate turned back to her typewriter. "Then I think you should have told him first."

She began pounding the keys, jamming some, typing letters and numbers that made no sense as her eyes blurred with tears. *The War Refugee Board*. She scoured her brain to remember what she'd read about it. Some agency FDR had approved to try to save whatever Jews were still alive in Europe. It was stupid; it could be dangerous. Why didn't he tell her?

Why did he have to go?

Then she thought of the last weeks, and she wished she could take them back. What difference did it make now? Married or not, she was going to lose him.

"What's wrong, Kate?"

She looked up and saw Robert, the same way he had stood by her desk the day she met him. Physically the same—the long face, the soulful eyes. But now so much dearer to her.

"Robert, could I speak with you?" Jason called from his office.

"You'd better go," she sputtered.

The walls felt as if they were closing in on her. "I have to run an errand," she told Delilah.

She dashed out the door and down the stairwell. She ran fast, as if it were possible to escape the news. But the questions still dogged her. How could he do this to her? Or had she done it to him?

She sat down on a park bench and put her hands over her face. She cried, quietly at first, then with great heaving sobs. Pedestrians passed by, but she didn't care who saw her. The pain was just too great.

She felt a hand touch her shoulder gently, and then heard his voice. "Kate, I . . ."

She whirled around, the tears streaming down her face. "Is it because of me?"

He shook his head. "I put in for it months ago."

"Then why didn't you tell me?"

He sat down beside her. "Because, frankly, I didn't think it was going to happen."

"Still, you should have told me."

He looked away from her. "I know."

She swallowed hard. "I'm happy for you." She struggled to sound brave. "I know it's probably what you wanted." She hesitated, then asked: "How soon do you leave?"

"Next Monday."

"Oh, God." She pressed her hands to her face, but nothing, not Robert's arms around her nor his soft words in her ear could make her stop crying this time.

"I won't be gone forever, Kate. Besides, it's not like I'll be fighting. They'll probably stick me behind some desk in Geneva."

"And if they do"—she sniffed loudly—"you'll be sure to find a way to get away from it."

"I'll be careful." He pulled out his handkerchief and offered it to her. "It's just something I have to do." He hesitated. "You understand that, don't you?"

Reluctantly, she nodded.

"There's something I want to say, though." He pulled her close, until her head rested on his chest. "I've been miserable these past few weeks, and I think you've been, too. I don't pretend to have the answer yet for us, but we can't stop trying to find it."

"Oh, Robert"—she put her arms up around his neck— "I've been such a fool." She held him tightly, and felt the joy, however fleeting, of being in his arms again.

He kissed her wet cheeks. "It would hurt me so to leave

you like this. I don't want the last few weeks to be our final memory."

He hesitated, then whispered close to her ear: "Come away with me, Kate. For the weekend. Just the two of us."

"But where?" she asked shakily.

"I don't care where." His voice grew more excited as his plan took shape. "I've been saving up my gas coupons. Let's just get in my car and drive as far as they'll take us."

She wiped away her tears—and all of her resolve to try to forget him. "All right," she said at last. "Let's do it."

Seventeen

They left right after work on Friday, stopping at Kate's house just long enough for her to pick up her bag and tell her aunt not to worry.

She had packed carefully the night before. She stuck in the precious pair of nylons she'd been hoarding and her new green taffeta dress. Then on top she gingerly placed the present she had received from her aunt and uncle on her last birthday: a nightgown and peignoir made of cream-colored silk.

Now, as they rode through the gentle hills of the Virginia countryside, she and Robert laughed and talked and sang silly songs from their childhoods. Kate had vowed to herself that she wouldn't cry this time, that she would try to make the weekend perfect. But they both knew, without discussing it, that it couldn't end that way.

It was dusk by the time they reached Fredericksburg. The gas station attendant said the hotel there would probably be full, but if they drove just a bit farther, they'd come to "Missus Hudgins's place." "She'll probably have a room or two."

It was not hard to find the white clapboard house. A wide

porch girded the front, with a swing swaying slowly in the breeze. In the freshly painted window boxes up front, the first yellow marigolds of the season were peeking out. Best yet, the "vacancy" sign was still posted.

Robert parked the car and reached down to turn off the ignition. He pulled the key out slowly, then turned and looked at Kate. "If you want," he said softly, "I'll see if she has two rooms."

It was a question, not a statement. A question Kate had asked herself many times since she had fallen in love with him. What did it mean to sleep with him? And now, what would it mean if she never did?

But she couldn't bear to think about that. All that mattered now was that they would be together, the way they should have been all those now-precious months.

"No," she said, "don't do that."

"I'll be back in a minute."

Up the street, a pigtailed girl was jumping rope, singing a rhyme to herself. Kate strained to catch it, wondering if it was one that she and Margaret used to chant. Then she looked back at the boardinghouse. Suddenly it seemed important to memorize every detail of this place, no matter how insignificant. *After he's gone, I'll be glad I did.*

Robert returned and opened the door on her side. "Our room, Mrs. Kaufmann, is ready."

They ate dinner at a little restaurant a few blocks away, where the chicken was deep-fried and the table laden with four kinds of vegetables. Then they downed thick slabs of apple pie with ice cream and weak cups of coffee ("Don't Forget Our Boys," the menu reminded them).

As they walked back to the boardinghouse, Robert reached into his pocket and pulled out the key. "Here," he said, handing it to her. "Why don't you go on up? She said it's the first room on the right. I'll be up with the bags in a second."

Kate asked no questions. She took the key and scurried up the stairs, hoping that she wouldn't run into Mrs. Hudgins.

She opened the door to their room and relaxed a little. It

was furnished simply, but with good taste. The chest and bed were of solid-looking maple, the mattress covered with an antique quilt worked in patches of white and navy. Framed embroidered samplers decorated the walls.

Why had Robert wanted her to come up here alone? Was he giving her one last chance to change her mind?

She would show him. She unzipped her dress and hung it in the closet. Then she undid her garters and carefully peeled her stockings off her legs. She reached into her purse for her hairbrush. There was a gentle knock at the door and then it opened.

Robert stood for a moment, drinking in the sight of her. He had known a few women before, but none like Kate. And no one had managed to stir him as deeply as she did now, just by standing there, waiting for him, in the fading twilight.

She was combing out her hair, slow strokes above her head that displayed the sinewy grace of her arms and exposed the long arch of her lovely neck. Her slip clung to her skin, showing off her curves; a strap slipped down on her shoulder, beckoning.

He closed the door and crossed the room.

"Here, let me." He took the brush and stroked it down through the auburn curls, then paused to kiss the nape of her neck. She shivered. He drew her into his arms to warm her, then slowly began to undress her.

He pulled down the straps of her slip, kissing her shoulders in turn as he passed them. He slithered the silken garment over the curves of her waist and hips, then let it fall to the floor like a puddle of moonlight. He unclasped her bra, then took her breasts in his hands, touching them carefully as if they were rare jewels.

The rest of her clothes disappeared quickly and Kate stood naked before him. But she felt no inhibitions, only a growing ache inside of her, a need to touch him—and love him.

"You're going to get cold standing there like that." He swooped her up in his arms and carried her over to the bed. Then he tucked the covers up around her carefully.

She watched him shed his clothes, thanking God one more

time that for whatever reason the U.S. Army had rejected the marvelous body now bared before her.

He crawled under the quilt and wrapped his arms around her.

"You know I love you, Kate."

"I love you, too, Robert."

He covered her with soft kisses, face, neck, breasts, and below. She pressed her body closer to him, wanting to be a part of him, wanting to know him completely. Desperately her hands struggled to touch every part of him. Was it the sexual longing he had awakened in her, or was it something else—a desire to know him, to memorize every part of his body before he went away?

As his long fingers explored every inch of her, his breathing grew more ragged, his face more flushed.

"Robert . . ."

He stopped and looked up the length of her body.

"Your lungs. Can they take it?"

He threw back his head and laughed. "If not, I can't think of a better way to die." He kissed the valley between her breasts, then brushed a tendril from her cheek. "And what about you, Kate?"

She reached up and pulled his head down close to hers. "Love me, Robert. Please love me."

He wasted no time then, but slipped inside her gently, growing bigger, hotter, faster, sweeping her along on a journey to an unknown place. *Oh, God,* he thought, *why did I wait so long?* He knew that it was right now. He could feel it. He could believe it. She was the center of his being. And all those lost weeks when he had tried to deny it! If he could only have them back now. Just a little more time.

She wanted to go with him. She wanted to ride with him, just as they were now. Their bodies melded into one, their hearts beating together. If she could go with him, she wouldn't worry. If she could go with him, she'd never lose him.

She felt an indescribable rush, and then, just as suddenly, a stream of tears welling up inside her. She squeezed her eyes tightly to stanch them. It was not the slight jab of pain, real as it had been. Rather it was remembering that he was about to leave. She was going to lose him just when she had finally found him. And there was nothing she could do to stop it.

He surged inside of her and then collapsed, his energy spent, into the soft fullness of her body.

"Kate, my darling," he whispered after a moment.

"Yes?"

"If I'm dead, I know this must be heaven."

Eighteen

"Good morning," he said across a sea of starched white sheets.

"Hi."

"Sleep well?"

"Yes," she lied.

In fact, she had lain awake for hours, watching the gentle rise and fall of Robert's chest, listening to the strangely satisfying sound of his snoring, reliving the memory of their lovemaking.

For it was not at all what she had imagined.

If they had told her sex would make a difference, if they had told her she would love Robert even more today than she had the day before, she would have told them they were crazy.

But it was true.

For as long as she had known Robert Kaufmann, she had never known him as well as she did at that moment. And now she felt she could open up herself completely to his love, even if she knew that it would hurt that much more when he left.

No, nothing was solved. The problems that were there

yesterday were still there now. But they all seemed so silly when the real problem was that Robert was leaving in forty-eight hours—and she didn't know when she would see him again.

He pulled her close, blanketing her with the velvety softness of his skin. And then, if she had any lingering doubt that the night before had only been a dream, he made love to her again, in the first pale light of the morning.

At nine they rose reluctantly, their growling stomachs demanding relief at Mrs. Hudgins's breakfast table.

Mildred Hudgins was a small stout woman, with wisps of gray hair at her temples that defied her repeated efforts to blend them into her bun.

"Good morning," she said, her blue eyes twinkling. She wiped her hands on her calico apron. "What can I get you folks this morning?"

"I'm hungry enough to eat a horse," Robert said, winking across the table at Kate.

"Horse?" Mrs. Hudgins repeated, pretending to be puzzled. "Well, let's see what we can do about that."

She retreated to the kitchen, then returned and loaded up their table with eggs, toast, grits, orange juice, and heartier cups of coffee than they'd had the night before.

"So what would you like to do today?" Robert asked as they dawdled over a second cup of coffee.

"Besides stay in bed?"

He laughed. "I suppose we ought to give Mrs. Hudgins time to change the sheets."

In the end, they borrowed bicycles and fishing poles from her and pedaled out to a wooded stretch of the Rappahannock River where she told them the fishing was good.

They rigged their poles with a weight and bobber, then added a minnow for bait. Then they plopped their lines in the water, and stretched out beneath a towering oak tree.

Kate closed her eyes and leaned back against Robert's shoulder, reveling in the warmth of the sun on her face and his arm around her. *Two days left*, a voice inside her brain reminded her. *No*, another voice admonished, *you must live these days as if they're your first together, not your last.*

"Wake up, silly, you've got a bite!"

That night they dined on their bass, which Mrs. Hudgins fried up especially for them. Then after coffee and strawberry shortcake, they rose and, without saying a word, went hand in hand to their room.

This time, Robert asked her to undress him. They laughed as her eager fingers fumbled with his belt and the buttons of his shirt. But when they were in bed together, there was none of that. Now they knew each other, if only fleetingly. But they were both determined to remember as much as they could for the time when their memories would have to suffice.

Afterward they lay together silently, their drowsy arms and legs intertwined.

"Kate?" His voice gently shook away the dreams.

"Yes?"

"Will you marry me?"

She opened her eyes, but could not see his face. "Why do you ask now?"

"I know there's not enough time before I leave, but when I come home. . . . I wanted you to know that I want to marry you."

She hesitated. "But nothing's changed, has it?"

"Yes it has." He rolled over so his face was next to hers. "These last few weeks showed me what my life would be without you. I decided that I could live without a lot of things; I could even live without my parents if I had to. But I couldn't face the prospect of living without you.

"But now I'm going to have to for a while. It would be so much easier if I knew you were waiting for me."

Her heart soared. The words she had longed so much to hear. He loved her. He would marry her. And once they were back together, they would never be apart.

She buried her head in his shoulder. "Come back to me," she whispered. "Come back to me and we'll get married then."

On Sunday, they went to church together.

From the street they heard the choir singing, and he suggested they go inside. They slipped into a pew in the back and listened. But Kate didn't follow the service; instead she kept repeating her own prayer: "Watch over Robert, dear Lord. And bring him back safely to me."

Afterward, Robert suggested they drive down Route 3 and visit the old Civil War battlefields. Chancellorsville, Spotsylvania, the Wilderness. The historical markers told of valiant men and brave deeds, but all Kate could see around her was death. Twelve thousand at Spotsylvania in one day alone! It didn't matter how history judged their causes when men on both sides still died.

"You've been quiet today," he said as he parked the car back in front of Mrs. Hudgins's place.

"Have I?" She willed herself to sound cheerful, even though she felt full of sadness.

Robert stared out through the windshield, his hands still clutching the steering wheel. "I'm glad we had this time together. . . . It's meant a lot to me."

"It's meant a lot to me, too."

He turned toward her. "Is there anything you wish we could have done?"

She thought for a minute. "I think I would have liked to have gone dancing. . . . Just one more time."

"C'mon," he said, opening the car door and pulling her across the seat. "I've got an idea."

He led her up to their room. There, under a pile of clothes, was a radio. He turned a knob. The dial lit up. He twirled the other knob, then gave the box a hard whack on the side. It sprung to life.

"Miss Callahan, may I have this dance?"

He took her in his arms, but they didn't dance so much as they clung together, holding each other as they swayed gently to the music. Fast or slow, it didn't matter. Until the announcer broke in, shattering their reverie. "We interrupt with this report, just in from the European front . . ."

Her body grew tense; Robert felt it, too.

He kissed her behind the ear, then turned off the radio. "Let's go to bed."

But this time, unlike the times before, something didn't

connect for her. Robert was gentle, and patient, and held off
his climax as long as he could. But she knew it wasn't going
to happen for her. Not tonight.

She needed something else instead. "Just hold me, Robert," she whispered at last. "Hold me very tightly."

She could not stop the hours from moving inexorably toward the dawn. She closed her eyes, but could not sleep.
The moon slipped by their window. Somewhere in the night,
a dog barked. Later a train whistle blew.

She realized suddenly that she didn't know exactly when
or how Robert was going to leave. But it didn't matter very
much anymore. It was Monday now.

In the gray light of the morning, she saw a figure moving
around their room.

"Robert?"

"I'm sorry," he said. "I didn't want to wake you."

"What are you doing?"

He sat down on the edge of the bed and took her hand.
"We've got to get going now. My train leaves Washington
at ten."

She nodded dumbly.

They picked up their things quickly. There was no time
left to make love, and nothing left to say.

Robert left to put their bags in the car, but she hesitated,
taking in every detail of the room one last time. Then, as her
throat began to tighten, she went to find Mrs. Hudgins.

"Thank you for a lovely time," she said, turning in their
key.

"Here," the older woman said, passing her a paper bag.
"I thought you might like these sandwiches for your trip
home."

"Thank you. That's very kind."

Mrs. Hudgins hesitated. "Tell me if I'm being too nosy,
Mrs. Kaufmann, but you seem kinda . . . What I mean is,
is your husband about to go off to the war?"

Were her emotions so obvious? Kate wondered. "He's not
a soldier, but yes, he's about to go to Europe."

"I remember when my Willie went to France in '16."
Mrs. Hudgins's thoughts seemed to drift for a moment, then

she added sprightly: "But don't worry. I know he'll be back soon."

"I hope so."

"An awful lot of people pass through here, but I'll remember you and your husband. Anytime you want to come back, you're welcome."

"Thank you," Kate replied, genuinely touched.

Robert reappeared in the front hall. "Take care then," the older woman said, giving her a hug.

There were no silly songs, no happy talk as Kate and Robert drove back north along the highway. It was shrouded in a soupy gray mist that made the trip longer, and also more tense.

"Will you write me?" she asked at last.

"You know I will. Just as soon as I find out my address, I'll send it to you."

She thought then of all the days they had wasted, the weeks and months when something, be it stupidity or stubbornness, had kept them apart. And now when they had only minutes left, she wished she could have all those days back again. She knew how she'd live them now.

She remembered the first time when they had really talked, sitting by the Tidal Basin. She had always known Robert had business to finish in Europe. And now the time had come to finish it.

He pulled up at Union Station, then handed her his keys.

"What am I supposed to do with your car?"

"Keep it," he said. "Or if you don't want it, let Elliot or my roommates use it." He smiled then. "But make sure they know I'll be back for it."

The station was filled with hundreds of people, but she never felt more lonely than she did as they crossed through the crowd. She wished for the train to be late. She wished for the war to be over. She wished for a voice to come on and announce that Robert should return to his office; it was all a mistake.

But it wasn't. The next announcement was for Robert's train.

He set down his bag, and took her into his arms. "Re-

member, darling, not to worry. I won't be near the fighting.
I'll be back before you know it.''

"I know," she murmured through her tears.

She clung to him, trying to soak up his strength, knowing
she would need it in the long months ahead.

Then he held her face in his hands and kissed her gently,
one last time. "I love you, Kate," he whispered. "I love
you now and I'll love you while I'm gone and I'll love you
when I come back. And I *will* come back."

She nodded. "I know you will."

"And when I come back, we'll get married."

"I love you, Robert."

He reached down for his bag, then gave her hand a squeeze.
And then she remembered something she'd learned a few
months back, when she'd tried to find out more about his
religion. A word, the book had said, that could be used as a
greeting or as a farewell. It had never seemed more appro-
priate than now.

"Shalom, Robert."

He smiled as the tears welled up in his eyes. "Peace to
you, Kate."

Then he turned and crossed the crowded concourse. She
almost lost him in the blur of her tears, but then she found
him, waving frantically, on the far side of the room. She
waved back, and then she heard his voice, echoing against
the station's towering arches:

"I love you!"

That night, she drove herself home, feeling tired and depressed. She yearned to go to bed, but the disciplined Kate
took over. "Unpack your bag," she ordered herself. "Better
to get it over with now than put it off until later."

She hung up the peignoir and the nightgown and smoothed
the wrinkles in her dresses. She pulled out the stockings, then
put the postcards she'd purchased away in her desk.

And then in a tangle of underwear, she found a forlorn-
looking undershirt. It was wadded in a ball, and not as white
as it once had been. She knew, without a doubt, that it was
Robert's.

She reached for it, then pressed it to her cheek. And then without warning, she began to cry.

Nineteen

Her world seemed to come to a halt on that Monday morning in June. Where there had once been warmth and light and laughter, there was now a chilling emptiness. A few days in which every moment was treasured turned into weeks when Kate had nothing but time on her hands.

She got up and went to work and she went home and went to bed. On Saturdays she worked or did errands, on Sunday she went to church. And two nights a week, she went to Union Station to work at the USO booth.

She had volunteered in the first days of the war as a way of helping "the cause." But now she did it in the fervent hope that wherever Robert was, someone was looking out for him, too.

She wrote him every night, long letters in which she tried to maintain a brave front. In return, she had received only two short letters, one from New York, one soon after Robert had landed on the Continent. The second one said he had a new "job," but provided no details. Because he told her not to worry, she did just that.

"Cheer up, old girl," Jason told her. "Remember, Robert's privileged to be able to go over there. As someone who will go nameless put it to me right after Pearl Harbor, at least he'll get his chance to stand up for the rights we all believe in."

She felt so low that not even Jason's sarcasm could make her feel any worse.

Now the summer days and nights seemed even more suffocating than usual. One night she stayed up late writing

Robert, hoping a breeze might be born. Half past midnight, she gave up and doused her light. But sleep did not come easily. She tossed and turned, transforming her neat bed into a pile of rumpled, sticky sheets.

When she heard the clock downstairs chime four, she sat up. It was useless. She might as well get up and go to work.

She walked down Connecticut Avenue briskly, appreciating the quiet of the morning—and the chance to think. She was hungry, but she could wait until she reached the office. There were some crackers in her desk, and she could heat a pot of coffee.

She entered the building. Without the throng of humanity that filled it each day, she was conscious of every noise. The click of her heels across the tiles. The chirp of birds outside a window at the end of the hall. The whup-whup-whup of the big ceiling fans, already waging battle against the heat.

The door to their office was locked, as it should be, so she reached inside her purse to get the key. Through the milky glass, she could see that Jason had left the light on in his office. Strange. That wasn't like him.

She opened the door quietly and put her purse down on her desk. She reached to flick on the light, but something stopped her. The door to Jason's office was closed, and someone, someone who looked shorter than Jason, was inside.

An inner voice told her to call a guard; another said that was silly. She crossed the room, knocked softly, then opened the door.

"Ohmigod," she gasped.

There stood Elliot, locked in an embrace with a young, dark-haired man—an embrace so passionate that neither of them looked up.

A wave of nausea rose inside her. This was all a bad dream. It couldn't be Elliot. Not their good friend Elliot. And the other man—she recognized him now—he was Ricky, the guy, a boy really, who brought the mail around each morning.

She didn't want to see this. She didn't want to know this. She walked backward quickly, but as she turned to dash for the outer door, she crashed into a metal wastebasket.

Elliot looked up, his face frozen in horror. "Kate. . . . What are you . . . ?"

She didn't wait to hear the rest. She turned and ran out the door, her hands covering her mouth, her purse swinging wildly. Down the hall, down the stairs, out of the building, away from that place. Away from that scene.

On Pennsylvania Avenue, she found a coffee shop that was open.

The man behind the counter looked up from his paper. "What'll it be, miss?" She didn't respond. "Miss? Are you all right?"

"Coffee," she said without thinking. "Very black. With toast."

She thought of all the words people used to describe men who loved men. Fairy. Pansy. Faggot. She couldn't think of Elliot that way. She saw the sandy-colored hair, always perfectly combed, his pudgy, freckled face. It was a face she'd describe as sensitive, not effeminate. He'd always carried himself with a sort of pugnacious swagger, not the oily glide she'd always imagined that homosexuals had.

She remembered the funny stories he told, the silly gifts he had given on her birthday, the times he had kept Robert and Jason from coming to blows. She closed her eyes. And she remembered how Elliot had always good-naturedly declined whenever she'd suggested that they double date.

She took a bite of the dry toast. But that was all yesterday; she had to deal with today. This was just the kind of thing the FBI had looked for before giving them their security clearances.

She thought of all the classified documents their office had handled. What if an enemy agent found out about Elliot's secret? His "tendencies"—she swallowed hard as the euphemism came to her—could be used to blackmail him into passing secrets along.

But if she told Jason or their section head, it would ruin him.

She took another sip of coffee, then placed a quarter under her saucer and left. She went home, and later in the morning, she called in sick. She did feel ill, but what she really needed was a chance to think.

It was the first time since the war had started that she had missed a day of work.

There was a knock on the door of Kate's bedroom. "A Mr. Ingraham to see you, miss," Tillie said. "Shall I tell him you're not feeling well?"

"No, don't do that." She thought for a moment. Stephen was out tonight. "Please show him into my uncle's study. I'll be down in a moment."

She thrust her feet into a pair of pumps, then ran a brush through her hair, more to delay the inevitable than to improve her appearance. Then she walked down the stairs, her hand tight around the railing.

He rose when she entered the study. "Hello, Kate."

She closed the door behind her. "Hello, Elliot." She struggled to dam the wave of revulsion that began building inside her again. Would she ever be able to greet him with the same friendly affection that she had before?

"Kate, I can ex . . ."

"Sit down, Elliot," she said firmly, "and listen to what I have to say."

He did as he was told, sinking deep into Stephen's leather sofa. Kate took a seat across from him.

"I've thought long and hard about you today, Elliot. My brain says to go tell Jason, or internal security or whatever, what I saw this morning. You're a security risk, plain and simple. You could be jeopardizing Robert, for all I know."

She hesitated. "But I can't do it. You've been a good friend, both to me and to Robert. I can't be the one to ruin you."

The tension drained from his face.

"However, if I ever stumble onto you again like I did this morning, I'll go to them without a second thought."

"I understand," he said quietly. He paused, then added, "I don't know how to thank you, Kate."

"Don't bother," she said, suddenly feeling very weary. "Now please. Just get out of here."

* * *

It seemed like an eternity since Kate had played tennis with her uncle. Was it the war, or Robert, or both? No matter. She was pleased when Stephen agreed to play a set, one July evening when a northerly had cleared away the thick summer air.

"So what do you hear from Robert?" he asked as they began warming up.

"Oh, he's fine," she said brightly. In fact, she was growing more and more concerned. A time was coming soon, he had warned her, when he wouldn't be able to receive her letters. His, meanwhile, were becoming less frequent.

"Are you sure?" Stephen pressed.

She nodded. "C'mon, let's volley for the serve."

She started off slowly. She felt rusty and wondered for a moment if she should have warmed up better first. Yet it felt good to be out, to work up a sweat, and run off her frustrations from one end of the court to the other.

She watched as Stephen prepared to serve. He seemed to take longer than usual, his head bowed for a moment, as if he were trying to summon up reserves of energy and concentration. Then he looked up and tossed the ball high, his right arm coiled back like a snake preparing to strike.

And then she heard it—an ungodly sounding groan that gurgled up from Stephen's chest. His racket clattered to the ground, the ball dropped at his feet. And then her uncle, her beloved uncle, crumpled to the ground.

She was beside him in a matter of seconds, searching for a sign that this was just a case of heatstroke, or Stephen's bizarre idea of a joke. But his eyes were closed, his face grew pale, and his pulse, when she could find it, was fading.

Helplessly, she wailed at the passing traffic: "Can't somebody get a doctor?" But she knew it wouldn't make any difference. It was already much too late.

Twenty

". . . We have come together today, O Lord, to bury your devoted servant, Stephen Matthew McNeil . . ."

They filled the front pew of St. John's, the old yellow church across Lafayette Square from the White House. Wife, daughter, and niece. Three women burying the man who had been their rock for most of their lives.

Kate had cried her tears before, hours and hours, behind the locked door of her room. But this was the public time for a very public man. For this hour, she must try to conduct herself with dignity. She knew Stephen would have wanted her to.

Nineteen years ago they had buried her mother. Now it felt as if they were burying her father. That long-ago wound still hadn't fully healed. Still, that was the confused pain of an abandoned child, not this adult kind of grief that seemed to come out of nowhere, knocking the wind from her lungs.

But Stephen had been more than a father to her. He had been her biggest champion and, next to Robert, probably her closest friend.

Her uncle wasn't a young man, she reminded herself. He had lived a long productive life, and died quickly, with little pain. Yet it seemed particularly cruel for him to be taken from her at this moment. With Robert gone, she felt achingly alone.

And she felt guilty. Had she pushed Stephen too hard to play tennis? Should they have spent more time warming up? Her guilt, her anger, were chewing her up inside because there was nothing she could strike out against. But when her anger did spill out, it was directed at Amanda.

Kate looked down the pew at her aunt, eyes fixed stonily

straight ahead. It seemed as if Amanda had slipped into her new role as easily as she had donned the stylish black sheath she had picked out for the funeral. No detail was too small for the grieving widow to oversee, from the musical selections for the church organist to the seating of dignitaries. It was as if she had been preparing for this day for years.

Kate tried to be sympathetic, to tell herself that it was just her aunt's way of coping with her loss. But Amanda didn't make it easy. Kate knew where her aunt placed the blame. "If you hadn't asked him to play tennis . . . If he'd stopped trying to pretend he was a younger man . . . ." She hadn't said it, but Kate knew she felt it.

And so, in the moment when the two of them might have drawn closer together, the gulf between them seemed to widen. And with it, the air grew chillier.

". . . he was a devoted husband, a generous father . . ."

Kate tried to shift her thoughts to Robert, to work, to counting the panes in a stained-glass window. Anything but the dear man whose lifeless body lay in the casket ahead of her. And as she forced her mind to wander, she began counting the days and weeks since Robert had left, then counted them again just to make sure. Yes, it was true. Her period was late. A day or two, she wasn't sure. She tended to be vague about such things.

No matter, she told herself firmly. It would be back next month. It was only because she was exhausted. First the strain of Robert leaving, then that scene with Elliot. And now Stephen.

Next month, she willed, it would return.

The law offices of Cadwalader and Cadwalader were located on the eighth floor of an ornate granite building on 14th Street. Kate hadn't planned on attending the formal reading of Stephen's will. But when George Cadwalader himself had called—"I really think you ought to be there, young lady" —she'd changed her mind.

"I'll try and make this brief," the attorney said, giving his vest a tug over his ample waist. "Mrs. McNeil, you probably know that your husband prepared a new will about four years ago. At that time, he made some changes in the disposition of his estate.''

Amanda clasped her hands more tightly in her lap. ''I was unaware of that.''

''To summarize, your husband has left your house, which I believe he owned before your marriage, entirely to you, Mrs. McNeil. As to that part of his estate that you did not own jointly, it is to be divided four ways. One-fourth will go to you, one-fourth to Margaret, and one-fourth to Katharine.''

The women said nothing.

''I might add that Judge McNeil managed to come out of the Crash in relatively good financial shape. While I don't know the exact amount you all will inherit, it will be substantial.''

Kate was stunned. She had thought Stephen might include some token for her—his books, perhaps, or enough money to make a trip to Europe. But one-fourth of his estate—she had never dreamed of anything like that.

And then it dawned on her. If she was getting more than she had expected, Amanda and Margaret were probably getting less.

''I find this a little awkward,'' the lawyer continued, ''but I know Judge McNeil took great care in drafting the language of his will. It is now my job to read it.''

He cleared his throat. '' 'To my dear wife, Amanda, I leave one-fourth of my solely owned estate, enough certainly to cover the costs of our house and her own expenses. Because she has her own sources of inherited wealth, I'm sure she will agree that the rest should go to the girls.' ''

Cadwalader paused, and looked over his glasses.

Amanda nodded, her face betraying no emotion. ''Go on.''

'' 'Another quarter of my estate is hereby left to my daughter, Margaret, in the hope that she can use my money more wisely now than she has in the past; that it will provide the seed with which she can harvest a productive life, rather than fertilize an extravagant life-style.' ''

''My father, the poet,'' Margaret said under her breath.

'' 'And to my dear niece, Katharine Callahan, another

quarter of my estate, for she has been all I could have hoped for in a daughter—and more.' "

Kate closed her eyes. *Oh, Uncle Stephen, I loved you so. And I knew you loved me, too. You didn't have to put it down in black and white for all the world to see.*

"That's three-fourths," Margaret said. "What about the rest?"

The lawyer pulled out a white linen handkerchief and patted his fleshy brow. "Your father has directed that the rest be donated to Vassar College, to create a scholarship in the name of his first wife."

They said nothing. Then Margaret sniffed, "I see."

The room seemed cramped now, the air harder to breathe. Kate wished she could escape to her room again and let the tears flow freely.

She recalled the obituary in *The Star*, the one that had praised Stephen for his fairness as a judge. Now it seemed as if he had worn his robes home, trying to make them all feel as if they were equal in his eyes. Amanda and Cecily, Kate and Margaret. Perhaps he had divided his estate the same way, giving each of them a share, never realizing that for his wife and daughter an equal share wasn't equal at all.

Why in the moment when he was giving her the world, did she feel as if it were caving in?

"Is that all then?" Amanda asked curtly.

"Basically, yes," the attorney replied.

"Then I think we should be going, girls. Good day, Mr. Cadwalader."

When it came time for Margaret to return to California, Kate and Amanda went to Union Station to see her off. The place swarmed with couples saying their good-byes. Kate remembered another one, too. Not even two months ago, yet it felt like an eternity.

Finally, the call came for Margaret's train.

Margaret turned and hugged her mother tightly. "Good-bye, Mama," she said, her eyes squeezed tightly shut. "Call me if you need me." She wiped her cheek, then turned to Kate, extending her hand rigidly. "Good-bye, cousin."

It was an odd gesture, but Kate tried not to let it bother her. "Good-bye, Margaret. I hope Jack comes home very soon."

Margaret nodded to a porter and picked up her makeup case. She took two steps, stopped, then turned, her face suddenly flush with a bitterness she could no longer contain.

"You know, Kate, I don't know why this has all been such a shock to me. You always were Daddy's favorite, weren't you? He must have lost track of where you came from."

She turned and headed across the concourse to her train.

"Come on," Amanda sighed. "Let's go home."

"But shouldn't I go after her and say something?"

Her aunt turned toward her, suddenly looking very weary. "Nothing you could say, Katharine, could make any difference at all."

Twenty-One

There was no denying it, no pretending anymore. Another month had passed. And the doctor had confirmed what she already knew was true.

Pregnant. With child. But not just any child—Robert's child. And that made all the difference.

She clung to her secret as if it were a newborn baby, examining all of its toes and fingers. Afraid to let others hold it for fear they would dampen her joy.

For she was happy. In this crazy, black world, she could now envision a future. Robert was gone, but he had left a part of him with her, in her. And now it was up to her to bring that gift into the world.

But could she do it? Was she ready to become a mother? She had always assumed she would have children, but not until she was older. Certainly not until she was married.

On and on, the questions spun around in her head. Would Robert be home in time for the baby's birth? And what if he wasn't? Would the child be branded as illegitimate? Would other children call him horrible names?

She had written Robert immediately to tell him the news. But since then she had fretted. What if he was angry? What if the prospect of becoming a father stirred up all his old feelings about his faith?

And what if he didn't find out? He had said he wouldn't be able to receive her letters for a while. From his letters, she could tell that he didn't know that Stephen had died.

But somehow she had to let him know. She needed his support. And more important, if he found out she was going to have a baby, he might be more careful. It just might bring him back to that safe desk in Geneva.

She put off telling Amanda as long as she could. And then she could wait no longer.

Since Stephen had died, they seemed to flail about in the evenings, not knowing what to do or what to say to each other. The house seemed so empty, the rooms so hollow. Gone, too, was the smell of her uncle's pipes and cigars, the musky scent that used to neutralize Amanda's too-sweet perfume.

Kate asked if they could talk in Stephen's study. Despite her uncle's absence, she still found the room strangely comforting.

"There's no easy way I can break this news, so I won't try. . . . I'm going to have a baby, Aunt Amanda."

"Oh, my God," Amanda gasped, her hands fluttering up to her face. "You picked a fine time for this, what with your uncle barely in the grave."

"I'm afraid there wasn't a lot I could do about the timing," Kate said quietly.

"You could have tried a little harder to remain a virgin. Who's the father? Robert Kaufmann, I suppose?"

"Yes."

Amanda shook her head with exasperation. "You're just like your mother was, wild and headstrong. No sense of family or reputation. . . ." She was silent for a moment. "Well, what do you intend to do?"

"What do you mean?"

"Are you going to have the baby?"

"Of course, I am. What do you think . . . ?"

"There are ways, you know."

"I'm going to have Robert's baby," Kate said defiantly.

"Well, you can't have it here!"

"I know that. I'm going to go away for a while."

She had already written Mildred Hudgins, twisting the truth a bit. Kate said she thought it would be better for the baby if she quit her job and spent her pregnancy away from Washington. Kate told her she was willing to pay for her room, or do light housework in exchange for it. She signed the letter "Kate Kaufmann," giving her a secret thrill.

Mrs. Hudgins replied before the fortnight was over: "Of course you can come."

Kate gave Jason two weeks notice, telling him that since her uncle had died, she had found it impossible to concentrate on her work. He studied her face, and she wondered for an instant if he could guess the truth.

Then he gave her a hug. "Take care of yourself," he said. "And remember, if there's anything you need, you know where to find me."

For a moment he was the Jason who had invited her to Cape Cod, the Jason who had led her onto the dance floor and into this job. But then she remembered all that had gone between them—and it chilled her.

She gave Delilah a long hug. Then she shook Elliot's hand, feeling sad as she remembered the happy times they had shared. Then she went home, loaded up Robert's car, and said good-bye to her aunt.

"Take care of yourself," Amanda said, giving her a quick kiss on the cheek.

"I'll try."

Kate savored the drive down to Fredericksburg. Somehow Robert's car—with its clanking engine and burnished leather seats—conjured up the man. She found herself talking out loud to him. "Do you like the name Elizabeth? What about Charlotte? . . . That was my mother's name, you know. . . ."

When she arrived, Mrs. Hudgins gave her the room that she and Robert had shared.

"But it's your best room, Mrs. Hudgins. I won't be able to afford it."

"We'll worry about that later. And please, call me Mildred."

The older woman was so open, so generous with her time and hospitality that Kate felt she couldn't lie to her anymore.

"I ought to tell you," she said one morning as they lingered over their coffee. "Robert and I didn't have time to get married before he left."

Mildred patted her hand. "I know, dear."

"But how?"

"One just has a feeling about these things." Then her eyes twinkled. "Don't worry. My Willy and I didn't get married until after our son was born either."

Kate filled her days now with helping Mildred, taking long walks and eating careful meals, and trying to twist yarn into a baby blanket. Mildred had taken it upon herself to teach her the finer points of needlework, shocked that Kate had reached the age of twenty-four without learning how to wield a crochet hook. It was the first time in her life that Kate had felt truly incompetent.

She fared better in the kitchen. If Amanda knew how to cook—which Kate doubted—she had never bothered to teach her niece. But Kate was eager to help Mildred in any way she could.

Mildred taught like she cooked, starting from scratch. She showed her protégé the proper way to make a white sauce, the best method for kneading bread. Then she led Kate through a syllabus of pies and pound cakes, molded salads and puddings, fish and fowl. And then she put Kate in charge for a weekend. It was exhausting, but by the time she had doled out the last piece of chess pie and poured the last cup of coffee, Kate knew she had mastered yet another foreign language.

Overnight, it seemed, her pregnancy had transformed her life, changing the way she looked at the world. She was slowing down, taking pleasure in the last of the year's flowers, the changing color of the leaves. She could laugh now at the silly things that used to aggravate her: a crowded trolley, a tear in her precious stockings, a worn-out typewriter ribbon. All of that seemed like a distant memory, of a time and a woman she no longer knew.

Now the months stretched before her with no deadlines, no reason to hurry. All her thoughts, all her energies, were directed toward helping Mildred—and nurturing the child that was swelling her breasts and belly. She no longer stayed up late at night, scribbling one more letter to her lover. Instead she went to bed early, nestling down in the bed she and Robert had shared, marveling at how a small fetus could make her feel so languid.

Dr. Chapman praised her good habits. When he peered over his wire-rimmed glasses and called her "Mrs. Kaufmann," Kate wondered if he could guess her secret. But then, there were a lot of young women whose husbands were away and a lot of fathers who didn't make it home in time for the birth of their children.

Each time she wrote Robert, she repeated her news, in hope that just one letter would make it to him. Amanda forwarded his sporadic letters to her, but they did little to quell her anxiety. He still said he missed hearing from her, and never spoke of the child.

It made her feel so crazy. A few months ago, she had spent every day with him. At most, he was a phone call away. But now, when they shared the closest possible bond between a man and a woman, he was beyond her reach. And nothing —not a phone call, nor a letter, nor a cable—could bring him any closer.

Still, she tried to remain optimistic. She tried to enjoy his letters. She tried to ignore the news reports about how the Allies had stalled in the middle of Europe. After all, she reminded herself, Robert wasn't really fighting. He was a government bureaucrat, not a soldier. He was working with the refugees, in places the army had already been.

All she had to do was give him a healthy baby. All she had to do was be patient. Of course, he would return. They were meant to be a family.

* * *

The holidays had come and gone. Kate had sent Amanda a package, but received nothing in return. Mildred was alone now, too, and so they had spent a quiet Christmas together, exchanging small presents and cracking nuts in front of the fire in the big room downstairs.

But now the days were gray, and the beautiful Christmas Eve snowstorm had been transformed into dirty little patches along the roadside. The decorations looked dated, the figures in the creche on the mantel needed dusting, the evergreen garlands down the banister were prickly dry to the touch. On the radio the news was grim: the Allies and Germans were locked in a do-or-die battle near the little Belgian town of Bastogne. And every time one side seemed to be winning, the other side managed to turn around and strike back.

Outside Hudgins's Tourist Home, they heard a car pull up.

"I'll go tell them we're closed," Kate said, putting down her crocheting. She looked out the window. "Why it's my aunt!"

Kate went out into the cold to greet her. Why had she come? she wondered. It was a long trip, especially driving alone.

"Hello, Amanda," she called. She hesitated, then added, "It's good to see you."

The two women hugged self-consciously, trying to ignore Kate's expanding figure.

"Come on in and get warm by the fire."

Kate ushered her in and introduced her to her hostess. Mildred retreated to the kitchen for tea and cookies.

"Here," Amanda said, thrusting a small package at Kate. "I brought you this."

"Why, thank you."

"I appreciated the shawl you sent."

"I'm glad you liked it."

"Kate made it herself," Mildred chimed in.

"I'm impressed," Amanda replied. She twisted her gloves in her lap, then said, "On Christmas Eve I wished I'd invited you home for the holidays. I'm afraid it was rather lonely this year."

"Yes, it must have been," Kate said. Suddenly she felt

sorry for her aunt. Stephen dying, Margaret leaving. It had not been an easy year for her either.

She pulled off the wrapping paper and opened the package. Inside was a pair of leather gloves.

"They're lovely," she said. "And I can certainly use them."

"Good," Amanda replied.

"Do you have any news from Margaret?"

"Not really. Jack's still away. She's taken a part-time job as a clerk in a shop."

"That's nice."

"How are you feeling?" The subject of her pregnancy couldn't be avoided any longer.

"All right," Kate replied. "My doctor seems to think I'm taking good care of myself."

"And you are!" Mildred said. She turned to Amanda. "She goes for a walk every day and I make sure she gets three big meals."

"That's good." Amanda took a sip of tea, then looked up from her cup. "And Robert?"

She asked the question slowly, sort of strangely, Kate thought. *Is she hoping he's abandoned me?*

"It's been a few weeks since I had a letter. . . . He's off doing a special job now. I'm afraid he may not have received any of my letters about the baby."

"I see." Amanda put down her teacup, and rose from her chair. She went over to the window and looked out for what seemed like an interminable moment. Then she turned back to Kate.

"I didn't want to be the one to have to tell you this," she began slowly. "But I decided there was no other way you would find out."

Kate's heart stopped.

"Jason came by the other day," Amanda went on. "He asked where you were, but I thought it best not to tell him. So instead he passed along his news." She paused, looking stricken. "Robert was killed, Katharine."

Her words floated across the room like heavy balloons, exploding just as Kate was about to grasp them. "It can't be true," she protested. "It's someone's idea of a sick joke."

Amanda shook her head. "Jason has a good friend at Robert's agency. He heard it from him. And I called the Refugee Board myself. Just to make sure."

"It's all a lie!" Kate screamed. "You're all just making it up so I'll get rid of our baby."

"No, Kate," her aunt said, looking straight into her eyes. "That's not true. What is true is that Robert is dead."

Kate heard the terrible words, but still they were only words, not the reality. The room started to sway. She clutched her chair for support. Then she heard her voice ask: "But how did he die? Where did it happen?"

"They said he was in Hungary, trying to help a group of Jews escape to Allied territory. That's all they know."

"I had thought he might be in France or Italy. What the hell was he doing in Hungary?"

Amanda shook her head. "I don't know."

Kate could see it then, like a movie they'd seen together, down at the Gayety Theater. Robert dressed in dark clothes and a cap, leading a band of ragtag peasants over a mountain, people jabbering away in a language neither he nor she would understand. A shot is heard. The people duck for cover. And then a grenade explodes.

She screamed, then started sobbing. All her dreams, shattered. All their plans, destroyed. And their child . . .

Why did he have to go? Why did he have to die?

Amanda hugged her tightly. "I'm so sorry," she murmured.

"I loved him so much. . . . It's just not fair!"

The three women sat there for hours, hugging and talking and crying some more. For Kate and the man she had lost. For the men all of them had lost.

Finally, Amanda turned to Mildred. "I'm afraid it's getting late. I have to get started back." She hesitated. "Would you like to come home, Kate?"

Kate didn't answer.

"Don't worry," Mildred replied quickly. "I'll take good care of her."

Kate embraced her aunt, but still couldn't speak.

"We'll talk more later," Amanda whispered. She let herself out the door.

The car pulled away, then Mildred said gently, "You ought to go upstairs and get some rest."

Kate didn't argue. She let Mildred lead her up the stairs and tuck her into bed. The bed where she and Robert had loved together. But she knew she would never really rest again.

If only I could see him one more time, to reach out, and touch his lips. Tell him about our child. But to vanish in some strange country? . . . Was any cause so great that it could justify taking my Robert?

Deep inside her the baby kicked. It was a jolting punch, up into her diaphragm, taking her breath away. She rolled onto her side and pressed her hands to her belly. The child kicked again, even harder this time, then several more times in rapid succession.

It knows, she thought sadly. *Even our child can't be shielded from the pain.*

She'd sit in the rocker, staring out the window, until the late-afternoon shadows crept across the frozen fields. She was filled with a wrenching emptiness, a feeling so intense that it seemed to have stripped her of her ability to cry, to move, to think.

She was angry with him. How could he leave her at a time like this? And then she felt guilty. How could she feel that way?

She'd stand under the shower until the water turned cold, the coursing water masking her tears but not the convulsive heaving of her chest. And just when she thought there were no more tears left to cry, they would creep up on her, running out of the corners of her eyes, prompted by who knows what? Except that she knew what. The memory of him, his touch, his smell, his voice, his laughter. The inescapable truth that he would never return, and that as much as she could wish it, nothing would ever change that.

She returned once more to the little church they had visited together. She had tried to pray, to achieve some sort of peace with herself. But all she felt was an uncontrollable rage, a desperate desire to lash out at whomever it was that had taken

Robert away. The Nazis. The bureaucrats who had given him a job. Jason for delivering the news.

Then she rose and declared to the empty church: "You have a lot to answer for, God."

Most of the time she stayed in bed, unable to face the days. Mildred brought her trays and urged her to eat, but she picked at the food, then pushed the dishes away. "But your baby," Mildred would say. "Remember your baby."

Yes, the baby.

The clock was ticking toward the day she'd have to make a decision, a decision she had never seriously considered before.

Should she put her child up for adoption?

Each night, she and Mildred stayed up late, sitting in rocking chairs in front of the fire.

"I just don't know if I could raise a child on my own, Mildred."

"You're a strong young woman, I know that."

"But it seems so overwhelming. Where would we live? How would I support him?" Kate stared into the fire. "Did you ever consider giving up your son?"

"Our situations were different." Mildred's voice was soft. "His father was alive. He hadn't come home yet, but I knew he was still alive."

"The baby is all I have left of Robert."

"That's true, too."

"What do you think I should do?" Kate pleaded, her eyes welling up with tears.

The older woman reached over and took her hand. "You must do what's best for you, my dear. I can't tell you what that is—only your heart will know. You're the one who will have to live with your decision. You're the one who should make it."

A part of Kate truly wanted to keep the child. It was Robert's baby. He would want her to raise it the way the two of them would have together.

But lying in bed, that idea exhausted her. The thought of becoming a mother had excited her, but the prospect of raising a child alone was overwhelming. She remembered the terrible days after her mother had died, and while she knew she could be a better parent than her father had been, she doubted she could be good enough.

Where would they live? Amanda probably wouldn't want them, but even if she did offer them a home the child would probably always feel the sting of Amanda's disapproval. Apartments were still scarce, and an apartment with room for a growing child—there was no point in even looking.

How would she earn a living? She could probably go back to work for the government. But who would watch the child during the day? She could fall back on Stephen's money for a while, but not forever. Certainly not until the child was grown.

And in the eyes of society, the child would be illegitimate. A bastard. The neighborhood children would point their fingers and call him names. She could remember what that was like. And people would talk about her, too. Was she willing to pretend to be married, to live out a lie for the rest of her life?

Remember, "Katharine Callahan" is a very nice name and it's the only name you'll ever have. So you have to be very careful not to do anything that will make people think that Katharine Callahan is a bad girl. . . .

Would the unbearable pain ever go away? she wondered. How many months, how many years would it take until Robert no longer was the first thing she thought of when she woke and the last thought she had before she went to sleep? How long would it be before other loves filled her dreams and other demons than his death filled her nightmares?

But finally, one long, lonely night, she decided. The only way she would be able to survive Robert's death was to pick up the pieces of her old life. A child would make that impossible. Each time she looked into its eyes, she would see Robert's. And each time she would know the despair all over again. She needed to get back to Washington, to her old routines and the people she knew. The child would force her to start all over again, to take on an enormous responsibility for which she had never been prepared. And she wasn't convinced she had the strength—or will—to do that now.

When she told Mildred, her friend said just the right thing: "I understand, dear."

She told Dr. Chapman the truth, and asked him if he would help her arrange the adoption. On a cold night in February, her waters broke. She rousted Mildred out of bed, and made it to the hospital in what seemed like record time.

That was all there was. They put Kate to sleep, and when she awoke, her womb was empty.

"Please," she begged the nurse who stopped by her bed to check her pulse. "Did I have a girl or a boy?"

The nurse hesitated, then lowered Kate's wrist and patted it gently. "You had a girl," she said. "With the most amazing crop of red hair I've ever seen."

The nurse turned off the light. Kate felt drowsy from the anesthetic, but knew that sleep wouldn't come. Red hair. Just like Charlotte. Kate started to cry, overwhelmed by her feelings of loneliness, the loss now of everything she loved.

It would take time, she reminded herself. Time to get over Robert. Time to get over the baby.

I did the right thing, she tried to persuade herself. *I know I did the right thing*.

Twenty-Two

Spring had come again. In the city around her, the daffodil and tulip bulbs were sending up their blossoms, the cherry trees were putting on their annual show, and couples were going for long walks along the river. The war would be over soon, you could feel it in the air.

But none of this cheered Kate. She gazed out the window of her tiny apartment, high atop Meridian Hill. But instead of the song of the nesting birds, she heard the muffled cadence of the drums that had led President Roosevelt's body on its sad last trip through the streets of Washington two weeks before.

Perhaps she should have stayed inside that day and unpacked another crate from Amanda's attic. But like everyone else, she was drawn inexorably to watch the caisson roll by. Around her women wailed and men cried without embarrassment. She wanted that kind of release, but even wanting it wouldn't make it happen.

She felt bitter and angry now. There had been no funeral parade for Robert, no flags or high-stepping horses. But in the end it made no difference. They all died the same death. And it was all such a waste.

The weeks passed, but Kate felt incapable of action. With Mildred's prodding, she had moved back to Washington. Then, with a little more work, she had found herself a place to live. It was a relief to escape Amanda's judgments, but now there was no one to nag her if she slept past noon, or didn't bother dressing, or left her dirty dishes piled up in the sink because she didn't have the energy to wash them.

She didn't bother to call Delilah, or look up any of her other old friends. There was no one who cared whether she worked or ate. No one who cared whether she lived or died.

V-E Day came, but it made no difference. New York had gone berserk, but in Washington, people seemed to remember that they still hadn't defeated Japan. Even so, the celebrations seemed like a cruel joke when men like Robert and FDR had died only weeks before they could enjoy them.

She told herself she couldn't go on like this. When she allowed herself to be pragmatic, she knew that she couldn't live off of Stephen's legacy forever. Each night when she went to bed, she vowed that tomorrow she would start looking for a job. But when morning came, there was always an excuse. She had a headache. It was raining. It was already three in the afternoon, and well, that was much too late in the day to start.

How long would it continue? The rest of her life? No, she couldn't imagine that. And yet the days passed and they never seemed to get better. The cloudy days were the worst. At least on the bright days, she could smile—briefly—at the sun. But then she'd remember. Why she wasn't working.

Why she wasn't living. And she'd get out Robert's undershirt one more time and bury her face in the remembered smell of him.

Then one night there was a knock at her door. She opened it just wide enough to take a peek.

It was a stranger, wearing the dark blue uniform of a naval officer. "Miss Callahan?"

"Yes?"

"I apologize for not calling, but I just arrived in town this evening. . . ."

As the man spoke, he took a step back, giving her a better view under the light of the hallway. His hair was brown, and his eyes almost hazel, but there was no mistaking the strong lines of his face, the nose, the cheekbones.

"You must . . . you must be Robert's brother."

"Yes"—he smiled—"I'm David Kaufmann."

"Won't you come in?"

She turned, then realized she had been sitting in the dark. She flicked on a lamp, then felt embarrassed at the clutter it revealed. The room was piled high with empty boxes, the chairs strewn with clothes she hadn't bothered to hang up.

"Please excuse the mess. I just moved in, and I'm afraid I haven't had time to put my things away." She patted the back of her hair nervously, wondering how disheveled she looked.

"That's all right. I should have called first."

She made room for him on Amanda's castoff sofa, then pulled up a chair close by. She studied his face for a moment—and didn't know whether to laugh or to cry. David sat like Robert used to, leaning forward, his elbows balanced on his knees, his whole body poised to move quickly. Their voices were similar, shaped by the streets of New York and a home where children never had to shout to get their parents' attention.

"Would you like a cup of tea?"

"Why yes, thank you."

She rinsed out two dirty cups and dried them quickly on a dish towel. "What brings you to Washington?" *And what brings you to my apartment?*

"I just got back from overseas. . . ." She remembered

now. He had been on a minesweeper in the Atlantic. "I had
some business to take care of here . . . and some business
for my brother."

"Oh?"

"He wrote me about you, you know. He wrote me long
letters about how he had met you and how you had changed
his outlook on life. He told me he was going to marry you
when he . . ."

He stopped, unable to say the words. And for the first time
it occurred to her that she wasn't the only person who was
grieving. Robert had a brother, a mother, a father. They all
had loved him. They all had lost him, too.

The kettle boiled, piercing the silence with its shriek. She
rose and poured the water into the cups. "Lemon? Sugar?"
He shook his head. She carried in the tray and set it down.

"How did you find me?"

"Robert had sent me your old address. Your aunt was kind
enough to tell me where to find you."

"I've been away for a while."

"Oh?"

She hesitated. Should she tell him about the child? Would
it make a difference? Would it lessen his pain? And what if
he thought she should have kept it—his family's only link
to Robert? No, she wasn't ready for a confrontation with
Robert's family—on any issue. But maybe Robert had
known. Maybe he had told David. . . .

"I'm not sure my letters were reaching Robert at the end."

"I don't think mine were either."

She took a sip of the tea, then braced herself to ask another
question. "I don't know much about how he died. Do
you . . . ?"

"I haven't learned very much." He set down his cup. "The
Refugee Board got word last year that Hitler was planning
to begin deporting the Hungarian Jews to Auschwitz. The
board tried a diplomatic approach. They asked the Hungarian
government not to cooperate and tried to find new homes for
the Jews. But the Germans controlled the borders and they
had no intention of letting any of them out."

He paused to take a sip. "Robert apparently got frustrated

and tried to lead a small group of them out on his own. He was crazy to try, but he did it. And then something went wrong."

Kate closed her eyes for a moment. Would it have made a difference if he'd known about the baby? Would he still have taken such a risk?

". . . I was able to confirm that he died on December fourth. I'm working now to find out what happened to his body. But it's hard, now that the Russians have moved in."

Neither of them spoke for a moment. Then David looked up. "What are you doing now?"

"Nothing right this moment. But I'm going to find a job very soon." If only she believed that.

"Robert wrote me that you're very good at languages."

"That may be overstating it a bit."

"The government's going to be needing people like you."

Why did she feel he was pushing her? "You said you had some business of Robert's. Do you want his car?"

"No. In fact, he told me where to find the papers to transfer it to you. What I really wanted to do was deliver this." He reached inside his jacket, then handed her a slim white envelope. On it was her name, written with Robert's looping "K" and "C."

It had been months since she had seen that handwriting, but she remembered the thrill she had felt when one of his letters arrived. But this one was clearly different from the rest.

"He sent it to me about eight months ago and asked me to hang on to it."

"Why?"

"He wanted me to deliver it . . . in case he died."

"I see." She felt her eyes begin to fill with tears.

David dabbed at his eyes and shuffled to his feet. "You'd probably like to be alone when you read it."

She put the letter aside for a moment and extended her hand. "I'm glad we got the chance to meet, David."

"I am, too."

He turned to leave, then stopped. "One more thing, Kate. A lot of my friends from law school are in Washington now—or will be when they get back from overseas. If you need any help—a job, money, contacts—give me a call.'' He took out a piece of paper and scrawled across it quickly. ''Here's my number for the next few days, and a number where you should be able to reach me after that.''

''Thank you. I appreciate it.''

''Good-bye, then,'' he said. ''Take care of yourself.''

''Good-bye.'' She closed the door behind him.

She picked up their teacups, then poured herself a glass of sherry. She settled back in her chair and picked up the envelope with trembling hands. She didn't rush to open it; rather she studied it with the deliberateness of an archaeologist who had just uncovered an ancient tablet. She wanted to read it, but she was also afraid of the secrets it might reveal.

Slowly she ran a fingernail under the flap. Inside were two sheets of thin white paper, dated October 1, 1944.

My darling Kate,

I'm writing this letter because I do not know whether I will see you again. If you receive it, you will know that I am dead. I am about to embark on a difficult mission and I felt I had to try to explain why I decided to accept it.

I did not lie to you; I had fully expected to come over here and sit behind a desk pushing papers. But the bureaucracy cannot move fast enough, and even now, as we close in on the Nazis, they are still killing Jews. I can't tell you the details of what we plan to do, but even if we don't succeed, I know I will have tried my hardest.

And if that means making the ultimate sacrifice? I am prepared for that, although I feel guilty that I could not have prepared you. But know this, dear Kate: In spite of the miles and traditions that separate us, I have never loved anyone as I love you. And your love was like a fire that kept me warm, even all these thousands of miles away, in my moments of darkest despair.

Do you remember what I was like when you met

me? I was grieving for my friends and relatives, but I was also grieving for myself. I was cold and empty, and if it had not been for you, I would have taken that darker side of me to my grave.

Grieve for me, Kate, but don't let your grief consume you like I let it consume me. Know that I believed in the cause for which I died; now you must live for the causes in which we both believed. And know, too, that I will always be with you.

All my love forever,
Robert

She turned off the light so the night wouldn't see her crying. She sat in the inky darkness, reliving her days with Robert, projecting her life without him, hearing the words he had sent her over and over, as if they were a litany from on high.

She had lost others before. Her mother. Her uncle. That was different, of course, and yet the process was the same. You picked yourself up and got through today. And then you worried about getting through tomorrow.

She had been lonely, too, before. A little girl in a motherless home. A little girl in a strange big city. A pregnant young woman without a husband. Each time, she just had to learn to dig down deeper.

Robert was right. It was easy to let grief consume you. She had known it before. Only this time she had to learn it from him.

When morning broke, she made herself a cup of coffee, splashed some water in her face, then searched for the scrap of paper that David had given her. She phoned the number and left a message for him.

It was brief, but she knew he would understand. "Tell him," she told the secretary, "that I'm ready to rejoin the living."

PART THREE

Washington, 1945

PART THREE

Twenty-Three

Phones rang. Doors opened and shut. Grim-faced aides rushed by with no time for even the simplest pleasantries. The United States had saved the world, now it had to lead it.

She had waited a half hour already, but Kate was determined not to let her impatience show. David had not exaggerated when he said he "knew some people." Within a matter of weeks, he had set up interviews for her at the Treasury Department, the SEC, and a congressman's office. But this job was the one that intrigued her the most.

"Mr. Harrison will see you now, Miss Callahan."

The secretary ushered her into a large, dimly lit room. One wall was covered with a huge map of the world. On the far side, sheer drapes billowed in the breeze off a small balcony. Beyond it was the White House.

The silhouette in the doorway surprised her: a thin man of average height. She had expected that an assistant secretary of state named John Phillip Harrison would have the stature to match his name and title.

"Ah, Miss Callahan. Won't you have a seat?"

"Thank you."

He sat down at his desk and riffled through a sheaf of papers. His face was pale, his hair sandy brown and thinning across his pate. In his neat, summer-weight pinstripes, he had the look of an academic or an aesthete.

"David Kaufmann and I are old friends from Harvard days. He speaks well of you. Have you known him very long?"

Kate winced. "Not terribly long, I'm afraid. I was engaged to his brother, but David was overseas then."

"Yes. I heard that Bob died. I'm very sorry."

She lowered her eyes, not sure what to say. It was strange to hear someone call Robert "Bob."

"I noticed on your résumé that you left your last job about a year ago. What have you been doing since then?"

She had her answer prepared. "It was a difficult year for me and so I took some time off. First my uncle died—he had been like a father to me—and then Robert. . . . But now I'm ready to come back."

He stretched back in his big leather chair. "Pretend for a moment, Kate, that you are secretary of state. What do you think the United States should be trying to do in Europe?"

She sat up in her chair, feeling as if she were back in the classroom. "The European people face enormous problems now. Their cities are destroyed, many of their people are homeless, their economies are near ruin. We can't turn our back on them now; otherwise, what have we been fighting for?"

"And the Russians, what do you think about them?"

"I'm not sure I trust them. I think they need to be watched . . . very closely."

"Now that help you mentioned for Europe. How do you propose to get it through Congress?"

"Am I pretending to be president yet?"

He put his head back and laughed. "A very diplomatic answer, even though you avoided the question. Never mind, that's to your advantage." He glanced down at her résumé. "How about your secretarial skills. Any typing? Shorthand?"

She bristled. "If you're looking for a secretary, Mr. Harrison, I'm afraid I'm not . . ."

"Now wait just a minute, young lady." He leaned forward in his chair. "It so happens that I'm not looking for a secretary. But you come to me with no experience overseas, or in the Foreign Service, or as a lawyer—all the usual places where I look for members of my staff."

Kate bit her lip.

"But on the other hand, you have an interesting background, an apparent aptitude for languages—and excellent references. I run the kind of office where titles are meaningless. Everyone does a little bit of everything—hence my seemingly impertinent question about whether you had ever met a typewriter before. But it's the kind of place where there's no limit to what a smart, hard-working person can do. You strike me as that kind of person. Are you?"

"I think I am."

"I think so, too." He smiled. "Do you think you could start in two weeks?"

John Phillip had been straight with her. On paper she was an administrative assistant, who answered phones and greeted visitors and typed letters and stuffed envelopes. But over the months and years that changed. Kate translated European newspapers and wrote reports. And eventually she was included in the early morning meetings of John Phillip's policy staff.

They all worked long hours—from seven or eight in the morning until well after dinner—but none of them seemed to care. They were imbued with a sense of mission, a feeling of destiny. It was up to America to lead the world back to a state of normalcy, and it was up to them to lead America.

John Phillip set the pace for those around him. His wife had died before the war, and although he owned an elegant Georgetown townhouse, he rarely spent any time there. He had two teenaged daughters, but they were safely installed at high-priced boarding schools in New England. His work, it seemed, was his life.

The same thing could be said of Kate. It was exciting to have to run a file over to John Phillip's home late at night, and wait, sipping a brandy, while he reviewed the memos. Or go into the office on a weekend to help hammer out the wording of the testimony he would deliver on Capitol Hill. She didn't mind skipping lunch or working past dinner for she found that when her mind was focused on England's troubled economy or the rumblings from Berlin, there was no time to think of Robert.

But late at night, the tears would sometimes return. As she

stood on her little balcony in the moonlight, she wondered
if she'd ever be able to feel the soft caress of the wind on
her cheek without experiencing a terrifying sense of emptiness.

Some nights she thought about her daughter, wondering
where she was and whether she would understand. Other
times Kate wondered if she would ever meet someone whom
she could love the way she had loved Robert. She doubted
she would. And she found she really didn't care.

"When are you going to take the Foreign Service exam?"
John Phillip had been after her for months to sit for it.

"Just as soon as I find the time."

"Well, take my advice and don't wait any longer. They
could throw me out of here in a second. And when I go, my
personal aides go with me."

Kate smiled. "So you've told me more than once."

It was strange, she thought. The department should be
heady with its successes. Europe was beginning to get back
on its feet, thanks to better harvests—and Secretary Marshall's "Plan." In Berlin, the Allies' airlift had demolished
the Soviet blockade.

Still, an undercurrent of suspicion ran through the place
that spring of 1949. Suddenly it became important how you
had felt about the Russians during the war, just how tough
you had been. Only a few months before, Alger Hiss had
been charged with lying to Congress about whether he had
passed confidential documents to the Soviets. Mao Tse-tung's
Communists were routing Chiang Kai-shek's Nationalists,
and it was all the State Department's fault. Some members
of Congress were even going so far as to question Acheson's
loyalties. It would have all been ludicrous except that the
carping voices were so serious, so intent on tracking down
every last "com-sym" in the department.

Even John Phillip couldn't escape them. Big chunks of
Europe had moved from Nazi to Soviet control without a
fight—and they blamed him personally.

When he was attacked, his response was the same: He'd
read the critique out loud to his staff members, playing the

role of the outraged congressman or columnist with such comic enthusiasm that he'd leave them close to tears. But Kate knew John Phillip well enough to know that the words stung him. He just wasn't about to show it.

She had grown to care for him over the time she had worked for him. He filled the role that Stephen had once played in her life. He encouraged her to reach higher, challenged her to think harder, rewarded her by always being there to listen.

And as summer approached, he surprised—and pleased—her by announcing at a staff meeting: "I've decided to take Kate along on my next swing through Europe."

"So," Avery Butler said one night as they packed up their things to leave, "you're going to Europe."

Avery was a go-by-the-books sort of bureaucrat who had moved over from the consular service the year before.

"I'm really looking forward to it," Kate replied.

"I'm sure you are." He wrinkled his brow. "But you know, I'm an old Foreign Service officer and I know something about Europe, too. And I've been asking myself, 'Why is John Phillip taking you instead of me?' "

Kate said nothing, bracing herself for his answer.

"I mean besides a little linguistic ability and a great set of legs, what do you have that's so great?"

"I think that comment is inappropriate, Avery." Now she was angry.

He barreled on, oblivious to her. "Well, I figured, from what I hear around the office, it must be the same reason he hired you in the first place—you've got the looks and you've got the connections. And the man's gone sweet on you."

He snapped his briefcase shut like an exclamation point. "Bon voyage."

Her throat burned with the words she wanted to throw back. How could he say such a thing?

But then, why *was* John Phillip taking her? Was there something between them that everyone but her had noticed? Something that—drowned in work and memories of Robert —she had never managed to see?

No, John Phillip was her mentor, that was all. And she

was not about to let some jealous Foreign Service officer ruin the trip she'd waited a lifetime for.

The London and Paris and Rome that Kate discovered that summer were not the unblemished cities of her girlhood fantasies. Nothing had prepared her for the devastation of Rotterdam, Le Havre, and Cologne. But still she could appreciate the determination with which all of Europe was struggling to recover from the horrors of war.

In between all the meetings, she found time for the British Museum and the Coliseum in Rome. She made John Phillip stop reading long enough to catch Olivier at the New Theater in London. And from Mainz, she took a boat trip on the Rhine, up past the Lorelei.

She wished that Robert could have been there to share it with her. Yet she felt that he was with her, that even from a passing train she could glimpse those things that had lured him back. There were the people, of course, but also the sights, the smells, the way of life, even though it had changed.

As they rode into Paris on the last leg of their trip, John Phillip looked up from his pile of cables. "Are you thinking of Bob now?"

The question startled her. "Yes. But how did you know?"

"You had a very sad look on your face. Very sad and faraway." He smiled gently. "Much too sad for a beautiful young woman who's about to arrive in Paris for the first time in her life."

She looked at him closely, wondering what he was thinking. It was a perceptive remark, but was it the perception of a wise friend or something more? Funny, but until now she had never really looked at John Phillip the way a woman regards a man. But now she saw the clarity of his blue eyes, the distinctive gray at his temples, the lines at the corners of his eyes and mouth that warmed his face when he laughed. It had been so many years since his wife had died. How did he cope with the loneliness?

He rose to stretch a crick out of his back.

"You've been very distracted, too," Kate said. "Is there anything I can do to help?"

He shook his head, then sat back down. He studied his papers for a moment, then said, "You know, you can work night and day for this country and some ass from the Midwest with a two-bit education who managed to get his neighbors to send him to Congress will start spouting off about how you're not perfect enough for him. It's enough to make you want to chuck the whole bloody mess and say, 'If you think you know so much, you come run the State Department!'"

She wished she could make him forget all that. He had done so much for her. Given her a new life, really. She wished she could just wave a magic wand and make all those crazy people disappear.

But she couldn't make them go away. All she could do was to be there when he needed her: to run an errand, discuss an idea, send a memo. And maybe once in a while to try to make him laugh.

"Gare du Nord, Gare du Nord." The conductor called out the station name in singsong French.

"Come on," John Phillip said, taking her by the arm. "It's about time we introduced you to Paris."

Twenty-Four

From his window office, Edward Feigan watched as the city of Washington passed below him. His vantage point was considered a perquisite of his job, earned by twenty years of work at *The Standard*, his stature as a columnist, and the writing awards that hung in the newspaper's lobby.

But today he felt like anything but a star. It was ten o'clock, only a few hours away from the deadline for tomorrow's column. And he didn't have a single idea.

It seemed to happen more these days, ever since he'd come home from the war. He had gone overseas in 1943 and cov-

ered the invasion, the march across Europe, the meeting with
the Russians at the Elbe. The war had brought out all that
was right about America, and covering it had been the high
point of his career.

But now that was all being frittered away. He had been
incredulous when American troops were ordered to stop at
the river. "That was Russia's territory," they were told. And
then he began to understand what Yalta was all about. Little
countries, all over Europe, given to the Reds without a fight.
Boys had died, American boys, from places like Little Rock
and Wichita and his hometown, Sioux Falls. Died thinking
they were defending democracy. Not knowing that when the
war was over, those smart fellows from the Ivy League would
turn their backs while the commies marched in.

And it was getting worse. Look what had happened in
Berlin. And China, too. But now people were starting to
figure out why. It wasn't just a matter of looking the other
way. Those Harvard boys were selling secrets to the Reds.
And he, Edward Thomas Feigan, wasn't about to let them
get away with it.

He stubbed out his cigarette. But first there was this pesky
little matter of tomorrow's column.

He could write about anything he wanted to—his bosses
were good about that. Politics, sports, his sons, the weather.
The problem was that August in Washington was a bore.
Especially when he'd squandered his annual diatribe on the
heat in the second week of June.

His phone rang underneath a pile of discarded paper wads.

"Feigan, here."

"Edward Feigan?" It was a male voice.

"That's right."

"I read your column the other day about the Hiss case. I
think I have some information you might be interested in."

"Oh?"

"Have you ever heard of a woman named Katharine Callahan. She also goes by 'Kate.' "

"No, can't say that I have."

"She's one of John Phillip Harrison's top aides. And she
has some interesting skeletons in her closet."

"Really?"

"Perhaps I could meet you somewhere to discuss it."

The caller could be a crank, Feigan thought, but then again maybe not. He checked his watch. "Could you be down here in half an hour?"

"Yes."

"Okay, I'll look for you out front of *The Standard* at ten forty-five. Do you think you'll be able to recognize me?"

"Do you look anything like the photo that runs with your column?"

"Yeah."

"Then I won't have any problem at all, Mr. Feigan. I've been a big fan of yours for years."

Despite John Phillip's pronouncements about being young and in Paris, it was clear to Kate that he was there for business, not play. Each morning they arrived early at the headquarters of the Marshall Plan. Some days he would get right to work at his desk, others he would disappear into meetings in the mansion's high-ceilinged rooms. Sometimes Kate was permitted to attend the sessions, but more often than not, she was forced to wait outside with the aides and secretaries to the other ministers.

Trapped as they were, the staff members formed fast friendships. At night, when John Phillip pleaded fatigue and returned to their hotel, she sat up late with the young men and women, arguing politics over coffee in the cafés of the Left Bank. On other nights, they led her on a tour of Le Tabou, La Rose Rouge, Les Deux Magots, and all the other new jazz clubs, where people went to be seen as much as they went to hear the music. She went cycling with one of the translators, Cecily LeBlanc, in the Bois du Boulogne, and then rode the train out to Chartres one Sunday to have dinner with Cecily and her grandmother.

By now, Kate had surveyed most of Europe's biggest churches, but the stately cathedral in the small French town overwhelmed her. Why? she wondered. Was it the height of its walls, its stained-glass windows, or the incongruity of its construction? She was eager to ask John Phillip what he thought.

As usual, she brought him a cup of coffee when she arrived at work on Monday. But this morning, it was clear by the look on his face that he was in no mood for small talk.

"What is it?" She took a seat on the other side of his desk.

"The embassy sent this over this morning."

He flung a paper across the desk. It was *The Washington Daily Standard*, with a column circled in ink. The headline jumped off the page.

Red Lady in the State Department?

Last week I wrote about the policies of Assistant Secretary of State John Phillip Harrison. Since then, new information has been brought to my attention that raises troubling questions about the loyalties of top members of his staff.

Mr. Harrison is now in Paris, ostensibly to review the progress of our European recovery program. With him is Miss Katharine Callahan, one of his top administrative aides.

It has come to my attention that during the war, Miss Callahan was a member of the local cell of the Communist party here in Washington. This is a woman who at this very moment is representing the United States as decisions are made in Paris about the very future of the European continent! The woman who sits at the right hand of the State Department official who is in charge of our policy on Europe!

Two weeks ago, "our" State Department announced that our old friend, China, had fallen into the hands of Mao Tse-tung and his Communist henchmen. Is it any wonder when Communist sympathizers like Katharine Callahan occupy offices at the top levels of the department?

Kate's hands started trembling. She couldn't believe what she was reading. She blinked several times, hoping that the next time she looked, the words would disappear. But instead they only seemed to grow bigger, darker, louder.

"I don't think I have to tell you how serious this is."

"No, sir."

"Is it correct?"

Did he have to ask? "No, sir."

He shifted in his chair. "Do you have any idea how or why Eddie Feigan would write this?"

She sat down slowly, the memory suddenly taking form. "Robert used to take me to meetings of liberal groups, left-wing groups. . . ."

"Like the Communist party?"

"Well, yes, but it wasn't a big deal then. Robert just called it 'part of my education.' We talked to people and signed petitions and things. But neither of us ever joined the party."

He sighed. "Do you have any idea who might be behind this?"

She shook her head. "There were dozens of people at those meetings. Robert had lots of friends; he introduced me around. But why now? . . . I just don't know."

John Phillip rose from his desk. "Your business is finished here. Pack up your things. You're going home."

"But why? Couldn't we just try to ignore it?" It was all happening too fast. Why did her trip have to end? Paris was a haven, an ocean away from this awful story. Why couldn't she just lie low in France?

"Whatever the truth is," he said, "I can't let your being here jeopardize these talks at a time like this."

"Now you sound like that columnist," she said with a trace of bitterness.

He ignored the remark as he reached over and scooped up the newspaper. "That's just the way the world is, my dear," he said, locking his briefcase with a definitive click. "And if you didn't know it before, you're going to learn it now."

Twenty-Five

It was as if the French had discovered she was a carrier of bubonic plague. There was no time for one last drink along the Champs-Élysées, no time even to say good-bye to Cecily and her other friends. There was a plane leaving for New York that afternoon, Kate was informed, and she was expected to be on it.

But first, John Phillip wanted to see her one more time.

"Think again," he persisted. "Who do you think is behind it?"

The question had consumed her since that morning. Who could have known she had attended those meetings? Only someone who was there. But why would they remember her? And why should they care now?

She remembered that man out of Robert's past. Karl . . . Karl . . . it had been so long she couldn't even recall his last name. Yes, he might still carry a grudge against Robert, but to connect her with all that? It seemed impossible.

Then there was Avery Butler. Should she tell John Phillip about their exchange? Was Avery jealous enough to ruin her? Or would he think he was protecting the department?

But how would he know she had gone to those meetings? Who could have told him?

She still had no answers so John Phillip stopped asking questions. He rose from his desk, but hesitated before leading her to the door.

"I hope you understand how much it pains me to send you home." His cool diplomatic facade began to crack. "Professionally *and* personally."

"Well," Kate replied with a sarcastic edge, "it'll be one less thing for you to worry about."

"I expect to be back in Washington in a few more weeks," he said, shuffling awkwardly to the door. "We'll talk more about it then."

"Yes," she replied in a wooden voice, "we'll talk."

The plane bounced through the turbulent skies over the North Atlantic, setting her stomach, along with her nerves, on edge. She tried to sleep, but rest eluded her. The night, as well as the flight, seemed to never end. But who wanted it to? What kind of future awaited her on the far side of the ocean?

She changed planes in New York City, then headed south. Her neck and back ached, her brain felt fuzzy from the lack of sleep. Her pink linen suit, freshly pressed in Paris, now looked like corrugated paper. She longed for a hot bath, the soft security of her bed.

But would Washington offer any security? She got her answer as soon as the plane landed.

The waiting room was crowded. Strange, she thought, for that time of night. And then she saw them, cameras poised, notepads at the ready. A room full of reporters and photographers, all waiting for the big story of the day—Katharine Callahan.

"There she is."

Kate's eyes widened in panic—like a deer caught by the headlights of a car or in the sights of a gun. And she felt the pain of the wounds before the first shot was even fired.

"Miss Callahan. . . ."

"Miss Callahan, over here. . . ."

"Miss Callahan, how long have you been a member of the Communist party?"

"What were you doing in Europe?"

She threaded her way through the terminal, the pack of journalistic wolves howling at her heels.

"When was the last time you attended a party meeting?"

"When are you going back to work at the department?"

She burst through the terminal's front doors. "Taxi," she yelled frantically. "Taxi!"

A cab pulled up with a squeal of tires. She jumped into

the backseat, then slammed the door on the mob's forward ranks.

"Sure are popular," the cabbie noted with a grin. "Where to, lady?"

"Anywhere," she replied. "Just get me away from here."

She sagged, exhausted, into the upholstery. *What do they want with me anyway*? She was a mid-level federal bureaucrat, after all. Why should anyone care what she did five years ago?

She breathed deeply, trying to slow her heartbeat. She didn't know who was responsible for the story. But someone from her office must have told the press what flight she'd be on. Probably Avery.

Kate closed her weary eyes, remembering that she'd left her luggage at the airport. There was no way she was going back for her bags now—even if it meant losing them.

The truth was, Kate knew, that she'd be lucky if her luggage was all that she lost in the next few weeks.

She opened her eyes as the reality sank in. Across the river, the old familiar monuments were coming into view. White and majestic, they represented the old Washington she knew. A purer place. A place of honor and principles. Not this sordid mess she had stepped into.

For she was the "hot story" now. The Washington papers ran her photograph on their front pages the next day. The readers saw a young woman, with a suit that was smartly cut, if slightly wrinkled. She looked like a proper sort, wearing gloves, clutching a purse. But the look in her eyes spelled panic.

There was little from that time that Kate would find to be grateful for. But the fact that her photograph appeared only once in the papers was one of them. For although her name would become engraved on the collective consciousness of the capital that autumn, her face never would be.

When she was very young and had a nightmare, Kate would climb into her mother's bed until Charlotte's hugs had dispatched all of the demons.

Later, after her mother died, Kate discovered that if she

was brave enough to get out of bed and turn on the light, she could make the monsters disappear.

But no matter what she did to try to shake this devil, no matter how hard she searched for the switch that would light up the truth, she could not bring the nightmare to an end.

She stayed in bed her first days back, after she had taken the phone off the hook (learning the hard way that her colleagues weren't calling, but the reporters were). She needed time for her body to adjust back to the American clock. But she also needed time for her mind to adjust back to America.

She didn't feel as if she were a different person. Yet she knew her life had changed, in a profoundly disturbing way. A change as dramatic as if she had been blinded or paralyzed. She felt as if she might as well have been.

But after a few days, she was eager to get back to work again. At least in her office, she thought, she'd find some sympathy. People who were her friends. People who understood what she was going through. People who knew better than to believe what the papers were saying about her.

"Hello, Grace," she called cheerily to the secretary in the outer office.

"Hello, Kate." The older woman looked up nervously, then bent back over her typing.

She spotted one of John Phillip's executive assistants. "Mary, it's good to see you again."

"Kate," the woman replied with a nod. She reached for her phone. "Excuse me, but I've got an important call to make."

It was as if a stranger had walked through the door. She had been gone for a month, yet no one, not even the lowliest filing clerk, asked her about her trip, or volunteered the latest bit of departmental gossip. No one asked how John Phillip was holding up, or how the meetings had gone.

She had hoped for a friendly greeting, a joke, an affectionate hug. Something for all those late nights and weekends they had worked together for their country. Anything but this.

"What's wrong with all of you?" she wanted to shout. But she knew what the answer was: "There's nothing wrong with us. But what about those stories we've been reading about you?''

At noontime, the pattern repeated itself.

"Janice, are you free for lunch?"

"Oh, sorry, Kate. But I've got some shopping I've just got to get done.''

"Ed, how'd you like to get a sandwich and sit outside in the park?"

"I'd like to, Kate, but I'm waiting for my wife to call.''

"Amazing," she muttered to herself. "In this whole office there's not a single person who can spare a lunchtime.''

"It's not you, Kate." She whirled around to see Grace Ackerman taking the cover off her typewriter. "I mean, it's not you personally. It's just that all of our jobs are threatened. Nowadays you have to worry about who you're seen associating with." She hesitated. "Even your old friends.''

Even a dead fiancé, Kate thought with a stab of pain.

And so she hunkered down alone in the foxhole of her apartment, carefully preparing her defenses. She kept her phone off the hook, she canceled her subscription to the paper, she thought up her own lunchtime errands so she wouldn't have to go searching for a companion.

For Eddie Feigan didn't stop with one column. Day after day he battered away at her reputation. The "facts," as he chose to portray them, didn't change. Only his conclusions and arguments did. Depending on the day of the week, she epitomized the decline of the State Department, the degeneration of the Truman administration, the wickedness of Washington. And no one spoke up in disagreement.

The following week John Phillip returned from Paris. Kate bided her time while the other aides battled for his attention. But then, before the end of the week, he summoned her to his office.

As she entered the familiar room, she looked for a knowing wink, a reassuring smile, anything that would be his way of telling her not to worry.

But there was no signal. Instead he looked at her warily and said, "Since the last time we talked, it's become clear to me that the department has to make some response to these charges." He picked up a sheet of paper from his desk. "Are you familiar with the procedures in cases like yours?"

So now she was a "case." "Only generally, sir."

"The department's loyalty review board will study your situation and make a recommendation to the secretary. If you wish to appeal it, you can go before the federal review board."

"Do you know how long that's likely to take?"

He shook his head. "But in the meantime, I think it would be better for all of us if we changed your duties somewhat. I'm going to put you back in the outer office."

She sucked in her breath. Four years of hard work. Written off in an instant.

"I have to ask you something, John Phillip."

"Go ahead."

"Do *you* doubt my loyalty? Do you think I'm a security risk?"

He leaned back in his chair. "No—on both counts. But I'm afraid, Kate, that these things aren't as simple as they ought to be."

His words resurrected her fears. "Is that all then?"

"For now, yes."

September came and Congress returned, scratching and sniffing and restless from its summer recess. Eddie Feigan had turned up another commie in the State Department for them. Soon the name "Kate Callahan" began popping up in speeches, from the floor of the House and Senate and around town as well.

She was, depending on who was talking, "Acheson's scandal," "an American disgrace," even "Katie, the Red Lady." And when politicians spoke, newspapers quoted. The other writers didn't display Feigan's audacity, but then they didn't have to. The congressmen had picked up the refrain. The newspapers merely supplied the music.

In the meantime, Eddie Feigan continued to spew out new details of her "leftist associations." He seemed to know more about them than she could remember now. And she decided it was time to tell him so.

She put on her most conservative suit, a navy blue gabardine, with a crisp white blouse and a pin at her throat. She rode up the elevator at *The Standard*, then asked the first person she met to point him out to her.

She saw a middle-aged man with rolled-up shirtsleeves and fleshy forearms. His raspy voice carried across the room as he talked on the phone; his hand punctuated the air with an ash-heavy cigarette.

She wasn't sure what she had expected, but certainly not this. This man was her nemesis—and he looked like somebody's uncle from out of town.

At last he hung up the phone. She took a deep breath, and approached his desk. "Mr. Feigan?"

He looked up from his typewriter.

"I'm Katharine Callahan."

His eyes widened with recognition.

Her words came out in a rush. "Mr. Feigan, you have to stop writing those stories about me. They're lies, every one of them. I don't know who told you that about me, but they're lying."

She stood by his desk, clutching her purse and gloves, while he remained seated, looking her over. It made her feel like she was ten again.

"Well, well, well, Miss Callahan," he clucked, opening up a notepad. "Why don't you tell me all about yourself. Starting with when you joined the Communist party."

"I was never a member of the Communist party."

"Is that so?" he said, arching an eyebrow. "But you attended their meetings, didn't you?"

"Well, yes, but . . ."

"And you signed their petitions and passed out leaflets?"

"Yes, but you see . . ."

"What I see, Miss Callahan, is that you were quite an active participant at party meetings."

"It wasn't like that all," she sputtered. "I went with a friend. Out of curiosity. It was ages ago. Five years to be exact. I haven't been anywhere near them since."

"Really?"

She tried again. "You don't understand. . . ."

"Oh, yes I do, little lady. It means nothing to you, that's perfectly clear. It's all just a lark. You and your friends."

He paused, then his eyes darkened. "Well, I watched brave men die fighting for their country. They didn't do it so lefties like you could turn around and give away the store."

How could she reason with this man? Somehow she had to find a way.

"Mr. Feigan," she began, trying to keep her voice calm. "I've worked for the United States government for seven years. I went to work right after Pearl Harbor, going to school at night so I could do my job. My fiancé died serving his country in Europe. I will repeat: I am not a member of the Communist party, I never have been and I never will.

"Your stories are ruining me. They are lies and you must stop publishing them."

He turned away from her. "I have nothing more to say to you."

"At least tell me who put you up to this!"

He looked up at her, his dark eyes boring through her. "Good afternoon, Miss Callahan."

It was hopeless. She should have realized that from the start. She turned, and with her last ounce of dignity walked back through the newsroom, her shoulders set back straight. This time she heard the voice of her mother, exhorting her to be brave: "Remember, Katie, you are a Dellaplaine. And Dellaplaines always hold their heads up high."

Twenty-Six

There was another option Kate had rejected until now. Should she go on the attack? Was it time to hire herself a lawyer?

Could she sue Eddie Feigan for libel? Or would hiring an attorney be tantamount to admitting she was guilty?

She called George Cadwalader, her uncle's executor, to seek his advice.

"That's not the kind of law I do," he replied after she outlined her situation.

"Isn't there anyone in your firm who could take it on?" she persisted.

His response was polite and circumspect, but she read its meaning clearly. "I don't think yours is the kind of case we'd be willing to take on."

Somewhat reluctantly, she called David Kaufmann in New York. She didn't mention Robert, but David seemed to understand.

"I can guess how you got yourself into this mess," he said. "What can I do to help?"

"I think I need a lawyer."

"I'd come down in a minute," he replied, "but I'm in the middle of a big antitrust case. It probably won't be wrapped up until December."

"I don't think this is going to wait that long."

"Let me call one of my friends," he offered.

"No, don't bother," she replied. Suddenly she had gotten cold feet. If she couldn't find a lawyer she already knew and trusted, she didn't want one.

And then a lawyer she did know phoned her.

It was Jason. "I've been trying to reach you since the stories broke."

"I took my phone off the hook."

"Is there anything I can do?"

She hesitated. But no, she didn't want Jason's help. "Thanks, but I'll manage somehow."

"Let me take you out for a nice dinner. Get your mind off all of this."

"I'm sorry," she said wearily. "I'm just not in the mood."

"But we've got so much catching up to do."

"Maybe another time."

She was beginning to feel she could trust no one. There were men waiting outside her apartment building when she left in the morning. Were they following her?

And if someone she knew as well as John Phillip wouldn't believe her now, who would?

At night she felt guilty, for her prayers had turned to one selfish theme: "Please, God, let them find a bigger fish. Turn up another spy with atomic secrets, find another Alger Hiss. Something, anything, to turn the spotlight away from me."

Something did happen, but not what she had hoped. One day in late September 1949, the president's press secretary summoned the White House reporters into his office, then shut the door. He passed out a mimeographed announcement. Its words were understated, but their meaning was clear.

The Soviet Union had exploded an atomic bomb.

It was only a matter of time, Kate knew, before she'd have to find another job.

She was definitely bruised, but still not beaten. She was a college graduate, she reminded herself. She spoke two foreign languages with near fluency. She had risen up the ladder at the State Department. John Phillip would certainly give her a good reference if she asked.

She went about her search systematically. David Kaufmann gave her the names of some more of his friends. She made a list of everyone she could think of whom her uncle had known. She scrutinized the want ads like a prospector.

It had been four years since she had looked for a job, and she quickly learned how much the world had changed in the meantime.

Some days she couldn't even make it past the receptionists. When she was asked to provide a résumé, she never received a phone call back. She knew she couldn't gloss over what she'd been doing for the past four years. But apparently as soon as any potential employer saw that this Katharine Callahan worked for the State Department, he knew that this Katharine Callahan was the one in the news.

And that meant this Katharine Callahan was not the kind of person he wanted to hire.

She called every name on the list she had made of her uncle's friends. A few were dead, a few were retired, a few politely demurred.

But she was hurt the most when she tried calling John

Carson, their old neighbor. He was a man who'd smoked dozens of her uncle's cigars and stayed up late with her, arguing good-naturedly about the future of Europe. But now, it was as if she had telephoned a stranger.

"How dare you call me!" he barked into the phone. "Don't you ever do it again."

"But, John, listen to me," she begged.

"I don't want you to call me, write me, come near me. Do you understand?"

"All right, I won't."

"I'm glad your uncle isn't alive to see this. If he had had any inkling of the kind of people you were involved with . . ."

She hung up quickly, but the cruel words still beat inside of her, stirring up a tide of despair.

Once she actually got called in for an interview. It was for a job at her alma mater, GW, and for a day, at least, Kate allowed herself a glimmer of hope.

She was surprised when "Miss Abernathy" turned out to be a receptionist, who asked her to pull up a chair next to her typewriting table.

The woman appeared to be about fifty, her scalp pulled back in a tight bun, her intense eyes poised, looking over the tops of her tortoiseshell glasses.

She reeled off a round of questions, which Kate tried gamely to answer: "What did you study at GW? What groups did you belong to? Did you have many friends on campus?" Then she shuffled some papers on her desk and said, "That's all for today."

"But what about the job?" Kate asked.

"Oh." The woman reddened. "Well, you see"—she laughed nervously—"when I opened the mail and saw your résumé, well, you see, I'd never met a Communist before. I just wanted to see if they're as bad as everyone says."

Kate snatched her letter out of the woman's hands, then rose slowly to her feet. *Keep calm,* she told herself. *It's a waste of emotional energy to respond to such gross stupidity.* Without saying a word, she turned and walked out of the room.

But all the snubs, all the thoughtless remarks, were wearing her down. She was growing more and more despondent. She knew that jobs in whole areas of Washington were off-limits to her: Congress, all the executive branch agencies. David tried another round of phone calls, but this time even he came back empty-handed. "It's the nature of the times," he told her over the phone from New York. Kate knew what he was too polite to say, that no one he had talked to was willing to talk to her.

He offered her a job as a typist at his law firm. He offered to lend her money. But she was too proud to accept either.

Then she heard from Jason again. Over the phone, his voice was kind.

"Look, I'm at the Commerce Department now. There are a million jobs there. I can find you one."

"You must be joking."

"No, I'm serious. Come on down and we'll talk about it."

She hesitated. Just how desperate was she? Desperate enough to work for Jason again? Would Robert forgive her if she did? Even if it looked like it was the only way out of this quagmire he had led her into?

No, she decided. As low as she might be, she still hadn't sunk that low. Better to wait on tables or work behind a counter than to work for Jason. She didn't have much of a reputation left, but she still had her principles—and her pride.

"Thank you, Jason, but . . . I really don't think the federal government wants me, and I'm beginning to think I don't want it now either."

"You'll be sorry, Kate." His voice rose. "You don't have many options left."

"I know that."

"But I'm prepared to help you!"

"I'll remember that, Jason," she said and hung up the phone.

A week later John Phillip summoned Kate to his office. It was a long walk now—as each week went by, her superiors kept moving her and her desk deeper and deeper into departmental Siberia.

A few years before she had lived for every summons into John Phillip's inner sanctum. But now she expected the worst.

She had come to love John Phillip almost as she had loved Stephen. He was the person, after all, who had taught her the ways of the State Department, the fine points of diplomacy. But now when he spoke to her, he wouldn't meet her eyes.

"We've learned from our friends in Congress—what few of them remain—that some members of HUAC want to hold more hearings on leftists in the State Department. They want to make you the center of the show. However, our supporters feel that if you were to resign, the committee might hold off for a while."

Kate said nothing. She realized that this was the end.

". . . It would be for the good of the department, Kate. Not to drag all of us up there again at a time like this."

"It won't make any difference, you know."

For the first time, John Phillip looked up at her.

"If it's not me today," she went on, "it will be someone else tomorrow. Just as long as no one has the guts to stand up to them." She paused. "Do you want me to resign?"

He nodded.

"Well, I won't. I'm innocent. I'm no more a Communist than . . . than Snow White is. And I intend to see that my name is cleared, even if I have to go to court against Eddie Feigan."

"It won't work." He spoke quietly. "Look at Hiss. He was a top department official, a well-respected lawyer. He'd been around the government for years. And they won't listen to him. Every time he tries to dig himself out, the hole gets deeper."

"I won't resign," she asserted.

He sighed. "Then I'm afraid I'm going to have to fire you."

Even though she had expected it might come to this, his words stung like a slap across the face.

She rose from her chair. "Tomorrow when I get up, John Phillip, I'll be able to look myself in the mirror. I wonder if you'll be able to do the same."

* * *

She packed up her desk quickly and left without saying a word. On the way home, it started to rain, a chilling rain that presaged the coming of winter. But that didn't stop her. She changed her clothes and grabbed her tennis racket, then headed for the neighborhood court that had a backboard.

There she stayed for the rest of the afternoon, a lonely figure in the rain, oblivious to the cold and the wet and the world around her. She pummeled the backboard with shot after shot, seeking an outlet for her rage. It boiled up inside her like a fever, numbing her brain and turning her limbs to steel.

At first she had no focus, flailing her tennis balls at a world, a God, that for some inexplicable reason had turned against her. But then slowly as she tired and the ball got wetter and heavier, her targets became more precise. She was angry at John Phillip, but she could not hate him. It was true he had betrayed her, but she could forgive him. In the end, he was weak, just like all the rest of them.

But she felt no mercy for Eddie Feigan. He had ruined her with a stroke of his pen, without the slightest regard for her or her story. How many others had he devastated? It didn't matter now. The only one she cared about was herself.

And what of the person who had given Feigan her name? She could imagine him, dangling the stories before the reporter like a butcher tempting a stray dog with fresh meat. Who was he—or she, for that matter? Feigan wouldn't tell her, and she knew the "process" wouldn't either. She'd seen enough of that already to know the accusers never had to show their faces.

She served once more, grunting with the effort. Her ball missed the backboard, and hit the fence instead.

She stared at it, lodged between the wires. She was alone now. She had no family, no husband, no lover, no child. As of this moment, she had no job. There was nothing anyone could do to her, no one they could take from her to hurt her any more than they already had.

She had lived her life as they had told her to; she had been loving, obedient, polite. She had worked hard at school, and

hard at her jobs. She had been loyal to John Phillip. She
had respected her relatives—and loved one man with all her
heart.

She had played by their rules—and this was what she had
earned in return. The world was not a kind, safe place. The
only person you could count on, the only person you could
trust, was yourself. And from now on, she vowed, she was
going to play the game by her own set of rules.

As she went to pick up her balls, she felt curiously calm.
She didn't have the slightest idea how she was going to get
back at Eddie Feigan. But she was determined now to do it,
even if it took the rest of her life to find a way.

She didn't have a job, she didn't have many friends. But
she still had herself. And she had an idea.

She had learned that the truth couldn't always protect her,
but there were two things that might. One was power, the
other was money.

You could inherit money or you could earn it. She had
inherited some, but not as much as she needed now. As for
power, when she looked around Washington, it seemed that
next to the politicians, the lawyers were the ones who had
it. Most of them had money, too. Lots of it.

And they had something else that appealed to her. They
had the law. "Learn the law," her uncle had told her once,
"and you'll always have it on your side."

She wasn't sure she'd ever be able to practice in Washington, but she couldn't let that stop her now.

First she needed a fresh start. She needed to disappear.
Once again, Mildred Hudgins was willing to take her in.

But before she left, Kate went to visit Amanda.

It had been months since she had walked up the steps of
her girlhood home. An unfamiliar maid asked her name, then
ushered her into the parlor. "I'll go tell Mrs. McNeil that
you're here."

Her aunt had redone this room since Stephen died. Now
it was a fuss of pastels and posies. The restrained good taste
of the Washington hostess had been overrun by the real
Amanda.

Her aunt entered the room, looking fragile, as if her fingers could be snapped off like the handles on a cheap tureen. She took a seat across from Kate, waiting while the maid passed a plate of cookies and cups of tea.

"How have you been, my dear?"

"Well, the last few weeks haven't been very pleasant. I'm sure you've seen the papers. . . ."

Her aunt nodded, then changed the subject. They made small talk for a while, of Margaret and Jack, of the weather and the latest fashions from France. Then Kate said quietly, "I'm going away again. Back to Mildred Hudgins's. I'm not sure for how long, but I'm sure you'll agree it's for the best."

Her aunt set down her cup. She dabbed her mouth with her napkin, then said, "I've always worried about you, Kate. You were smart and you were pretty, and because of that, I always worried that you were going to turn out to be just like your mother.

"You see, all of New Orleans society was scandalized when they found out she'd married your father. It about killed your grandparents. But I'd always held out hope that by raising you in a proper home, in proper society . . ."

"It's not as if I chose this fate, Amanda."

"I know that," her aunt replied. "However, we do choose the company we keep." She sighed. "I'm just grateful your uncle didn't have to suffer through all this with you. Your pregnancy was bad enough. But this would have killed him.

"Fortunately, most people probably won't make the connection between your name and his."

Yes, Kate thought bitterly, wasn't it fortunate that her name was Callahan and theirs was McNeil?

Amanda knew her too well, she thought. Her aunt knew the names to invoke, the ghosts to conjure up, all of the tender spots that could be used to make her feel guilty. And Charlotte and Stephen were two of Kate's tenderest.

Kate gathered up her things and rose from her chair. "It's so comforting, Amanda, to know that at times like these, you can always count on your family."

* * *

Her aunt made it easier to go, reminding her yet again that there were no ties left, no reasons to remain. And so she packed up her car and moved to Fredericksburg.

Unlike the others, Mildred asked no questions and required no explanations. Her old friend Kate was back.

But in Kate's heart, the hatred burned quietly, like a dying fire. Yet she didn't want to focus on it. There was no point in blowing up the flame. Not here, not now. She would save that energy for later, when she needed it.

At night in her room, she pored over applications to law schools. But she had a new worry. What if they recognized her name and refused to admit her?

She picked up one form, but couldn't get farther than the first line. It was waiting for her name. The name that all of Washington had pilloried. She stared at the blank space for some time, then picked up her pen and wrote: "Callahan," followed by "K. Aurore."

She held the form out at arm's length. It might make the difference. Her transcripts would still have "Katharine" on them, but maybe no one would notice.

"Aurore Callahan." She said the name out loud. She rather liked it. It was unusual. Distinctive.

"Katharine Callahan" is a very nice name and it's the only name you'll ever have. So you have to be very careful not to do anything that will make people think Katharine Callahan is a bad girl.

She had tried—very hard, in fact. But people still thought "Katharine" Callahan was bad. So she would begin again. She would throw away her name along with her past. She would never use it again.

Twenty-Seven

Aurore paused in front of the statue of Thomas Jefferson as she headed toward the Rotunda. The tall bronze figure gazed down at her, a curious expression on his face.

"Do *you* think I'm crazy?" she asked aloud.

She was thirty now. She had not been in a college classroom for eight years. And in the virtually all-male world of the University of Virginia, she was bound to stick out like a mismeasured pillar in a colonnade.

But Tom's face was reassuring. She remembered his words from the catalog she'd devoured after she had been accepted. His school, it said, was to provide the quiet needed to study, "and lessen the dangers of fire, infection, and tumult."

That's what she needed now, more than anything. An escape from the tumult of Washington, until she was ready to return.

She stepped back into history as she passed through the gate and out onto the Lawn. Centuries-old brick, made of red Virginia clay, shaded by towering trees that knew stories even older than the buildings. A place where honor meant something—they had a code to prove it. And on a sunny September day, it was a place where she knew she could start over.

She headed down the road and entered Clark Hall. She'd already found the classroom—two days ago. Now she had to laugh at herself. She was acting just like a nervous freshman.

She took a seat in the middle of the room. But no matter where she sat, she wouldn't be able to hide—she was the only woman in the class.

"Good morning, I am Professor Anderson." A white-haired man in a three-piece suit had taken his place at the lectern. "And this class, in case you are lost, is Criminal Procedure."

He pulled out a sheaf of papers. "A good part of your success here will depend on your participation in class. So I have to know who you are. Please bear with me while I run through my seating chart."

He adjusted his glasses on the bridge of his nose. "First row: Adams, Alberts, Beamon . . ." He rattled off names as he pointed to seats. "Bromwell, Callahan, Cronin, Davenport . . ."

Aurore took her seat and opened her notebook.

"Excuse me." She turned slightly to the voice from behind her. "Cronin," she discovered, was a man who appeared to be as old as she was. "Do you have a pen I could borrow?"

She dug through her purse. "Will a pencil do?"

"Sure."

She handed it to him. His hair was the color of honey, his blue eyes seemed to light up his face. He smiled easily, like a little boy. Like those around him, he wore a jacket, but its shiny newness set him apart from all the other Harris tweeds.

"Thanks."

"Forget it." She turned back to the front of the room. Sandy hair, blue eyes. What had gotten into her? She didn't want a man, didn't need a man. She was here for one purpose and one purpose alone: to become the best damn lawyer she could.

She picked up her pen as the professor began writing an outline on the board. Yes, it was all coming back—it was even easier now. Working for John Phillip, she had picked up shorthand.

The hour flew by quickly. "Read the first five chapters," Professor Anderson concluded. "That's all for today."

She closed her notebook and rose to leave.

"Oh, miss." It was Cronin again. "Here's your pencil."

"Thanks."

"No, thank you. I would have been dead without it."

"Well, anytime. Just yell."

She turned to leave, but he didn't stop.

"I'm Andrew Cronin. And you must be . . ."

"Aurore Callahan."

"That's a pretty name."

She smiled, wondering if it was a gambit he always used. "My mother thought so, too."

He followed her down the hallway and out into the sun. She paused for a moment, not sure where she wanted to go next.

"Can I ask you a question?" he said.

"Sure."

"Do you feel out of place here?"

She couldn't help but smile. The only woman in the class, and he had to ask?

"I'm sorry," he said. "That was stupid, wasn't it?"

"I don't feel out of place. Just sticking out, I guess. Why?"

"Because I feel like I don't belong here. Everyone I've met so far went to Harvard or Princeton or Yale. But me, I'm an overaged vet from a little town that's about as far west in Virginia as you can get."

There was something about Andrew Cronin she couldn't help but like. In the past few years, she had spent too much time around too many stuffed shirts.

"Well, I'm not an Ivy Leaguer either, so you can stop worrying."

"Good." He checked his watch. "Oh, damn, I'm going to be late for my job. I'll see you on Thursday." He ran a few steps, then whirled around and saluted her. "And I promise next time I'll remember my pen."

She laughed. "At ease, Cronin." He turned and sprinted down the street.

As he disappeared, she thought back over the past few years. It had been a long time since she had had a really good laugh.

Or, for that matter, a man.

Aurore had taken two rooms above a store at "The Corner." Even though the first wave of GIs had graduated, the school was still crowded—and housing was at a premium. Her apartment was noisy, and strange smells wafted up from the grocery store below. But the price was right. She didn't want to have to take a job—anything that would distract her from her studies.

The professors might confuse the Cronins and the Smiths and the McIntyres for a while, but they wouldn't forget that "Callahan" was the woman in their class. If she wanted to practice law in Washington, it wouldn't be enough to be good. She had to be the best.

And so Aurore bypassed the boozy fraternity parties and the Saturday morning football extravaganzas. She stayed in the library as long as they would let her, then worked even later in her rooms.

But so, apparently, did Andrew Cronin. As Socratic debates raged around her in class, she began to realize that he was one of the smartest people she had ever met. Others might be able to drop their Latin phrases with more savoir faire, but Andrew always trounced them with the force of his argument and his straightforward country talk.

He was disorganized. He had forgotten his pen so many times that she always made sure she had two. But when it came to organizing a line of attack, he was brilliant. He knew how to think on his feet. And whether it was a point of evidence or an offer of a cup of coffee, she always found him very persuasive.

"But you promised," he said, following her out the door of their classroom one day a few weeks after school started. "You told me, 'I can't today, Andrew, but next time, I'll have lunch with you.' "

"I did; hmm?"

He raised his hand to take an oath. "The truth, the whole truth, and nothing but the truth."

She smiled. "All right, then. Today it is."

They had started studying together. Aurore was grateful because Andrew drilled her mercilessly—and always knew the right answer. But she enjoyed the camaraderie, too. She had met very few people since she had arrived in Charlottesville; he was the only one who came close to being a friend.

One day when she was sick, he phoned her. "I was worried when you didn't show up for class."

"I came down with a virus. I didn't think I could move."

"I'll be right over."

"No, don't bother. . . ."

But he came, and fixed her some tea and hot soup.

"Now, I'm going to make you a copy of my notes from today."

"You don't have to, Andrew."

"How are you going to learn them otherwise?"

Once again, she couldn't argue with him. She watched him from her bed, hunched over his notebook, copying quickly but carefully. Through the haze of her fever, it seemed as if he belonged here. She nestled down under her covers and fell asleep again, this time with a smile on her lips.

When she awoke, he was gone. Beside the notebook, he'd left a handwritten sign: "You'd better get well soon. I forgot my pen again today."

But that wasn't all. In a mayonnaise jar by her kitchen sink was a big bouquet of daisies.

One afternoon Andrew looked up from his books. "You know everyone else here is so much smarter."

"Don't be silly," she replied. "All their big-city talk is bull. You're the smartest one of the bunch."

He was smart all right, but Aurore was always amazed at how unaware Andrew was of what other people thought of him. He still was insecure about his clothes, his education, his drawl. But she knew all their classmates looked up to him. He was destined to be number one.

He also seemed to be totally unaware of the effect he was having on her. It was different from the way she had felt about Robert at first. That had been like jumping off a cliff. This time she just felt good about herself again.

And maybe that was enough. It had been six years since Robert had died, but she wasn't sure she was ready to give him up. She cried every year on his birthday and on the day David had found out he'd died. She knew she should let go, but a part of her didn't want to. She didn't want to abandon him.

Yet she knew she was drawing closer to Andrew. And she

wondered how he felt about her. Would they ever put their law books down long enough for her to find out?

One day after class, she thought the time had come. They paused outside the law building and he asked: "Would you be free for dinner on Saturday night?"

She was, but she didn't want to sound too eager. "I think so."

"Great," he said, "Ellie's been looking forward to meeting you."

"Who's Ellie?" she asked.

A look of embarrassment washed across his face. "Oh, I'm sorry." He kicked away a stone with his toe. "I guess I forgot to tell you. . . ."

"Tell me what?"

"Well, you see . . . Ellie's my wife."

Aurore fumed as she drove out to Copeley Hill. She was angry at Andrew, but she was angrier at herself. Looking back on the few weeks she had known him, she could recall nothing he had done that was out of line or disingenuous. The time they had spent studying? Just a conscientious student. The flowers? Just a gift for a sick friend.

And if he had neglected to mention one rather important detail of his life—well, Andrew was forgetful. And besides, what did that have to do with studying law anyway?

No, she told herself, she should be mad at herself. She had begun weaving Andrew Cronin into her fantasies, before he'd given her any reason to. So if it hurt that their "romance" was over before it had begun, she had no one to blame but herself.

The apartments for married students were clustered on the hillside just beyond the C & O tracks. The buildings were grim, temporary things, with the rubble of small children scattered about outside.

She found a parking space and then the apartment. The paint on the front door was blistering, but inside, frilly white curtains framed the windows. She knocked on the door, and almost immediately it swung open.

"Hi," said a petite woman, who extended a tiny hand. "I'm Ellie Cronin. You must be Aurore."

"Hello, how are you?"

"Come on in. Andrew has told me so much about you. I've been dying to meet you."

Aurore wasn't sure what to say. *Either she's incredibly secure with her husband or incredibly innocent. Probably a little of both.*

Ellie took her coat and ushered her into the living room. There was not much beyond the standard-issue laminated furniture—a bookshelf fashioned out of orange crates, some pillows that Ellie must have embroidered, an afghan that probably covered a bare spot on the sofa.

"There you are," Andrew called from the doorway of the bedroom. He straightened his tie. "Did you have any trouble finding us?"

"No, I just turned left at the first sandbox."

"There are a lot of children, aren't there?" Ellie said. "I like it, but it makes it hard for Andrew to study here. That's why I'm so grateful he's been able to study with you."

"It's made it easier for me, too," Aurore said quietly.

As they sat down, she took the opportunity to observe Andrew's wife. She was not at all what Aurore had expected. Ellie was attractive, but you wouldn't pick her out in a crowd. She couldn't be an inch over five feet, and her large eyes, framed by a jet-black bob, made her look younger than she probably was. She fussed about Andrew like a hummingbird in heat, making sure he took the best chair, making sure he had a drink. It would have driven Aurore crazy, but Andrew seemed to revel in it.

They chatted about inconsequential things—the rigors of law school, the balmy fall weather. Then Andrew pulled up a third chair to the small table in the corner, while Ellie dished up plates of fried chicken and mashed potatoes and gravy.

"So," Aurore said, trying hard to be pleasant, "how long have the two of you been married?"

With a slight nod, Andrew signaled Ellie to answer.

"Since Andrew came home from the war. But really, we'd been engaged since we got out of school."

"High-school sweethearts, hmm?"

Ellie giggled. "I'd guess you'd say so. We come from a very small town, Aurore. It was so small, our graduating

class only had six people in it—six, can you imagine? Andrew
and five girls.'' She giggled again. ''I guess I was the lucky
one.''

The puzzle of Andrew was starting to make sense. If you
grew up in a small town, and went to a small college, and
never had any challenges by which to measure yourself, you
might never know that you were really head-and-shoulders
above the rest.

Certainly, Ellie couldn't tell him that—she had no way of
judging. Andrew was undoubtedly the smartest person she'd
ever known, but like him, she probably assumed that the rest
of them were even smarter.

As the evening wore on, one other thing became clear.
Ellie and Andrew were deeply in love. You could see it in
their eyes, the little private jokes they chuckled about, the
way she knew exactly how to fix his coffee, the way their
hands gravitated together across the table.

Driving home, Aurore felt drained, and she wondered for
a moment if Andrew had staged this evening for her benefit.
But no, it was not like that at all. He had displayed no
awkwardness, no embarrassment over his relationships with
her and his wife. The Cronins' friendliness had been genuine.

She couldn't help but like Ellie Cronin, but she doubted
they would ever become very close friends. They were just
too different. Ellie had goals, but they were Andrew's goals.
She wanted him to complete law school, because that's what
he wanted. She wanted to have children, because they wanted
a family.

But there was another reason they would probably never
be close: Aurore was beginning to want Andrew, too. Not
as a man, but as a partner, to share in her work.

For she hadn't been deterred from the quest she had started.
With Andrew, she knew she could build that law firm in
Washington. The law firm that would give her security. The
law firm that would give her the power to strike back.

Twenty-Eight

A brash guy from Harvard had been elected president of the Student Legal Forum. But instead of proposing the usual round of lectures by retired profs, Bobby Kennedy had used his father's connections to produce a speakers' series that was worth attending. William O. Douglas and Ralph Bunche and his brother, the congressman.

And Senator Joe McCarthy.

"Are you coming with me tomorrow night?" Andrew whispered across the table in the library. Since Ellie wasn't interested, he and Aurore had gotten into the habit of going to the speeches together, then stopping for a bite afterward.

Aurore looked up from her book. "Actually, I thought I'd pass this time."

"Why?" He marked his place in the torts book. "Don't you want to see McCarthy in action?"

"I'm not about to give that man an audience."

Andrew shook his head, puzzled. "I didn't say you had to agree with him. I'm just curious what the American public sees in him."

"I said no, Andrew. Now please drop it."

"Okay, what is it?"

"What do you mean?"

"Tell me why you're so upset."

"I don't want to talk about it."

But he did. He reached over and took her book away. "This is Andrew, remember. Andrew Cronin? Your closest friend. Your best buddy."

She couldn't help but smile.

"There, that's better. Now tell me what's bothering you."

Still, she hesitated. As close as they had become, as much as she trusted him, she still wasn't sure. She had kept her secret all this time. Why should she tell him now?

But she knew she'd have to eventually. Otherwise he'd never go along with her plan.

"I was run out of Washington by McCarthy's boys."

"You?" His voice betrayed surprise, but no sense of moral outrage. "Why didn't you ever tell me?"

"It's not something I talk about."

"I wish you would."

It was hard to get started, to make sure that he understood. It was a time that seemed so long ago now. Robert and the State Department and dreams that would never be fulfilled. The world was so much blacker now.

"Back during the war," she began, "my boyfriend took me to the meetings of some leftist groups. I never joined or anything like that. But a few years later, when I had a job pretty high up in the State Department, somebody decided that fact was vitally important to the security of the nation. A newspaper columnist got hold of it, and the next thing I knew, everyone in town was calling me a Communist. Some congressmen wanted to haul me up to the Hill to testify, and I wanted to, to try and clear my name. But my boss wouldn't let me. He was too worried about his own position. And so he fired me. But even before that it was like I was damaged goods. No one else would hire me."

"So you came here?"

She nodded. "I took some time off. Things quieted down a little . . . Somehow I got past my interview with the dean of women. I used a different name back then. I used to go by Katharine. Did you ever read about me?"

He shook his head.

She hesitated. "Does any of this shock you?"

"Me? No, not at all." His words were gentle. "Mad at them, yes. But remember, Aurore, I know you. I know that you're honest. I know we share the same goals, the same ideals.

"No, I know who you really are." He winked. "Even if I don't know every episode of your sordid past."

He touched her cheek, as if to wipe away an imaginary tear. She trembled slightly at the feel of it.

"Where is the boyfriend now?" he asked pointedly.

"He died in Europe. In the closing days of the war. . . . We had planned on getting married when he returned."

"That must have been hard for you. . . ."

She shrugged. "You learn how to survive."

"I wish I could go in there tomorrow night and punch out Joe McCarthy, just for you. Tell him, 'Here's a message from your old friend, Katharine Callahan.' "

She had to laugh, in spite of herself. "Promise me you won't do it."

"Why not?"

"They say he used to be a pretty vicious boxer. And I've sort of grown to like your face the way it is."

"Well, then. . . ." He smiled, the smile that always made her feel better. "I promise to check with you first before I try to defend your honor."

Once again he had managed to find her tender spot. She lowered her eyes, unable to look at his. "I guess," she said quietly, "a girl couldn't ask for more."

A semester passed and then another. And sooner than Aurore would have thought possible, their final year arrived.

Over the months that her plan had taken shape, she had never mentioned it to Andrew. She was afraid of how he would react, afraid that she would push him too soon. She needed his help too desperately.

But time was running out. There were decisions that had to be made.

They had stopped for coffee after studying for an exam. They were tired, but confident that they had mastered their material. Ellie was at home, which was exactly where Aurore wanted her now.

"Do you think you're going to apply for Judge Taliaferro's clerkship?" Michael Taliaferro was a judge on the federal appeals court in Washington and an alumnus of the law school. For the past decade, he had always hired one of his clerks from the U-Va graduating class.

"I don't know. I don't think my chances are very good."

"Don't be silly. You're near the top of our class, you're editor of the law review, and the judge comes from your part of the state. Tell me who has a better chance."

He couldn't produce a name. "But anyway, all Ellie and I wanted to do is go back to Ewing so I can start a practice there."

Aurore had been afraid it would come to this. She bit her lip, marshaling her forces to present her most convincing argument.

"Is that really what you want?" He looked surprised at her challenge. "Would that really make you happy? Spending the rest of your life writing wills and handling real estate transfers? You could be a brilliant lawyer, I know it. But all your talents would just go to waste down there."

He arched an eyebrow. "And what do you suggest I do instead?"

She took a deep breath. "Come to Washington. Open up a law firm with me."

"Do you really want to go back after all that's happened?"

She swallowed, then said softly, "More than anything else in the world. I'm not about to let them keep me down." Then she looked up at him. "But I can't do it without you."

"Why do you say that?"

"I still can't be too visible. I'm still afraid someone will recognize my name or my face."

"Go on."

"But we both know that there's more to law than standing up in the courtroom," she continued. "You could be the visible one. You're better on your feet than I am, anyway. But I know Washington—that's my strong point. I can write the briefs, help you plan strategy, run the office, hire the staff. We can hunt down all the best of our peers—people who'd rather be big fish in our little pond than lost in a big firm." She hesitated. "What do you say?"

A smile crossed his face. "You obviously have done a lot of thinking about this."

"I've even come up with a name for the firm." She raised her hands, as if spelling out the words on a theater marquee: "Cronin and Associates."

"I think I could grow to like that." He thought for a moment as he sipped his coffee. "What if I don't get the job as Taliaferro's clerk?"

She shrugged. "Then we'll get started sooner. If you do get the job, I'll get the firm organized until you can join me."

He thought for a moment. "It is tempting. But I'll have to talk it over with Ellie."

"Of course. . . . But Ellie will want what you want, Andrew—you and I both know that. If you want to go to Washington, she will, too."

Later, after he had walked her back to her rooms, she tried once more. "Think about what we talked about. I know it's a risk, but we could be great, Andrew, working together. Don't settle for the easy way out."

He looked away quickly. "I'll see you tomorrow, Aurore."

Upstairs, she undressed and climbed into bed. In her mind, she could see Andrew returning home. Would he mention it to Ellie? Probably not tonight. He'd think about it first and make up his own mind. Then he'd pick his moment to take it up with her.

She remembered how Ellie always talked about going home and how much she missed her family. But she also adored Andrew. Would she still be willing to bend for him?

Aurore had never contemplated what she'd do if Andrew said no. But now she did. She would never be able to work in Washington by herself—at least not until enough years had gone by that people would have forgotten. By then, she figured she'd be close to forty. It was not the age to be starting out as a lawyer in the nation's capital. Not if you wanted to be a player, that is.

Still, she had given it her best shot. Andrew was not her husband; she could not tell him what to do. All she could do was hope that he would choose what she knew was best—for both of them.

PART FOUR

Washington 1953

Twenty-Nine

Commencement arrived on a warm, sunny day in early June. As she rose and donned her rented cap and gown, Aurore felt a rare sense of satisfaction. For the first time in nearly four years, she felt in control of her life. For a change, the fates were smiling on her.

It was all because Andrew had decided to join her. He had won Judge Taliaferro's clerkship, and that made his decision easier. But Aurore felt it was a vote of confidence in her and her dreams.

She was going to take on Washington again, as she had promised herself she would. She didn't know what awaited her there—McCarthy, for one, was still on a rampage. But even if she couldn't make a name for herself now, she was determined to be a success. With Andrew's help, she was certain she could.

And when she had security—money and powerful friends and a law firm with a top-notch reputation—she would await the day when she would settle her score. Then it wouldn't matter whether Andrew was willing to help her. She was prepared to do it all alone.

She sent out half a dozen invitations to the ceremonies, more as a ritual than because she thought anyone would come. She was hurt, but not surprised, that Amanda said she couldn't make it, and Margaret didn't reply. But it did surprise—and please her—that Mildred Hudgins rode the train down from Fredericksburg for the day. And she was touched that David Kaufmann swung by on his way home from his honeymoon. He brought his new wife, a pretty, dark-haired woman named Rachel, whom Aurore liked immediately.

The day was perfect in nearly every way. Andrew captured two of the law school's top prizes and Aurore was surprised to hear her name called out for another. But the surprises weren't over yet.

When she returned home that night, she found a letter waiting. She checked the postmark, and saw that it was from Mississippi, from a special person she had decided, at the last minute, to invite.

> *Dear Katie,*
>   *Forgive me if I don't call you Aurore, but I still think of you as my little girl. I asked Lucy to write this for me to thank you good and proper for inviting me to your graduation. When I think of the last time I saw you, that tiny little girl by the railroad track, I know that my prayers that day were answered. And I know that if your mama was alive today, she'd be so proud of her girl.*
>   *I hope that one day before I join the Lord I'll get the chance to see you again. But I hope you'll forgive me if this old lady doesn't feel up to making a trip up north for the occasion.*
>   *I look forward to hearing from you again, child.*
>   *Love,*
>   *Matty*

As she read the letter over a second time, a tear formed in the corner of Aurore's eye. No matter how far she had sunk or how deep her despair, there would always be people like Matty and Mildred. People whose love was complete, unquestioning, unending. People whom you could count on.

The year did not go by quickly. Aurore was still afraid of running into people at the courthouse who might remember her. So she tried to keep busy doing paperwork—real estate transactions, wills, patent filings—exactly the kind of things she had convinced Andrew he *didn't* want to do. But for now, she had no choice. These days even the U.S. Army was getting dragged up in front of McCarthy's committee.

She had hunted carefully for an office, a job that had produced their first major disagreement. Aurore had insisted on four rooms: an office for each of them, a reception area for clients and a secretary, a fourth room for meetings and their law books.

"It's too extravagant," he protested. "I'm already paying a fortune for our apartment."

"But no one will take you seriously unless you look serious," she replied.

Eventually, he gave in, more out of exhaustion, she suspected, than anything else.

She found a suite of rooms in an old office building that faced Pennsylvania Avenue. It was slightly seedy, but it would have to do. There was room to expand, but she hoped that wouldn't be necessary. When the time came to grow, she intended to move.

She spent her weekends with Ellie, checking the sales and sifting through secondhand shops for usable furniture. It was there that Ellie taught her the subject of Andrew, the kinds of lessons a woman only learned by living with a man. That his favorite paintings were nature scenes. That he preferred green to brown. That he hated prickly upholstery. That he always forgot to rinse out his coffee cup.

As the weeks went by, Aurore could see subtle changes in Andrew. He was picking up the jargon of Washington, feeling more at home. He seemed more self-confident, as if he had finally accepted the fact that while the guy in the next office might have a framed diploma from Harvard, that didn't mean he was a better attorney.

Aurore repainted the walls of their office when the landlord wouldn't, then found two area rugs to cover the bare spots on the linoleum. She turned up two good desks, bought shelves for their law books, framed and hung their degrees, along with some paintings of the Shenandoah Valley. Only then was she ready to show the office to Andrew.

She would have preferred to unveil the office alone, but she could hardly make Ellie stay home. And besides, the finished product was the result of Ellie's work almost as much as her own.

They conspired to show it to him one Saturday morning. They blindfolded him in the car, then led him up in the elevator, finally unmasking him in front of the glass door that had the firm's name stenciled on it.

He smiled. "I like it. It has a nice ring to it."

She took one hand and Ellie took the other, and they ushered him in, like Santa's elves, leading a boy on his first trip through Toyland. "This is great," he murmured over and over. "This is perfect." Ellie winked at Aurore. They had done it.

"Now a surprise," he said. He reached into the bag he had been carrying and pulled out a bottle of champagne. He launched the cork up to the ceiling, then filled three glasses.

"A toast," he said, lifting his glass. He turned to Ellie. "To a great partnership that's still going strong." Then he turned to Aurore. "And to a great partnership that's just beginning."

As the bubbly drink slid down Aurore's throat, Andrew's eyes never left hers. She shivered slightly, a sensation, she realized later, not unlike one she had experienced many years before, the first time an aloof young man had let her know he cared for her.

"To partnerships," Ellie said, breaking the tension. "And," she added with a giggle, "may they be very profitable!"

Gallagher's was a sort of demilitarized zone, halfway between the courts and the press club. It might not have survived except that Joe Gallagher was willing to stay open longer than anyone else. And so at a certain time of night, there was nowhere else to go.

Aurore had never hung out in bars before. But now, when Andrew went home to Ellie, she went home to Gallagher's. There she'd nurse a beer and a hamburger for a while. And sometimes, if she got lucky, she'd find herself a client.

One autumn night, when she was feeling lonely, a rumpled-looking man took over the stool next to her.

"Good evening," he said.

"Hello."

"Joe said I ought to talk to you."

"Oh, really?" Some nights Joe seemed to send every semi-desperate man her way.

"I need a lawyer."

"Well, then maybe I can help you."

"My wife and I are getting a divorce. And she's about to screw me."

"I'm really not a divorce lawyer. . . ."

"Yeah, and I really can't afford one either."

Aurore smiled. Joe had a knack for sending her the real gems. But a client was a client. "Tell me a little about yourself."

He signaled the bartender to bring him a beer. "My name is Jerry Pieczenik. I'm a reporter for *The Daily Standard*. My wife is going to make me pay. . . ."

He babbled on as if she were the bartender. But she heard nothing beyond the newspaper's name. An idea took hold, but this was not the place to pursue it.

She reached into her purse. "Here's my card. Come see me tomorrow. We can talk about it then."

He checked the address. "What time?"

"About two?"

"I'll see you then."

Twelve hours later, with a clearer head, and by the light of day, she regarded Jerry Pieczenik. He was not exactly what Amanda would describe as a classy-looking human being. His hands were stuffed in his jacket pockets, his hair was mussed by the wind, and a toothpick was lodged nonchalantly between his teeth.

But that suited Aurore just fine. She wanted someone whose loyalty she could earn, and who would place it above loyalty to any other person—or institution.

She did not tell Andrew about her appointment. He would wonder why she wanted to take on a divorce case. He would be annoyed that she was going to do the work for nothing. But mostly she was afraid he would disapprove if he knew the way her mind was whirling.

It was clear that Jerry Pieczenik was a desperate man. He was supporting two women, one who wanted to marry him, one who wanted to bleed him dry. The case didn't look very promising—except for a vague suspicion he had that his wife was carrying on a secret affair of her own.

"So, we'll tail her," Aurore announced.

"But I can't afford detectives," he protested.

She laughed. "Who said anything about detectives? We're talking about me."

"But I'm broke!"

She shook her head. "Here's the deal. I don't want your money. But I do want to know what's happening at *The Daily Standard*. Don't ask why, just accept it. If I represent you —and if I succeed in getting your alimony payments lowered—will you agree to meet with me from time to time and tell me what's going on there?"

Pieczenik looked puzzled, but didn't argue. "Sure. Why not?" They sealed their agreement with a handshake.

It took Aurore two months, but she finally caught Dorothy Pieczenik at her game—late-afternoon trysts in a suite at the Wardman Towers. Dorothy was careful, but not careful enough. And when she tried to press her case, the judge was unimpressed. Aurore's own photographs of the lovers, strolling hand in hand through Rock Creek Park, were grainy but clear enough. Jerry was still going to have to pay for his freedom, but the price would not be as high as he had feared.

That night, the two of them celebrated at Gallagher's.

"I still can't believe that we won, Aurore. Or that you're not going to soak me."

"Don't worry," she said, "I'll get my payment." She downed the last sip of her drink, then contemplated her empty glass. "I don't know how long it will take, Jerry. But I do intend to collect."

Aurore and Andrew would always look back fondly on their first years together. They'd laugh, remembering their arguments over which bill they could ignore—the one for the phone or the one for the electricity. Or the time they had to let their secretary go—and how Aurore had played her part. The days when a night on the town meant a big vat of spaghetti and a bottle of wine at Aurore's.

But those days didn't last long. Andrew began making his reputation as a trial lawyer—his low-key, country-boy style put jury after jury in his pocket. Then his contacts from the federal courthouse started to pay off, just as Aurore had known they would. The network produced new clients, small-business men mostly, who had a case to make before Congress or an agency and couldn't afford the hourly rates of Covington & Burling.

Aurore took some of those clients, and after her first nervous weeks walking the halls of Capitol Hill, she began to relax a little. No one there seemed to recognize her or her name. But, after all, five years had passed. The Korean War was over, the mood of the country was changing. The Senate had finally censured McCarthy.

Still, the wound remained. Aurore still felt as if she were a nonperson, that the young woman she had been that summer in 1949 had disappeared, along with all of her hope and optimism. A new woman was left in her place, one who was cynical and suspicious, a woman who was forever looking over her shoulder. A woman who had come to expect the worst.

There was that other person, that nameless, faceless person who had brought her to Eddie Feigan's attention. As long as he or she was still out there, she couldn't feel completely safe.

One balmy summer night, Andrew offered to drive her home. They had both found homes in Arlington. For the Cronins, the price had been right. As for Aurore, she felt safer on the other side of the Potomac, away from the people and the neighborhoods of her past.

"Are you in a hurry tonight?" Andrew asked as they headed up the George Washington Parkway. When she shook her head, he pulled off at Theodore Roosevelt Island. He parked the car, climbed out, and took a seat on the hood.

"We don't have many summer nights like this, do we?" he said. There was none of the usual stickiness, just a gentle breeze that whispered down the river, caressing their faces and bare arms.

"No, we don't." She climbed up beside him. The metal was slippery, slightly hot to the touch.

"I ran into Tommy Brown today."

So that was why he wanted to talk. Tom Brown was his archrival in law school. "What's he doing now?" She tried to keep her voice light.

"He's still with that big firm in Richmond. They made him a partner last year."

She drew a circle in the grime on the hood. "Are you sorry you came here with me?"

He looked away from her, up the muddy river to where the spires of Georgetown University could be seen above the trees. "Ellie misses Ewing. She misses her folks and her brothers and sisters. Course, if we could just have a baby, I think she'd be happier."

Aurore hesitated, then said quietly, "I didn't ask about Ellie. I asked about you."

He looked at her then, and smiled his silly, half-cocked grin. He took hold of a hank of her hair, giving it an affectionate tug, as if it were a pigtail about to meet an inkwell. But then his faced turned serious, and his hand slid down and gave her hand a squeeze. "No, I don't regret it. Tom Brown may have all the money, but we both know you and I have all the fun."

Fun, she thought. Yes, they did have fun. Fun, but nothing more. Perhaps she should be touched. Touched that even now, knowing what he had given up, he would still come with her again.

"You know," he said, "I worry about you."

"You do?"

He nodded.

"Why?"

He was silent for a moment. "I worry that you're lonely, that you cut yourself off from other people. . . . I wonder why you never think about getting married."

Her heart sank. Didn't he know?

"I haven't met anyone I'd want to marry." It was a lie, of course. There was a man who was dead and a man who was alive. And she no longer knew which caused her more pain. Her throat was tight. "But I do okay. I have my work and I have my friends. I don't need a ring around my finger."

He looked at her again, feeling hurt and confused. It hadn't come out the way he had meant it, but then he wasn't sure what he had wanted to say. Just that he was concerned about her. Just that he cared about her. But how could he tell her that? Aurore was his partner. And he had a wife.

"I guess I'd better be getting you home." He hopped down off the hood, then turned to help her. He reached out for her waist, her hands touched his shoulders. Funny, but he'd never noticed how tiny her waist was, how light she could be. When he thought of Aurore, he thought of her strength, her intelligence. He never thought of words like fragile. Soft. Tender. Not until this very moment.

He set her down, her face a few inches from his own. How could he read those eyes, so green and intense, half crying, half daring him? And was he prepared to give what they wanted?

He spoke, but the words were hard to put together. "Please don't misunderstand, Aurore. It's just that I care about you very much. I want you to be happy."

"I understand, Andrew." It was not much, but it was something. A very small something.

Reluctantly, she returned to the car, and climbed in beside him. For a moment she thought he had misplaced the key. But then he produced it, and the sedan sprang to life.

He waited for one car to pass, and then another. Perhaps he had changed his mind about leaving. But then he pulled into traffic and drove them home: to a wife with a hot dinner waiting, and to a solitary glass of wine on a lonely summer night.

Thirty

The telegram came on a Monday, from a law firm in Mississippi.

REGRET TO INFORM YOU THAT YOUR FATHER HAS DIED STOP PLEASE CONTACT EARLIEST STOP (SIGNED) JAMES COWPET.

They wanted decisions. Decisions on the funeral. Decisions on his house. Decisions about a man she hadn't heard from in more than twenty years.

Andrew looked over her shoulder. "Why didn't you ever tell me about your father?"

"I didn't know he was alive."

"Would you like me to go with you?"

She was touched by his offer. But no, this was a trip she had to make alone.

Another death to grieve. Ah, but this one was so different from the others. Robert and Stephen were real to her, but her father was little more than a dim memory. That part of her life was over long ago.

Yet Emory Callahan *was* her father. And even after all these years, that still meant something.

James Cowpet met her plane at the small airfield in Jackson. He was a few years younger than she was, tall and earnest-looking.

He led her to his car. "I appreciate your coming so quickly."

"I'd like to get it over with."

"I understand." He climbed in on the other side of the car. "Would you like to go straight to the funeral home? The interment is set for three."

"That would be fine."

She gazed out the window as he started up the car. She

thought her parents had taken her to Jackson when she was about four. But all she could remember was a never-ending road through acres and acres of fields, not the growing city she had just flown over, nor the busy highway that stretched north to Homer.

She turned back to the lawyer. "There's one thing I'm curious about. How did you know where to find me?"

"Mrs. Brown—Matty Brown—told your father, several years ago, I believe. After that, he drew up a will and left us with instructions on what to do if he died."

"His fortunes must have improved since the last time I saw him."

"Oh, he's done all right. Of course, the money from Judge McNeil helped."

She looked at him sharply. "What are you talking about?"

The young lawyer stared back at the road, swallowing hard. "I didn't intend for it to come out this way."

"I think you'd better explain, Mr. Cowpet."

He glanced at her quickly. "I guess so." His hands clenched the wheel more tightly. "From about the time you were twelve or thirteen up until his death, your uncle was sending your father a check every month."

"But why?"

"To keep Emory out of your life. I guess he was worried about the competition."

"Over me?"

Cowpet nodded. "He made your father believe that it was better for you if he stayed away. And he said he'd pay him if he did.

"Still, the arrangement bothered your father. He accepted the checks, but saved them up so he could buy back your old home. He kept it up so that you could have it one day."

It was too much to take in all at once. "What about his drinking?"

"Did he have a problem? I didn't know about it. Maybe my father did. He used to handle your father's affairs. No, as far as I know, your father lived a pretty quiet life. He was the kind of man who paid his bills on time and kept to himself."

He hesitated. "After your father became ill, we urged him to try to contact you. But he wouldn't hear of it. He said too much time had passed."

If the attorney said anything more, Aurore didn't hear him. The scenery whizzed by, houses and fields and stores, carrying her back, not just to Homer, but to another time and place. The summer she was twelve. The last time she had seen her father.

So Stephen had paid him off. All these years he had kept her from knowing her father. Did he think that was what she had wanted? Was he right? Or did Stephen have his own reasons?

Suddenly the pieces fit together. The letters to her father that never were answered. The attention Stephen had lavished on her, the lessons and schools and presents. And most of all, an inheritance as big as his daughter's. She was Stephen's daughter—he had made sure of that.

But she had lost something, too. She had never known her father. The man she remembered was a drunk who wouldn't take care of her. But it was a different man who had died. A man who was quiet and temperate, who had taken his brother-in-law's bounty, but had saved it all for her.

Why had he stayed away? Did he think that would make her love him more? And Stephen—she had idolized him for as long as she could remember. *He* had become her father. But he had also kept her from knowing the truth, even when she was no longer a child. Had he been that unsure of her love?

And what about herself? Aurore wondered. She could have looked for her father; there had been nothing to stop her.

But the truth was, she had never wanted to.

"We're here," the lawyer said.

She had always dreaded funerals and funeral homes: black-suited men; hushed, strangely perfumed rooms; waxy-faced bodies laid out in white-pillowed coffins. She preferred to remember friends and relatives as she had seen them last, in the warmth and fullness of life.

She had planned to ask that her father's casket be closed, so that her memories could be sealed up neatly with him. But the father she remembered was a troubled young veteran, not the quiet man who had saved so carefully. Now she wanted to see him.

"If I could be left alone for a few minutes."

"Of course," the undertaker replied.

She approached the bier slowly, steadying herself for the painful reunion. Yes, it was as if her father were sleeping. She remembered how she would find him sometimes, long after the sun had come up, flopped in his bed with his clothes on, while outside the cows complained about their tender udders.

She wondered if she would have recognized this man. The dark brown hair had turned to gray, his bushy mustache was shorn. He looked frail, a wisp of the man she remembered. It was probably the disease, the disease that had lingered. She could have helped him; she could have made it easier. If only he had let her. If only she had tried.

"Oh, Daddy," she whispered, "why did we do this to each other?"

It was then that she started to cry. They were tears she had never expected to shed on this trip, tears for a man she had never been allowed to know, and the daughter she had never been. Tears for a man whom she must have hurt, unwittingly but still cruelly, for all the years of her life.

The unflappable Washington lawyer metamorphosed into a five-year-old girl. She touched her fingers to her lips and then to his cold cheek. And then she cried for as long as they would let her.

She had a vague memory of the little church, and the spot where her mother was buried. A granite marker had been added, with both of her parents' names, waiting only for the year of her father's death to be chiseled in.

Now at last her parents would be together again. How different her life would have been if they had never been parted! She would have been a country girl, she thought with a twisted smile. Would she have gone to college? Or would she have married some local boy and raised a family by now?

Would that have made her happier?

The minister cleared his throat noisily, then began a final prayer. It was over, done with. One part of her felt limp with relief; the other, not ready to let go, wanted to cling to whatever was left of her family. But there was nothing.

The minister mumbled something to her, and she turned to walk away. James Cowpet took her elbow to steady her, then pointed her in the direction of his car.

As they approached the fence that defined the cemetery, Aurore noticed a beat-up Chevy, parked away from the other cars. A tall black woman got out and stood with the door open, watching her. There was something familiar about her, and Aurore couldn't help but stare back.

As she drew closer, the woman called out, "Katie!"

It could only be one person. "Lucy?"

The woman nodded.

"I can't believe it," she cried as she ran to give Matty's daughter a hug.

If there was a family in Homer that she belonged to, it was the Browns. Even now, when their situations were so different, she still felt close to Lucy, and still remembered the games they'd played and the dolls they had shared.

And Matty? Well, Matty, she realized now, had made motherhood easier for Charlotte. If a high-spirited five-year-old girl had needed an occasional whupping, it was Matty who delivered it, letting Charlotte dry the tears when her daughter was ready to be good again.

Now, as Lucy led her into Matty's darkened room, Aurore remembered what she had told her on the ride from the cemetery: "Mamma has good days and bad. She'll drift in and out of sleep. . . . I'm not sure whether she'll remember you."

"Mamma," Lucy called softly, touching Matty on the arm. "We have a visitor today."

The plump old woman shifted in her seat, trying to straighten up. "Who issit?"

Lucy waved Aurore to come closer. "It's an old friend of ours. It's Katie, Charlotte Callahan's daughter."

Aurore knelt beside her. "Hello, Matty."

The old woman's face lit up. "My baby!"

"Yes," Aurore said as she took the old wrinkled hands, then kissed them. "Your baby has come home again."

They talked for several hours, about her father and Amanda, about Robert and her baby. After a while, Matty's eyes closed and Lucy signaled that they ought to let her rest. Aurore kissed the old woman's warm cheek softly, then turned and followed Lucy out of the room.

It was growing dark now. Lucy paused to turn on a light, casting a warm glow across the living room. It was neat, but furnished simply, probably with some pieces handed down from the white families Lucy used to work for. Outside, her son, Eric, was finishing mowing the lawn. He was tall and thin, rather like a wild weed that had sprung up along the highway. There was no sign of a father, and Aurore didn't ask why.

"You're gonna stay for supper, of course?"

"I don't want you to go to any trouble."

Lucy silenced her with a wave of her hand. "Don't be silly. We gotta eat, too, don't we?" She opened the refrigerator and studied her choices.

"I'm sorry you didn't come inside the cemetery."

Lucy snorted. "Don't let your Mr. Cowpet hear you say that. The good white folks of Homer have decided that they don't want none of us colored folks hanging around their church."

"It didn't used to be that way, did it?"

"No, but times have changed. We're makin' 'em real nervous. . . . You heard about the bus boycott in Montgomery?"

Aurore nodded.

"The colored people are starting to get angry. And they're going to get a whole lot angrier before it's over." Lucy looked out the window. "Like my Eric. He's a bright boy, he works hard. Where does it say in God's law that he can't go to Ole Miss 'cause he's a different color than the white boys?"

Aurore couldn't answer that.

Lucy looked up. "You could help us, you know. We're going to be needing more help in Washington."

Getting involved. Sticking her neck out. Was she ready

for that? Even though Lucy was her friend, the thought made her feel uncomfortable. Yet she heard herself say, "I'll think about it." A moment passed and then she added, "I'll see what I can do."

He listened to the two women, and Eric felt uneasy. He had never seen a white person in his home before, much less passing platters around his dinner table.

Just because this woman was from up north, just because they had been friends, was that supposed to make a difference? Well, he had friends, too. Friends he'd made out back while his mother was inside cleaning their parents' houses. Friends who didn't want him in their schools or looking at their girlfriends. Friends who were always happy to remind him which part of town he belonged in.

So he listened to the women, but said nothing. He knew this Miss Callahan wouldn't be back. She'd go home to her nice house up north and think about it again. And maybe then she'd know there was nothing in this town that she wanted badly enough to come back for.

They talked long into the night, and promised each other to try harder to keep in touch. And when the cab arrived to take her back to her hotel, Aurore gave Lucy a long hug.

"Take care of yourself," she whispered.

"You, too, Katie."

She settled in for the long ride back, and closed her eyes wearily. It had been a long draining day. It felt as if a part of her had died, and yet, a part of her had been reborn, too.

But she still wasn't finished.

In the morning, James Cowpet came by to take her to her father's house. The house she was born in. Her house now.

It hadn't changed much from the way she remembered it. The sycamore trees were taller and the yard seemed smaller. The white shingles had been repainted a pale green, the shutters and trim no longer looked weather-beaten.

The lawyer found the key, and opened the glass-paned back door. The kitchen was completely different; the antiquated appliances had been replaced, and green-and-white linoleum covered the floor. She opened a few drawers and cupboards to satisfy her curiosity. No, her mother had brought no china or silver to the marriage, and her father certainly wouldn't have bothered to acquire them on his own.

They climbed the stairs to the second floor. Her old room was empty now. It did not surprise her, but still it was a shame. She might have saved the rocker, or the old rag rug if it was still in one piece.

She walked down the hall to her father's room. She opened the door, then stood for a moment, stunned. It was as if nothing had changed since the day she had left.

She walked over to the dresser and picked up the photograph of the young soldier and his bride, so much in love and so proud of themselves. How she had longed to see that picture her first months in Washington! Beside it was a portrait she had forgotten, of an infant girl in a frilly white dress. Her father had kept it all these years.

She tucked the pictures under her arm and met Cowpet on the landing. "I've got the things that I want."

"Are you sure?"

She nodded. "You can give my father's clothes to the church or a charity. Then I'd like you to auction off the rest."

She thought that would be the end of it. She flew back to Washington, unpacked her bag, and went back to work. But the ghosts of Homer followed her.

It was a busy time for Cronin and Associates. They were getting more clients than they could take care of; they were ready to expand.

As always, Aurore took charge of the real estate. But they had also decided to hire six associates, and it was her job to find them.

She was glad to have a project to delve into, yet she found it didn't help. Her mind wandered, her appetite died. She lay awake most of the night.

"What is it with you?" Andrew asked one day when he found her staring out the window. "You haven't been the same since you got back from Mississippi. Do you need some time off?"

She shook her head.

"Then get back in gear. I can't carry us alone much longer."

She would be thirty-eight next year. She had achieved a measure of financial security. She doubted that she would ever marry, but that didn't bother her. She had her work, she had her friends, she and Andrew had the firm.

And she still had the emptiness.

Until she had returned to Homer, she hadn't realized how strong the ties of blood could be. Seeing her father again had stirred something inside her, some powerful emotion that neither time nor Stephen McNeil's money could suppress.

But her father and mother were gone now, her little brother, too. An aunt and cousin should count for something, but they didn't, not anymore.

She needed someone to love, but there was no one to love, no one who needed her.

Sure, Andrew needed her, but for what? He had a wonderful wife, and he could always find another bright lawyer to manage his law firm.

But there was someone. Someone else to whom she was tied. It was a crazy idea, and it could backfire. But the more she thought about it, she knew she had to do it.

She entered Andrew's office and shut the door behind her. "There's something I need to talk to you about."

He put aside a brief. "What is it?"

She looked down at her hands. "There is no easy way to tell you this . . . something I never told you before." She hesitated for a moment. "I have a daughter."

She watched his eyes widen and waited for the words to sink in. Then she spoke, in a voice that was soft and yet strong, so there could be no mistaking that she meant what she said. "I want to see her, Andrew. I don't care how long, or how much money it takes. But I have to find out where she is."

Thirty-One

Aurore licked her fingers and peeled off a bill. "One hundred for you, one hundred for me. Two hundred for you, two hundred for me. . . ."

They giggled like children who had just landed on Boardwalk. But the money was real, their cut of a big liability suit they'd taken a gamble on—and won.

"I still can't believe you got it in cash."

"Enjoy it while you can. I promised the bank I'd bring most of it back tonight."

"But what if you get robbed on the elevator?"

She shrugged. "Then I guess Ellie won't get her three bedrooms and three baths, will she? Eight hundred for you . . . eight hundred for me. . . ."

"And you won't get your farmland out in God knows where."

"Fairfax County, Andrew. And someday you'll be sorry you didn't buy a couple of acres, too."

He laughed. Aurore and her secrets. It was one of the things about her that he liked the most. Her personal defenses were as well practiced over the years as her legal ones. But now and then, she showed that other side of herself: the part that was moved by her heart instead of her head. The one that was willing to take risks.

Secrets. When she wasn't snatching up real estate, she was meeting with that newspaper reporter. She never told him what that was all about and he never asked. She would tell him when she was ready. She had told him about McCarthy, hadn't she? And when she needed to, she had told him about her child.

He knew where she could find her daughter now. He had

hired Mike Packard, and as always, Mike had been discreet. Once Dr. Chapman's old nurse had pointed him in the right direction, it was amazing what a little cash could accomplish around a Virginia courthouse.

That was four days ago, but he still hadn't told her. Why? He wasn't sure. Except that he already had to live with Ellie's obsession, and he didn't want it to become Aurore's, too.

They had read the books and talked to the doctors. One month he and Ellie would make love every night, the next one, only a couple of times. Still nothing worked. They swore they didn't blame each other, but down deep they knew they did. And it wore them away, little by little, day by day. Sex became programmed, mechanical, something you did because you were supposed to, not because you wanted to. It lacked all the joy he had known when they were newlyweds.

He had always been able to count on Ellie then. Never complaining, never changing. But now she was turning into a stranger, and he knew it was all his fault.

He held the key for Aurore now, too. It was in a manila envelope in the middle drawer on the left side of his desk. It could stay there forever. He could tell her he had struck out.

But she had trusted him. She had believed in him. Just the way Ellie had. He couldn't deprive her, too.

"Fifteen hundred for you, fifteen hundred for me. Sixteen hundred for you. Sixteen hun . . ."

"Stop, Aurore."

"What?"

"Please . . . stop." He opened the drawer and pulled out the envelope. "I should've told you about this on Monday."

She put down the pile of bills. "What is it?"

"I've got the information you wanted."

"About my daughter?"

He nodded.

She grasped the arms of the chair and took a deep breath. Perhaps, he thought, she really wasn't ready.

"So tell me," she demanded.

"Are you sure you want to know?"

She blinked. "There's nothing wrong with her, is there?"

"Oh, no," he said quickly. "I'm only thinking of you, Aurore. You put this all to rest a long time ago. Do you really want to open it up again?"

She nodded. "I'm sure."

He fumbled with the metal clasp, then remembered he had sealed the flap shut. He pulled open his top drawer and riffled through it for his letter opener.

"Andrew, rip the goddamn thing open."

"All right." He tore open the corner, then pulled out the sheaf of papers. It took him a moment to find the right one.

"Her name is Martha Beauchamp. She lives in Gloucester, Virginia. Her parents"—he stumbled on the word—"her parents' names are Acel and Ruth. They're in their fifties. Her father is a farmer."

"Any brothers, sisters?" she asked.

"She is their only child."

Aurore said nothing for a moment. Now she knew. Her daughter, a vague sort of notion that had drifted away in a cloud of anesthesia one morning fourteen years ago, was real. She was alive. She had an address.

She also had a mother and father.

But Aurore had something more now, too. She had flesh and blood.

"Is there anything else?"

He shook his head. "Not much. Of course, Mike could probably find out more—if he had the time and money."

"Never mind, it's not necessary."

Thank God, he thought. Now they could get back to business.

"Actually, there is one more thing I need to know."

"What's that?"

She smiled. "Tell me how to get to Gloucester."

No, she had told him, she didn't know what she was going to do or what she was going to say once she got there. Of course, she wasn't going to just march up to the Beauchamps' door: "Hello, you don't know who I am, but . . ."

The truth was she didn't know what to expect. She was excited and yet terrified. Afraid of what she might find and yet knowing she couldn't go back to Washington without finding it.

But how was she going to do it?

She asked herself the question once again as she waited in her car, parked along the side of State Road 615. The kids go to school by bus, the real estate agent had told her when she had asked. "It usually starts its run around eight."

The Beauchamps' house was nothing fancy, but clearly well cared for. The lawn was freshly mown and dotted with new daffodils. In the backyard was an old swingset and a birdhouse on a tall pole. There was a boat by the barn, and all around it stretched chocolate-brown fields.

The wait seemed like an eternity. Perhaps there was no school today. Perhaps it was a local holiday, a crab festival or something. Maybe Martha had missed the bus. Maybe she was sick.

Aurore ticked off the alternatives and then . . . down the road, just ahead of a cloud of dust, lumbered a big yellow bus. The front door of the house swung open. A gray-haired woman handed a girl a lunch box. She had red hair, pulled back in a ponytail. She was wearing a green dress. She ran down her driveway. The bus stopped. The front door opened. She disappeared inside.

And that was all.

The bus passed her car. Aurore checked every window, hoping for one more glimpse of her daughter. But the faces whizzed by, and the bus was gone.

She waited a moment before starting her car, not knowing what to do next. She felt guilty, almost unclean, as if she were some sort of voyeur, or worse—a molester stalking her prey.

But she had seen her daughter. A red-haired girl with a spring to her step, a girl who looked eager to go to school.

A girl with Charlotte Callahan's flaming hair and perhaps her own love of learning. And Robert's, too.

But did she love English more than math, or history more than science? Did she swoon for Elvis Presley, or did she prefer Mozart? Did she have a favorite boyfriend or did she still think boys were silly? Did she like chocolate cake and ice cream and pretzels and popcorn and . . .

Aurore turned the key in the ignition. The questions would all have to wait. Just like she was going to have to.

Andrew settled into his favorite armchair, took a sip of brandy, and pulled out the letter one more time. He was puzzled that she had written instead of phoning. But then, it was probably easier for Aurore to say it this way.

I have not been able to reestablish contact with my daughter yet. I'm not sure why I thought it would be easy, but I'm still determined to try. I've decided that the only way I can do it is to become a member of this community, not just a visitor. By that I mean to live here for a while. Then in time, I will meet Martha. It may be at church or a school function, but I WILL meet her.

I'm not sure how long I'll be gone. I feel guilty about the load this will put on your shoulders, but I know you will understand. Whatever formula you want to work out for dividing the firm's profits this year will be fine with me. In the meantime, wish me luck. . . .

He folded up the letter angrily. He should have never helped her find her daughter. It had turned Aurore into a kind of crazy woman. And what would her daughter think when Aurore suddenly turned up in her life?

But no, that wasn't why he was angry. Aurore had been gone only two weeks, and already his work was in a state of chaos. He needed her to set priorities. He needed her to screen clients. The pile of applications for summer work was growing deeper every day and he needed her to figure out whom they should hire.

But that was just Aurore's efficiency. He could replace that if he had to. But he couldn't replace her.

He missed the way she turned up her nose when he pulled out a cigar. He missed the laughter in her eyes and voice when she started to tell him the latest joke from the U.S. Attorney's office. He missed the way she'd stop him before he left the office so that she could straighten his tie. He missed the fearless way she'd tell him that his brief was full of bullshit.

But how could he convince her to return? He could stomp his foot and say that she was violating their partnership agreement. But no, he didn't want her that way. He only wanted her if she wanted him. She had a daughter now, and there was nothing he could offer that came close to that.

"You look tired."

Ellie stood in the doorway, silhouetted by the light of the entranceway beyond.

He rubbed his eyes. "I guess I am."

"Why don't you come to bed then?"

He looked up at her, more closely this time. She was wearing the blue peignoir he had bought for her birthday last year, the fabric that had seemed so inviting when the clerk at Garfinckel's had persuaded him to stroke it. Underneath she'd be wearing the nightgown, the one with the tiny little straps that showed her breasts so nicely.

Her eyes were alive and her lips parted in expectation. It could only mean one thing: Dr. Greenberger had told her to do it tonight.

Oh, not tonight, Ellie, he pleaded silently. *Can't you see it won't make any difference?*

"Andrew?"

But he couldn't tell her that. And so he quaffed the last of his drink, and turned off the light. Then he took her hand and followed her up the stairs.

She climbed into bed and he started to undress. He did it slowly, deliberately, one shoe after another, one sock at a time. He put his shirt in the hamper and hung his suit up. He checked to make sure the pleats of his pants were straight.

It was too much to hope that Ellie would fall asleep, but maybe she would grow weary. God knows, he felt that way. He went to the bathroom, brushed his teeth, and washed his face. Then he sat on the toilet, his head in his hands.

"Andrew?"

"Coming."

He trudged back to the bedroom. She looked tiny in their

double bed, her arms like two thin white sticks lying on top of the beige blanket. He turned off the light, and traced the old familiar path to her side.

But as he climbed in beside her he heard a laugh, a strange laugh, a laugh that was low and sultry. Ellie's laugh was high-pitched. Or at least it seemed that way to him. She tended to giggle up into her nose, like she was still a schoolgirl.

No, this laugh was different, and it ricocheted around in his brain.

"Eight hundred for you, eight hundred for me. Nine hundred for you, nine hundred for me . . ."

"Andrew, did you hear the one about the three lawyers who went to heaven. And the first lawyer . . ."

He felt his penis growing harder, in spite of himself. And as it did, he grew angrier, the rage and the hurt building up inside. He was angry with himself, and he was angry at her, the woman with the low laugh that was driving him mad. There was only one way to make it stop.

He rolled over on top of the woman beside him, then brusquely spread her legs apart. He wasted no time, but plunged inside her, over and over and over again. Deeper and deeper, trying to obliterate whatever it was that was haunting him. And each time he smothered his face into her breasts, he pleaded with her: "Don't leave me, don't leave me, don't leave me."

The release came, an explosion deep inside of her. It came sooner than he was used to lately, but it drained him more. He rolled over to his side of the bed, spent and sweaty, his eyes glazed over by the mists of dreams.

And then he heard a voice.

"What got into you tonight, Andrew?"

It was not the voice he had expected. And now he realized the difference. Her hair grazed her chin, not her shoulders. The hips were wider, the breasts plumper. His toes stretched down a foot beyond hers. She smelled of popcorn, not Fabergé.

He knew what he had done. On his wedding night, he had vowed that Ellie would always be the only one who was in his heart and his head. He wasn't like all the other guys in

his outfit, who knew a woman in every port that they could
pop. He was better than that.

But now he knew. He was a man, a man just like all the
other men he knew. He knew the words he could say that
would reassure Ellie, that would make her believe she had
driven him wild. He would take her in his arms, and cuddle
her and kiss her and stroke her until she slept.

But now he knew. He could make love to one woman
while he thought about another. And, for tonight at least, it
didn't bother him a bit.

Thirty-Two

As the afternoons in Gloucester grew longer and hotter, Aurore liked to stop at Siler's Drugstore for a root beer float or
a shake. Back in Washington, the drugstores were ripping
out their soda fountains, but Mr. Siler kept his red-topped
stools and fountain equipment shiny bright. He was usually
good for a tale or two about the town and its residents. And
most days, Aurore had discovered, the kids dropped in after
school.

The door swung open behind her, and a gaggle of teenagers
entered. 3:10. Just like clockwork. She didn't bother to turn
her head. She'd been coming here for a week and a half, but
still there was no sign of Martha.

Aurore stirred her chocolate soda with her straw as the
kids rattled off their orders.

"A cherry Coke for me."

"A banana split . . . With two spoons."

"A lemonade."

"Small or large?"

"Large, I guess."

There was a pause. "And how 'bout you, Martha?"

Time seemed to stop.

"A lemon Coke, please."

Aurore sipped slowly on her straw, regaining her breath. She didn't dare look; she didn't dare move.

The voice was soft, but there was a sureness to it. A trace of a southern accent, and a lilt that made you smile.

Aurore lifted her head and glanced in the mirror that covered the wall behind the fountain. Yes, it was the redheaded girl. It had to be Martha Beauchamp.

She wanted to take a longer look, but was afraid to be caught staring. She didn't want to frighten Martha. So she contented herself with watching in the mirror as she sipped the last of her soda.

The kids were huddled down at one end of the counter. Aurore could only glimpse Martha's back. She was wearing what Aurore supposed was the "girl's uniform" at Gloucester High School this year: tennis shoes and bobby socks, a plaid skirt, a cardigan buttoned down her back, a scarf around her neck. The sweater was forest green, a good shade for Martha's coloring.

"Here you go, kids." Mr. Siler spread their orders out along the counter and they took their seats behind them. The lemon Coke was last. He set it down next to Aurore.

"Thank you," Martha said.

Aurore's head felt light, her limbs grew weak. She had waited so long for this moment that she was terrified that it would slip away, that she would ruin it.

"Would you like anything else, Miss Callahan?"

"A . . . a cup of coffee, I think. Thank you."

As she pushed away her dirty glass, Aurore realized Martha was looking at her. At first the girl didn't say anything. Her parents had probably warned her about talking to strangers.

But then she said, "Hi." Her voice was tentative, shy.

"Hi." Aurore felt shy, too.

"You must be new around here."

Aurore nodded.

"My name's Martha Beauchamp."

"I'm Aurore Callahan."

"Pleased to meet you."

The name seemed to have no effect on Martha, but then there was no reason it should. In fact, for what seemed like an interminable moment, she turned back to her friends and rejoined their conversation: "No, Frankie, you've got it all wrong. Alice's older sister is going to the track meet with Ralph."

Then she took a sip of her drink and returned to Aurore.

"What brings you to Gloucester?"

Aurore's heart skipped a beat. No, now wasn't the time. "I—I—I wanted to get away from the big city," she said slowly. "I'm thinking of moving down here and practicing law."

"You're a lawyer?"

Aurore nodded.

"Where are you from?"

"Washington."

"Oh," Martha squealed with delight, "that's one place I've always wanted to visit."

Aurore hesitated. "Maybe you will someday."

"What's it like up there?" Martha's eyes were gleaming.

"Well, compared to Gloucester there are a lot of cars and a lot of people. Most of the people who work, work very hard. But there are plays and concerts and nice stores, too."

One of the boys tapped Martha on the back. "We're going over to Julie's now. You coming?"

Aurore held her breath. Martha seemed to waver for a moment. But then she said, "No. I'll see you later."

She had won—at least temporarily.

Martha turned back to her. "This question may seem silly."

"Go ahead."

"Have you ever met the president?"

Aurore smiled. "No, but I saw him once. It was a big dinner, with hundreds of people. He was at the head table."

"Oh." Martha took a long draw on her straw.

At last Aurore felt free enough to study her daughter more closely. She did not see herself in this young girl, but she saw her mother again, the hair and her eyes, and—with a pang in heart—she realized she saw Robert. Martha had his nose, long, but not as large, and the angles of his cheeks and jaw.

She could remember running her palm along that same jawline. The first time, the last time, she could remember it as clearly as if it were yesterday.

But then she stopped herself. This was today. She couldn't let this moment go adrift in a sea of memories.

"How about you? How do you like to spend your time?"

Martha shrugged. "Gee, I don't know."

"Do you like school?"

"Yes."

"What subjects do you like best?"

"I like history, and I like English a lot—the books, not the grammar."

"What about after school? What do you like to do then?"

"Well, in the fall and winter I'm busy with cheerleading."

"A cheerleader, that's great."

"It's just JV."

"Still, I'm sure almost all the girls want to be cheer-leaders."

"I guess you're right . . . And next year, I'm going to be secretary of my class. But this time of year, I'm mostly busy helping my parents around the farm."

"My parents." She said it matter-of-factly, without a trace of hostility. How far could she push? Aurore wondered. She stirred her coffee, then took a sip. She set her cup down. "I know a lot of teenagers who don't get on with their parents."

Martha said nothing for a moment. "Actually, I think I get along pretty well with mine. Oh, that's not to say we don't have our arguments, but they've been pretty good to me."

She hesitated. "They're older than most of my friends' parents. They waited a long time to have me—I'm adopted, you see. But because of that, I think they appreciate me more. I can tell they really love me. And, well, I love them, too."

There was nothing Aurore could say. She felt her throat go dry, she fiddled with her cup. And she waited too long.

"Well, I guess I'd better be going." Martha climbed off her stool. "I enjoyed talking with you, Miss Callahan."

Did she have to go already? Aurore tried to think of something, anything, that would make Martha stay. But their meeting had been perfect, and she didn't want to ruin it now. She didn't want to scare her daughter, and so she knew she couldn't push her.

"I enjoyed it, too . . . And please, call me Aurore."

"All right then. See ya' around." Martha turned and headed for the door.

"Good-bye"—Aurore's voice trailed away—"my dear."

She closed her eyes and tried to remember every word, every phrase, the sound of her daughter's voice, the color of her eyes and skin, the texture of her hair.

If she could have she would have folded it all up into a locket that she could wear close to her heart. But she couldn't. She had nothing as simple as a photo, or an offer of an address or phone number to keep in touch. She was afraid that if she opened her eyes, it would all be a dream, and she'd still be sitting at Siler's, waiting for Martha Beauchamp.

No, not Martha Beauchamp. She remembered now. Ann Marie Kaufmann. She had picked out the name while she had waited at Mildred's. Waited for Robert and waited for the child. A girl's name and a boy's name, added onto Kaufmann. No, that wasn't her last name, but it would be soon. As soon as the war was over. As soon as Robert came home.

"She's a nice girl, that Martha."

Aurore opened her eyes. Mr. Siler smiled as he picked up the dirty dishes and wiped down the counter with a wet rag.

"Smart as a whip, too."

"Oh?"

He nodded, and stopped wiping for a moment. "I remember when she won the sixth-grade spelling bee a few years back. Now you gotta understand, that's a big deal in this town. And there she was up on the stage, just a little slip of a girl, reeling off those words like she was some sort of human dictionary."

Aurore smiled. Yes, she acknowledged, she was proud. So this is what they call parental pride.

But that made her wonder. "What do the kids around here do when they finish high school?"

"Well," he said, turning over his rag, "I guess they do what kids everywhere do. Some of them get jobs, some of them get married, some of them go into the army."

"Do any of them go to college?"

"A few. The really bright ones."

"What about Martha? Do you think she will?"

He stopped and squinted, as if puzzled that she would ask. "Oh, she could do it, no doubt about that. I guess the only question is, whether her family will be able to afford it."

"I see," she murmured.

Another customer came in and Mr. Siler turned away to greet him. Aurore downed the last of her coffee, then paid her bill. There was no point in staying any longer.

She stepped outside. The clouds had rolled in and the late-afternoon humidity prickled her skin. Would it rain? Probably. Maybe even a thunderstorm. Still she turned away from her car, preferring to walk for a while.

It was over now. The moment she had been waiting for for weeks. For years, too, probably. And now that it was over, she felt a curious sense of disappointment.

Not in her daughter, certainly. Her daughter was beautiful. Her daughter was intelligent. Her daughter was polite and friendly. But most important, her daughter was happy—and obviously loved.

All of that should have pleased Aurore, and yet it didn't. The moment had played out differently in her dreams. Martha was neglected and Martha was deprived and Martha was so grateful that after all these years her real mother had returned to take her away from her miserable existence.

That was the way she had dreamed it, and that was why it had seemed so easy. But while Aurore desperately needed a daughter, Martha Beauchamp didn't need her. And up until this moment, that prospect had never occurred to her.

As she strolled on through Gloucester, she remembered another walk she had taken, when she was just a little younger than Martha. A summer day in 1932 when her father reappeared in her life. It was a long time ago, but she could still remember how confused, how frightened she had been. She was not sure what she was supposed to feel. Love? Hate?

Anger? It had taken her months to sort it out, months before she had stopped dreaming about him. Months before she had felt her life could go on as it had before.

What would Martha feel if she just reappeared like that? Did she ever wonder who her real parents were and why they had abandoned her? Could she possibly understand how it felt to be pregnant and alone?

Or, Aurore wondered, *would she judge me?*

If you loved me, you never would have given me up.

If you loved me, you'd stay out of my life now.

Aurore stopped. That was the painful truth of it.

She had reached the point where the sidewalk ended, so she turned around to go home. The wind blew up through the oak trees, beckoning the watermen home. They would come home from tending their crab traps, home to simple houses where people still played cards and read books, instead of watching the TV shows the stations in the big cities showed.

Andrew was right. She didn't belong in Gloucester. And she didn't belong in Martha Beauchamp's life.

Still, she thanked God she had had the chance to meet her, to know her, if only briefly. Now her dreams would be filled with the face of a real girl, a red-haired cheerleader in a little town in Virginia. And maybe someday, when Martha was no longer a child, she would be able to see her again.

But she longed to do something now. And as she walked on it occurred to her what that something could be.

In the morning she paid a visit to Willis Flood, the lawyer who had an office on Main Street. Yes, he agreed, it could be done. She would send the money, he would be the trustee, and a few years from now, Martha would never have to know why some stranger was willing to give her the money to go to college.

Before leaving town, Aurore stopped at Siler's for one more sundae. Then she drove out past the Beauchamps' farm one last time. As she did, she thought of another farmhouse, a house down in Mississippi. She thought of the man who had left it to her, and wished again that she had known him better.

For she understood now why she had started this quest.

She had not wanted to lose her daughter the way her father had lost her. To go for years without knowing her, without seeing her.

But most of all Aurore understood what her father must have learned: how it hurt to give every gift you could, except the gift that really mattered, the gift you most wanted to give.

The gift of a parent's love.

Thirty-Three

For the first time in five years, Aurore regarded their office from an outsider's point of view. Yes, it was time to be moving. And this time, those Shenandoah Valley scenes would have to come down. They needed something classier.

Where was the receptionist? What about the procedures? Had the office managed to go to hell in six weeks?

The door to Andrew's office was open. She could hear him dictating. She knocked lightly, then entered.

Andrew stopped in midsentence. "That will be all, Sherri."

The secretary smiled as she passed. "It's good to see you again, Aurore."

"It's good to see you, Sherri."

She shut the door as she left.

"Well," Andrew said, getting up from his desk, "shall we bring out our lawyers to handle our negotiations?"

"It won't be necessary. I'm coming back."

His face started to break into a smile. "What happened?"

She sat down in a chair.

"Well, I did meet my daughter. We had a very nice conversation. Big-city lawyer to teenager, that is. And I came to the conclusion that it would be better for her if I stayed out of her life right now."

"I see," he murmured.

She smiled. "You're being uncharacteristically restrained, Andrew. I think a loud 'I told you so' might be in order."

He shook his head. "You won't get it from me." He searched his desk for a file. "No, what matters is that you're back." He stood up. "And we've got a lot of work to do."

He took her by the arm and led her to the door. But he didn't open it. Instead, he turned and gazed down at her, his eyes wistful and yearning. "It just wasn't the same without you, Aurore."

"It feels good to be back."

He said nothing more, but took her in his arms and held her close for a moment. That was all—nothing more, nothing less. But it was enough for now. And for the first time in what seemed like a very long time, Aurore felt as if she had come home.

In the fall of 1960, they moved the firm closer to the White House, to a gleaming new building that was hungry for tenants. The time seemed ripe for expansion. Washington had been sleepwalking through the Eisenhower years and no matter who won the election, things were going to start happening again. Cronin and Associates was determined to be ready when they did.

They had already hired ten associates, and in a few years, some or all of them would have to be made partners. Andrew and Aurore knew they both dreaded that day. While it would be a signpost of their success, they would lose something, too. It would no longer be just the two of them.

As a result, they scouted their prospects carefully. They knew they couldn't begin to compete with Arnold & Porter or Wilmer, Cutler & Pickering for the cream of the Harvard graduating class. But they could still afford to be choosy. They offered a young attorney the chance to practice law, not just proofread briefs for a senior partner. They offered the chance to make an impact and—if the lawyer worked hard—the chance to make money.

They found Peter Mitchum at Duke. His class rank wasn't as high as some students Aurore had interviewed, but, she had discovered, that was because he had come down with hepatitis his first year. Ken Noble was from Virginia, Richard

Kalinsky from Georgetown. David Bauer, meanwhile, came over from the FCC, with plans to build a communications practice.

For the fifth opening, Aurore had some definite ideas.

"I want to hire a woman."

Andrew began to smile.

"Seriously, Andrew, there are a lot of good women out there—with credentials that are much better than mine were. But the Cravath Swains and the Arnold & Porters won't hire them—and if they do, it's just one notch above the typing pool."

He leaned across the desk, his lips forming a mocking grin. "I don't suppose you have anyone particular in mind?"

She smiled. "As a matter of fact, I do."

Her name was Jane van Rippen. Aurore had found out about her from the placement office at Harvard when she'd made a trip to Boston last month. Jane, it turned out, was ranked twentieth in her class. As of last week, she didn't have an offer.

Aurore invited Jane to come down to Washington for an interview. It was important for the chemistry between them to be right. Aurore was not about to give up her role as the firm's grande dame.

Jane was tiny with hair that a catty person might call "mousy brown." But behind her unassuming exterior she hid a formidable intellect. Aurore's instinct was to offer her a job on the spot. But she sought Andrew's opinion first, and he, too, agreed.

Over crab salad and wine at the Willard Hotel, Aurore spelled out their offer.

"That's very generous," Jane acknowledged. "But, if I may be blunt, who the hell has ever heard of your firm?"

Aurore smiled tartly. "If I may be equally blunt, outside of the placement office at Harvard, who the hell has ever heard of Jane van Rippen? Face it, how many big Wall Street firms already have their one woman partner? How long do you think it will take you to make that happen there?"

Jane took a bite of the salad, mulling her choices. Finally, she said, "There's one thing that's puzzled me, Aurore."

"What's that?"

"If you and Andrew Cronin are truly equal partners in this firm, how come his name is the only one that goes on the door?"

Aurore took her white linen napkin and carefully wiped her mouth. "There's a reason for that that I don't care to go into. That has always been the name of this firm and it always will be." She paused, then added, "If you're worried about getting your name on the door, then I suggest you find a job somewhere else. But if you sincerely want to practice law, I think you should come with us."

Jane smiled. "Actually, I was just thinking what a perfect name it was. Rather all-purpose, you might say."

"So will you accept our offer?"

Jane nodded, and Aurore extended her hand.

"Welcome aboard. I think you and I are going to have a lot of fun together."

That night she met Jerry Pieczenik at Gallagher's.

Over the years, it had become a ritual for them. Every three or four months. Drinks and dinner in the same booth.

Jerry's gossip had proved to be more useful than she had expected. The firm had more contact with reporters now, and it was helpful to know who was covering what, who was in, who was out. Aurore was never quite sure how she would use the information, but it made her feel more secure to have it. A phone call to the right reporter, a story that helped a client's cause. A tidbit dropped at a dinner party could turn into a call from someone who wanted a lawyer who "knew the town."

"What about Eddie Feigan?" she asked after a while.

"It always comes around to that, doesn't it?"

Aurore shrugged. "Well, he is the paper's most important columnist."

Jerry signaled for another round. "Actually, Eddie's talking about retiring at the end of this year."

Aurore froze. "Are you serious?"

"Now, would I lie to you?" Jerry waited as the waitress set down their drinks. "He's got this back injury that's been bothering him. Says it hurts when he types."

The martini burned her throat. It couldn't be true. Feigan couldn't retire yet, not before she'd had her chance to get back at him.

But she hadn't figured out how yet. She'd lie awake at night and try out different ideas. But nothing was right. Either she knew it wouldn't work—or, worse, that it wouldn't quench the fire that still burned inside her.

Sometimes, when she was handling a tough case or struggling to keep up with their workload, she could forget about it for a while. But then something would happen: Feigan would write a column attacking some other poor soul, or an older lawyer would say, "Don't I remember your name from somewhere?" Then the bitterness would well up in her, the lost years, the lost opportunities. And she would renew the pledge she had made to herself a decade ago.

Jerry cleared his throat. "The word's going 'round, though, that they're about to hire Eddie's son."

"I didn't know he had one."

"He has two actually. But Tom—the younger one—is the one he's closest to."

"What else do you know about him?"

Jerry shrugged. "Not much. He's about to graduate from college. I think they may put him to work covering the cops. Sort of a favor to Eddie, if you know what I mean."

She nodded, but her mind was racing ahead of him. So it wasn't hopeless after all. Eddie Feigan had a son, a son who wanted to go into journalism. Maybe there were a few lessons she could teach him. It would be more complicated, infinitely so. But what was the old saying? The sins of the father shall be visited upon the son?

"Aurore."

"Hmm?" She looked across the table.

"Remember, we reporters don't make very much." He nodded toward her plate. "I bought you a nice dinner. Why don't you eat some of it?"

The new president was inaugurated on a bitter January morning. Snow blanketed the city, but Cronin and Associates still managed to open its doors for a small parade-watching party. First came the ceremony: an aging poet, struggling to read his offering in the sunlight's glare, then the young president, laying down a challenge to his generation.

My generation, Aurore thought. *Our time has come.*

The new administration meant new business for the firm —and something else.

"I had a meeting over at the Justice Department today," Andrew came in to tell her one night a few months later.

She was rushing to pack her briefcase. "Oh?"

"With the attorney general."

She looked up. "And how's our old law school buddy? Has he organized any more speaking engagements for McCarthy?"

Andrew snorted. "You're never going to forgive him, are you?"

Aurore shook her head.

"No, actually, he had a proposition for me. He wants me to be head of the Civil Division."

She gasped, then threw her arms around him. "Andrew, that's wonderful! . . . What did you tell him?"

"I told him I'd have to think about it. Discuss it with my wife—and with my partner."

It was beginning to sink in. Of course he'd have to sever his ties to the firm. Could they survive without him?

"Well, what do you think?" he asked.

"It's a terrific opportunity . . . and it'll be great for the firm in the long run. . . ."

"But?"

"But"—she flashed a smile of resignation—"how will we manage without you?"

"It won't be forever," he reminded her.

"I know."

He smiled. "Look at it this way. For the next few years you'll be able to run this firm any old way you want!"

Yes, she thought, that would be fun. It would be a challenge, too. But for the first time since law school she really felt she could handle it alone.

She smiled. "So when do I start cleaning house?"

* * *

Andrew sailed through his confirmation hearing, but Aurore hadn't doubted that he would. He had a squeaky clean reputation and good Democratic connections, developed over the years. His answers to the senators' questions were straightforward and confident, and yet he also managed to convey the right amount of respect for the members of the Judiciary Committee.

She was proud of Andrew, and proud of what the two of them had accomplished. Yet the hearing depressed her. She listened carefully as the senators probed every aspect of Andrew's past. And she was reminded once again that she would never be able to withstand that kind of scrutiny. Times had changed, but they hadn't changed that much. All she'd have to do would be to put her State Department job on a résumé and someone would remember. Most of the senators were around then. Eddie Feigan certainly was. And that nameless, faceless other person, too.

It had taken a matter of weeks to destroy her old life. It wouldn't take much now to dismantle the new one she had built.

So Andrew would taste the power, a job that was so important that the United States Senate had to take the time to review his qualifications. But Aurore knew that she never would. And the realization made her sad, and more than a little bit bitter.

She was forty-one now, and while she didn't exactly feel old, she was feeling her age. She didn't think of herself as a matron yet, though she supposed it would come to that. She thought of names for women who never married. Spinster. Old Maid. None of them seemed to fit. She had her career, after all, and as the years passed, she was surprised to discover how much pleasure it could give her.

Enough pleasure, in fact, that the prospect of spending the rest of her life alone did not concern her. And had it not been for two serendipitous weeks in the summer of 1961, she might have been able to go on feeling that way forever.

Thirty-Four

For as long as Aurore had known her, Ellie Cronin had wanted a child. Now, after years of frustration, she apparently had decided to adopt one instead: a forty-one-year-old single woman named Aurore Callahan.

Ellie reminded her when it was time to see her doctor and dentist. Ellie called when she heard about a great bargain at Woodie's. Ellie kept an eye out for Aurore's china pattern when she went to estate sales. But most of all, Ellie was determined to find her a husband.

It was her latest project, almost like the annual Junior League bazaar or the March of Dimes dinner. She held innumerable dinner parties to introduce Aurore to good-looking men. There was Joe Something-or-other, a divorced man who lived down the street from the Cronins. There was Benjamin Alexander, Ellie's internist, whose wife had died a few years before. And then there was the Cronins' stockbroker.

Aurore actually liked Malcolm Scofield quite a bit. He was witty, and a good dancer, and wealthy enough to indulge her with dinners at the Jockey Club and plays at the National Theater.

But both of them recognized early on that they would never be more than good friends. Perhaps it was simply a matter of chemistry, or because each of them had been single for too long. But they were old enough to agree that that was certainly no reason they couldn't go on seeing each other.

So when Ellie first suggested that they all go on vacation together, it seemed like a great idea. They could swim and fish and read, and play bridge together at night. But most of all they could relax.

"You all haven't had a proper vacation in years," Ellie

reminded them over dinner. "It's always been work, work, work—and it's going to get worse once Andrew moves over to Justice."

"What do you think?" Andrew asked Aurore the next morning.

"I don't know. Who would look after the firm?"

He shrugged. "We'll postpone the cases we need to and let the others fill in. It's dead around here in August anyway."

"What does Mal say?"

"Ellie talked to him again this morning. He said that if he can rearrange his schedule, he'd love to join us."

She looked at Andrew closely. There was something about the arrangement that made her wary. She liked Ellie a lot— but in small doses. Could she take two weeks of watching Ellie flutter around Andrew—and hover over her?

"Wouldn't the two of you rather get off by yourselves than have me and Mal tag along?"

Andrew spoke slowly, with no trace of a smile. "I think Ellie knows exactly what kind of vacation she wants."

"And what about you?"

He stretched back in his chair, lacing his fingers behind his head. "All I want is a sunny day and a gentle breeze and my fishing pole in the water and an ice-cold beer in my hand." He looked at her intently. "Simple, isn't it?"

She laughed. "I guess when you put it that way, I can hardly refuse."

It was settled then. With the help of a real estate agent, Ellie found what they were looking for: an old rustic cabin on the shores of Canandaigua Lake in upstate New York. It had three bedrooms, a spacious living room with a kitchen attached, and a wide screened porch that straddled the house on the lakefront side. The photographs showed a yard dotted with big trees and a wooden dock. A boat and hammock were included.

Andrew and Aurore swapped the pictures back and forth. "I know one thing," he said.

"What's that?"

He looked up. "I get first crack at the hammock!"

Aurore had wrapped up most of her cases and Jane had

promised to water her plants. Her bills were paid, her paper boy and postman notified. And then Mal called.

"I can't go."

Her heart sank. "Why not?"

"We've got a big bond issue coming up, and at the last minute New York decided they needed me. The way they put it, I couldn't refuse."

"But it hardly seems fair!"

"I know." He paused. "I hope this doesn't disrupt your vacation."

"Oh, don't worry about me. We'll just have to try to do it again sometime."

But it did disrupt her plans. Four was two couples, but three was a crowd. She tried to explain that to Ellie, but she wouldn't listen.

"Of course you're still coming. You're like family to us, Aurore. We wouldn't think of leaving you behind."

It was easier just to go along with Ellie than fight her. "If you really mean it," Aurore said at last, "then I'll come."

They had planned to all drive together, but in the end they were forced to take separate cars. The jury that Aurore had thought would decide by Wednesday kept at it until the next Monday afternoon. She was embarrassed that her prediction was so far off the mark. But then the judge had made a muddle of his instructions. At least, in the end, her client had won.

She set off early Tuesday morning. It was a long drive, but she didn't really mind. It was a good time to think.

It was nearly suppertime when she finally arrived.

"You made it!" Andrew said as he came out to greet her.

"Your directions were perfect."

He led her up the stairs and through the porch. Ellie looked up from the kitchen counter, where she was juggling four mixing bowls and three saucepans. "Hi, how was the drive?"

"Not too bad. Who are you feeding tonight, an army?"

"I tried to remind her she's on vacation," Andrew said, "but she won't let up."

"I just figured it would be nice to have something special tonight. It won't take much longer."

Aurore glanced around the room. The house smelled of wood. Cedar, hickory, she didn't know which kind. But it was a warm country smell, the antithesis of metal desks and file cabinets.

The rooms were simply furnished; primitive watercolors hung on the walls, all apparently painted by a mysterious "B.L." A rag rug warmed the plank floor in front of the fireplace. A nearby shelf overflowed with a five-year supply of *National Geographics* and *Reader's Digest Condensed Books*.

"Come on." Andrew put down her bags and took her by the arm. "I'll show you the best part."

He led her down across the yard, past the hammock to the dock. The sun was dropping down behind the hillside, casting their shadows on the green-brown water at their feet. The waves lapped at the scrubby shore and tiny fish—hardly big enough to call them that—darted among the rocks, searching for dinner.

"I like it here," he said. "I've been gone two days and I already feel more relaxed than I've been since before law school."

He picked up a flat black stone and skipped it across the water. "I got up early this morning and went fishing. Before sunrise even. It was great. Just me and the boat, alone on the lake." He paused. "You can get a lot of thinking done then."

"Oh?"

He smiled. "Don't worry. Nothing too profound."

"Yeah," she said softly. "That might be dangerous—especially on a vacation."

"Andrew, Aurore." Ellie's voice sailed down through the trees. "Are you down there? Dinner's ready."

"Coming," they replied in unison.

Ellie had outdone herself: breaded pork chops, mashed potatoes, green beans, a molded salad, and strawberry pie. Aurore listened as Ellie described her trip into Canandaigua to buy the groceries. She tried to pay attention, but she found her mind wandering. The drive and the food had made her sleepy.

When they'd finished dinner and cleaned up the dishes, Ellie said, "We can't play bridge without Malcolm, but what about a round of Parcheesi?"

"I hate to be a party pooper," Aurore said, "but what I'd really like to do is go to bed. Will you forgive me?"

"Sure," Ellie said.

"But up and at 'em in the morning," Andrew ordered.

She said good night then, and went down the hall to her room. She unpacked a few things and slipped into her silk nightgown. Then she had to laugh at herself. What could have possessed her to bring it? It was getting cooler now. She would have been better off in flannel.

She got an extra blanket down from the closet shelf, then climbed into bed. She left the light on, wondering if she felt like reading, then thought better of it and turned it off.

It was dark in the room, and quiet, too. Outside, she could hear the chirp of a lonely cricket, the distant hum of a motorboat crossing the lake. She heard the murmur of the Cronins' voices, then the door to their room shut.

She closed her eyes and said a prayer: *If Andrew and Ellie make love tonight, please, dear God, don't let me hear them.*

Aurore awoke the next morning to an extraordinary sound and an extraordinary smell. It was bacon sizzling on the stove.

"I fixed it for Andrew," Ellie explained, "but before I knew it he had taken off in his boat." She passed the plate over. "Have a piece."

"This is a real treat," Aurore said. "I never bother cooking breakfast at home."

"Well, you should. My mother used to always say, 'Breakfast is the most important meal of the day.' Why don't I fix you some eggs, too?"

"Oh, I can do it, Ellie."

"No, it's no bother. I'll just whip them up while you're getting dressed."

"I hope you're not going to wait on me for the next two weeks."

"I won't," Ellie insisted. "But you know how it is. Old habits die hard."

Yes, Aurore thought ruefully. Already she missed her *Star* and her *Wall Street Journal*. She wasn't used to making conversation before she'd downed her first cup of coffee.

"Now Andrew on the other hand . . ." Ellie looked out across the lake. "He doesn't seem to have any trouble adjusting." She sipped her coffee in silence, watching her husband. "Say," she said suddenly, her eyes lighting up. "When I was in town yesterday, I heard there was going to be an art fair today. How would you like to go?"

All Aurore really wanted to do was to climb into the hammock and open one of her books. But she felt sorry for Ellie. Away from her home she was like a lost child. She couldn't have cared less about swimming or fishing or swinging in a hammock. She had come up here for Andrew's sake. And Andrew was having the time of his life, alone on a boat in the middle of the lake.

"Sure," Aurore said. "Just let me get dressed."

The "fair" wasn't exactly an extravaganza, just a couple dozen card tables and spread-out blankets arranged in haphazard rows. In the end Ellie bought Andrew a new humidor, and Aurore bought a set of hand-woven placemats.

"You know," Ellie said as they walked back to the car, "there was a time when I thought of opening a store that specialized in mountain crafts."

"Really?" Aurore was genuinely surprised. "When was that?"

"Oh, a long, long time ago. When Andrew first came home from the war."

"Why didn't you?"

Ellie looked at her a moment. "I wasn't brave enough."

"Didn't Andrew encourage you?"

She laughed softly. "You don't know how it was, do you?"

"What do you mean?"

"I'm surprised Andrew never told you." She hesitated. "No, I guess I'm not. He doesn't like to think about those days."

Ellie was silent for a moment. "Andrew came home in the spring of 1945. Except he didn't really. Oh, they had patched

him back together all right—his stomach looked like a piece
of Swiss cheese from the shrapnel wounds. But that wasn't
what bothered me.

"All through the war I'd bought my war bonds and tended
my victory garden, and planned what life would be like when
Andrew returned. And then my husband came home and I
hardly recognized him. This was the man I had been counting
on to take care of me, and he couldn't figure out what to do
when he got up in the morning. I mean, did he put his left
shoe on first, or did he put on his right shoe?—it was that
bad.

"I was panic-stricken. What was I going to do? I could
be a nurse or a teacher, but I'd have to go back to school for
that. And we didn't have time for that. We had bills to pay.
I'd been working as a clerk at the general store, but that
wasn't enough to feed a family.

"So I started thinking about running my own store. It was
a silly idea. I mean, I had no money to buy a building or an
inventory. And besides there probably wasn't enough tourist
business in Ewing for the thing to succeed. In the meantime,
Andrew's mother insisted we move in with them. She said
someone needed to look after her boy properly. That he
needed to rest. That the stress of having to earn a living would
do him in."

Ellie dug into her purse for a minute, then pulled out a
tissue. It was as if she thought she had told too much, but
didn't know how to stop.

"At first it made sense to me. I could work, and Mother
Cronin could look after Andrew. I mean, all he wanted to
do then was sit on the porch all day and stare up at the
mountains. Then one day, I figured it out. I don't know what
changed, but I suddenly realized that if Andrew stayed in his
mother's house, he might as well shrivel up and die. What
he needed was a good kick in the pants.

"So I announced we were moving out, and I told him that
I was married to a man who had always had his heart set on
going to law school and so he had better get his fanny in gear
and apply. It took a while, I threatened, I pleaded, I cried.
I ignored his mother, who accused me of trying to kill her

little boy. And one day he got up and got dressed, and sat down and sent off for his applications.''

"I never knew . . ." Aurore said. "I always thought . . . I mean, Andrew always seemed like someone who knew exactly what he wanted, even when he wasn't exactly sure how to get it."

"But he was," Ellie said quickly. "He was that way growing up. No one ever doubted that Andrew would go far. He just got sidetracked for a while."

"But what about your crafts store?"

"Oh, that," she said with a wave of her hand. "No, I realized early on that being Andrew's wife was going to be a full-time job. He likes things a certain way. He needs to have things taken care of. He needs to save his energies for work, not the dry cleaner or the yard work . . ." She smiled. "Or even to plan a vacation."

"And why do you put up with it?"

Ellie looked as if she didn't understand. "Because that's Andrew. . . . And I love him."

Yes, Aurore thought, she knew exactly what Ellie meant. Andrew needed them both, wife and partner. But like Ellie, she didn't resent it. She received so much in return.

All these years she had never figured it out. The hold that Ellie had on Andrew. The bond between them. Now it started to make sense. And she realized that she didn't know Andrew half as well as she thought she did.

Andrew caught three bass that day. "Stick 'em in the oven with some lemons," he told Ellie.

But she would have no part of it. She made another trip to the store, for spices and something to stuff the fish with. "You worked a long time for these," she told him. "They deserve something better."

It was a grand meal. They shared two bottles of white wine, and reminisced about the times they had shared together: their student years in Charlottesville, the lean years in Washington, and the past few months when they could sit back and acknowledge that yes, their firm had become a success.

"I don't know about you two," Andrew said, pushing his chair away from the table, "but I need to walk off some of this food. Care to join me?"

It was a cool, quiet night, and the full moon lit their way like a flashlight. They walked side by side until a car came. Then Aurore stepped quickly ahead so they would clear the road. Ellie slipped her hand through her husband's arm.

"What are you going to do tomorrow, Andrew?" Aurore tried to keep her voice light. "More fishing?"

"No, not like today," he replied. "Now that I've caught us a dinner, I'm happy to do whatever the two of you want me to."

"Well, for starters," Ellie said, "I would be satisfied with conversation." Aurore turned and Ellie winked at her. "The fish can't be that interesting!"

"Tomorrow you will have my undivided attention, dear." Even in the moonlight, Aurore could see his teasing smile. "After I catch breakfast, that is."

They turned to head back, this time with the moon following them home. When they reached the cottage, Aurore didn't want to go back inside. There was an awkward moment. Then Ellie said good night, and Andrew followed her inside.

Aurore strolled down to the dock and sat down on the rough-hewn planks. It felt good to get away. She hadn't thought about the office all day.

She never could have done it without Andrew's help, that was for sure. What would she have done if she hadn't met him? Funny, she had never thought about that, even while she was waiting for him to make up his mind about practicing with her. She probably would have moved back to Fredericksburg, become the country lawyer that he had been destined to be. But Washington? No, she was sure she never could have dared it alone.

"Mind if I join you?" He stood above her, holding two glasses.

"Of course not."

"Here," he said, handing her one of the drinks.

"I'm not sure I need this."

"Don't worry. Just a little club soda." He smiled. "Besides, I'm not that kind of guy."

She took a sip as he sat down beside her.

"Did Ellie go to bed?"

He nodded.

"I had fun with her today."

"She did, too. She told me so."

"And how 'bout you? Did you have fun today?"

He nodded.

"What do you do all day when you're sitting out there?"

"Think mostly."

"About what?"

"Oh, nothing in particular."

The lawyer in her couldn't give up so easily. "You don't expect me to believe that, do you?"

He hesitated. Then he said, very softly, "I was thinking about my new job, and how much I was looking forward to it."

"I see." She turned her face away.

"And I was also thinking how much I'm going to miss working down the hall from you."

"Well, I guess we're all going to have to adjust." She struggled not to show her emotions. "I mean I'm not sure that I'm ready to be the head of a Washington law firm at the tender age of forty-one."

"Is that how old you are?" he teased. "I had assumed you were at least fifty. Maybe I'd better think twice about this."

She slugged him playfully.

"Ouch!"

"And there's more where that one came from."

His face grew serious. "I know," he said, his voice barely a whisper. "There's lots more."

A few houses away, a party was breaking up. The fare-wells, the laughter, seemed to drift on the air along the lake's edge. Did sound travel better across water or land? She tried to remember her high-school physics. Could Ellie lie in bed and hear every word they were saying?

"Ellie may be wondering what's keeping you."

He looked at his watch, but it was too dark to read it. "You may be right." He stood up. "Good night then."

"Good night, Andrew."

He turned and walked up the slope toward the house. As he did, she was struck by a memory, as clear today as it had been a decade ago. She saw them studying together, and possibly stopping for coffee. And then the inevitable moment would come when he would leave to go home to Ellie.

She knew it was her own fault. Their law school had been filled with smart, good-looking men. And she was a smart girl, all right. She had the brilliance to fall for a smart, good-looking man . . . who happened to be married.

That was her choice. It didn't have to be that way. And now all she had was her work and her friends. And herself to fall back on.

That had been enough the past few years. It had seen her through tough times. But was it enough to sustain her for the rest of her life? That she wasn't sure.

She took a sip of the drink he had left with her. It was club soda, just like he said. She was just a little disappointed that it wasn't wine or whiskey. She smiled. Yes, if pressed, she could become that kind of girl. But no, Andrew was definitely not that kind of boy.

Thirty-Five

It was Thursday or Friday, Aurore had lost track. One day slid into the next, distinguishable only by a change in the cloud pattern, or what they had for dinner, or the book she was reading.

Once or twice a day, she'd stop reading long enough to go for a swim, a long leisurely journey toward the center of the lake. It felt cool and liberating and she loved the sensation of the water streaming over her warm arms and legs.

One morning she went out early, before the others had

gotten up. The water was cold at that time of day, but after a few quick crawl strokes she hardly noticed the chill.

Ellie noticed her, though. "You know," she said when Aurore returned, "you really shouldn't go out there alone."

"Why not?"

"You know why not. You could get a cramp or something and drown. And we wouldn't even know that you were out there."

"Then it wouldn't ruin your breakfast, would it?"

"Be serious, Aurore."

"I'll try and be good."

She changed out of her wet suit, grabbed her book and a couple of plums, and headed for the hammock. A breeze rose up off the lake, rustling the leaves that shaded her from above. It had the makings of another beautiful day.

A half hour later Andrew came out to the dock, carrying his pole and tackle box.

"When are you going to join me?" he asked.

"When you start catching more fish in an hour than the number of books I can read in a day!"

He laughed, a good strong laugh that rumbled out of his chest. Then he plopped his line into the water.

She remembered going fishing once before and trying desperately to have a good time. It was the first time, the only time. The time she and Robert had borrowed bikes and ridden out to a grassy bank above the Rappahannock River.

She turned back to her book, but the words blurred before her eyes. How do you slow time? she wondered. Did it help to put away your watches and calendars and pretend that one day was no different from the next? But you couldn't stop it completely. Tomorrow would always come. And "tomorrow" Andrew was moving to the Justice Department.

Up in the house, the phone jangled.

Andrew groaned. "I told you we shouldn't have given the office our number."

But it was clear it wasn't the office. Ellie answered the phone and stayed on the line for a long time. When she hung up and rejoined them, she looked stricken.

Andrew put down his pole. "What is it, Ellie?"

"My mother."

Aurore sat up. "What happened?"

"They think it's her heart. She's resting at the hospital now, but Sissy thinks I ought to come home."

"Then I'll come with you." Andrew began reeling in his line.

"Don't be silly, honey. There's no reason you have to give up your vacation."

"If it's serious enough for you to go, it's serious enough for me."

So much for the vacation, Aurore thought, marking her place in her book.

"Besides," Andrew added, "how were you planning on getting home?"

"I already called the airline. The quickest way is to take an afternoon flight back to Washington, then transfer through to Roanoke. I can have Sissy meet me at the airport."

"Then I'll drive you, and we can leave the car at the airport. And once you know that things are under control we can fly back and pick it up."

Ellie was silent for a moment. "I still hate to drag you away. You know how Mama is. It's probably not *that* serious. Just her way of letting me know she still hasn't forgiven us for leaving Ewing."

"I don't think you should go alone."

"But I hate for you to miss out on your vacation. . . ."

He shrugged. "There'll be other times. . . ."

"Yes," she said, "years from now." She started to turn back to the house. "What about Aurore?"

Aurore swung her legs to the ground. "Aurore's a big girl. Don't worry about me."

"Are you sure?"

"I *have* spent vacations by myself before."

Aurore fixed sandwiches for them to carry, while Ellie and Andrew packed their bags.

"Don't worry about rounding up all your gear," she said. "If you don't make it back, I'll just bring it with me."

"You really are a dear," Ellie said.

"I hope your mother's going to be all right."

She smiled. "Knowing Mama, she'll probably recover about twenty-four hours after I arrive."

Time, in this case, sped forward. In what seemed like a matter of minutes, they had changed into their "city" clothes and loaded their bags into the trunk.

"Take care," Ellie said, hugging Aurore tightly.

"You, too," she said.

Andrew helped his wife into the car, then put his arm around Aurore's shoulders.

"I want you to know I left you my fishing rod. . . . It's in your bedroom."

"Oh, Andrew"—she laughed—"I'm touched."

He brushed his lips across her cheek. "Good-bye then."

He climbed in beside Ellie, and started up the car. Aurore waved as Andrew drove up the gravel driveway and pulled out on the highway that skirted the lake. The car accelerated, and then it was gone.

It was quiet then, eerily quiet. Even the wind and the birds seemed to have hushed out of deference to her mood. There was an empty feeling, an acute sense of loneliness.

She walked inside to get her sandwich and a drink, then paused outside the door to her bedroom. She smiled when she saw the fishing rod.

It wasn't as if she had never gone on a vacation alone. She usually traveled that way—and had the journals to prove it. Books were her companions, and when she tired of them, she found she enjoyed sitting back and watching the rest of the human parade go by.

But this vacation was different; the Cronins had been a part of it. Gingerly, she picked up Andrew's fishing rod to see how much it weighed. They'd been gone what?—five minutes?—and already it seemed strange without them. But she was being silly, and she knew it.

She finished off *To Kill a Mockingbird*, ate her lunch, then decided to go for a swim. She heard the voice of Ellie— "you shouldn't swim so soon after a meal, Aurore"—but she ignored it. She left her towel on the dock and dove in.

She started out with crawl strokes, crisp and neat, then

switched to breaststroke when she began to tire. For some reason, she thought of that movie she'd seen a few years before, the one where the Hollywood star's has-been husband commits suicide by swimming out into the ocean.

She didn't feel suicidal, not the least bit. But she didn't feel she had to be responsible either. *If I were somebody's mother or wife, I probably wouldn't swim so far out alone.*

But she had no husband nor, in truth, any children. She didn't even have an aging parent to watch over. No one would grieve a long time if she died. Andrew and Ellie and Mal would probably mourn her passing. And her death would probably throw the firm into turmoil. But that was different; she was not responsible for making those people happy.

She accepted her life. There were things she would have changed if she could have, but they were done now, and there was no point in ruminating on the might-have-beens. She was free, and if she felt like swimming alone across Canandaigua Lake on a full stomach, by golly she was going to do it.

But it was a long swim back to shore now, and she knew she had gone far enough. She treaded water for a moment to get her bearings, then turned and headed back to the cottage. Her mind drifted with lazy thoughts that matched the pace of her strokes. She would read another book today, she decided. Maybe take a nap. Go into town. The possibilities, she thought with a chuckle, were endless.

She switched back to breaststroke again, swimming this time toward the sun. The bright light was disorienting. It transformed the water in front of her into a dark mirror, glinting with points of light. She could pick out the house now, the wooden cottage over there among the trees. She saw the white speck of the hammock. And on the dock, there was a man.

She blinked quickly, several times. It must be some sort of mirage. But no, the figure stayed there, and as she came closer she knew without a doubt that it was Andrew.

How much time had passed? Three, maybe four hours. Had they missed their flight? She didn't quicken her strokes, but she felt her limbs surge with renewed energy.

"You shouldn't be swimming alone," he called out as she drew near.

"I'm afraid there isn't any other way." She tucked her head down for the final flurry of strokes. Then she looked up and found him sitting with his feet dangling in the water.

"I could accuse you of sounding like Ellie," she said as she tried to regain her breath. "Where is she anyway?"

"On her plane."

"Why didn't you go?"

He hesitated, then said, "All the way to the airport, Ellie kept drumming away that there was no reason for me to leave. That her mother would probably turn out to be all right. That it was a shame I had to give up my vacation. She kept at it so long that by the time we got to the airport, I thought, 'Screw it. If that's the way you feel, I'll stay.' "

Aurore climbed up the ladder and squeezed the water from her hair. "What did she say?"

He shrugged. "She gave me a kiss. She said she'd call me when she knew more. She told me to have a good time." He turned to Aurore and smiled. "Which I intend to do— starting right now." He scrambled to his feet. "I feel like a drink. How about you?"

"What are you having?" She tried to keep her voice light.

"A gin and tonic."

It seemed early for a cocktail, but suddenly she didn't care. "I'll have one, too."

He handed her the towel, then headed up to the house. She watched him as she dried herself off. What were the ground rules now? she wondered.

The screen door slammed shut. Why had he come back alone? Probably Ellie had convinced him that he really did need this vacation. And what better way to spend it than with a good family friend.

She was being silly. After all, it wasn't as if she and Andrew had never spent any time alone together. But they'd never spent a vacation together, just the two of them now, in a remote summer cottage.

"I didn't make them too strong," Andrew called out from the porch. He brought down a tray with two tall, frosty glasses. She smiled. He'd even gone to the trouble of cutting up limes.

"Was the traffic very heavy?"

"Not too bad—until we hit town."

"I hope Ellie's mother will be all right."

"Ellie said she'd call once she had a better idea."

"I hope she can come back before we have to go home."

"Yeah," he said slowly. "I hope so, too."

There was an awkward silence.

"Did you go fishing yet?"

"No, not yet."

"Then I guess I'll have no choice but to take you out to dinner."

She was touched that he offered, but it didn't feel right. "Thanks, but . . . Ellie left us with an awful lot of food. It might be better to finish it off first."

"Whatever you say."

"In fact," she said, standing up, "I'd probably better get something started."

She walked up the path, then stopped and turned toward him. "Do you need your pole?"

"No," he said, heading for the hammock. "Since you've finally gotten out of this thing, I think I'll give it a try."

Ellie had already decided that Aurore was going to have ground round for dinner—it was defrosting into a puddle on the countertop. Aurore put it back in the refrigerator. Maybe for lunch tomorrow, but not for dinner tonight.

No, she decided, she would make Mildred Hudgins's fried chicken recipe, with a tossed salad and corn on the cob. Then she'd whip up a shortcake to go with the berries they'd bought yesterday from the stand down the road. You could always find the recipe on the Bisquik box.

She went about her work quickly, then set the table on the porch for two. There was a pair of candles on the counter by the stove and she was tempted to put them out, too. But no, that was ridiculous. Andrew would wonder what had gotten into her. She was beginning to wonder, too.

Thirty-Six

He awoke to the sound of running water, rattling the metal walls of the shower inside the cabin. He had fallen asleep, but he wasn't sure for how long.

He stretched out his legs. It had been hot driving back, and now his shirt was a mass of wrinkles. He rubbed his hand across the light stubble of his chin. He must look like shit.

The water stopped. Aurore must be finished. As he walked up the path, he caught a whiff of dinner. She had been working hard.

"Do I have time for a shower?" he called out.

"About fifteen minutes," she replied.

He shut the door to the small room, filled now with steam and the smell of women. No, he corrected himself, a woman. How quickly the traces of Ellie had disappeared. Gone were the stockings, hanging like limp rags in the shower, the jars of creams and potions cluttering up the sink. In their place was a single flowered makeup case, neatly zippered shut.

He stripped off his clothes and turned on the spray. The bracing water coursed down his back, reviving him and clearing his head. He felt like a kid again—just a few days here had done that to him. But he was puzzled by Ellie. Was this supposed to be some sort of test of him and their marriage? If so, he might have already earned an F. But right now he didn't really care.

"Five minutes, Andrew."

He heard her voice over the roar of the shower. He knew the voice, there was no mystery in it. And yet it enticed him. It reached out to him in a new and disturbing way.

"I'm coming."

255

But where was he heading? He turned off the water. That, he knew, was where the mystery lay.

Her hair was pulled back in a ponytail and she was wearing a pale blue dress, one of those flimsy summer dresses that made a man think he could see through it even when he couldn't. Her eyes were bright when she glanced up from the table, her cheeks flushed with pink. She hadn't bothered with lipstick, but still her lips looked moist and inviting. All of it, he realized with a jolt of remembrance, made her look ten years younger.

She had set up the table out on the porch and pushed it up against the screen. There they could watch as the darkness marched up the lawn, enveloping them in the sweet smells and gentle sounds of a warm summer night.

"You've outdone yourself," he said, as he took his place.

She smiled. "It wasn't that difficult."

"Still, I'm impressed. I miss your old dinner parties."

"You could hardly call them that—the three of us, around a big plate of spaghetti."

"That's not how I remember them."

"Well, that was back before I got so busy."

"No, back before you got so successful." He took a bite of a drumstick. "Where'd you learn to cook like this anyway?"

"Mildred Hudgins. I used to help her out in the kitchen. I had a lot of time on my hands that winter when I . . ."

She stopped at the memory.

"When you were pregnant?" he asked.

She nodded slowly. "I've never told you much about that time, have I? About Robert, I mean."

"No, you haven't."

"But then you never asked."

He set down the piece of chicken. "I guess I figured that if you wanted to tell me, you would."

He was right, and that annoyed her. But not for long. She felt close to him tonight. She could share things she hadn't wanted to before.

"Sometimes," she said softly, "I wonder how my life

would have been different. If he had lived and we had gotten married. Not often, mind you, but sometimes. When I'm relaxed and alone, and have time to think about things other than work.''

"I can't imagine you staying home with kids.''

"Funny. I don't think the women in my family ever wanted anything more than that. But I never saw myself that way. At least, not until I met Robert. Not until I became pregnant.''

"Did you ever talk to him about it?''

She laughed, a little bitterly. "There never was time for that. You remember how it was. People were coming and going and you never knew how long the war might last and what would be left after it was over. The truth of the matter is that he only got around to proposing the weekend that he left.''

She stared at her plate for a moment, trying to stab a piece of lettuce. "But you know, I can look back now and wonder if it really would have worked. We were so different. I didn't care that he was Jewish, but it bothered him a lot that I wasn't. But we were young, and it was an emotional time, and . . .'' She stopped before she went too far. "It's hard to remember now.''

He wasn't sure what he was supposed to say.

"Do you ever wonder,'' she asked, "how your life might have been different?''

"What do you mean?''

She meant if he hadn't married Ellie, but she couldn't say that. "Oh, for instance . . . if you'd never gone to law school. If you'd never left Ewing.''

"I don't really feel that I left Ewing.''

"Why not?''

He smiled. "I married Ellie, didn't I?''

She wasn't sure what he meant by that. A simple recitation of the facts? A wry observation on the state of his life? Or something else? A hint of dissatisfaction?

She knew she ought to try to sort it out. But the wine he had poured was working now, and the words that she might have kept back before could no longer be corraled in her heart.

"I remember back in our first year of law school when I found out you were married. I was furious."

He chuckled softly. "Why didn't you say something?"

She leaned forward. "Because I wasn't sure that it was your fault. I was never sure whether you had led me on or whether it was just another one of those things you forgot to mention." She paused. "You want to tell me now?"

He studied his wineglass for a moment. "Actually, I think it was a little of both. I think I forgot at first and then, when I realized you didn't know, I guess I figured it couldn't hurt to keep you in the dark a little while longer."

"Thanks a lot."

"Well, I wanted to get to know you better. Face it, would we have become such close friends if you'd known I was married?"

"Probably not."

"So there. I spotted you that first day in class. I liked your style. I liked your sense of humor." He hesitated. "Frankly, you were the first woman I'd met that made me wonder why I had gotten married so young."

There. He'd said it. He'd cared for her as long as she had cared for him. But why had she doubted it? He was her closest friend, after all. Brother, father, husband, friend.

But not lover.

"I never took advantage of you, did I?"

"No."

"There, then." He raised his glass to her. "All it did was pave the way for a great friendship and a very profitable partnership. That's not so terrible, is it?"

"No, I guess not." The subject was growing dangerous. "We've changed a lot, too."

"Do you think so? I don't. You still like Gershwin, and I like Benny Goodman. You like . . ."

The phone rang. Once, twice, three times. They stared at each other, saying nothing but knowing that they both were willing it to stop. But the longer it rang, the more insistent it became. At last Andrew rose to answer it.

"Hello? Oh, hello, hon." He tried to muffle the conversation, but it was no use. Aurore could hear him, and in her mind she could hear Ellie.

"What's the verdict? . . .Uh-huh. . . .Hmm. . . . Sounds like they're doing everything they can for her. . . . Give her my love. . . . She said that? . . . Yes, that sounds like her. . . . Hmm. . . . I'm sorry to hear that. . . . Well, keep us posted. You know I can be back at the airport in an hour or so. . . . What have we been up to? Not much. I fell asleep in the hammock. We were just finishing dinner. . . . Okay, I will. And give my love to your family. . . . I love you, too."

He put down the phone. "Ellie sends her regards."

"What about her mother?"

"She really did have a heart attack, but the prognosis is good. They're keeping her in the hospital for now. But Ellie doesn't know if she'll be able to get back. Her father has taken it kind of hard."

"Do you have any second thoughts?"

"About staying here?"

Aurore nodded.

"Actually, no." He drained the last of the wine bottle into his glass. "Around Ellie and her sisters, I'd be just another son-in-law getting in the way. She made up some story explaining my absence to placate her mother, not to mention mine. And it seemed to satisfy them."

He paused. "Maybe next week I'll feel guilty. But on a beautiful night like this, I can't imagine a place I'd rather be."

The talk was unsettling. They needed a dose of reality. "You know," she said, "one day you and I are going to have to sit down and hash out what's going to happen when you leave the firm."

"I'm not looking forward to that."

"Nor am I."

The words floated on the air between them.

"We don't really have to do it tonight, do we?"

"No, I guess not."

"Well, then." He rose from his chair. "I was just thinking of pouring myself a brandy. How about you?"

"All right."

She cleared the table while he found the bottle. He filled two tumblers, then took her by the hand.

"Come on," he said. "I had a crazy idea this afternoon."

He led her down the steps and out onto the lawn.

"The hammock?" she asked.

"We can sit, side by side. See, like this." He took his place, facing the lake with his feet still on the ground. "Then we can rock back and forth, like it's a garden swing."

She sat down carefully, surprised to discover it was big enough to hold both of them. The ropes cradled their backs as they rocked slowly, hips pressed together, feet firmly on the ground. Saying nothing.

Is this what married people do? she wondered. Sit around after dinner, sipping their drinks? Dissecting their days or not, as they choose? Needing nothing more than the presence of the other to feel secure?

Where was Andrew now? Following Ellie to Virginia? Decorating his new office? Or here, with her? On a night that had grown so quiet you could almost hear the stars whisper.

But she could hear something else. It was the voice of Ellie. A spirit that hung over the lake, low like a cloud. Dulling the sounds. Hiding out the moon. Threatening rain.

This is madness, Aurore thought. She had known it from the start. And there was only one place it could lead.

He turned to her. "I really enjoyed your dinner."

"Thank you."

"It was very special."

"Why?" She laughed. "Because you remembered that I knew how to cook?"

"I think you know what I mean."

She did, but she tried to ignore it. She stopped the swaying, and steadied her legs. Then, as gracefully as possible, she rose from the hammock.

"I was up early this morning. I think I'm going to go to bed."

He said nothing for a moment. "Maybe tomorrow I could take you fishing."

"I'd like that."

He stood up beside her. "See you at sunrise then."

He made no move toward her, no touch, no kiss. And she could not be sure if she was relieved or disappointed. "Good night," she said and turned and walked to the cottage. The screen door slammed behind her with a crack. And the house had never before seemed so suffocating.

It was impossible to sleep now. The chilly evenings that had welcomed them to the Finger Lakes had given way to a hot, humid night. Her limp sheets had become hopelessly twisted around her legs like a length of thick rope.

But that wasn't the real problem. The real problem lay sleeping in the next room. Just a few steps away, though it might as well have been miles.

She closed her eyes for a moment and imagined tiptoeing into Andrew's room. Should she stop and call out to him? Or having gone that far, should she climb right in beside him?

But no, she was not about to take a risk like that. There was too much at stake. The firm, for one. Their friendship. It was too easy to be wrong about what a man really wanted.

Across the lake she heard a rumble of thunder. The noise was low like a grunt, but then it grew louder. Suddenly her room lit up, an image frozen for an instant as if caught by a flash camera. There was another flash, and then another, and the thunder seemed to march across the lake like row after row of drummers.

The rain came then, pelting against the windowpane, driving through the open window below it. She rose and slammed the window shut. The storm answered with a clap of thunder that seemed to crack the roof above.

There was no point in trying to sleep now. But perhaps a glass of milk would help. She pulled on her silk robe and gave the belt a tug.

She stepped out into the hall and found her way to the fridge with a flash of lightning. She opened the door. It was dark inside; the power had gone out. She found the milk, then turned to find a glass. There was another shot of light.

And then she saw Andrew.

He was standing on the other side of the room, arms crossed, watching her. He was naked to the waist, wearing only his pajama bottoms. He looked tired, his hair rumpled. She had never seen him like this before.

"I couldn't sleep," she said nervously.

"Neither could I."

She took a sip of milk. "I've always been afraid of thunderstorms. I . . . I think it's because there was a storm the night my mother died."

"Really?"

"Uh-huh."

He took a step toward her. "I think, madame counselor, that for such a good attorney, you make an awfully lousy liar."

"What do you mean?"

"The reason you and I can't sleep has nothing to do with thunderstorms." He took another step closer. "It has nothing to do with mothers." Another step. "Nor does it have anything to do with hot summer nights or indigestion."

He was beside her then, and his fingers reached out to stroke through her hair, carefully, tentatively, as if the night might be shattered if he moved too fast.

His hand grazed her shoulder, then both hands traced the lines of her lapels, coming to rest just above her breasts. "I can't promise anything, Aurore. I feel like a madman, I can't think. All I know is that as I sat across the table from you tonight, something deep inside of me clicked. And I realized that for as long as I've known you, I've wanted you."

Was it all just a dream? How long had she yearned for those words? And yet there was an instant's hesitation. There was so much to lose.

But the instant passed, washed away by a tide she could not have controlled if she had tried. Her arms slipped up around his neck and there was no more need for words.

He slipped off her robe, then pressed her naked skin against his own, tracing his way down her neck with fiery kisses. But she did not want to play the seduced coquette. She drew away, then took his hand to lead him back to the bedroom.

But which one? Andrew's had the double bed. But it also had the ghost of Ellie. She hesitated, but he didn't. He led her into his room, then lowered her tenderly onto the mattress. It didn't matter who had been there before. She was the woman in his bed now.

"I have dreamed of this moment," he said, "without even recognizing the dreams."

"Ssh," she said, pressing her fingers to his lips. "No more words now."

"Only three," he said. "I love you."

And with those words she felt alive again, the hunger she had learned to ignore became sated, the emptiness became full. She felt like a flower, feeling the first raindrops that would end the long drought, opening up her petals, one by one.

He took them in turn: her lips, her neck, her breasts, the silky path down to the center of her need. The place that had slumbered for so many years since Robert had died. And now it wanted Andrew so desperately that she could not think. She could only touch. She could only feel. She could only love.

They came to his bed not just as man and woman, but as equals, as partners. He gave and then she gave. He paused to bring her to the brink with kisses that fluttered like butterflies. Then she made him lie back and enjoy hers, too.

The storm raged in her like a fever; her heartbeat answered his like a thunderclap. And when she came, it felt like a warm spring rain that flooded a meadow with flowers. The bloom would last forever.

They made love, over and over and over again throughout the night. But it was not as strangers to each other's bodies. They were longtime lovers. They had not ' wn the exact planes, dimensions, moles, or scars. But y had known each other in another way, and that made tne physical so much richer now.

The storm outside passed, and they clung to each other, as if afraid that the dream would come to an end. There were questions to answer, there was no denying that. But for now he was here beside her. And that was all that mattered.

The light intruded too early, bringing the morning after. She looked across the bed and smiled when she saw him. He took her hand and kissed it. "Remember," he said, "I told you I'd see you at sunrise."

* * *

He took her fishing that day, and they laughed at how his luck changed. When he'd filled up the bottom of the boat with bass, he put down his pole and let the boat drift on the blue water.

They talked about nothing important, but everything had a deeper meaning now.

"Was there anyone besides Robert?"

She shook her head.

"Not even Mal?"

"No"—she laughed—"not even Mal."

"That's a long time to go . . ."

"I guess it was."

Now it was her turn. He had raised the subject, after all.

"Was there anyone besides Ellie?"

"No. . . . Does it make a difference?"

"No. But it makes it harder."

He put the oars back in the oarlocks and rowed back to shore. He said nothing, but she could see the tension in his shoulders and feel it in the air.

"Why don't I take you out to dinner tonight?"

"But we've got a boatload of fish."

He dismissed them with a wave of his hand. "I'll fry 'em up in the morning."

He wants to get away from here, she thought. *He doesn't want to be here when Ellie calls.*

Did she blame him? No. But how much longer could they go on pretending his wife didn't exist?

They found a quiet restaurant by the side of the highway, with red vinyl tablecloths and candles dripping down the sides of wine bottles. They stayed as long as they could, and it was long enough. The phone didn't ring after they returned.

They needed no words this time. They left their clothes in a heap on the kitchen floor. They knew their destination. But it was different now, more desperate in a way.

And Andrew seemed different, too. Wilder, crazier. He called out her name over and over. As if he were trying to forget that other woman by becoming lost in her.

But they couldn't forget, either one of them. She lay beside him and for the first time saw the scars against the whiteness of his belly. She reached out and traced them lightly with her fingertips.

"Why didn't you tell me?" she asked.

"Tell you what?"

"About the war. About when you came home."

He hesitated. "Because I was ashamed."

"Ashamed?"

"Back then I was afraid you'd think less of me if you knew."

"And now?"

He kissed her on the forehead. "Now you know me, warts, scars, and all."

They said nothing for a moment, and then, across the darkness, she heard his voice.

"She told you, didn't she?"

"Yes."

"I thought so."

Aurore had trouble falling asleep, but once she did, she slept soundly. When morning came, and she could no longer ignore the racket of the birds, she rolled over to greet Andrew with a kiss.

But he was gone.

She rose quickly. "Andrew," she called as she swooped into the kitchen. But it was empty.

It was then she noticed that the boat was gone. She looked out across the lake, and in the distance she could see him, a lonely figure hunched over his fishing pole.

This time, she knew, he was searching for something other than dinner.

She had known this had to happen; she just hadn't counted on it happening so soon.

She flicked on the stove to heat her water. One thing was for sure. If Andrew was deciding what to do, the time had come for her to decide, too.

Thirty-Seven

She watched as he tied the boat to the dock, slowly, methodically, double-checking to make sure the knot would hold. He'd been gone all morning, and it had given her time to think.

She knew Andrew had three choices. He could choose her and reject Ellie. He could choose Ellie and reject her. Or he could try to love them both.

She couldn't live with the last option. She was not prepared to be a mistress, least of all Andrew's. And the other choices . . . ?

He didn't see her watching as he walked up the path. But as she waited, her heart sank. His step was not the skip of a young man with a newfound love. Instead, it looked like the death march of a man consumed by guilt.

But over whom?

"Hi," he said softly as he entered the house.

"Hi."

"I'm sorry I disappeared on you."

"That's okay."

"I had to have time to think."

"So did I."

He looked surprised, then nodded toward the cup of coffee she was cradling in her hands. "Do you have any more of that?"

"Sure." She knew he was trying to buy some time.

He took a seat on one of the stools at the kitchen counter and she joined him.

"We have to talk."

"I know," he said. "Let me try first."

He finished off the drink, then put his cup down. "When

266

I woke up this morning, I had two women in my heart and in my head. I wanted to love them both, but I knew that wouldn't be fair either.''

One choice down.

"I love you, Aurore. I love you in a way that is totally new and different to me, even though I've probably been in love with you for years."

There was pain in his eyes. "And yet I also know that I can't leave Ellie. Call me a cad, call me a coward. But somehow over the years, she's becoming an essential part of me. And I could no more cut her off than I could cut off an arm or a leg."

She had prepared herself for this, steeled herself the way her clients did when the jury had reached its verdict. Even so, it took all her reserves of courage, all her years of hiding her emotions, to look him in the eye and say very softly, "I accept that, Andrew."

"But I'll hurt you," he said. "And I can't bear the thought of that either."

She swallowed hard. "I've been doing some thinking, too. . . . About what I need."

"I'm trying to find an answer."

She looked down at her hands. "These past few days have been like a gift to me, Andrew. A gift from a God that I thought had forgotten about me long ago.

"I love you, Andrew. I'm not ashamed of that. And you, thank God, turn out to love me, too. But we have a life away from all this. You have a wife. We have a law firm. We have a friendship, a friendship that is also very important to me."

She looked up at him. "We have another week here together—that is, if Ellie doesn't come back. Could you give that to me? One week of loving me freely, without any of this guilt? One week—out of a lifetime?"

"And what happens when we go back to Washington?" he asked.

"We go back to the way we were before. I'm not saying it will be easy; in fact, I know it will be hard for me. But it won't be impossible. You'll be going over to Justice—that'll give us time to adjust. And by the time you come back to the firm, I hope this will be a distant memory. And yet it could be something that both of us could treasure.''

''What if Ellie comes back?''

''Then I'll leave,'' she said. ''I'll make up some story. But I won't stay here with the two of you.'' She paused. ''Ellie is my friend, too. I'm not setting out to hurt her.''

He hesitated. ''Is this what you really want?''

She nodded. ''But on one condition.''

''What's that?''

''For the next week, I have to be the center of your universe.''

He smiled. ''I can't stop Ellie from phoning.''

''No, but you can pick your time to phone her. All I'm saying is that if you're here with me, I really want you here with me.''

''What's my choice?''

''If you say no, I'll leave. There's no point to it. It would be agony to stay.'' She hesitated. ''You don't have to tell me right this minute. Think about it. Could you do it? I think I can. I've known a lot of pain in my life, Andrew. But I've learned how to cling to what's good, and try to bury the rest.''

He went to pour himself another cup of coffee. ''I'm not sure I can turn my emotions on and off so easily.''

''No matter what happens, Andrew, I'm going to have to.''

She picked up her book and headed for the hammock. She would give him until supper, that was fair enough. And if he didn't know by then, she would decide for him. She would leave. There was no sense spending another night together. It would only make it worse.

She searched for her place in the book and struggled to pick up the threads of the plot. But her mind couldn't focus beyond her own drama, playing out there beside the lake.

Was she mad to suggest this denouement? Did she know herself well enough? She had to believe that she did. But when had the bashful debutante begun demanding what she thought a man owed her? And did Andrew really owe her something?

Overhead the birds cackled, and the sun felt hot on her

skin. The breeze made the hammock sway gently. Then she opened her eyes and saw that it was Andrew who had given her a push.

"I've decided," he said.

"That was quick."

"I think there are times when you have to listen to your heart instead of your head." He reached down and pulled her to her feet. "We'll have our time together, Aurore. It won't be easy later on, for either of us. But if you can do it, I can do it, too. . . . And I want to."

He pulled her close and kissed her, then looked at her and said, "Now, I've managed to waste five or six hours of our precious time, so I think we ought to see what we can do about making that up. What do you think?"

She nodded, then nuzzled her face into his neck. He was right, of course. It *would* hurt later on. But it felt so good right now, she couldn't bear to let it stop.

Andrew kept his word. For the next week, they loved and laughed, talked and played. Ellie phoned to say she would not be able to return. And then they really felt free, like children let loose in paradise, with no rules, no limits, no preconceptions.

If Andrew spoke to Ellie after that, Aurore didn't know. And if she didn't know, she didn't care. For once again, she had managed to stop time in its tracks: a week this time instead of just a weekend.

Each morning when they woke, they made their plans for the day. They swam and they fished, but they also sailed and hiked. They found cozy country restaurants and held hands at the movies. And they talked, about things that were not consequential and things that were.

"I think we should rename the firm."

"Why?" she asked.

"If you're going to run it, I think it ought to carry your name. Cronin and Callahan."

"No."

"Why not? You're not still worried about some commie hunter coming out of the woodwork, are you?"

"I just have my reasons, Andrew."

So he dropped the subject. Instead they talked about how they wanted the firm to grow over the years he would be gone: how many partners, how many lawyers, how many clients, how big a gross.

"You'll do fine," he said.

She smiled. "I know."

They talked about things they'd never had time for before.

"Why did they name you Aurore?" he asked.

She was thoughtful for a moment. "It was my mother's idea. I think she thought it was exotic. I remember one night, right before she died, she took me out in the backyard and we looked up at the stars. And she told me about the aurora borealis. 'You will light up the skies,' she said."

Aurore turned to him. "Silly, wasn't it?"

"No," he said, "she was right."

At night when Aurore lay awake, savoring the feel of Andrew's skin for just a few minutes more, she wondered if many couples could love as intensely as they did, when they all knew they had a lifetime in which to do it. And she tried to convince herself that this was the best kind of love to share.

But she didn't really believe it. The hours slowed, but they didn't stop. Wednesday turned into Thursday. Thursday turned into Friday. Friday turned into Saturday. A new family would inhabit the cottage, just as "new" people would have to learn how to inhabit their old bodies.

Aurore remembered now when Robert had left, that acute unbearable pain that had numbed her and colored her vision for years to come. It was not going to be that way this time, she vowed. Andrew would not disappear completely. He would still be a part of her world.

She would not be able to touch him, she would have to be wary of every glance, every word. And yet, when she heard him speak, she would remember words of love. When she heard him laugh, she could smile at the memory. When she went to bed at night, she could fall asleep, dreaming of her lover.

And now the dream was about to end.

The last night, she insisted on fixing dinner again, spaghetti and Italian bread, like the old days. Andrew bought a bottle of wine and they sat on the porch, picking at their food, holding hands, and saying little.

When the darkness came, he pushed his chair back and took her hand. "Indulge me," he said. "I have a crazy idea."

He led her down across the lawn. The sliver of moon was obscured by the clouds and so they picked their steps carefully, until their eyes grew accustomed to the dark.

She expected him to stop at the hammock, but he kept going, down to the dock. One last boat ride? But no, he stopped and turned her toward him and gave her a long, lingering kiss. Then he slipped down one strap of her sundress, then the other, and in moments the dress was discarded. His clothes came off just as quickly, and they stood face-to-face, naked in the night air.

"What about the neighbors?" She giggled.

"Screw 'em."

He took her hand and pulled her into the lake. She shrieked as she met the chilly water, then laughed as she tried to escape. He caught an ankle, then a wrist, then she didn't want to fight anymore. He was hard against her, and she wanted him.

"My beautiful Aurore. The light of my life."

"I love you, Andrew."

"I love you, too."

He came inside her then and it was impossible to tell where she ended and he began, the boundaries of the water and their bodies, the limits of their love and their lives. It was different from before, and yet so familiar. And she tried desperately not to cling too tightly, for she knew that if she did, she could lose him forever.

Afterward, he chased her up to the house and they made love again, this time on a mattress with a squeak and newly dampened sheets. She closed her eyes tightly to remember: the curve of his buttocks, the breadth of his shoulders, the softness of his cheek, the taste of his lips. She knew what he liked now. She knew how to make him come, fast or slow, wild or laughing.

And she knew she would never forget.

He held her tightly. She rested her head on his shoulder.

"We have a long drive tomorrow."

"But I don't feel like sleeping."

"Nor do I."

The night was silent, except for their heartbeats.

He spoke next. "I wish we could drive back together."

"It might be better this way."

"Why?"

"It's like when a mother has to wean her baby from her breast. It's easier to do it gradually." She hesitated. "I'm going to have to be weaned from you, Andrew. It might be easier to drive for ten hours, all the while looking ahead and seeing you, than to turn around suddenly and find that you were gone."

"I know how you feel."

They got up early the next morning. She had thought of taking one more swim, one last boat ride. But it was a gray day and they faced a long drive, so there seemed no point in delaying. They closed up their suitcases—and a chapter in their lives.

She waited as Andrew locked the cabin door, then turned to gaze at the hammock, the boat, and the water one last time. She blinked back her tears—*Remember, you told him you'd be strong*. But still her heart twisted with pain, an ache not unlike that of a little girl, standing on a train platform, leaving behind everyone and everything that she loved.

"Good-bye, cottage," she whispered. "I'll always remember you."

They climbed into their cars, then headed south, Andrew in the lead. They stopped briefly for lunch together, but otherwise there were only long stretches of time in which her mind wandered, playing off the love-lost songs coming over the car radio.

You could keep your life under control, she thought. You could go along, never taking chances, never taking a risk. You could be reasonably happy. But wasn't it better to take the risk, even if it meant that inevitably there would be some pain?

She wasn't sure now; it was too soon to tell. For as she drew closer to Washington, the image of the cottage receded and the image of her own home, dark and empty, loomed larger. And on Monday, she would go into work and pretend that nothing had changed when, in fact, her whole world had.

Up ahead of her, Andrew looked in his rearview mirror and wondered if he'd ever feel normal again. Thank God, Ellie wouldn't be back until tomorrow. He'd need the time to adjust.

Would she be able to tell? he wondered. Would she sense the difference in him? God, he hoped not. For all of them.

Now, they were almost home. Up ahead, the traffic slowed, as it threaded its way through construction projects. The flashing neon caught his eye—and seized his imagination. He pulled into the parking lot and smiled when she followed.

"What's the matter?" she asked.

"I've been kept apart from you all day and I want to say good-bye properly." He nodded at the motel's office. "Will you join me?"

She was tired, but there was no way she could say no. He got out of his car and went to get a room.

It was motel-strip ugly. Overhead, a light shone too brightly. The drapes clashed with the bedspread. It smelled musty, of truck drivers and fast-talking salesmen and one-night stands.

Andrew undressed her slowly, worshiping her body with gentleness. He took her under the cold sheets and hugged her and caressed her and didn't rush to come. And perhaps she should have enjoyed it more than she did.

But she knew this was the end, and prolonging it for a few more hours wouldn't make a difference. She had lost out to Ellie, and nothing Andrew could say would change that fact.

"I think you'd better go now," she said across the darkness.

"Why don't I follow you home?"

"No, you don't have to." She hesitated. "Besides, I think I'd like to stay here a little longer."

"Are you sure?"

"Yes."

And then he understood.

He found his clothes in the dark and dressed quickly.

"You can leave the key in the room," he said as he came around by the side of the bed. He sat down beside her and took her hand. "Aurore, I . . ."

"Don't say anything, Andrew. Please, just go."

And so he did.

She buried her face in her pillow. Outside the neon light flashed on and off, a beacon to tired travelers. It filled the room with flashes of white. Flashes like lightning.

Lightning. The memory of their love.

And then, like a hard summer downpour, the tears followed.

Thirty-Eight

In the middle of the night, her thoughts always turned to Andrew. And Aurore wondered why she was different from other women. She had passed the age of forty and had loved only two men, neither of whom could—or would—marry her. She was a daughter without a mother, a mother without a daughter.

But she had her work, and in the lonely hours of the early morning, Aurore found it strangely comforting. She was in charge, and deep inside she found the reserves of energy and skill that she needed now more than ever.

The easiest way to avoid the Cronins, she decided, was to move out of Arlington. But she didn't tell them that. Instead she said she needed more space and that she had discovered an "excellent investment opportunity"—a modest townhouse in Georgetown.

She had purposely avoided John Phillip's old neighborhood when she'd moved back to Washington. But now she felt differently. A house on P Street was a symbol that she had arrived. And she didn't mind flaunting it.

She was forced to endure a dinner party at the Cronins', where Ellie wanted to hear "everything" about the vacation she'd missed. So they talked about the fish Andrew had caught and the books Aurore had read and the restaurants they had discovered. Through it all, Aurore tried to keep her voice even, to remember how they had talked in "the old days." Andrew played his part, too, but she was still afraid to catch his eye.

Finally, when Ellie went to check on the roast, they looked at each other, a long smoldering gaze that said more than words ever could. And Aurore resolved that she would not do this again, at least not anytime soon.

Andrew phoned the next week, and asked if they could get together for lunch.

"No," she said, "it's too soon."

"But I miss you, Aurore. When will you see me?"

"I'll let you know."

For weeks she didn't call him. She filled up her calendar with lunches and dinners and an occasional outing with Mal. She hosted fund-raisers for the Democrats. She didn't miss a chance to recruit new clients. And all of it began to pay off.

"Admit it," Jane said when they met for lunch one day to review her current cases. "You like being in charge."

Aurore smiled. "Yes. I have to confess, I do."

"Do you miss Andrew?"

Aurore looked up at the younger woman who over the years had become one of her closest friends. Was there more to her remark? Did she sense what had passed between them?

But no, it was an innocent question. "I think we all do," she replied.

"You may get used to running things," Jane said, probing deeper. "How do you think you'll adjust when he comes back?"

Aurore looked away. "I guess we'll just have to face that when the time comes."

The phone call stunned her, for it had been years since she had talked to her aunt.

"How are you, Katharine?" a frail voice asked.

"Fine, Amanda. And you?"

"I would like to see you again." She coughed to clear her throat. "Could you come Saturday? Perhaps about two?"

"Certainly."

"I'll see you then." And with that, the older woman hung up.

What does she want? Aurore thought of all the bitter words she and her aunt had exchanged over the years. Yet Amanda was the closest thing to a mother she had had for most of her life. And even after all these years, a part of her still yearned for her aunt's approval.

Saturday dawned chilly and gray, with a drizzle that seemed to find its way inside her fall raincoat. It was a good day for an elderly woman to stay inside and keep warm.

The old, familiar house, Aurore thought, was showing signs of its occupant's age—and probably her finances. The bricks needed a fresh coat of paint, the flower boxes were a tangle of ivy. Above the door frame, where the wood was beginning to splinter, one of the house numbers hung upside down for want of a screw.

She rapped on the door, wondering who would answer. To her surprise it was Margaret.

"Come in, Kate." Her voice was warm. "It was good of you to come."

"It's good to see you again." Aurore stomped her feet on the rug, then handed her damp coat to her cousin. "Where's Amanda?"

"In the morning room. But I wanted to talk with you before you saw her."

Margaret went to hang up the coat in the hall closet, then returned.

"I think it's best to be honest with you. She's dying, Kate. She's been sick for a long time, but the doctors have told her they can't do anything more for her. They don't expect her to make it through another winter.

"It's taken her a while to understand what they were telling her, but I think she accepts it now. I think that's why she phoned you."

Of all the reasons her aunt might have called, Aurore hadn't suspected this one. "I wish I'd known sooner."

Margaret took a deep breath. "She's resting in on the couch now. She doesn't have much energy these days, so you won't be able to stay long." She paused. "I just thought you should know before you saw her."

"I appreciate that."

Margaret led her down the hall to the room that had always been Amanda's domain. As she did, Aurore regarded the rooms around her. The house seemed so much smaller now. Oh, the walls still stretched up ten feet or so, but she no longer viewed the place with the wonderment—or the fear —of a child.

Margaret knocked on the door softly, then opened it.

"Come in, girls," Amanda said, gesturing with her hand.

She was propped up with pillows on a flower-sprigged couch, and covered with a pile of afghans and quilts. Amanda had never been a large woman, but now she made Aurore think of a baby bird. Her skin was white, almost transparent; bones jutted out at her wrists and pale blue veins at her temples.

"Hello, Amanda." Aurore bent down to place a kiss on her cheek. It felt soft, delicate, but also strangely cool.

"It's good to see you again, Kate." Then she turned to her daughter. "Why don't you leave us alone for a bit?"

Margaret left quietly, closing the door behind her.

"Won't you sit down, dear?" Aurore looked around for a chair, then decided to kneel on the floor right beside her aunt.

"How have you been?" Amanda asked.

"Fine," she replied, wondering where this conversation was headed.

"Tell me what you've been up to."

Amanda asked the question casually, as if it had been days since she had seen her, rather than years. "Well," Aurore began slowly, "you probably know that after I graduated from law school, I came back to town and formed a law firm with . . . one of my friends from school. It was a struggle at first, but the firm—we call it Cronin and Associates—has become quite successful.''

''I'm proud of you.''

The statement was simple, but Aurore had never heard those words before, at least not from this person.

''And how about your life away from work? Has there been anyone for you since Robert died?''

''No,'' she lied.

''I'm sorry about that.''

''Yes, so am I.''

Amanda pulled her blankets up closer to her chin. ''I've had a lot of time to think lately. A lot of time to try to make sense out of my life. And I came to realize that one of the things I most regretted was losing touch with you over the past few years.''

''I've regretted it, too.''

''There were things you did that I could never condone—and I'm sure you know what they are. But I also know that I wasn't a very good mother for you. And I wanted to tell you I was sorry, while I still had a chance.''

''I'm sure you did the best you could.''

Amanda closed her eyes and shook her head. ''No, no. I should have done more. I owed that to your mother.'' She hesitated, as if gathering her strength. ''But the problem was, I could never seem to get over how jealous I was of her. And that always kept me from giving you the love you really needed.''

Her gaze drifted up to the ceiling, her mind back dozens of years.

''She was so beautiful. Too beautiful, I used to think. God had wasted beauty that he might have divvied up among the rest of us. And that red hair—it was like a beacon to all the young men. Calling them, welcoming them, pulling them into her orbit.

''I was the oldest.'' Amanda's voice became stronger, her head more erect. ''I was supposed to be first. Except I never was. She was Papa's darling, and I was just the other daughter.''

She folded her fingers over the edge of her quilt. ''And so

when we discovered she had gotten married, we were all shocked. It was a family scandal, a scandal for the whole town. But secretly, I loved it. For I thought that all of them—Charlotte and my father, even all the boys in New Orleans—got just what they deserved. Their little sweetheart didn't turn out to be so sweet after all.''

She paused for a moment, then gestured for the cup of tea just out of reach on the table. Aurore held it for her, stunned by the depth of her aunt's emotions, silenced by Amanda's new ability to strip away old layers of deceit.

''And then you arrived, a poor, motherless little girl. It was my chance to try and make it up to Charlotte. And I did try at first. But that didn't last for long. For it turned out you were pretty and you were smart, much smarter than my own daughter, in fact. And, silly as it may seem, I felt like I was competing with Charlotte all over again, and once again I was going to lose.''

Aurore remembered her aunt's harsh rebukes, the chilly, disapproving glances, the sense that no matter what she did, Amanda would find something to criticize. But underneath, she must have known there was love. For why else would she keep coming back, hoping someday to find it?

''The truth was,'' Amanda continued, ''that I was very proud of you. The grades you got in school. The work you did during the war. Your job at the State Department—at least until that terrible mess erupted around you. But I just never seemed capable of telling you that I cared about you.

''Like your graduation from law school. I should have gone. There was no reason not to. Except that something inside just stopped me.''

''I was disappointed you didn't come,'' Aurore said. ''I guess that's why I stayed away these last few years.''

''I don't blame you,'' her aunt replied.

There was another subject Amanda hadn't raised. But if she was opening up, Aurore decided she might as well broach it. ''I think I always felt that you resented the fact that Stephen and I were close.''

Amanda smiled weakly. ''Yes, there was that, too. His affection for you only made it worse. It was yet another place where I was losing out to Charlotte—my own husband. Lord knows, he never gave me any reason to doubt his love. But I couldn't help it. That was the way I felt.''

She looked away. ''And Stephen used to nag me all the time: 'Why do you have to be so hard on Kate? Why can't you show her that you love her?' But that only made me more jealous.''

Aurore hesitated, wondering if the question on her lips would cause her aunt more pain. But they'd stripped away so many secrets already, what was one more?

''Did you know that Stephen sent money to my father?''

''Only after he died. Cadwalader told me. He wanted to know if he should continue making the payments. But I stopped them. You were a grown woman. I didn't see any point in paying your father to stay away any longer.''

''But you didn't tell me. . . .'' For the first time, Aurore's voice took on the tone of an accusation.

''No, I didn't,'' she acknowledged. ''Because it was your uncle's secret. I didn't think I should be the one to divulge it.''

''But it kept me from knowing my father. . . .''

''Yes,'' her aunt sighed. ''I don't think I realized that could hurt you. I suppose I just never really forgave your father for your mother's death.''

A pain contorted the lines of her face.

''I should be going,'' Aurore said quickly. ''You're probably getting tired.''

She rose to her feet, but her aunt reached out to stop her.

''Wait,'' she said. ''There's one more thing.'' She propped herself up on her side, then pointed across the room. ''Go over to the desk and look in the second drawer on the left. You'll find a bundle of old letters.''

Aurore did as she was told, and found the cache of envelopes, tied together with a pale pink ribbon. ''What are they?'' she asked.

''From your mother,'' Amanda replied. ''From the time I left home until she died. I want you to have them.''

''I can't believe it,'' Aurore murmured.

''I reread them the other day and remembered that there

was something else about your mother that I had envied. Your father may have been nothing but a drunk of a farmer in my book, but, oh, did your mother love him! When she loved, she didn't just love with her heart or with her head, but with her whole being.'' Her eyes grew watery. ''I just wish I had been able to love like that, too.''

Aurore turned the bundle over and over in her hands. ''Why didn't you show them to me before?''

''Because you wouldn't have understood. But you're older now. You know what love feels like. You know the twists and turns that a life can take.''

''But I knew that fifteen years ago, Amanda!''

Amanda closed her eyes, then said softly, ''You have to remember, Katharine. She may have been your mother, but she was my sister, too. And the letters were all I had left of her.''

Aurore looked down at the thin, yellowing sheets of writing paper. *All I have left of her. All that anyone has left of her.*

When she glanced back at Amanda, she saw that her aunt had drifted off to sleep. Carefully, she readjusted her blankets, then kissed her one last time. She could forgive her now. She hoped her aunt could understand that. For as imperfect a mother as she had been, as silly as her hobgoblins now might seem, she had done the best she could. She had opened her house and opened her arms. And, in time, she had finally learned how to open her heart.

Aurore took a deep breath to regain her composure, then went out into the hallway.

She found Margaret in Stephen's old study, looking out the window at the thickening clouds.

''She's sleeping,'' Aurore reported.

''She often does that at this time of day.'' Margaret motioned toward a tray with a crystal decanter. ''Would you like a sherry? I know I would.''

''Yes, thanks.''

Margaret got out two glasses and filled them. ''Did you have a good talk?''

''Yes.'' Aurore wondered if her cousin would probe further, but Margaret didn't follow up.

"How's Jack?" Aurore asked, trying a different tack.

Margaret snorted. "We were divorced five years ago."

"I'm sorry."

"Don't be. It was never a very good marriage."

"We really have lost touch, haven't we?"

Margaret nodded. "And you? I knew about Robert, of course. But after he died, did you ever marry?"

Aurore shook her head.

"We're a fine pair," Margaret said. "Who would have thought at our deb ball that we'd wind up this way. A couple of old maids!"

Aurore winced. "I don't think of myself that way."

Margaret laughed and finished off her drink.

Aurore looked out the window. "It's getting late. I'd better be getting home." She hesitated. "I know the next few months will be difficult for you, Margaret. I'd like to help."

"I appreciate that." She went to retrieve Aurore's coat. "Thanks again for coming." She hesitated, then added, "I guess at a time like this, we should all try to put the past behind us."

Aurore gave her a hug, then whispered, "I think you're right."

She felt guilty about leaving, but she was eager to get home. She wanted to devour the letters.

But first she lit a fire and made herself a cup of tea. Then, settling into her favorite armchair, she untied the knotted ribbon.

To her delight, the letters were in chronological order. They took her back to New Orleans, to a time of cotillions and courtesy, when the South was still struggling to recover from the wounds of war.

They took her into the mind and heart of the young woman who a few years hence would become her mother. A carefree girl whose laughter jumped off the page, whose intelligence abounded in the precise words she chose to describe the world around her.

She wrote of her excitement at meeting Emory Callahan. She said she was worried he wouldn't return from France, but never told Amanda that they were married. Then, when

Emory did come back, there was a new defiance. She was leaving New Orleans "and Mother and Daddy be damned!"

The letters touched Aurore's heart. Her mother had been so optimistic that it would all work out, just as she had been with Robert.

But then the letters took on a new tone, as if her mother was trying to persuade herself that everything was going to be fine. There was the birth of a daughter: "a scrawny little thing, but beautiful to me." Aurore felt the tears well up in her eyes.

The letters became franker then. Emory's fields weren't producing like they should. She was pregnant again, she hoped for a boy. Maybe a new baby "would make him happy again."

The last letter closed: "Must run. There's a picnic tomorrow and Matty and I still have to bake the pies."

That was all. Of course, it was.

Somewhere in her heart Aurore felt a sharp stab of pain. She could remember the day now, as clearly as if it were yesterday. The pies, the parade, the picnic. And her mother's death.

Amanda was right: she never would have understood the words when she was younger. But now she did. Every one of them. The hope and the pain. But most of all the love.

Amanda lived for three more weeks. It wasn't very long in the course of a lifetime, but Aurore tried to make the most of it. She shared Margaret's chores, fed her aunt meals and gave her backrubs, passed the hours by talking or reading to her. They buried their difficult past by sharing what was left of the present.

Then one evening, Amanda slipped off to sleep and never woke up again.

The night of the funeral Aurore went home and got out her mother's letters. She read them once more and thought about the two Dellaplaine girls, their triumphs and their mistakes, their loves and their disappointments. And she reflected on her own life and what her mother might have thought of it.

And as she did, she realized that Amanda had succeeded in bringing her mythical mother to life. Seventeen years before she had received Stephen's legacy. Now she had received Amanda's.

Time, Aurore had learned, could be a great healer. The passage of years had allowed her to mend her rift with her aunt and cousin. And as the weeks went by, she found that the pain in her heart labeled "Andrew" seemed to diminish, too.

She missed his love, and yet she carried it with her. She felt more attractive, and that made her feel more secure. Just at the moment when she needed more confidence, she was able to find it.

The firm was flourishing. The news of Andrew's appointment had undoubtedly attracted some new business, but that alone couldn't account for all of their new clients. Even without Andrew's fees, the firm would close 1961 with record profits. Everyone, from the secretaries on up, was going to get a big Christmas bonus.

And now, she decided, she could risk seeing him again.

This time, he suggested the Sans Souci. The choice amused her—it was "in" with the Kennedy crowd. But it also was civilized, not at all clandestine.

The restaurant stretched out below her—a place to see and to be seen. As she entered, the diners all seemed to turn to look at her. And then she saw him, on the platform on the far side of the room.

For a moment she felt weak. Then she grasped the banister and fixed a smile on her face.

The maître d' led her back to "Mr. Cronin's table." Andrew kissed her on the cheek. It felt hot, burning her skin with a memory that couldn't be washed away.

"You look wonderful," he said.

"Thank you."

"You must be happy."

"Well, I am," she lied. "Maybe not 'very happy,' but at least 'happy.' "

"Good. I'm glad to hear that."

"And you?"

"Fair," he said. "Not happy."

The waiter arrived and gave them menus.

"It's over, Andrew. You've got to accept that."

"I know. I do. That doesn't mean I have to like it, does it?"

"No."

"I told Ellie we had a fight."

"Why?"

"I had to. Did you want to have to go through another evening like that last one every month or so?"

"No, but . . . what did you tell her?"

"I told her we had had an argument about what kind of clients the firm should go after now. But that since you were in charge, I had to stay out of your way. She was pretty upset."

"Actually, I'd wondered why I hadn't heard from her."

"She misses you, but . . . you know Ellie."

"As far as she's concerned, you come first. And if you're not talking to me, she can't either."

"Something like that."

"Didn't she think it was odd, coming so soon after our vacation?"

"I told her we had avoided talking about the firm then, because we knew this might happen."

"Will you tell her we had lunch today?"

"Depends how it goes. And how we feel after it's over."

She consulted her menu, he consulted the wine list. It seemed strange sitting across from him, calmly reading down a list of French dishes. A mélange of images rocketed through her brain, pictures of them eating and sleeping and loving.

She closed her eyes for a moment. She mustn't think of that. The memory was still too fresh, the potential for pain too great. This was a test today, and she wanted desperately to pass it.

He was talking again. "I would be lying if I said it's been easy. The new job helps."

"My work helps, too."

"But things haven't been the same with Ellie. She knows it. She blames the job, the long hours, the pressures."

Aurore didn't want to listen.

"Still, I guess we'll work it out."

"I guess you'll have to, won't you?"

He looked at her then, and for a moment she thought he would speak up, that he would tell her he had made the wrong choice.

But she knew Andrew too well—and so did he.

"Do you regret last summer?" she asked.

"No. Do you?"

"No, not at all."

"I just wish that we could be close without hurting each other. That we could find a way to be friends again."

"So do I, Andrew," she whispered. "So do I."

They kept it light after that. She swapped gossip about their firm and other lawyers, he talked about what it was like to work for Bobby and the latest scuttlebutt from the White House.

And then it was time to leave.

He walked her back to their old office. There was a nip in the air, but the scent of Christmas, too. Shoppers surged by on their lunch hour, oblivious to the couple who paused for a moment outside the double glass doors.

"You ought to come up," she said. "Say hello to everyone."

"I will," he said. "Another time." He reached inside his overcoat and pulled out a small square package. "Here, I want you to have this."

It was wrapped with gold foil and tied with a red velvet ribbon. Obviously, the store had done the wrapping.

"You shouldn't have!"

"Well, 1961 was a very good year for me. I wanted you to have a remembrance of it. . . ."

She examined the box closely.

"Don't open it now. Put it under your tree."

"All right, I will."

He rebuttoned his coat against the wind. "I enjoyed lunch."

"So did I."

"When can we do it again?"

She looked at the gift again. "Let's not push it, okay?"

He smiled wanly. "Okay."

She took the present home and put it underneath the small artificial tree she had set up on a table in her living room. She stepped back and laughed at the sad state of things. There were only four presents: a small package, a surprise from Margaret; a large box, probably a blouse, from Jane; a heavy package, probably a book, from Mal.

And the present from Andrew.

Last year, she had spent Christmas Eve with the Cronins. *I wonder what they're doing this year*. She picked up the small package and shook it. She smiled, musing whether Ellie would get one just like it.

She worked late on Christmas Eve, but instead of going home, she went to the service at the National Cathedral. It was purely on a whim, but the old familiar carols, the warm glow of the candles, and the red-cheeked crowd around her made her feel less lonely.

She went home and opened her presents, saving Andrew's for last. She pulled off the paper and opened the box. Nestled in a square of cotton was an exquisite gold bangle bracelet.

When she picked it up to study it more closely, she saw the inscription. The message was subtle, but she understood. "1961."

Yes, Andrew, she thought, it was a pretty good year.

Thirty-Nine

In most matters of business and law, Jason Rush preferred to hold his cards close to his chest. By nature, he was a man of action, bordering on the impulsive. Yet over the years he had learned the strategic value of going second, of letting the other fellow decide whether to kick or receive.

But this wasn't a matter of business, and he had already

waited fourteen years. And now that he was back in Washington, he was determined to see Kate Callahan again.

He knew his best hope, as always, was Amanda McNeil. The old woman had kept mum when he'd pumped her after Kate had disappeared. He could tell she was mortified by all the headlines and the speeches about her niece. But perhaps enough time had passed. . . .

He realized he still remembered the number when he found it in the phone book. He was surprised, however, when Margaret answered the phone.

"Jason, how are you?"

"I thought you were living in San Diego."

"I was . . . up until my divorce."

"How's your mother?"

"She died last fall. . . . She'd been ill for some time."

"I'm sorry. I wish I'd known."

"You always were one of her favorites, Jason."

"Have you been in touch with Kate?"

"Yes."

His spirits lifted. "Where is she?"

"In town."

"Can you tell me how to find her?"

"It'll cost you."

He tried not to show his impatience. "Okay, Margaret, how much?"

Her price was dinner for two at the Hay-Adams. After sharing a rack of lamb, a bottle of wine, and the long tale of how she'd spent her life since the war, Margaret finally explained how her cousin had changed her name and opened a law firm.

"Aurore Callahan," he repeated. Such a simple change, but a critical one. Because of it he had lost track of Kate for more than a decade.

Margaret had "dessert" in mind, too, but that didn't tempt Jason. She bored him now even more than she did when she was a dizzy debutante. He'd been willing to spring for one dinner in exchange for a precious nugget of information. But now that he knew where to find Kate, he had no need for a sun-fried divorcée from California.

* * *

Aurore was surprised when Jason Rush called her, but even more surprised when she agreed to see him.

It must be some kind of perverse curiosity, she decided. Certainly, she no longer felt any affection for Jason. But an attraction? Well, possibly. He was, after all, a man she once thought she could marry.

It was a ridiculous notion now. And yet Jason was the kind of man who made you wonder how his life had turned out. Had he made a killing in the market? Had he met the perfect woman? Or was he still the same old Jason?

"Why don't you come by my office around two?" She made no suggestion of lunch—by design. She wanted to keep their meeting formal—and on her own turf.

For she was proud of that turf. She had come a long way since the days when she was just another government girl. And she wanted to make sure Jason knew that.

Most mornings she didn't spend much time fussing over what she would wear to the office. But this time she did. After several changes she settled on her Chanel suit, black and white with a smart cropped jacket and a bright red scarf at the neck. It bolstered her sense of confidence. More important, she knew Jason was the kind of man who would recognize the designer—and appreciate the price tag.

He arrived five minutes past the appointed time. It annoyed her, but she knew better than to show it. She suspected he had done it on purpose.

"Jason." She rose as her secretary ushered him in.

"It's good to see you again, Kate." He paused, then added, "I mean, Aurore."

"Call me whatever you like." She led him over to her couch and sat down across from him.

For a moment they were like two street-smart kids sizing up each other on a playground, wondering if they could be friends or whether too much was at stake.

He had aged well. His hair was still jet-black, but his skin was no longer so pale. He was sporting the tan of a recent warm-weather vacation. He had the look of wealth, but not the prep-school kind. He had kept trim, but then he could probably afford whatever club membership he needed—if not the club itself.

And what does he think of me?

He looked around her office. She was glad she had used some of last year's profits to refurbish the room with some choice antiques.

"Nice office."

"Thank you. We've done all right."

"The 'we,' I take it, is Andrew Cronin."

"And myself." There was no point in trying to hide behind the firm's name for Jason's sake. "We went to law school together, then formed the firm."

"He's at Justice now, isn't he?"

"Yes. And where are you now?" She remembered from the stories that appeared when he first got the job, but didn't want him to know that.

"SEC," he replied. "Chief of enforcement."

"Sounds impressive."

He shrugged. "I like to say that I'm right for the job because I'm going after the kind of people I grew up with." He paused. "You changed your name."

"Not really. It's my middle name."

"Why did you do it?"

"I don't know. I suppose I thought it sounded more elegant."

"I wondered if it was because of those stories that came out when you were at the State Department."

She bristled. "Perhaps it was."

He rose and wandered over to study her framed law degree. "I guess you really didn't need my help back then, did you?"

What could she say? That she had needed it, but didn't want it. That as desperate as she had been, she still knew the cost would have been too great.

She tried not to dwell on that time anymore. But when she did, the anger still bubbled out of her like a nascent volcano. She could cool the fire. She could always remind herself of what she had managed to achieve. But the bitterness still boiled beneath the surface, waiting for the fissure that would let it escape.

"I appreciated your offer, Jason, but I guess I decided there wasn't anything anyone could do to help."

He turned around to face her. "When you changed your name I lost track of you."

For a moment she saw that old wildness in his eyes. "I really didn't mean to hide from my old friends." She tried to keep her voice calm. "It just seemed simpler that way." She hesitated. "Anyway, it all seems like such a long time ago now."

"And you never married?"

She shook her head. "What about you?"

"Once. But it was a mistake."

"Where did you meet her?"

"You'll laugh."

"No I won't."

"At a debutante ball."

She did laugh.

"See I told you!"

"You always said you found those parties boring!" She paused. "Do you have any kids?"

"No, thank God."

"I thought you'd want to make sure the Rush line survived."

"Well, I do, but . . . when my marriage broke up, I was glad I didn't have all that baggage."

"How about Delilah and Elliot? Do you know whatever happened to them?"

"Delilah, no. But it's funny about Elliot—I keep running into him. After the war, we both ended up at the Commerce Department. And then the other day I ran into him on the elevator. What can I say? He's a government bureaucrat."

"Somehow I never pictured you that way, Jason."

"I don't either. The trick is, to go in and out, in and out. Every time you come out, you make more money than you did when you went in. I'm sure Andrew Cronin understands that."

Did he? If so, he certainly wasn't as cynical about it as Jason was.

For a moment she compared the two men. They could both

be charmers, with all the right words. Yet Jason still had that slickness about him, that slickness she had failed to see when she was young and didn't know any better. But she had learned a lot of lessons over the years, and one of the most important was to beware of men with the gift of gab.

"I'd like to see you again, Kate."

She had wondered if it would come to this. Flattered in a way that it had. But she was a different woman than she had been at twenty.

"I've enjoyed seeing you, Jason. But we have a history, you and I. And maybe it's better just to leave it at that."

Her rejections still stung him, but not the way they used to. He had missed his chance, and he knew it. When she was down, she might have listened. He should have pushed her harder then. She would have been dependent on him. She might have married him.

For he had been right about her. The woman of forty validated the judgment of his twenties. Beautiful. Brilliant. Better than the rest. He had been obsessed with her, and he still understood why.

But that, as she had said, was a long time ago. He cared about other things now. Money, for one. Power for another. Chasing difficult women—especially those approaching middle age—was well down the list.

He rose. "Perhaps we can have lunch sometime."

"Who knows?" she said. "Maybe we'll meet in a courtroom."

"Now that would be interesting!"

"Good-bye, then."

"Good-bye."

She watched as he walked down the hall to the reception area. He took his time, surveying the paintings and prints that hung on the walls. As he did, she could almost hear the whir of the adding machine in his head.

As a lawyer, she had learned to be analytical, to try to put emotional reactions aside. Yet after all this time, her reaction to Jason was totally subjective, totally visceral. And all the years, all the pleasant small talk, even all the flattery and flirtation, still couldn't dispel the bad taste that was left in her mouth after sampling him one more time.

* * *

It had taken Aurore a while to learn to love the Kennedys. Perhaps it was because Andrew seemed to adore them so slavishly. Or because of her memories of Bobby from law school. Or simply because she had learned not to grow too attached to anyone or anything.

But as the years went on, she found it impossible not to like the First Family: the vibrant leader and his rapier wit; the lovely young wife with her sense of style and culture; the beautiful children and their antics.

But there was more than that. Washington had changed during his term—and for the better. The traditions of the old-fashioned southern town were tumbling down, slowly but irrevocably. And gradually the city was becoming a capital worthy of the world.

So when the awful news came on that November afternoon in 1963, it felt as if a member of her family had died. Like everyone else, she would always remember where she was when she heard it: in Judge Granelli's courtroom in the Federal Courthouse. A bailiff passed the judge a note, and turning ashen, he read it aloud. He declared the trial in recess.

She walked through the courthouse in a daze, not sure where to go or what to do. And then she knew.

It was a warm afternoon and she could have easily walked. But it was faster to hail a cab. She was at the Justice Department in minutes.

Secretaries milled about, hugging and crying openly. She could hear phones ringing in every office, but going unanswered. When she reached Andrew's office, she started to explain to his secretary, but she waved her on in. It was obvious why she had come today.

She found him staring out his window, the big, wide window with the grand view of Constitution Avenue. She had looked out this window with him before and laughed at the effect it had: with this vista, you could feel powerful and in control.

But now, everything seemed out of control.

He turned to face her and she could see the grief that was already etched onto his face.

"I came as soon as I heard."

"I can't believe it's over."

She went to him then, and held him, tightly. And as she did, he started to cry.

At first he tried not to, but he couldn't hold back the tears. Tonight he would go home to Ellie and be brave and male for Ellie's sake. But with Aurore, he could show his real self. And for now that person wanted to cry.

He cried for a long, long time. He cried without shame, without embarrassment, great heaving sobs that shuddered through his body. The whole building seemed to cry. The whole country. The whole world.

She cried, too, and yet she was moved that he would let her try to comfort him. It told her that this love of theirs would still endure, no matter what form it was forced to take.

When at last he gained control of himself, he spoke very, very softly.

"There'll never be another like him."

She squeezed him tightly one more time. "I know, Andrew," she murmured. "I know."

PART FIVE

Washington, 1964

Forty

The gray days were more depressing than usual that winter. The city seemed out of sorts with itself, refusing to accept the fact that the president had died and a dog-faced Texan had taken over his office.

The attorney general had turned over his department to his deputies while he wrestled with his grief. They tried to carry on the best they could, but Aurore knew that all the joy had gone out of Andrew's work. There were rumors up and down the halls of Justice that Bobby might run for office, maybe even for president. And if he left, Aurore was sure that Andrew would, too.

Could she work with him again? She thought so, but until he came back, she couldn't be sure. Even as the firm had added partners, everyone knew who was still in charge. She had gotten used to making decisions on her own. It would be hard to give that up.

Then there was that other, more delicate problem. The problem that she and Andrew could not bat around at a partners' meeting. The problem of loving each other, and never being able to show it.

Even though the warm memories of a summer by a lake were fading now, those days had changed their relationship forever. It would be good to have him back, but it would hurt, too. His presence would be a constant reminder of what she could—and couldn't—have. A flesh-and-blood remembrance of the fleeting loves she had known.

Sometimes she felt restless, that it was time to try something new. Now and then she thought of making another trip to Gloucester to see how Martha was getting on.

But no, Aurore had made her decision. And though it was difficult, she knew it was the right one. Martha was not the answer to filling her emotional vacuum, any more than Andrew could be.

But what was the solution? She was forty-four now, probably past the midpoint of her life. Would there be time left for love? Time for another man? Probably not. And that was why, she knew, that the firm always felt like family. Jane and the others, they were colleagues of course, but they also felt like brothers and sisters, sons and daughters, with careers that needed to be guided and shaped. In a way, she was mother to them all.

And their long-lost father was about to come home.

He asked her for an appointment, and even though his name was on the door, she treated him like an important client. A two-hour block of time, an offer of coffee or tea, an admonition to her secretary to "hold all my calls."

It did not take Andrew long to get to the point.

"I'm leaving the Justice Department."

"Do you want to come back?"

He smiled. "If you'll have me."

She set down her coffee cup. "Of course, I will."

"I know it will be an adjustment for you."

"I'll manage."

"But you've gotten so good at running the place—maybe I should just stay out of your way."

"But then we wouldn't have any fun."

The words had a double meaning that she hadn't intended. She held her breath, his teacup stopped in midair. His blue eyes darkened, capturing hers. For a moment neither of them spoke.

Then he put down his cup. "I think we needed the break," he said softly. "I think it will make it easier now."

"I think so, too."

He took out a pipe—a new habit he'd acquired—and filled it and tamped down the tobacco and lit it with a match. This was a different Andrew. An Andrew who had been apart from her. An Andrew who had been places where she couldn't go.

He had aged some over the past few years. The tawny hair was laced with gray, his eyes framed by lines of concern. His lanky, youthful figure had filled out to a more middle-aged measurement.

He took a puff of the pipe, then held it in both hands. "I think I ought to tell you that Ellie and I are—how should I put it?—better now."

"I'm happy for you."

"There was a time"—he hesitated—"I used to wonder why you never pressured me to leave her. I used to think that if you had ever asked me to, I would have."

She rose and turned away from him, struggling to keep her emotions buried. "If I had pushed you to leave her, Andrew, I never would have been able to live with myself."

She stared at her hands for a moment, then turned back to him. "It had to be your decision," she said softly. "It always was."

The firm welcomed Andrew back with balloons and a banner and a big cake that read "Andrew Who?" He gave a short speech, saying how good it was to be back, and then good-naturedly admonished everyone to "get to work."

He needn't have worried. Cronin and Associates was growing now, faster than Aurore had ever anticipated. Someday soon they'd have to open an office in New York. And on the West Coast. It was just a matter of time.

They had seventy-five lawyers, and thirty of them were partners. Got a messy divorce? Call Paul Johnson. Patent law? Murray Feldman. A case before the ICC? Alice Rampling. But Aurore still liked dabbling in everything—and keeping her eye on it all.

That included real estate. Those farms out in Fairfax County that she'd bought a few years before were worth ten times what she'd paid for them. Highways, shopping malls, tract homes, they were all going in, and developers were phoning, telling her to name her price. But she wasn't in a hurry. She knew she was sitting on a gold mine, and as Washington grew, her land could only become more valuable.

Her knowledge of the media had become a valuable commodity, too. Over the years, she had studied it like an academic discipline. It had started with her lunches with Jerry Pieczenik. She loved the newsroom gossip: who was "in," who was "out," who was covering which beat. At first, all she'd really cared about was following Eddie Feigan. But now her attention had turned to his son.

She dissected his stories with the precision of a surgeon and the mien of a frustrated English teacher. He seemed, from Aurore's critical viewpoint, to have graduated from the same school of journalism as his father. She combed through his stories, cataloging his apparent biases. She cackled whenever one of his articles required a correction the following day. She empathized whenever an aggrieved official complained in a letter to the editor that Tom had misquoted him. She wondered how long he'd keep getting handed the choice stories he'd been getting.

She focused on the Feigans, but she had learned that Jerry's information could serve a more immediate purpose, too. She got to know the reporters who covered the courthouses and learned how to win them to her clients' side. And when the firm was doing a lobbying job, it helped to know where the chances of planting a favorable story were best.

She explained all that to Andrew, trying to bring him up to date on everything that had happened in the years he'd been gone. Despite the passage of time, it still felt like the old days, starting the morning with a cup of coffee together. Their offices were plusher now, their staffs bigger. But there was still the swapping of gossip, the sharing of advice.

"Peter Raymond called me yesterday." He dropped the name casually, in between sips of coffee.

"The White House guy?"

Andrew nodded.

"What did he want?"

"They've got a seat opening up on the National Labor Relations Board. Your name came up."

"Me? But I've never done much labor law."

"Apparently it doesn't matter. They'd like to appoint a woman for a change. You've built a good reputation in this town, and you've been a loyal soldier for the party."

"It's that simple?"

He nodded.

She smiled. "I'm flattered."

"He wanted me to sound you out. What shall I tell him?"

A presidential nomination. The kind of job she'd never dared to dream about. The chance to clean the slate, once and for all. "Tell him I'm interested . . . if you think it would be all right for the firm."

He grinned. "I'll call him right now." He headed for the door.

"Wait a minute."

Andrew turned around.

"What about the trouble I had at the State Department?"

"What about it?"

"I think you'd better tell Raymond about it. If it comes out, and someone makes a big deal of it, there'll be hell to pay. I think they should know about it."

"But this is 1964, dammit!"

"Still, I think you should tell him."

He shrugged. "If you insist. But no one will care."

She managed to smile. "Let's hope not."

But she wasn't sure. Fifteen years had passed, but was that long enough? If it wasn't, she wanted to know now, not after her name had gone before Congress, not after she'd been called to testify. She was not about to be humiliated again.

Then she smiled to herself. But, on the other hand, if someone wanted to reward her . . .

Peter Raymond met her for lunch at Trader Vic's. His suit had a Brooks Brothers polish, but his Texas drawl gave away his backcountry roots. Aurore judged that he was a few years younger than she was, with virtually no respect for his elders.

"We were pleased when Andrew said you were willing to

come on board." He summoned the waiter with an impatient gesture.

"Tell me what your timetable is."

"The term expires September thirtieth. We hope to get you through the FBI clearance in time so that Congress can act before it goes into recess."

The FBI clearance. Of course she'd known about that, but still it sounded ominous. "Did Andrew talk to you about my background?"

"You mean that stuff at the State Department?"

She nodded.

"Yeah, but I'd like to hear what you have to say about it."

"There's not much to say." She picked up her spoon and fiddled with it. "Eddie Feigan—you remember him, the old *Standard* columnist?"

Raymond nodded.

"Well, he wrote a column claiming I was a Communist. At the time I was an aide to John Phillip Harrison. It was true that I had attended some party meetings back in the forties—I had trouped along with my fiancé. But I certainly never joined the party or made any sort of commitment to it.

"Still, it was a sensitive time and my boss asked me to resign. I refused because I knew I was innocent. So he fired me."

"Did you file any sort of appeal?"

She laughed. "Obviously, you weren't around in those days."

"You changed your name then, didn't you?"

"Well, I began using my middle name. Why?"

He shrugged. "Some people might wonder what you were trying to hide."

"I was trying to save my reputation." She realized, too late, that her voice was rising.

"Well, naturally, we wish your résumé didn't include that little episode, but we don't see it as a major obstacle. Christ, in some circles now it's a badge of honor to have been tarred by McCarthy."

She allowed herself to relax a little.

"But get this straight," he went on. "We don't intend to

bring it up. We'll have to have a strategy to deal with it if it does comes up. But, of course, we hope it won't.''

She smiled weakly, lifting her glass. "I'll drink to that.''

It was one of those Washington receptions she had come to dread. Too many people crowded around a table laden with crumbly canapés. Still, it was supposed to be good for business.

She was nursing her second glass of wine when she felt a hand placed on the bared part of her back.

"Congratulations!''

She turned to find Jason, offering up his martini in a toast.

"What are you talking about?''

"The job at the NLRB.''

He was better connected than she gave him credit for. "It's not really official yet,'' she cautioned. "Who'd you hear it from?''

He smiled. "The FBI.''

"The FBI?''

"They tracked me down as part of your background check.''

"I'm impressed,'' she said warily.

"Well, there was a time when I was your boss. And, depending on whom you asked, possibly something more.''

She would have drawn away from him if she hadn't been desperate to find out more. "Did they . . . did they ask you about why I left the State Department?''

He nodded.

"What did you say?''

"That I was sure you had never been a member of the party, but that other than that, all I knew was what I read in the papers.''

"Great,'' she groaned.

"Well, face it, Kate, you weren't confiding in me much back then.''

"No, I wasn't.''

"Don't worry,'' he said. "I've been through one of these. Those guys ask a lot of questions, but nothing much ever comes of it. It'll be a piece of cake.''

"Hmm." She stuffed a canapé in her mouth. "I wonder. . . ."

He checked his watch. "I've got to run to another reception. But say, no matter what happens, good luck."

"Thanks." He patted her arm, then disappeared into the crowd.

She wondered what he had told the investigators. The truth was, Jason didn't know very much about her. He knew where she'd gone to school and where she'd gone to work. How she'd disappeared for several years, then just as suddenly popped back into the headlines.

All I knew was what I read in the papers.

Unfortunately, she thought, that was all that anybody knew.

She cut back her caseload to make more time for "cramming." Supreme Court decisions, newspaper clips, law journals—she was going to be prepared. She might be a neophyte in labor law today, but she was determined to sound like an expert by summer's end.

And then a diversion turned up—in the form of a phone call from Lucy.

Matty had died two years before. So now her daughter was the only tie Aurore had left to the little country town of Homer, Mississippi.

Lucy was agitated. "Have you been following the news down here?"

"Who hasn't?" Civil rights groups had launched "Freedom Summer" and thousands of college students were streaming south to help Negroes register to vote.

"I'll get right to the point. Do you remember when you were down here the last time and I said we could use your help?"

And I never called you back to volunteer. "I'm sorry, Lucy. I really did mean to get back in touch with you."

"Never mind. You aren't the first. But I could use your help now."

"Tell me how." Aurore pulled out a yellow pad to make some notes.

"We need a flood of lawyers down here," she said. "It's the only way we can protect these kids. We gotta keep challenging the police. Make 'em know someone's watching them. Do you think you could give us a week or two?"

Aurore hesitated. She had already cleared her calendar, but for the purpose of preparing for the hearings. She wanted to help Lucy; it was just that the timing was so bad.

"Can I get back to you? I'll need to check with my partners first."

"Sure. And if you can come, you can stay at my place if you like."

"Thanks for the offer. I'll get back to you soon."

She hung up the phone, feeling guilty for having lied to her friend. She did not intend to check with her partners. She was going to check with a self-important young man who just happened to work for the White House.

It took Peter Raymond twenty-four hours to return her phone call. That was not, she decided, an auspicious sign.

"What can I do for you?" he asked.

"I was trying to make some travel plans so I wanted to know the status of my nomination."

"We're still working on the clearances."

"Any problem?" She tried not to display her fear.

"No, just the routine political stuff."

"The reason I ask . . . I've been thinking of leaving Washington for a few weeks. A friend asked me if I'd come down to Mississippi and do some legal work."

"Civil rights stuff?"

She took a deep breath. "Yes."

There was a long pause. "I wouldn't if I were you."

"Why not?"

Again, he hesitated. "The president is getting pretty steamed up about the credentials fight those Freedom Democrats are planning for the convention."

"I see." It was starting to become clear.

"The other thing is, with your kind of background, I don't think you ought to be running around sticking your neck out for a left-wing cause right now."

With your kind of background. The words made her shiver. *What kind of background?* She was no lefty. She'd never been.

"I'm not sure I'd characterize the civil rights movement as a bunch of left-wing radicals," she said quietly.

"Look, I'm just trying to make you understand the facts of life, Aurore. You've already got one strike against you. Okay, we're willing to overlook that. Just be careful that you don't end up with two or three."

Was it a warning—or a threat? And where did that leave her? She wanted to help Lucy. She knew she ought to go. And yet the job was so close she could taste it.

How many chances like this could she expect to get in a lifetime? She had lost so much fifteen years ago—her job, her dignity, her identity, really. Now all she wanted was the Senate's seal of approval. She had waited so long for it, a few more weeks wouldn't matter now.

"All right," she said at last. "I'll stay put."

"You're no dummy, Aurore."

"Right," she said as she hung up. Then she muttered to herself, "But am I something worse?"

Later that afternoon she gathered up her courage to make the call to Lucy.

"I'm sorry," she said, "but I can't get away right now. I really wanted to but . . ."

"That's okay."

Aurore could hear the disappointment in her old friend's voice. "Look," she said quickly. "I know Thad Walker at the NAACP's Washington office. I'll call him tomorrow. Maybe I could give them some help with the lobbying on the civil rights bill."

"Sure," Lucy replied. "If it'll make you feel better, fine."

The words stung. "If my situation changes, I'll let you know. Maybe later in the summer. Maybe things will let up."

"Katie, cut the crap." Lucy's voice set the phone crackling. "There comes a time when you have to take a stand. People are putting their lives on the line down here this summer. Kids like my Eric. White boys and girls. If you're not willing to do that, fine, I'll stop asking. But don't waste my time pretending to be too busy. And don't waste my time pretending to be something you aren't.''

Lucy hung up the phone with an angry crash. Aurore stared at the handset for a long moment, then heard the dial tone return. Across the miles, a phone went dead. And in the same moment, Aurore felt that a part of her soul had died, too.

Forty-One

The weeks went by, and still there was no word from the White House. As the summer heat descended with a vengeance, Aurore knew there was no way her nomination—whenever it came—could clear Congress before the August recess.

Meanwhile, the news was full of stories from Mississippi, horrible stories, dreadful stories. Three civil rights workers, young men, black and white, disappearing in the night. Then, weeks later, the harrowing discovery of their bodies, buried in an earthen dam.

The stories never let up. And they all seemed to taunt her for watching from the sidelines in the capital's sluggish summer heat.

Finally, to keep from going stir crazy, she'd agreed to take on a new client—a father, fighting for the custody of his children. She'd known the case would be tough, but it was worse than she had expected. This time, she lost.

As she sat in her office afterward, she reviewed the strategy she had followed. Had she given it her best shot? Or had she been too preoccupied with her own trial?

There was a knock at the door. Andrew peeked in. ''Got a second?''

''Got a revolver?''

"That bad, huh?"

"You know me. I hate to lose."

He hesitated. "I'm afraid I'm not going to help your mood."

"What do you mean?"

"Peter Raymond just called."

"Why didn't he call me?"

"A coward, I guess." He hesitated. "I don't know how to tell you this. They got cold feet on your nomination. . . ."

She sat, not comprehending at first, as Andrew rambled on. "They're worried about the election. Johnson's completely paranoid about Goldwater. They're not looking for new problems now."

"But this isn't just any problem, is it?" She said sarcastically. "A woman who was in bed with the commies fifteen years ago. That would drive the right wing wild, wouldn't it?"

"You said it, I didn't."

"But it's true, isn't it?"

"They're afraid it would just provide more ammunition for the folks who think LBJ's being too soft on Vietnam."

She threw up her hands. "Gosh, I'm honored. Who knows, maybe next month I'll be responsible for the whole future course of East-West relations!"

"I'm sorry," he said quietly. "You know I never would have pushed you if I'd thought this would happen."

"You never did pay enough attention to politics, Andrew."

She rose and went to the window. All those weeks, she thought. Wasted, playing Peter Raymond's lapdog. She could have gone to Mississippi. She could have helped Lucy.

She could have been true to herself.

She turned back to Andrew. "Fifteen years, Andrew, and it still won't leave me alone. Except what is it? I followed my boyfriend to some meetings he was interested in. Maybe I told him we shouldn't go. Maybe I argued with him on the way home. Nobody knows but me. But it was enough to ruin my career back then and it still follows me now."

"You didn't have to tell Peter," he reminded her. "You built a new life. You'd managed to escape it."

"You may be right. I probably could have gotten away with it. Maybe I used Raymond as a test, to see if anybody still cared. Because the truth is I'm getting tired of running. Half the people in my life know me as one person, and half know me as somebody else. And the worst thing is, sometimes I'm not sure which person I really am."

She looked back down at the street. "A long time ago my uncle told me to make sure to keep my name clean because you only have one name. So what's my name? Am I the Kate Callahan who was drummed out of town in 1949? Or am I Aurore Callahan, the Washington lawyer who didn't exist before 1950?"

She fiddled with the cord to her venetian blinds. "Sometimes I don't even know."

"There'll be other jobs," he said.

"It's not the job. Hell, if I sat down and analyzed it rationally I probably would have turned it down 'cause it would have meant a salary cut. No, it's the wounds, Andrew. Every time I think it's over and done with, something happens and I feel the hurt and the anger all over again."

She threw up her hands in despair. "And the stupidest things will do it. I'll see a story about how 'unidentified sources' have accused somebody of doing something and I just can't finish reading it. Or I'll read something about an American ambassador and I'll think, 'Whatever happened to my wonderful career in the Foreign Service?' "

"You don't regret everything that we've built together, do you?"

"No. It's just . . . it's just that I wish I could have been the one to control my life."

He came over and placed his hands on her shoulders. "You know, don't you, that if I could do anything to set it all straight, I would."

She managed to smile—for his sake—but then she turned inward again. "There's only one person who can set it straight. The person who was at those meetings and knows that I wasn't really involved with them. But it's been fifteen years. And if they haven't come forward yet, I don't see any reason why they should do it now."

* * *

Andrew invited her out for a drink, but Aurore declined.
She felt alone again, but at this moment the only person she
wanted to be with was herself.

As she unlocked the door to her townhouse, she experienced, for a fleeting moment, the comfort of familiar sur-
roundings. Plants she had nurtured from seedlings. Paintings
of favorite places. One-of-a-kind pieces of furniture, carefully
acquired over the years.

Yes, she thought, she had money now. She had friends in
high places. But still she couldn't escape the past. And even
if she hadn't told Peter Raymond, what was to stop that other
person? How could she be sure he wouldn't come forward
to sabotage her again?

Maybe she should have tempted him this time. At least
she might have found out who he was. Now she wasn't sure
she ever would.

Fifteen years had gone by, and she was no closer to the
answer now than she had been that long-ago summer. Back
then she could remember the faces at the meetings if not the
names. Now she couldn't even remember the faces.

But she blamed the two of them more than ever, Eddie
Feigan and his "source." They had ruined her once before.
They had cost her a career then; they had cost her a job now.

But more importantly they had made her forsake everything
she thought she believed in. Friends. Justice. Fighting against
prejudice. That's what her battle had been all about up to
now, but they had co-opted her.

She kicked off her shoes, mixed herself a stiff gin and
tonic, then began riffling through the mail. She hesitated when
she came to the copy of *Life*. The cover photograph was a
scene from Mississippi, a long line of black people, waiting
patiently to register to vote.

She began thumbing through the pages, as if she were
performing a penance. She stopped when she came to a photo
of a young black man being led out of a police station in
handcuffs, with blood streaming down his face.

She stared at the photo and sipped her drink. And then, in
a horrible instant, she realized who it was. It had been years
since she had seen him, a young teenager, mowing the lawn

of his mother's house. But if she had any lingering doubts, the cutline dispelled them. It was Lucy's son, Eric.

She thought of the murders earlier that summer, the lynchings of years gone by. Every day now Lucy faced the prospect of losing her son. A young man about the age of Martha. A young man who had his whole life before him.

And yet she hadn't been willing to sacrifice a stupid job for her old friend. A job that had seemed important only because important people had wanted to give it to her.

Know that I believed in the cause for which I died; now you must live for the causes in which we both believed.

Robert's final words cut through to her heart. How had her life gotten so out of synch? What had happened to her values, her ideals?

Yet she hadn't really changed. She still knew who she was, even if the rest of the world didn't.

She went to her desk and dug out the phone book. She placed a call to the airline, a call to Andrew, and then, the most difficult, a call to Lucy. And in the morning, she did what she knew she should have done months before.

She boarded a plane to Mississippi.

Forty-Two

The older Aurore got, the more sentimental she felt about coming back home to the firm.

The sights, sounds, even the smells came back to her in a rush. The chill of the marble lobby. The rat-tat-tat of high heels rushing to work. The faint smell of cigars in the elevator. The press of bodies and rain-soaked wool. A formidably paneled wood door, still emblazoned with only one name. And in the reception area, that same scene of the valley that he was never going to throw out.

She waved at the redheaded receptionist juggling phone

calls and breezed down the hall to her office. It was silly, but she was always relieved when she found it exactly the way she had left it.

She had traveled almost nonstop for the past two years. First had been two months in Mississippi, winding up cases that other lawyers had begun. She was there long enough to see Eric released from prison, his arm broken in two places but not his spirit. She'd made up with Lucy, and promised that the next time her old friend called for help, she'd come. This time, they both knew that Aurore meant it.

When she returned to work, she decided to tackle the job she had postponed while Andrew was gone. If the firm was going to grow, it had to expand.

She drafted a plan that the other partners approved: New York, Chicago, Los Angeles. New offices, opening in rapid succession over the next two years. And who better to open them, they all agreed, than Aurore.

So she had hit the road, locating the real estate, recruiting the lawyers, finding the clients and tying it all together. It was exhausting—a sort of state of perpetual jet lag—but exhilarating, too. It reminded her of the early days of the firm, landing in a new city and starting out. It made it easier to forget the disappointments, to put the Peter Raymonds, the Eddie Feigans, the John Phillip Harrisons out of her mind.

She suspected that the travel made it less awkward with Andrew, too. It was easier to be friends at the other end of a transcontinental telephone connection than it was from an office down the hall.

But the work was done now. It was time to come home.

There was a knock at her door, and Jane poked her head in. "I thought your secretary said you'd be back today."

In her office, a sanctuary from the protocol of their very male profession, they felt free to give each other a hug.

"I got in this morning on the red-eye from L.A."

"And now you're back for a while?"

"I hope so." She eyed the mail that awaited her. "So what's new around here? Anyone getting restless to move?"

"Actually, there is something I've been wanting to talk to you about. I would have phoned but . . ."

Aurore looked up. "What is it?"

"It's Andrew." Jane began pacing across the room. "He just hasn't been himself lately. Distracted. Lethargic. We've all had to keep an eye on his cases. But if you ask him, he'll say nothing's wrong."

When had she last talked to him? Now that she thought about it, it had been weeks. That wasn't like him either.

"I just thought . . ." Jane began. "I mean, you probably know him better than anyone. I just figured if anyone could get to the bottom of it you could."

Yes, that was probably true.

"I'll see what I can find out."

"Well, even if you don't turn up anything," Jane said, heading for the door, "it's good to have you back again."

"Thanks."

Aurore opened her briefcase and began sorting papers. But she stopped before she reached the bottom. There was something more pressing to attend to.

She turned left out of her office, passed three doors, then knocked lightly on the fourth.

"Come in," a tired voice said.

She found him hunched over a set of documents, pen held in one hand, lost in concentration.

"Hello, Andrew," she said softly.

He looked up. "Aurore!" He rushed over and put his arms around her. "It's about time you came back. You don't know how . . ." The rest was lost in his embrace.

"Let me look at you." He held her at arms' length. "You look fabulous."

She wished she could say the same for him. He had lost weight since she had seen him last—too much. An ineffable sadness colored his eyes.

"I'm glad to be back," she said at last.

"I think we pushed you too hard these past few months."

"Me? Never!"

She waited for him to say his next line, the innocent bantering they fell into when they were playing professional partners. But he stopped and turned away, saying not a word.

"What is it, Andrew?"

He pulled open a drawer of his desk and dug in it aimlessly. "Where's that damn . . . ?"

She leaned across the desk toward him. "You won't tell the others. But I'm not 'the others.' You can tell me."

He slammed the drawer shut, then covered his eyes. "It's Ellie," he said, his voice cracking.

"What?" Aurore persisted.

"She has . . . She could die, Aurore. . . ."

"Oh, Andrew." She went to embrace him.

His arms found their way around her again and held on tightly.

"I've needed you, Aurore. In so many ways. Not just the firm but . . ."

"That's all right," she whispered. "I'm back—and this time I'm not going to leave."

He pulled away. "It's okay. It's just that sometimes. . . . But she's going to come through it all right."

Aurore looked into the depths of his eyes. "Really?"

"Really," he replied with determination.

But Ellie was not, really.

Aurore turned to Mal Scofield for the facts. Ellie had been diagnosed with cervical cancer four months before. After years of trying to have a baby, she'd gotten fed up with gynecologists. She'd simply stopped going for checkups.

The prognosis? She was not expected to live much past the new year.

She was back home now, which made visiting a little easier. Away from the shiny white walls, the jolting fluorescence, the squawking PA systems that made hospitals so depressing. Andrew had put a bed in the dining room so Ellie could look out the French doors and watch the crocuses and daffodils and tulips come up next spring. If she lived that long.

The nurse led Aurore in, into a house that smelled of alcohol and antiseptic. Not cinnamon and baked apples and roasting lamb. Ellie kind of smells. It was ironic, Aurore thought, for Ellie to be lying in bed in her dining room, the hostess who had filled her guests with so much good food and so many good times.

Now the table was gone, the room dominated instead by a bulky hospital bed. In the center of it lay a tiny woman who was only a memory of her former self. Like a bright pink balloon that had nearly deflated.

"Aurore!" she said, her eyes glistening.

"Hello, Ellie." Aurore wanted to hug her but was afraid to disturb the tubes that were threaded into her arm. Finally, she kissed Ellie's cheek and squeezed her shoulders. She was shocked to discover how little there was left to squeeze.

"I'm so glad you're back," Ellie whispered. "It's been a long time."

There were no long times anymore. "How are you doing?" Aurore asked. She reached up and brushed her friend's bangs back from her forehead. What would Ellie want her to say?

"I'm dying," Ellie said. There was no emotion in her voice. It was as if she were announcing the time of day or the temperature. "I've made my peace with myself. I've done what I need to do. I'd still like to see the spring flowers. I'm glad I got to see you again."

Aurore swallowed hard, struggling not to cry. "I would have come sooner if I'd known."

"I know. That's Andrew's fault." She turned to look out the window. "Sometimes I think that if I could just hang on a little longer he would learn to accept it. Other times I think that the longer I go on, the more it makes him think I'm not really going to die. It only makes him deny it more.

"I try and talk to him about it, but he won't listen. 'Don't be silly,' he'll say. 'You're going to get better. I know you will.' He tries to be strong, for my sake. But all you have to do is look at him to see how torn up he is inside."

She coughed slightly. Aurore looked at her hands, pretending not to notice. When she looked up again, she saw not the Ellie of old but a woman with a fierce determination.

"Will you do something for me, Aurore?"

"Whatever you say."

"Will you watch out for him when I'm gone? I know you always did, but he's going to need it now, more than ever."

"Don't worry, Ellie, I will."

She smiled wanly. "Thank you."

She closed her eyes and the nurse stepped forward. "I think Mrs. Cronin ought to rest now."

"I understand." Aurore leaned over and whispered in her ear: "I'll come again soon."

She went outside and got in her car, but she didn't try to start it. It would be easy to cry, it would probably make her feel better. But she found that she couldn't. She felt empty inside, stripped bare of all emotions, except one: guilt.

In all her years of loving Andrew, she had never felt what she did now. It was a creepy sensation that seemed to flow through her veins and consume her, filling her with self-hatred.

She closed her eyes. "Watch out for him when I'm gone," Ellie had said. Up to now, Aurore had kept herself from thinking of that future. She had never fantasized about Ellie's death. The Cronins' divorce maybe, but never her death.

And now she was filled with an overwhelming feeling of dread. She was about to lose one of the sweetest, most selfless women she had ever known. And nothing would change with Andrew. She knew the kind of people they were. Ellie's death would never liberate them. It would only entrap them with the guilty secret they still shared.

"You know, it's funny," Jerry Pieczenik told her over drinks. "I never realized how much I enjoyed our lunches until you disappeared. What's it been now, more than a year?"

She nodded.

"You wouldn't have believed the rumors that went around the courthouse press room. Somebody said you had a nervous breakdown. Somebody else was putting out the word that you'd run off with some European prince."

"And to think I was working my butt off!" She motioned to the waiter. "But now that I'm back, I just want to get into the swing of things as fast as I can. Like, what's new at *The Standard*?"

"Let's see. We've got a new city editor. A new guy at the

White House. They've put me over on the national staff. General assignment. I guess they figure I can't do much damage there.''

"What about Tom Feigan?''

"Up to his old tricks. Looking for the quick hits that make a big splash. I can't say he's very well liked around the newsroom.''

"Why's that?''

"Well, there are some people who think he wouldn't have gotten hired if it wasn't for his father. And I know more than one reporter who's pissed 'cause Tom stole a story he was working on. He stole one of mine, but I'm too old to get worked up about it anymore.''

"I actually got a chance to see him in action when I was down in Mississippi in '64.'' She took another sip of her drink. "No, that's an exaggeration. I knew some people that he interviewed that summer. They thought that he, shall we say, spent too much time drinking with the courthouse crowd instead of trying to report their story.''

"I think his editors thought so, too.''

"Well,'' she muttered, "it's good to know that another Feigan is setting the world on fire.''

"What?''

"Nothing,'' she said. "Have another drink, Jerry.''

He smiled. "Like I said, Aurore, it's a pleasure to have you back in town.''

Eleanor Miegs Cronin died on the morning of February 10, 1966. The snow had melted two days before; although she never saw her flowers, Ellie thought she had lived to see the spring.

Like everything else in her life, Ellie had planned her funeral down to the last detail. She had chosen selections from Chopin and Mozart, asked friends to read poems, and picked out the Scripture for the minister to read.

"For everything there is a season, and a time for every
*   matter under heaven:*
A time to be born, and a time to die. . . ."

Aurore thought of the others who had gone before. Her mother, her father, Stephen, and Amanda. Robert. And now Ellie. The rituals were the same, and that was comforting in a way. Yet each funeral had been different, with a pain or emotion that set it apart from the rest.

> *". . . a time to weep and a time to laugh;*
> *A time to mourn, and a time to dance;"*

Ellie had made the service a celebration of her life, of praise to God and thanks for the beautiful things of nature. Aurore tried to focus on that, to be happy that Ellie was no longer suffering.

But she couldn't forget Andrew. She knew how much he was hurting. And that made the pain worse for her.

Back at the house, friends and colleagues clustered around him. "I know how you must feel." . . . "At least she didn't suffer any longer." . . . Aurore knew the expressions were meant well but she knew they couldn't make it right.

She stayed close to Andrew, wishing she could help. Finally, when nearly everyone had left, they stood together in the dining room. The bed had been removed, the table was back in place. Andrew was staring at the flower bed where he had planted the still-slumbering bulbs.

She put her arms around him and held him tightly.

"She was such a wonderful wife," he said, finally breaking down. "She deserved better than I gave her."

Aurore closed her eyes to stanch her own tears. "Ellie was a good wife. But you were a good husband, too."

"Oh, God, there were so many things. . . ." He cried harder then, and she understood. The guilt was killing him.

A time to embrace, and a time to refrain from embracing. Andrew would need both, but which did he need now?

"None of us is perfect, Andrew. None of us is a saint. We just have to try as hard as we can and hope that that's good enough."

I've been there, Andrew. I believed that God punished me by taking Robert, just as you believe that he's punishing you

*now. But it won't bring her back. Nothing will bring her
back.*

"Be gentle with yourself," she whispered at last. "It's
going to take a long, long time."

It *would* take a long time—for both of them.

Forty-Three

It was time for the firm to move again, and this time Aurore
had a strong opinion: no more renting. There was money to
be made in downtown office buildings. This time they were
going to own one.

She had just bought a new house in Georgetown for herself,
one that came with a dream of a live-in maid, Inez Garcia.
This time she also treated herself to a decorator to take charge
of furnishing the place.

Sometimes she wondered where she used to find time to
manage her personal life. But she knew what the difference
was now: she was handling the work of two lawyers.

Andrew showed up in the office each day, but he couldn't
seem to get interested in his work. She tried to involve him
in the plans for the new building, but he'd shrug and say,
"Do whatever you want."

She urged him to go out, to see friends or take in a movie.
But so far, the result had been disastrous.

At a birthday dinner at Cantina d'Italia, he had picked at
his veal and stared at his wineglass morosely. "Ellie was the
center of my life," he said. "And I let her down so many
times."

Aurore couldn't be hard on him. She knew what he was
going through. But it had been more than a year since Ellie
had died. Someone needed to tell Andrew to snap out of it.
But she just couldn't bring herself to be the one.

* * *

The building was finished, the new offices were ready. It was time to go through her personal files and weed out the papers that didn't have to be moved.

There was a file of yellowing newspaper clips: Andrew's nomination, the cases that had been worthy of a story. There were programs from bar association dinners she had helped organize. She'd even kept a file on Jerry Pieczenik's divorce.

She riffled further back and came across another file that she'd almost forgotten about. It was filled with sheet music, pages she couldn't interpret, except for the words across the top of the first page: "Elegy for Katharine."

In the months before he had died, Robert had fleshed out his composition and sent it to his brother. After they had met, David had passed it on to her.

Back then she'd had an idea, but she didn't have enough money. Now she had the money. And, she thought with a smile, for a change money might be able to buy her at least one thing she'd always wanted.

"I appreciate you meeting me for lunch, Mr. Stein." Aurore had picked the Rive Gauche for the lunch, hoping it would impress the orchestra's manager.

"It's my pleasure, Miss Callahan. I've heard of you and your firm, of course, but I was not aware that you were a music lover."

She strongly doubted he had heard of her before her phone call last week. But she was confident he had determined she was not currently a subscriber to the orchestra's season.

"Well, I do love some kinds of music, Mr. Stein. Music that I can connect with on a personal level."

"I understand."

"I might as well get right to the point of my phone call. I am prepared to make a sizable contribution to the National Symphony in whatever form would be most useful."

"That's most generous of you," he said. "What amount were you thinking of?"

She named the figure.

"That *is* very generous," he said.

"There is one condition."

He smiled. "There usually is."

"In the coming season, the orchestra must perform a composition of my choice."

"What did you have in mind?"

" 'Elegy for Katharine' by Robert Kaufmann."

"I've never heard of it."

"It's never been performed publicly."

Stein shifted in his seat. "This is somewhat irregular."

"But there's always a first time, right?" She flashed an unctuous smile. "The music was written as a violin sonata. I have had it arranged for a small orchestra with violin solo."

He was silent for a moment. "I can't give you an answer today. The program committee will have to review the music. See if it is acceptable."

"I understand." She picked up her iced tea. "There's one other thing I ought to mention. Next year will be the thirtieth anniversary of the start of World War II. Robert Kaufmann died in 1945, working to help save Jewish refugees in Europe. If you like the piece, that might give you an even better reason to include it on your program next season.

"But don't forget my offer," she added with a sly smile. "I understand you're trying to raise money for a tour of Europe."

"You've done your research, Miss Callahan."

She smiled. "It usually pays off."

"Elegy for Katharine" was premiered by the National Symphony Orchestra at Constitution Hall on the evening of January 11, 1969. David, Rachel, and Jane joined her for the performance, and at the last minute, Andrew did, too.

The program noted that the sonata was composed by Robert Kaufmann at the age of thirty, before he died in Europe in the closing days of World War II. The program also noted that "the performance was made possible by a generous contribution from Miss Aurore Callahan."

A young musician played the solo, reminding her of the night when Robert had picked up his violin for her. Aurore listened to the music she had not heard for more than a quarter century with a mixture of sadness but also satisfaction. She didn't know if Robert had ever dreamed that his music would have an audience of more than one. But now that she had shared it with the world, she felt as if she had brought a part of him back to life.

The applause was enthusiastic, but Aurore was still eager to see what the critics had to say. It didn't matter to her, one way or the other. But for Robert's sake, she wanted someone else to like the music, someone other than the person to whom it was dedicated.

The next morning she got her answer.

The Standard's reviewer dealt first with the Tchaikovsky symphony and the tone poem by Richard Strauss. And then he turned to "a rather strange addition to the orchestra's repertoire, the 'Elegy for Katharine,' by Robert Kaufmann.

"This reviewer asked himself what such a piece was doing on the orchestra's program. But when he listened, and allowed himself to become lost in its haunting refrain, its sense of *tristesse*, he could only think how tragic it was that such a promising composer had to die so young."

How tragic it was. Yes, the reviewer was right. And yet her heart swelled with love and with pride. Robert had been a brilliant young man. And he had loved her, loved her enough to take up his violin again and write music for her.

He had given her so many gifts, gifts that had endured long after he was gone. Gifts he had never even been aware of.

And now, at last, she'd been able to give him something in return.

The day after the reviews appeared, she received a phone call.

"It's a man named Elliot Ingraham," her secretary said. "He says he's an old friend of Kate Callahan's."

"Put him through," Aurore said. The phone rang and she picked it up eagerly. "Elliot?"

"Kate? Or do I call you Aurore?"

"Actually, we're one and the same. How are you?"

"Fine," he said. "And you?"

"Twenty-five years older, I'd say."

He laughed. "It has been a long time, hasn't it? Actually, I tried to look you up years ago—without any luck. And then I went to the concert the other night and heard Robert's piece. When I got home and read the program more closely, I noticed the other name. I figured if it wasn't you, it had to be a relative. So I decided to give it a shot."

There was a time when she had been torn over Elliot. He was a good person, someone she had wanted very much to like. But the memory of that morning in their office had always colored her feelings.

But the rules had changed some, and she had changed, too. Now he was a link to a time in her life that she always wanted to remember.

"I'd really like to see you," she said. "Could you stop by for a drink tonight?"

"Sure."

When she got home that night, she lit a fire and got out a bottle of Courvoisier and two snifters. He arrived just after eight, and when she saw him, they embraced.

He hadn't changed much over the years. His hair was thinner on top, his sideburns longer. Just the same, she didn't think she would have recognized him if she had passed him on the street.

They took seats by the fireplace. He proposed a toast to Robert, which touched her. He asked about her law firm; she asked about his job.

"I've been at the SEC for the past fifteen years, and in the government ever since I last saw you." He took a sip of his drink, then added, "That's long enough for my pension—a fact I've got you to thank for."

"Oh, I don't know about that."

"I do," he said. "You could have ended my career, Kate. All you had to do was speak up, and I would have been out of there. But you kept quiet. And I've been grateful to you ever since."

He looked off into the fire. "All these years, I've always wished there was something I could do to repay you."

She spoke up. "It was nothing more than what anyone

would do for a friend." She tried to change the subject. "How about our old colleagues? Do you keep in touch with any of them?"

"I lost track of Delilah ages ago. But I used to run into Jason when he was at the SEC."

"He looked me up a few years ago," she said.

"I'm surprised you would still talk to him."

"What makes you say that?"

"After what he did . . . when you were at the State Department."

He said it so casually, she couldn't be sure she had heard him right. "What do you mean?"

"You know, when those stories came out about you being a Communist."

"I still don't understand."

"You mean you don't know?" She shook her head. "I can't believe it," he said, looking her straight in the eye. "Jason was the one who spread the stories about you."

"Jason? Jason was the one?"

He nodded.

She felt a rush of heat, but it wasn't the drink. It was her rage, unbottled at last with the pop of a cork. A cork made of all her trust—and naïveté.

She felt her stomach churn and her limbs tense. Jason! Why hadn't she suspected him?

It was always easier to believe that it was someone else. Someone in her office. Some disaffected party member. Someone who hadn't liked Robert. Well, that was Jason, certainly. But Jason had loved her once. Could love turn into such a bitter hate?

And then she remembered with chilling clarity how he had offered to help her back then. The gall of the man! Offering support, offering a job. Reaching out to her even as he was destroying her.

And the job at the NLRB. He was interviewed by the FBI. What lies had he spread this time?

"You didn't know, did you?" Elliot asked.

She shook her head. It was almost too much to absorb all at once. But she had to find out everything. "How did you know it was Jason?" she asked.

He rose to stretch his legs by the fire. "God, it's such a long time ago. . . ."

"Try to remember, Elliot. Everything you can. It's important to me."

"Okay." He thought for a moment. "When the war was over, I remember now, I lost track of Jason for a few years. Then one day he called me up. He had a job at the Commerce Department and wanted to know if I'd like to join his staff. I didn't like Jason very much, but the job was a good one and the money even better. He made it hard to refuse."

"What year was that?"

"1949, I think."

"How do you know he was responsible for the stories?"

"Give me a second. I haven't thought about this in years." He sat back down across from her. "I guess it was a few weeks after you were forced out. We went out for a drink together. He had one drink and then another and then another and before too long he was pretty plowed. And then he started to offer toasts to himself, congratulating himself for doing you in. He said that maybe now you'd know how he felt when you chose Robert over him. I remember it now. He called him 'that Jew boy.' "

"Go on."

"At first I thought he was crazy, that he was just making it all up to impress me. But then I started asking him questions and he laid out the whole thing. How he had called up that columnist—what was his name?"

"Eddie Feigan."

"That's right. And then he told me how he had met with him and how easy it was to persuade him to do the story.

"I remember thinking, 'This guy is really sick.' I'd always known he was obsessed about you and Robert. He'd make cracks about the two of you when you weren't in the office. I think that sometimes he used to follow the two of you when you went out. . . ."

Now it started to make sense. He had seen them go to those meetings. Maybe he'd even taken notes. Notes that he'd passed on to Eddie Feigan.

"I used to wonder how much Jason had to do with Robert deciding to go back to Europe," Elliot continued. "When you weren't around, he used to egg him on so. You know, rub his nose in the fact that the Jews were dying and all he was doing was sitting behind a desk.''

''That doesn't surprise me.''

''And then when Jason found out that Robert had been killed. . . . Well, what he said doesn't bear repeating now. But he never could get over the fact that you had loved Robert and not him. He tried to find you right after Robert died. He always thought you would come back to him eventually, but of course you never did. And so a few years later, when he found out you had that good job at the State Department— and that you had managed to survive without him—he decided to strike back at you.''

''And he succeeded.'' She downed the rest of her drink, sending fire down her throat. ''I should have known,'' she said flatly. ''I was too trusting back then. And to think Jason could calmly call me up and offer to help!''

''I tried to find you then,'' Elliot said. ''I wanted to let you know. But it never occurred to me you'd change your name and move back to town.''

He took a sip of his drink, then studied the snifter. ''Jason is a lowlife. At the SEC, they still talk about how he worked his way through the secretarial pool. I certainly endured my share of taunts from him over the years. But what he did to you was . . . was totally unforgivable.''

''Still,'' he said, glancing around the room, ''as an objective observer, I'd have to conclude that you've managed to survive.''

''Does it look that way?'' she asked. She retraced the path that his eyes had taken around the living room, from the rare prints to the period furniture to the oriental rug, all carefully gathered over a lifetime of hard work. ''I guess, in some ways, I have survived. I went to school and I got a law degree and I helped build a firm that made a lot of money along the way.

''But it changed me, Elliot. The old Kate that you knew died that day I was forced out of my job. I never trusted people the way I once did. I always felt that it was me against the rest of the world, and I was probably going to lose. And it still comes back to haunt me. There were jobs I didn't get because of those stories. They were lies, but they trailed me, no matter where I went. Even if I changed my name.''

The fire crackled like a Greek chorus behind them. She was quiet for a moment. Then she rose and picked up the fireplace poker. ''So it was Jason,'' she hissed as she stabbed the fire.

''You know, there are rumors around the SEC that he's going to end up as one of Nixon's ambassadors.''

That piqued her interest. ''I thought Jason was a Democrat, at least on paper.''

''If you give 'em a big enough campaign contribution, they don't care,'' Elliot replied with a laugh. He set down his glass. ''Look, I'd better be leaving. I know this has upset you, and I'm sorry. But let's stay in touch, okay?''

''Okay.''

''I plan to retire from the government pretty soon. My roommate and I are thinking of moving to Greece.''

''That's nice,'' she said politely.

He got up to leave. ''I meant what I said, Kate. If there's anything I can do, all you have to do is ask.''

''I'll remember that.''

She showed him out, then refilled her glass and sat back down by the fire. She was angry, bitterly angry, but she didn't curse or throw things. Rather she stared at the flames for a long, long time, letting her rage grow hotter. Thinking of Robert and Martha and the years she had lost. Thinking of Jason and Eddie Feigan and how they had hurt her. Thinking of all the times she had vowed she would get even.

And now, after more than twenty years, she could.

What did she have to lose by trying? She had no family, no commitments. Material things meant nothing to her now. She had been patient. She had waited. And now she had been given her chance.

But how?

She put another log on the fire and got out a yellow legal pad. She started jotting down notes, notes and ideas, things she knew about Jason. Ways to show him what she had gone through.

She didn't rush. She took her time. She carried the kernel of her idea around in her brain for several days: when she worked, when she went home, when she slept. The idea took hold, growing bigger, taking shape.

It was a shame that Eddie Feigan had retired before she could pay him back. In her mind, he was almost as big a culprit as Jason was. But then it occurred to her: she could bring Tom Feigan in on her plan. If he practiced journalism the way his father had—and everything she'd heard said he did—he could be the instrument of Jason's demise.

She analyzed the scheme over and over, trying to anticipate what could go wrong. It was not a perfect plan. It relied too heavily on luck—and her ability to judge human nature. Tom Feigan would have to bite, Jason would have to react. But if they did, Jason would know how it felt to flail against a story you couldn't control. And Tom might learn what his father never did: the price of running a story that was too good to prove.

But it all depended on Elliot. He'd have to manufacture some sort of agency document and plant it. If he wouldn't —or couldn't—help her, she'd have to start from scratch. There was a risk involved for him if he got caught, and maybe it was unfair even to ask.

But he owed her one, he'd said so himself.

So she invited him to dinner, and outlined her plan. He tossed out some ideas of his own, the things he remembered from Jason's days at the agency, the rumors that had gone around among the bureacrats. As he talked, he suggested some refinements of her scenario.

Then, after several hours, she asked, "So what do you think?"

He smiled, and reached out to shake her hand. "We're going to pay him back, Kate. I'll get started on it first thing tomorrow."

Forty-Four

Over coffee and a cold fried cake, Tom Feigan sulked over that morning's *Standard*. Sometime between eight and ten last night, the Maryland legislature had decided to pass some stupid piece of legislation, bumping his story off of page one.

And not just any story. The one he'd spent two weeks working his tail off for. The one he'd wasted a full day on, trying to get an interview at the Pentagon. The one he'd labored over all weekend, trying to make it sing.

And what had he gotten for his trouble? A one-column head buried back in the truss ads.

His dad had always made it seem so easy. He was home on time, he never worked weekends. Yet his column had always appeared, just like magic. And they were good columns, too. Good enough to win him a huge following. Good enough that a son would dream of being just like him.

But now Tom wondered when his time would come. He had been on the national staff for more than five years, but the really big stories still weren't coming his way. No one had suggested that he should go cover the White House. Or even Congress for that matter. And he didn't understand why. He knew he could do it, just like his dad had. They just didn't know it.

The phone on his desk rang. He dug through the pile of newspapers to answer it.

"Tom Feigan."

"Mr. Feigan?"

"Speaking."

"My name is Aurore Callahan. I'm a lawyer here in town.

I just wanted to tell you that I thought your recent series on
the interstate highway system was fascinating.''

"Why, thank you.'' He was surprised to discover someone
had actually read the thing.

"My firm represents some trucking companies so I found
it particularly interesting. I was wondering if I could talk to
you more about it.''

"Certainly, Miss . . . Miss . . .''

"Callahan. Aurore Callahan.''

"Would you like to get together for lunch?'' He never
missed a chance to make *The Standard* pay for a meal.

"Lunch would be fine. How about next Monday?''

"Sure. What time?''

"Why don't we say about one? I'll have my secretary call
you that morning to reconfirm.''

"Okay.''

"Fine. I'll see you then.''

Aurore recognized Eddie Feigan's son the moment he walked
into Harvey's. He, too, had the physique of a street brawler,
with broad shoulders and strong arms. And he carried himself
with the same rest-of-the-world-be-damned bravado.

For a moment she wished that it were Eddie who was taking
a seat across from her. After all, he was the one who should
have to pay. But no, she would have to be satisfied with this.
If Tom Feigan was a careful reporter, he wouldn't fall into
her trap. But if he took the same kind of shortcuts his father
did, he would.

As they ordered their steaks, she tried to curb her excitement. This was no different, she reminded herself, from all
the other lunches she had had with reporters over the years.
If her scheme was going to work, Tom would have to think
of her as just another one of his sources.

"Based on your reporting,'' she asked, "do you think
Congress is likely to increase the gasoline tax this year?''

She listened carefully, treating him with respect. She kept
the conversation on highways and trucking and Tom's series,
nothing else. It was not until the waiter brought the bill that
she played her card.

"You know, Tom, I've been fascinated by everything you've said today. I was wondering . . . I'm planning a small dinner party a week from Friday. Just a few friends. I'd love to have them meet you. Could you join us?"

She held her breath as he seemed to hesitate. Then he said, "Sure, why not?"

"Great. I'll send you an invitation so you'll have all the details." She stood up. "I really enjoyed our lunch."

He shook hands with her. "See you a week from Friday."

Tom wasn't sure what the hell he'd gotten himself into. But he got an inkling two days later when his invitation to the party arrived in the mail. It was a heavyweight, ivory-colored card, engraved with Aurore Callahan's name. The specifics were listed in dark black ink. Georgetown address. Black tie requested. Who was this woman anyway?

He called the library for her clip file, but it was a disappointment. She was a lawyer, like she'd said. A Democratic party activist. That was about it.

Well, what did he have to lose? He might meet some people, get a good dinner. It would only cost him his time and the price of a tux rental.

And besides, he thought with a smile, he could probably get away with deducting the tux on his income taxes.

It still might not work, Aurore told herself as she waited for Andrew to get off the phone. The only thing she could count on was that Tom Feigan was coming to dinner that night. He would eat her food and drink her wine, but he could still say good night and that would be the end of it.

But it wouldn't be, not for her at least. She would find another way of getting back at Jason. Tom, she could give up on, but not Jason. The wounds were too deep now. And they had been allowed to fester for too long.

Had she thought of everything? Had she underestimated Jason? Or overestimated him, for that matter?

Andrew hung up the phone and rejoined her in front of the fireplace.

"You're crazy, you know."

It was clear he wasn't about to let the subject of their talk drop. "Maybe I am," she replied.

"All these years I've known you, I don't think I ever accused you of that. But now I will."

He settled back into the Queen Anne chair and stared into the fire. "I don't think I've been very easy on you since Ellie died."

"I never expected you to be."

"Still, you must have wondered. We loved each other once, you and I. My love for Ellie was the only thing that stood in the way then."

"But we're different people now, Andrew."

"You think so?"

She nodded. "And even when you're ready to love someone again, I may not be."

"What do you mean?"

"I've become much more skeptical about love and commitments," she said, turning away from him. "Love, trusting people, has hurt me too many times. I think I'm getting too old to hurt like that again."

"You'd rather devote your energies to hurting other people."

"You may look at it that way, Andrew. I don't."

"Settling the score, getting even. An eye for an eye. Call it whatever you like, that's still how I see it."

"Yes, but you don't understand how I see it."

He sighed. "Think of it, Aurore. You've already won. You came back to Washington. You were successful. Jason Rush doesn't matter anymore."

"He does to me." She looked down at her hands for a moment. "All these years, I've carried around that anger. It was muted at times, but only because I'd given up hope that I'd find out who was responsible. But now I know. He ruined me. Think of the lawyer I might have been if I hadn't been hiding out those first years we were together. Think of the jobs I missed out on.

"Elliot thinks Jason may have even pushed Robert to go back to Europe. He could have been alive today. We could have had children . . ."

"That's a lot you're laying at Jason's feet. It's not very rational."

"The world isn't very rational, Andrew. That's one thing I've learned over the years."

He turned away from her, lost in his own thoughts.

"You'll be there tonight, won't you?"

He turned back and managed to smile. "Of course, I will. After all, somebody's got to keep you in line."

She greeted Tom effusively, complimented him on his tux, introduced him to her guests. She didn't fail to catch him eyeing her living room appreciatively—or admiring the cut of Jane's bodice. She loosened him up with a couple of drinks, but not so many that he would forget the evening.

In addition to Jane and Andrew, she had invited five close friends, just in case she had to enlist their help later on. Andrew had refused to play a role in the setup, so she had turned to Jane instead.

Jane was playing it just right, Aurore noted. Fawning over Tom, treating him as if he had already won the Pulitzer Prize. And Tom, Aurore noted, was enjoying every minute of it.

So far, so good, she thought as she looked down the length of her dining-room table. Everything according to plan.

As Inez cleared away the plates, Jane turned to Aurore. "I was talking to my friend Michael at the State Department the other day and he said the word's going 'round there that Jason Rush could wind up as the next ambassador to England."

"Really? Did you hear that, Andrew?" She couldn't resist lobbing the ball into his court. "Do you know anything?"

"No," he said with a scowl. "I'm not very plugged in at the State Department."

She turned to Tom. "What's the word around *The Standard*?" It was important to draw him in, make him feel important.

He shifted in his seat uncomfortably. "Uh, Rush is, well, I guess he's one of the names that's being mentioned."

"Rush is an interesting character," Aurore said as she

signaled Inez to begin pouring coffee. "He's been in and out of Washington several times since I've lived here. Always seems to leave some questions behind him."

"Like what?" Jane asked.

"I'm not sure about all the specifics. But someone I know at the SEC was telling me that when Rush was chief of enforcement there, he was involved in some dubious activities."

"Such as?" Tom asked, leaning forward.

Aurore took a moment to compose her thoughts. It was important not to appear too eager. "Apparently Jason's family owns a company that ran into some trouble with the SEC. And then suddenly the investigation was called off."

"Why?" Tom asked.

Aurore shrugged. "Like I said, I don't know the details. But my friend said it was unusual, at least on the surface." She winked at Tom and Jane. "Not what you'd want to hear about someone who could be the next ambassador to the Court of St. James!"

She let it drop then, she couldn't push too hard. It would all depend on how hungry he was . . . and whether she had played him right.

The conversation shifted to the new Congress, a rehash of the Redskins' season, who the Democrats were likely to run the next time. She moved her guests to the living room for after-dinner drinks.

She usually enjoyed this time the best: when the anxiety of dinner was over, when her guests were full and in good spirits. But tonight she couldn't wait to get rid of them. All of them, that is, but Tom.

Slowly, one by one, they said good night. Even Andrew, who sensed she didn't want him to stay late. But Tom seemed to linger, and Aurore allowed herself to hope.

He rose when Jane did and helped her with her coat. He opened the door for her, then let it close behind.

"A very pleasant evening, Aurore."

"I'm so glad you could come, Tom. I know everyone enjoyed meeting you."

"Before I leave, I wanted to ask you one thing." She held

her breath as he pulled out a cigarette. "Your friend at the SEC. Would he be willing to talk to me?"

She hesitated. "I'd have to check with him. He's in a sensitive position. He might prefer to call you."

"Whatever you think."

"I'll ask him though."

"I'd appreciate it."

She opened the door, then smiled as seductively as she could. "One thing I do have to ask though. If this does turn out to be a story, I hope you'll keep my name out of it. Everyone knows lawyers gossip like this, but I wouldn't want anyone to know I was the source of your tip. And besides," she added, "the story could turn out not to be true."

"I understand."

"It's been a pleasure, Tom." She extended her hand. "I look forward to seeing you again very soon."

"Thank you for inviting me."

He skipped down her steps to the street. Aurore waved, then closed the door.

She sagged against it, then clapped her hands. He had taken the bait.

In the morning she phoned Elliot.

"We caught him," she said. "Now he's waiting for your call."

"Good work. I'll put the finishing touches on the file, then I'll phone him."

"Let me know what happens." She paused. "And thanks, Elliot. For everything."

"Like I said before, Kate. I owed you one."

Forty-Five

The phone rang on Tom's desk. He reached to answer it.

"Mr. Feigan?" a voice said.

"Yes?"

"I understand you may be interested in Jason Rush's tenure at the SEC."

This was it! Tom grabbed a pen and flipped open a notebook. "Yes I am. What can you tell me, Mr. . . . ?"

"Let's just call me Darryl," the voice said. "I have access to a lot of documents from top officials at the agency and I wouldn't want anything you wrote to get traced back to me."

"Okay, Darryl." Sometimes this cloak-and-dagger stuff drove Tom crazy. "What can you tell me about it?"

"It's all in the files. All you have to do is ask for it. The files of the Boston regional director. They're at headquarters. The month of June, 1962. The regional director called off an investigation of Jason Rush's company on Rush's orders. Then you also might ask for the agency's travel records for 1962. You'll see that Rush was going up there a lot to check on what the regional office was up to."

"Anything else?"

There was a pause at the other end of the line. "I've seen the documents. They speak for themselves. I think that you'll find everything you need."

"I'll get right on it, Darryl. . . . But tell me: how can I reach you if I run into a problem?"

"I'd feel better if I call you. I really don't want to jeopardize my position."

Tom scowled. He didn't like it, but he didn't have much choice. "Okay, but call me back. Please. Anytime, day or night."

"Don't worry, I will."

They hung up. Tom went to the national editor's secretary to get the forms for a Freedom of Information request. Across town, Elliot dialed another number.

"I called him," he said.

"What do you think?" Aurore asked.

"He sounded interested."

"Good. Now we sit back and wait for the wheels of government to turn. I guess it could turn out to be months, huh?"

"I've thought of that, too."

"What do you mean?"

"We've got a backlog of FOIA requests. So three weeks ago I brought it to the attention of the top administrator. Now the branch has been told to hire some temporaries until they're caught up."

"Elliot, you're a genius!"

He laughed. "I'd say we bring out the best in each other."

The Freedom of Information Act request had produced a memo and the travel records. The meaning of the memo was perfectly clear. So what was the problem?

The problem, Tom reminded himself, was that his editors were full of chicken shit. They wouldn't move his story.

It wasn't like that in his father's day. "I'd write 'em the way I saw 'em," his dad told him, "and they'd print 'em the way I wrote 'em." He thought now of calling his father for some sympathy. But no. He was close to breaking this, and he'd rather give the old man a thrill by surprising him with his scoop.

Okay, he acknowledged to himself, there were a couple of holes in his story. But do prosecutors always have their entire case pinned down the moment they walk into court? He knew how the system worked. A reporter writes a story. It alone might not nail the official, but the next one would. Another story runs, then another, all variations on the first one, all bringing out new details. Eventually, the official can't keep up with the stories. Eventually he has to yell "uncle."

And Tom wanted to get Rush now. He hadn't felt that way at first. He wasn't after the man, only a good story. But that was before he had had to battle through the secretaries guarding the phones at Rush's law firm. Before Rush had put him off for a week before calling him back. Before Rush had treated him like he was a pile of shit.

And then Rush's defense, he thought, remembering the conversation. So contemptuous. So transparent.

"A fabrication!" the lawyer had bellowed. "I never ordered Blunt to call off the investigation."

"Let me read it to you again. The document is on SEC letterhead, dated June twenty-eighth, 1962, and addressed to you from George Blunt, regional director of the Boston region. It says, and I quote, 'Per your recent instructions, I have called off my office's investigation of JVR Enterprises, effective immediately. If questioned, I will cite budgetary constraints as the reason for this decision.' "

"You already read it to me once, goddammit. And I'm telling you I never told Blunt to call off any investigation."

"It's true, isn't it, that in the six months prior to this letter, you made repeated visits to the Boston office?"

"I don't recall."

"I have the agency travel vouchers to prove it, sir."

"I may have visited the office, but I never talked to Blunt about any investigation like that."

"Why did you go to Boston then?"

"I'd . . . I don't remember."

"JVR Enterprises was your family's company, wasn't it?"

"Yes, but look, this just doesn't make sense. I'd really rather have you sit down with my attorneys. I'm sure there's an explanation."

"Well, you can start by explaining how the document—if it's a fake—got into the SEC's files?"

"How the hell do I know since I've never seen the damn thing? I'll tell you one thing, though, Mr. Feigan. That document better not make it into your paper, or I'll sue your ass."

Even now, as Tom reread the transcript, he shivered with the thrill of the hunt. "The guilty ones always threaten you," his father had told him once. "If they're really innocent, they've got an explanation."

Of course, it would have been better if George Blunt hadn't died last year. Tom had spent a week asking questions around the Boston office, but hadn't flushed out much. Not many people were still around from 1962. No one remembered the JVR investigation. A few of them had a vague memory that Jason Rush had visited a lot when he was enforcement chief. And one person thought it had something to do with Jason's mother. She was chairman of the board of the company. Close enough, right?

Not for his editors. He hadn't told them about Rush's threats. That would queer it for sure. Everyone had gotten so damn timid lately. All the guts had gone out of the paper.

But this one was so close he could taste it. What did it need now? He thought a minute, then snapped his fingers. He picked up the phone and called the paper's White House correspondent.

"Do me a favor, Paul. Ask around over there and get me a quote about where Jason Rush stands on the president's short list. No, tonight'll be fine."

Then he called Mike Mobley, a House committee staffer he used to play tennis with.

"Whatcha got?" Mike asked. "I'm in a hurry."

Tom described the story.

"Sure. Send me a copy. It might fit in with what we're doing."

"How can I describe your investigation?"

"Gee, it really hasn't gotten off the ground yet."

"How 'bout if I say it's a quote 'wide-ranging probe of SEC enforcement practices' unquote."

Mike thought for a moment. "Hmm, I kinda like the sound of that."

Yeah, Tom thought as he hung up, *so do I.*

"It's taking too long," Aurore said when she met Elliot for lunch. They sat upstairs at The Astor, a little Greek place near Connecticut and M where they wouldn't run into anyone they knew.

"It takes time," he said. "You've got to be patient."

"But if it takes too much time, it's going to die. Feigan

will get other assignments. Or the president will nominate somebody other than Jason. Or more and more editors will take a look at the story and decide it just doesn't fly.''

"But what can we do?"

"I've got an idea."

Two hours later Tom Feigan's phone rang. He recognized the voice immediately.

"Look," Darryl said, "I'm not going to start telling you how to do your job. But I thought you ought to know something.''

"What's that?" Tom asked.

"There's a reporter from *The New York Times* sniffing around here now. He's been asking questions about Rush and his time at the SEC. I don't know whether they're onto this or not, but I thought you'd want to know.''

"Thanks," Tom said, "I appreciate it."

He hung up and smiled. Nothing like some competition to put some ants in the pants of his editors.

Then he cursed under his breath. He'd forgotten to try to get Darryl's phone number again. The guy had always refused, but he really ought to have it. Just in case he needed to find him.

But then, he didn't actually quote Darryl, did he?

He went to find his editor. Bob Weston was hunched over a story, marking it up.

"You know that Jason Rush story you guys have been sitting on?"

Bob looked up. "Yeah, what about it?"

"My source tells me *The New York Times* is onto it now. I'd hate for us to lose it.''

"*The Times*, huh?" Bob rubbed his jaw. "I guess we could make room for it tonight." Then he hesitated. "I had our lawyers look it over. There was one thing they flagged. That source of yours, the guy who put you onto the documents, can he be trusted? Does he have any ax to grind?''

"As far as I know," Tom replied, "he's a high-level agency official who doesn't want to see a crook become ambassador to England.''

"And you can reach him again if we have to?"

Tom swallowed hard, then forced a smile. "Sure," he said. "No problem."

Aurore's phone rang at 6:30 the next morning.
"Have you seen today's paper?" Elliot asked.
"No, why?"
"Bingo!"
The story was the off-lead of the paper, underneath a two-column head.

Jason Rush, an attorney who is under consideration to be the next ambassador to England, called off a federal investigation of a family-owned business when he was chief of enforcement for the Securities and Exchange Commission in the early 1960s, agency documents show.

In a memo dated June 28, 1962, George Blunt, then the Boston regional enforcement director for the SEC, wrote Rush: "Per your recent instructions, I have called off my office's investigation of JVR Enterprises, effective immediately."

At the time Rush was named to the SEC post, JVR Enterprises was a publicly traded company controlled by the Rush family. Rush's mother, Audrey, served as chairman of the board.

Rush denied that he had ordered Blunt to call off the agency's investigation. "It's a fabrication," he said in a telephone interview. Blunt died in 1969.

Rush now practices law in New York City. At the SEC, he was a political appointee of President Kennedy, but over the past decade, he has become increasingly active in Republican politics.

Earlier this week, a White House source said Rush was "a top candidate, if not the top candidate" to be the next ambassador to the Court of St. James. A White House spokesman said yesterday that he had no comment on the allegations.

The episode is now being studied by the House Permanent Subcommittee on Oversight and

Investigations as part of a wide-ranging probe of SEC enforcement practices.

Rush visited the Boston regional office thirteen times in the six months before Blunt wrote his memo, agency travel vouchers show. Rush denied that the trips had anything to do with calling off the investigation. But when asked last week why he had made the the trips, he replied, "I don't remember." . . .

"You did it!" she said.

"No," he corrected her. "We did it."

"Still, your 'memo' was convincing. And Blunt was the perfect name to put on it. And the crowning touch was the fact that you remembered Jason's travels after all these years."

"Like I said, we always thought all those trips were suspicious. The rumor was that Jason was visiting his mother at agency expense. That may be why he says he can't remember why he was up there—he doesn't want to acknowledge the real reason."

"I love it," she said.

"What do we do now?"

"We sit back and watch Jason squirm. Feigan still doesn't know how to reach you, does he?"

"Nope."

Aurore laughed. "Then I think it's possible he's even sloppier than his father was."

Later that morning, she met with Andrew.

"I see by the morning paper that you've accomplished your mission," he said.

"Actually I just set the wheels in motion. It always depended on whether Tom would take the bait. He didn't have to write that story. He did it to himself. And Jason, well, Jason brought on his own problems a long time ago."

"Are you satisfied?"

"I think the fun's only just beginning."

Forty-Six

The stories started then. With Congress out of town, it seemed that every reporter in Washington had time on his hands. Time to mosey on over to the SEC and ask a few questions about Jason Rush.

They found out about the secretary who'd filed a harassment complaint against Jason. They heard the stories about how he had dipped into the travel budget to throw a Christmas party for his friends from New York. Feigan's story proved maddeningly difficult to duplicate—the records seemed to have dried up. But that didn't stop them from repeating it.

"Jason Rush, who, it is alleged, called off an investigation of his family's business . . ." said *The Washington Star*.

"Jason Rush, reportedly the subject of a congressional probe of SEC activities," wrote *The Wall Street Journal*.

At Cronin and Associates, a researcher was assigned to clip all the newspaper and magazine articles that referred to Jason Rush. Each afternoon, a manila envelope was delivered to the desk of Aurore Callahan.

"So," Andrew asked her, "do you feel better now?"

"As a matter of fact, I do," she replied. "But not the way you think."

She opened the latest envelope and spread the clippings across her desk. "You know, it's different now than it was back then. My story was all over Washington, but that was about it. Now a story starts here and spreads all across the country. Just when you think you've got it stopped, it will pop up in another place. Jason's got his hands full."

"And that pleases you."

"He's an evil man, Andrew. Sure, this story isn't true. But the other ones are. Maybe they should tell those other stories, but they won't. They're not sexy enough. They don't sell papers. Robbing someone of her reputation may not be the same thing as robbing a bunch of shareholders. But it's all robbery in my book.''

She paused and looked at him intently. "I don't view this as getting even. I view this as justice being done.''

At *The Standard*, Tom Feigan was enjoying his work. Now, for a change, his editors were paying attention to him. What was he going to write today? Did he have anything more on Rush? But that was the problem. He wasn't sure where the story was going to lead next. And if he didn't come up with something, somebody else would steal it away.

His phone rang. It was Gloria Seymour, the managing editor's secretary. "Douglas would like to see you in his office,'' she said.

"Sure. I'll be right over.''

Tom smiled as he loped across the floor to the suite of executive offices. It had been months since Douglas Bowman had been willing to give him the time of day.

"Sit down,'' Bowman said as he showed Tom in. He sounded graver than Tom had expected.

He sat down behind his large, cluttered desk. "I got a call from Jason Rush's attorneys today. They've raised some questions about your story.''

Tom tried to act blasé. "That was to be expected.''

"Their position is that the memo was never written. That it was a forgery. That you don't have anything to back it up.'' He hesitated. "How did you find out about it?''

"A Freedom of Information request.''

"Who told you what to look for?''

"A source.''

"Contact him again.''

Tom shifted in his chair. "I'm not sure I can.''

"What do you mean?'' Bowman bellowed.

"He wouldn't give me his phone number.'' Then Tom added quickly, "But I may have another way of reaching him.''

Bowman's eyes narrowed. "You've been on my shit list

for a long time, Feigan. You'd better come up with that number or it's going to be your ass.''

At the house in Georgetown, a telephone rang. Inez knocked on Aurore's bedroom door. "A Mr. Feigan on the phone, ma'am."

This was a critical moment. The heat must be on Tom Feigan. The only question now was how hard would the paper push?

They could summon her to testify. But she was gambling they wouldn't. From all her years of studying *The Standard*, she knew it had always protected its sources. And hidden behind them, too.

She reached for the phone.

"Tom? What can I do for you?"

"It's about the Jason Rush story, I need to talk to your friend again. Can you tell me how to reach him?"

She paused, putting on the sweetest voice she could muster. "I'm afraid I can't help you. I told you my friend was in a very sensitive position. And you promised me you wouldn't drag me into this. I'm a little disappointed in you, Tom."

"But I have to talk to him!" Now he sounded desperate.

"I wish I could help you," she said gently. "The truth is I tried to contact him myself this week. You know, after your stories started to run. . . ."

"And?" he demanded.

She closed her eyes, grateful that she had anticipated this. Grateful that Elliot was prepared to go ahead with his plans. "Like I said, Tom, I wish I could help you. But they told me he had left the country."

There was a long pause. Then, just before the phone slammed down, came an anguished expletive.

"Shit!"

The stories kept up, but the allegations grew thinner and thinner. Tom couldn't sleep. At work, he tried to tough it out, cheering on each new fragment of the Jason Rush story. Secretly, he hoped the whole thing would go away.

His father called each day from Florida, eager for every

new detail. And Tom gave him what he was looking for: gossip, the tips that were too hot to print, and the key role his son had played in ferreting it all out.

He just prayed to God he could keep the old man happy. Rush had already threatened to go to court. If it came to that, Tom didn't want to have to explain his story. He knew its weaknesses, and now his editors were discovering them, too. But he didn't want to be forced to spell them out to the world—or to his father.

Two weeks after the first story appeared, Bowman summoned him back to his office. Sitting beside his desk was an ominous figure: Bradley Moore, a lawyer the paper called in when it had a legal problem on its hands.

"We've just been on the phone with Rush's attorneys," Bowman said. "We offered them a retraction."

"Without consulting me?" Tom demanded.

"I've gone over your story with your editors," he said. "Unless you can produce some more evidence, I thought it was the best approach."

"But I know I've got that guy. . . ."

Bowman raised his hand to silence him. "It doesn't matter anyway. *The Times* reported this morning that Rush is no longer under consideration for the ambassadorship. And Rush has notified us that he's suing us for libel."

Now the battle was joined, Aurore thought with satisfaction: sleazy reporting on one side, Jason and his lies on the other.

As she waited in the booth at Gallagher's, she read the story one more time. Now Jason would know how she had felt. Tom would pay the price for rushing into print. And perhaps even Eddie Feigan would feel a little pain.

"A great day for *The Daily Standard*," Jerry said as he joined her.

"I imagine things aren't very cheery around the office today," she said.

"Well, Tom Feigan's not in very good shape, but then Tom's not one of the best-liked people around the place. There are a few of us who think it couldn't happen to a nicer guy."

Aurore took a sip of her wine, saying nothing.

"I wondered if you might feel the same way, Aurore."

"Me? Why?"

Jerry's voice lowered. "All these years we've been meeting like this, you always seemed particularly interested in the Feigan family. And so it surprised me one day when Tom Feigan came in and started bragging about how you had invited him to a black-tie dinner at your place. . . . I mean, all these years we've been friends and you never invited me to one."

"That was different," she said quickly.

"Don't worry, it didn't bother me. But it did make me curious. You see, I like snooping around my office as much as I like snooping around Washington. And I wondered what it was about Tom Feigan that you found so interesting."

"Get to the point, Jerry."

"Well, just on a lark, I asked the library to dig out the clips we had on you. . . ."

"What?"

"Bear with me. There wasn't much there, but as I was riffling through them, I discovered the librarian had made a mistake. She'd given me the envelope on another Callahan, too."

Aurore held her breath.

"A woman named Kate Callahan."

"So?"

"I looked in the file and read the stories. She worked at the State Department back in the forties. I saw that Eddie Feigan had written some pretty nasty columns about her. I read the vicious names that the congressmen called her. I read how she lost her job.

"There was a photo with one of the stories. It was yellowed now, and hard to make out . . . but I thought it looked an awful lot like you."

"Me?"

He nodded. "And so Tom Feigan goes to dinner at your house and a few weeks later he turns up this hot story, a story that seems to have a few problems with it. And so I ask myself, 'Is it possible that Aurore set this guy up for a fall?'"

She said nothing. For the first time since she'd started all this, she felt genuinely afraid. She had been afraid that Tom might blab about her. But how could she have anticipated that Jerry would figure it out? And what was he going to do about it now?

He lit a cigarette and took a long drag. "You don't have to answer my question, Aurore. In fact, I don't want to know the answer. But I'll tell you one thing." He leaned back in the booth, his lips twisting into a smile. "You oughtta consider yourself lucky that I owe you a lot more than I owe my bosses."

Forty-Seven

It was spring again, the season of flowers in Washington. The season when, no matter how depressing the headlines, there were still bright pink azaleas in the parks—and hope in the fragrant air.

Andrew was just back from a trip to the other offices. He had balked at first, but Aurore had pushed him. Now she was glad she did. He had returned with a briefcase full of memos and ideas and a new kind of energy. It had been three years since Ellie had died. And for the first time since then, Aurore caught a glimpse of the Andrew she remembered, the eager, fun-loving young man with whom she had shared a dream.

"New York is ready to grow, and Los Angeles will be next year," he told her as he came to the end of his list. "This environmental business is really booming now."

"I knew it would."

"So tell me," he said, his eyes teasing her. "What's new with *Rush* v. *The Daily Standard*?"

She smiled. "I thought you'd never ask." She settled back in her chair. "As best as I can figure out from talking to Jerry Pieczenik and reading the briefs, the paper is going to try to ignore the inherent flaws in its story and argue that Jason's a public official. And then they'll cite the Supreme Court's ruling in *Sullivan* and say he's got to prove a malicious disregard for the truth. If the jury buys that, then Jason will have to prove that the paper knew the story was wrong but went ahead and printed it anyway.''

"Why haven't they just tried to settle?"

"I don't think Jason will let them. And Jerry tells me that *The Standard* is under a lot of pressure now from other newspapers to defend the thing. They're afraid that if Jason succeeds, they'll all have a much more difficult time going after government officials.''

"Any chance you could be subpoenaed?"

"I don't think so. Since they're making this into a big First Amendment case, I think they'll take the position that Tom can't identify his sources.'' She laughed. "I think at this point Tom would rather take the names of his sources to jail with him. At least that way he could become a media hero.

"In any case, I made sure Elliot never told me exactly how the memo turned up. And I never told him just what to do. And if they want Elliot, well, he and his lover are well installed in Greece. The court can't get him now.''

"You've thought of everything, haven't you?" For the first time, she detected a little admiration in his voice.

"I tried to," she said. "And you, Mr. Counselor, helped.''

"Please!" he said, rolling his eyes. He reached into his jacket and pulled out his pipe. "Of course, Jason could still get some money out of this.''

"True. But it's going to cost him a lot in the process. No, I realize there's a chance he could win. If not before the district court, he might get it on appeal. But it's put him through the wringer. He's lost the chance for his ambassadorship, and whatever that would have been worth to his law practice later on. And no matter how the trial turns out, I don't think it's going to do a lot to improve his reputation.

"As for Tom Feigan, Jerry says the paper will continue to pretend he's one of their best reporters. But once the trial's over, he says Tom will be lucky to wind up on the obit desk.''

"So, that's that."

"Except . . ." She hesitated. "I still wish there had been a way I could have gone after Eddie Feigan. And I wish there was a way I could let Jason know that I was the one behind all of this. You know, a sort of coup de grace."

"That's kind of risky, isn't it?"

"Yes," she said with resignation. "So I guess that's one satisfaction I'm just going to have to live without."

The trial began in July. Already, one newspaper reported, the two sides had shelled out more than $100,000 in lawyers' fees.

Aurore longed to attend the opening arguments, but knew that was foolhardy. Instead she devoured the stories of all the reporters covering the trial. And there was an army of them, attracted by the prospect of a no-holds-barred battle between a prominent Republican lawyer and a major American newspaper.

Andrew and Jane dropped in when they could—and when they could find a seat. Tom Feigan, they reported back to her, seemed on the verge of a breakdown. Jason, meanwhile, was no longer pretending to be charming. He seemed, Jane said, like a man intent on getting even.

But he wasn't having an easy time of it. *The Standard* was calling witnesses from Jason's days at the SEC. They didn't know much about Tom's story, but they had plenty of tales to tell about Jason: secretaries he'd propositioned, subordinates he'd fired without cause, questionable things he'd done with his expense account.

Still, the case moved slowly and when the hot, slow days of August rolled around, Andrew came to Aurore with an idea.

"Let's get away from here. Just the two of us."

Had she heard him right? "What did you have in mind?"

He smiled. "I was thinking of renting a little cottage on a lake. Somewhere different this time."

"Since when do you plan vacations, Andrew?"

"Since I decided my partner desperately needs one."

She hesitated. There were so many things that could go

wrong. So many memories that could become painful. "Are you sure this is a good idea?"

He looked at her closely. "There's only one way to find out."

He arranged for a place on Deep Creek Lake, out in northwestern Maryland. It was newer than the other cabin, but still rustic. And it had a dock, a hammock, and a bedroom for each of them.

Even now, as she looked around the place, she was dubious. If he had really wanted a vacation, they should have gone someplace else, someplace with a beach and a pool and tennis courts and a good restaurant. The only thing a place like this could provide was memories of Ellie.

And memories of the two of them.

But she was too old for that now. Her life had developed a rhythm; she had gotten used to being on her own. And every chapter of her life had only convinced her that the only person she could really count on was herself.

"Rest if you like," he said as he carried in their bags. "I'll fix dinner."

But she didn't feel sleepy, she felt like a swim. "Don't swim alone," she remembered Ellie telling her. What Ellie hadn't realized was that all her life she'd gone swimming alone. Sometimes it seemed that was the only way she knew how.

She swam out about a third of a mile, then turned around to head back. She remembered that long-ago day when she had seen Andrew, standing alone on the dock, and wondered why he had returned.

What would have happened if he hadn't been there that day? If she had spent that vacation alone, would she have learned eventually to open her heart to someone else? Someone who would have been free to love her, too?

A man came out on the dock. His hair was silver now, his body fuller around the middle. But it was the same man as before. He had hurt more, but then she had, too. Those lazy, happy days of fishing and swimming and swinging in the hammock now seemed like they belonged to another lifetime.

"Dinner's ready," he yelled.

"Coming."

She swam back quickly, then changed into dry clothes. There was no need to make a fuss of it. This was Andrew, after all. He had seen her at her best—and at her worst.

He had fixed a big pot of spaghetti. Had he remembered their last vacation dinner? Was he that much of a romantic? Or was it just the only thing he knew how to cook?

He filled her wineglass, then sat down beside her.

The silence made her uncomfortable, and so she spoke first. "When I was swimming out there, I couldn't help remembering the afternoon when you came back to the cottage after putting Ellie on the plane."

She hadn't meant to bring up Ellie, at least not so soon. But she couldn't help it. She felt Ellie's presence here and she was sure he did, too. She wanted to know, right from the start, what that meant to him.

"You know," he said, "sometimes I wonder whether Ellie knew about us."

She closed her eyes, bracing herself for another round of guilty recriminations. But he went on, more calmly than he had in a long, long time.

"I've thought about it a lot the last few years, working out my feelings about her death and all. I've pretty much decided that she knew we had some sort of special relationship. And I think she accepted that. She might not have accepted the sexual side of it. But I think she knew that you provided me with things that she couldn't. And because she loved me, and was generous to a fault, I don't think it threatened her."

Aurore said nothing. It had been hard to escape Ellie on their vacation before; it was even harder now.

"Ellie taught me an important lesson when she was dying." He picked up his wineglass and studied it. "We had to try to live each day like it was going to be her last one. It sounds trite, but it does make a difference. You get your priorities straight. You don't get upset over the things that aren't really important."

He looked at her. "I guess that's why I had trouble understanding the thing between you and Jason. Why did it matter now? You had survived. He couldn't hurt you. But then I decided it wasn't for me to say. If it was important to you, it didn't matter how I felt about it. It was what you had to do.''

"But I got impatient. I got impatient with you and then I got impatient with me. I realized I had been wasting the last few years. I guess I had my reasons, and I guess they were valid. But now I want to stop wasting them.''

He put down his glass. "You and I aren't getting any younger, Aurore. We might have thirty more years together, we might have one. But no matter how many years we have, I think we ought to spend them together.''

She closed her eyes for a moment. How many times had she longed to hear him say those words? How many times had she dreamed of the two of them being together? But still she hesitated. "Are you sure?" she asked. "Are you sure that I'm the same person you fell in love with before?"

"The thing with Jason hasn't changed you. Not in any way that matters. I was just afraid that you would get caught up in it, that you would get hurt.''

She rose and went over to the screen to look out on the lake. Darkness had fallen and the air was soft and languid. Just like that summer on Canandaigua Lake. She remembered that now. And if she could still remember the magic of that summer evening when they had first loved, didn't that mean something?

"After Robert died," she said softly, "after you went back to Ellie, I swore I was never going to love anyone again. I knew that love was wonderful, but it was just too painful when you lost it. And now that I had nobody, it was better just to leave it that way.''

He came up behind her and put his hands on her shoulders. "But which would be worse?" he asked. "To love me and to lose me? Or to lose me, and to know that we had never finished what we had begun?"

He turned her toward him. "It's not an issue with me, Aurore. It's not a question of loving you. I've always loved you, and no matter what happens, I always will. But now I want to live with you. And yes, I'd rather live with you and love you for a day, than go the rest of my life without having that.''

She felt the tears on her cheek. Was he really saying it? Was there no catch this time?

He bent his head and kissed her tears away.

"Before Ellie died," she said, "she made me promise I'd take care of you. I don't think I've done a very good job of that."

"But I didn't let you, did I?" He held her close and whispered, "There was a time when my despair was so deep that I thought I'd never want to know a woman again. But I was wrong. There is a woman I want to know. And if you're ready to live again, I am, too."

He kissed her again, full and soft on the lips, then harder and deeper and faster. And when he took her hand to lead her back to his room, she didn't hesitate anymore. She knew it was right, just as it had been that stormy night so many years before.

From the moment you were born, were you destined for one man? She had always felt that way about Andrew, even when he belonged to another woman. And now she knew that it was true.

Their lives had been spun together since the day they started law school. Their passage had been marked by fits and starts and hurdles. But they had begun the journey, and now it was theirs to finish.

Their bodies were older now, with more pains to bear. But the fire was still there. And there was something more now, something better than the passion she had known before. This time, the man wanted a commitment. This time, the man wasn't leaving. And this time she wasn't either.

They were married Labor Day weekend in the chambers of U.S. District Judge Howard Wachtman. Aurore wore an off-white silk dress with a scalloped hem and carried a single orchid. Andrew wore the navy blue pin-striped suit she'd helped him pick out.

Their closest friends were invited to hear them say their

vows. Jane, David, Rachel, and Mal. Mildred Hudgins and Lucy. And now, even Margaret.

"I, Katharine Aurore, take thee, Andrew . . . In sickness and in health. . . . As long as we both shall live."

Who knows how long we'll have my darling? But you were right. I'd rather be yours for a day than spend the rest of my lifetime without you.

Then she listened as Andrew said his vows. She remembered listening to him in court and in law school. Calm, self-assured, the man who knew what he wanted.

That was the voice he spoke with now: a serious voice for a serious time. But she remembered his words of love, too: whispers in the darkness, the passionate cry of her name, the little-kid giggles when they were through.

And then, like in the dream she'd had so many times, she heard the judge say: "I now pronounce you man and wife."

Their friends applauded as he kissed her, first gently and then with a full embrace. She felt tears begin to form in her eyes, but, as always, he knew just what to say.

"Don't cry now, you'll ruin your makeup!"

And as always, his wisecracks did the trick.

Afterward, they moved to a party at the Metropolitan Club. They cut their cake and danced on into the night. And when their feet could take no more, they sped away to the Hay-Adams in a limousine, under a shower of rice.

When she awoke the next morning, Andrew was gazing at her.

"Happy, Mrs. Cronin?" He pulled her into his arms.

"Yes, Mr. Cronin."

"I've been lying here thinking. And I've got an idea. It's time to add your name to the firm's name. The only reason we didn't do it at the start was because you didn't want to attract attention. But it's time you got the recognition you deserve."

"Cronin and Cronin," she mused. "Sort of distinctive."

"No, Mrs. Cronin." His tone was insistent. " 'Cronin and Callahan.' Anything short of that isn't worth reprinting the stationery for."

She smiled, her heart warm with love. "As you always used to say, dear, it has a nice ring to it."

The jury in Jason's case had been out for four days when Jane's call came: "It looks like they're coming back in."

Aurore hurried over to the courthouse. She had made up her mind that morning: she had to be there. Jane would hold a seat in the back row until she arrived.

She slipped in just as the jury was taking their seats.

"Have you reached your verdict?" the judge asked.

"We have, your honor," the foreman replied.

The bailiff handed it to the judge. He read it and handed it back to the bailiff.

She watched the backs of the two men before her, the two men who represented the central struggle of her life. She could imagine what they were thinking as they waited for the decision. She'd been there before with so many clients.

Fear. Expectation. Dread. Hope.

But was that all? Did Tom wonder what his father would think of him now? Did he ask himself why he had decided to go into journalism?

And Jason. Did he think of her in this moment? Did he wonder how she had felt when he had ruined her?

The bailiff cleared his throat. "On the first question, the jury finds that the defendant, Thomas Feigan, did libel the plaintiff, Jason Rush."

Tom slumped to the table, holding his head in his hands. Jason reached over to shake hands with his attorney.

"As to the question of damages"—the courtroom hushed again—"in view of the testimony presented, the jury finds that the plaintiff's reputation was not materially damaged by said libel. Thus it awards him damages in the amount of one dollar."

The Standard's attorney slapped Tom on the back. Jason stared at the judge in shocked disbelief.

As she rose to leave, she saw Tom turn to join a spectator in the front row. He was an old man, hunched over with his head buried in gnarled hands. Tom patted him on the shoulder, looking lost and desperate. Then the old man peered up and wiped away a tear behind his glasses. And even though she'd only met him once, she knew she'd never forget Eddie Feigan.

Now he would know how dreams were dashed. When bright promises were snuffed out. But most of all, he would know how it felt when his name became synonymous with shame.

She had hoped she might be able to teach one of them a lesson. But she had managed to catch them all. And now, after twenty years of nursing a very deep wound, it was time to go home and open the champagne.

A week later Aurore was walking through the restaurant of the Mayflower Hotel when she saw Jason, lunching with his attorneys. He waved her over, then introduced the others.

"I heard you got married," he said. "Congratulations."

"Thank you. I followed your case. Sorry it didn't turn out the way you had hoped. Are you going to appeal?"

"That's what we're trying to figure out now. Whether it's worth making the effort."

Aurore started to say good-bye, but something stopped her. There were so many bitter speeches she had delivered to him in her fantasies, it was hard not to launch into one now. But she controlled her anger. She looked at him closely, then said very evenly, "I want you to know, Jason, that I understand how you feel. You may remember what Tom Feigan's father did to me back in '49. By the sounds of it, Tom's story was as shaky as his father's was then."

She paused, then added, "I guess you might say that what goes around comes around."

He stared at her for a moment, quizzically, as if he were trying to fathom what she meant. Then he shrugged. "Yeah, sort of a coincidence, I guess."

Later, over dinner, she told Andrew about it.

"More than that's going to come around for Jason," he said.

"What do you mean?"

"I was talking to one of my old colleagues at the Justice Department today. It seems that when all those reporters were trying to dig up stuff about Jason, some of them went over to the IRS. They got some auditors interested in looking at the records of JVR Enterprises. It seems Jason and his mother haven't done a real good job of paying their taxes over the past few years. The feds are about to go after them for tax evasion.''

She closed her eyes and then she raised her wineglass. "Indulge me while I offer a toast." She hesitated, then said in a clear, strong voice: "To Robert. And to those who struggle for the truth."

Andrew lifted his glass. "And," he said, "to justice."